LUMI'S SPELL

To Kevin

Happy reading!

Ulana Dabbs
05/12/22

Also by Ulana Dabbs:

Storms of Tomorrow

Lumi's Heart

LUMI'S SPELL

Ulana Dabbs

LUMI'S SPELL

Copyright © 2022 by Ulana Dabbs

All rights reserved. This book or parts thereof may not be reproduced in any form, stored in any retrieval system, or transmitted in any form by any means (electronic, mechanical, photocopy, recording, or otherwise) without prior written permission of the author.

This novel is entirely a work of fiction. The names, characters and incidents portrayed in it are the product of the author's imagination. Any resemblance to actual persons, living or dead, events or localities is entirely coincidental.

For more information, contact:
ulana@ulanadabbs.com

Cover Artwork © Mario Wibisono
Developmental Edit by Fiona Longsdon
Line Edit by Philip Athans
Proofreading by Lauren Nicholls

Connect with the author on:
Website: www.ulanadabbs.com
Twitter: https://twitter.com/ulanadabbs

Bonus Content:

Get your free fantasy adventure!

*"An emotionless warrior.
A journey across four lands.
A quest to uncover the power of the human heart."*

Visit ulanadabbs.com to subscribe and receive your free copy of:

Storms of Tomorrow

To Fiona.

Thank you for your coaching, insight, and inspiration.

I

Serfs rushed around the courtyard lighting torches and lanterns to chase away the evening gloom. Their heightened voices, mixed with the scraping of shovels, carried into the night as they worked their way through snowdrifts to clear out a path. With a flurry of snowflakes, the wind fought against the torches, tugging at the flames, trying to extinguish them with each gust. Secured with bolts and latches, the iron gates loomed over the courtyard, strong against the blizzards of Nordur, warding off trespassers. The sentry upon the tower sounded his horn, announcing the arrival of my father and his warriors.

The riders drew near, surrounded by a dust of snow, and my heart quickened when they reached the gates. I hadn't seen my father in weeks, but his deep voice still rang in my ears, asking me to take care of Mother in his absence. 'Jarin, you are a man now,' he said, and I remembered the pleasant shiver deep in my belly caused by those words. Every few months he would gather his most skilled warriors to ride against the Varls and Mother grew lost in prayers, locked in a world filled with worry and fear, reading scrolls about the Day of Judgement and the Wrath of Skaldir while I filled my lonely hours practising with a pine-wood sword Father had carved for my eighth birthday. For the past two winters, this blade was my companion as I scoured Stromhold, fighting imaginary foes hidden in the hallway tapestries, or challenging the wooden statues of the gods with my battle cry. They would wake, beg for mercy, and surrender their powers, but like my father, I would be ruthless and end their lives with the slice of my blade. I couldn't wait to be old enough to join my father on one of his adventures, to fight beside him in a real battle against the Varls. Being ten felt like a hindrance, a waiting game until the day I was a warrior like them.

Serfs unbarred the gates and let the warriors into the courtyard. I searched for my father, scanning each silhouette whilst serfs tended the horses and took charge of swords and axes. My breath caught at the possibility that Father was not among the living, but then I saw him, wrapped in furs and looking as powerful as ever, and I heaved a sigh of relief. Broad-shouldered with an overgrown beard, he sat in the saddle with his head high, the wind tearing at his long hair. He reminded me of the warriors I read about in the scrolls in our library, proud and fierce. His black horse, bigger than the rest, seemed as dominant as his master, stomping the ground. It looked as though the long and treacherous journey had barely left a mark on them.

The skies darkened and the last of the evening light drained away, turning warriors into black shadows. Father motioned one of the serfs his way and when he unfolded his cloak, I glimpsed a small person nestled between the furs. He lifted his passenger with ease and handed him over to the serf. Once they had blended with the nightfall, I ran to the main hall where Mother stood with a silent prayer on her lips, hands pressed to her chest, waiting for the men to enter.

'They're coming.' I ran circles around her.

'Shh…Jarin. Not so loud. Show some respect,' she said with her eyes fixed on the entrance.

The door swung open and my father crossed the threshold followed by his warriors. In the candlelit hall they looked tired and battle-worn. Even Father had not been spared, his cheek ruined by a gash, daubed by an angry scab. His hand rested on his sword, its hilt pointing at me like a shaft from a stray arrow, silver glinting in the light from the fireplace. And not for the first time, I found myself enthralled by it. The blade of Stromhold Guardians—one of a kind.

'Aliya,' Father said, taking my mother's hand.

She reached for his face and ran her thumb across his scab but no words escaped her. She concealed her emotions like a true warrior's wife. She relaxed against him and the silent moment stretched between them.

I gaped in awe at the ugly stump that replaced Argil's left arm, wrapped in rags with dried blood embedded in the fabric. My own hand twitched at the sight, an image of it laying, severed, on the ground made me shudder. But despite this, I wanted to see what hid beneath the material covering his wound. Perhaps if I asked, he would show me. Orri stood next to him, the left side of his face mangled and his eye lost amidst the scars. He looked like a monster from the Nordern tales that spoke of frost giants and ocean creatures feeding on human flesh. Pride filled my heart. I had visions of the fallen Varls they left in their wake and I dreamed of having scars of my own.

'You have grown, son.' Father placed his hand on my shoulder. 'At this rate, you'll soon be ready to ride with us. Have you been practising during my absence?'

'Yes, Father.' Thrusting my chest out, I stepped forward, hoping to impress him with the moves I learned. 'Let me show you.'

'There'll be plenty of time for that.'

Before I could voice my disappointment, Mother motioned to the serf and his charge. 'Who is she?'

A girl in a white gown stood surrounded by Father's men, looking small and fragile with her bare feet and bluish lips. Black hair framed her pale face. Judging by height and the size of her feet, she was about my age, but the resemblance ended there. I never saw a Nord with a face like hers, but it was her eyes that fascinated me the most—large and lifted at the corners, they held vivid images of deep, blue waters, shifting and changing as she focused on the flames in the hall's fireplace. Though frost was thick on the shutters and wind howled outside, she didn't seem to be bothered by the cold.

'We found her lost in the blizzard,' my father said. 'She hasn't uttered a word during the ride. There was no one around and we couldn't leave her alone in the cold.'

'She is not dressed for the snow. Anyone wearing a dress on the plains, without shoes or a cloak, would freeze to death within moments,' Mother said, her voice tinged with suspicion. She approached the girl and touched her cheeks. 'Icy cold!' She turned to the serf, standing in the shadowy corner of the hall. 'Selma, take care of her. Make sure she is warmed and fed.'

Selma, a woman from the South who had been sold as a serf by her parents and brought from Hvitur to serve my mother, trotted up to us. Her left leg was shorter than her right and she moved with great difficulty.

'Come, child,' Selma said, offering her mottled hand.

'Where is she from?' Mother asked again when the door closed behind them.

Father shrugged. 'We found her wandering in the forest. At first, we thought someone was pursuing us, but then we saw her, wading through the snowdrifts.'

'But you know nothing about her.'

'Aliya, she is a child, no older than Jarin, for sure.' They exchanged glances, a subtle message passing between them.

'Still—' Mother shook her head—'these are dangerous times. She isn't a Nord, that's for sure. Have you ever seen features such as hers?'

'To put your mind at rest, I'll send a scout at first light to search the forest and the plains.' He turned to his warriors. 'You have proven yourselves again and I'm proud to be the Guardian of Stromhold with you at my side. Let us rest and celebrate our victory. We have managed to drive away another wave of Varls and show Hyllus that his magic is no match for the forces of Nordur. Some of you paid a heavy price—' he regarded Argil's stump—'and such are the pitfalls of war, but your sacrifice wasn't in vain, for we fight for our land and people.'

The road-weary men acknowledged his words with a cheer and shuffled outside into the night. Father caught Orri on the shoulder.

'Send scouts and look for footsteps or signs of life,' he said, lowering his voice. 'Report any findings.'

Orri nodded and followed the warriors out.

'Can you tell me about the battle?' I asked. 'I want to hear about your adventures.'

'It's late,' my mother said, steering me towards the door. 'Your father needs rest. There will be plenty of opportunities for stories in the days to come.'

'But—'

'Mother is right,' Father said. 'I have many tales to tell, but they can wait.' He ruffled my hair and lowered himself, so we faced each other.

'Did it hurt?' I traced his scab with my fingertips.

He waved his hand. 'It's just a scratch.'

I threw my hands around his neck and buried my face in his furry cloak. It smelled of damp and felt cold against my cheeks. For all the stories I conjured up, no warrior ever matched my father in greatness and the only thing I wanted was to be like him.

'Come now.' Mother's voice broke the moment, and I pulled away from him.

'We'll talk tomorrow,' he said. 'I promise.'

I sighed and followed her out.

* * *

I waited for my mother's footsteps to fade before I snuck out of bed and tiptoed along the dark hallway towards my parent's chamber. Careful to not make any noise, I perched on the stairs with a clear view of the fireplace. My father stood watching the flames and Mother sat on a chair, hair cascading down her back in a golden wave, fingers curled around a black pearl hanging down her neck on a silver chain.

'How bad is it?' she asked.

'We're outnumbered and the forces from the west are gaining power. Hyllus is creating an army of Varls with his magic, turning people into beasts, twisted in their once human bodies, howling with pain and rage. I can still hear them ripping through the bodies of our men.' He turned to face her. 'They're so strong and every time we clash I lose more men than I can replace.'

'May the gods have mercy on us all,' she whispered. 'How are we to withstand such horrors? What will become of us, of our son?' Her voice caught in her throat and she turned her head to the fire.

'The gods are sleeping, Aliya. We fight this battle alone.'

My mother's lip quivered. 'They may be asleep, but they can still hear us. Don't lose faith, for Jarin's sake. We must do all we can to keep him in Stromhold, out of harm's way.'

'I know what we must do, but Hyllus is relentless. I'm surprised we have managed to keep him at bay for so long, with such limited forces.'

Mother inhaled deeply. 'There is still time. Your brother—you can ask him for help. He will not turn you away if—'

'Never.' Father tightened his fists. 'I will never bow to Torgal.'

'Perhaps now is the time to forget the past and join together against our enemies? We won't always be around to protect our son. One day he will learn the truth…'

'I'd rather die than ask Torgal for help.' He slammed his fist against the wall and I winced at the depth of anger in his voice.

'You can't keep blaming him for what happened,' my mother said, and she crossed the room to stand beside him. She lifted a tangled lock from his face.

'We swore an oath to protect our father, but he chose to spill his blood. It's because of him you set foot on that forsaken hill. This betrayal can never be forgiven and if I ever see my brother again, we'll cross swords until only one of us is left standing.'

I knew little about the war and even less about my cousins dwelling far north. They lived on the edge of Nordur, in the settlement of Hvitur, and sailed vessels decorated with the heads of mysterious serpents. My father once told me the serpents' song can kill a man, enticing him into a storm created by its sweet melody. I imagined myself steering a boat through the ocean storms, fighting serpents and adorning my ship with their heads. Everyone would bow to me—the first warrior that survived the insidious songs of the Great Atlantic. I grinned at the thought of bringing glory to my name.

'What about the girl?' Mother's voice brought me back and I shrunk further into the shadows. Father had caught me eavesdropping in the past, and the experience left me with a burning backside.

'What of her?'

'Who is she? How did she come to be in the wilds?' Aliya looked at her hands. 'She could be one of them. We know nothing of Hyllus's magic. Is she dangerous? Working her own illusions?' She pointed towards the window. 'How could anyone survive the bitter colds of Nordur in a cotton dress?'

'The war is raging at our door and you're worried about a child?' he asked, lifting his eyebrows. 'It'll take more than a girl to take down Stromhold.'

'Doesn't it strike you as odd that you found her alone, wandering the plains? She doesn't resemble any of us, a clear sign that she is not from here.'

'It is odd that she didn't freeze to death, I grant you that. We need to learn more about her before we decide what to do.' Father kissed her cheek. 'Tomorrow, at first light, Orri will scout the forest. Have patience. We can't just throw her out now.'

The girl I saw earlier had looked frightened and alone, so this exchange between my parents didn't make sense. Dangerous? My mother didn't know much about war. It was unlikely that a little girl would be capable of inflicting any kind of damage, and besides, what could be more powerful than my father and his sword? With the warriors at his command, he could defeat anything.

'I can't understand how you can be so calm and trusting of her. After all you have seen, would it be any wonder if something dark came this way?' Mother paced around the room with her nightgown sweeping across the floor. 'Senia softened your heart, but she is gone and will never be replaced.' Her voice wavered. 'There isn't a day that goes by that I don't weep for our daughter. I pray to Yldir to keep her safe in the Fields of Life until I can hold her again.' She wiped at her cheek.

My father caught her arm. 'Do not speak her name. I can't bear it.'

They stood silent. The fire crackled softly, filling the room with an orange glow.

'There is nothing to fear,' Father said after a few long moments. 'The girl is no threat to us.'

'What about Jarin? How will he react to having a girl around?'

'The boy has no siblings or other children to play with. She may prove good company for him when I'm away.'

Mother shrugged. 'As you say.'

Father wrapped his hands around her waist. 'I have missed you so much.' He kissed her on the lips.

The way they looked at each other made me cringe. A silly smile replaced my father's frown and Mother laughed softly as he pulled her closer. I slipped away, ears impossibly hot as I sprinted across the hand-knotted rugs in the hallway, under the guilty looks of the wooden gods.

II

In the morning I hurried into the dining hall and my stomach rumbled at the smell of freshly baked bread. I always looked forward to the first meal of the day. Truth be told, it was a wonder that I still woke up every morning following so many hours of sleep without a meal in between.

Mother and Father were engrossed in a conversation and the girl was also there, staring at the food on her plate. She paid no notice to me as I took my place at the table. Sven, a serf brought from the southern borders following a battle that wiped out his farm and family, placed a steamy bowl of porridge in front of me and I tucked in without delay, letting the warmth fill my belly and pacify the hungry noises within. He winked at me and placed a heel of loaf on my plate, knowing from my many ventures to the cooking quarters that it was my favourite part.

Sven was a funny man. He laughed at his own jokes and his bulbous nose reminded me of the potatoes he peeled daily. Unlike other serfs who were captured or sold into servitude, he took an oath of his own free will to serve my father and to lay down his life for Stromhold.

'You'll burn your tongue,' my mother warned me then turned her attention to the girl. 'Aren't you hungry, child?'

The girl didn't respond and continued mixing her porridge with a wooden spoon.

'How are we going to communicate with her?' Mother asked. 'The girl hasn't said a word to me, or to Selma. We don't even know her name. Someone might well be looking for her.'

Father frowned at that. 'Winter storms are coming in full force and we're away from the main settlements. I don't see how anyone could get here without being noticed. The scouts have returned this morning with no news. The plains and the forest are quiet.' He took a swig of mead from his wooden cup and regarded the girl. 'Are you afraid of us, child? There is no need.' He leaned across the table. 'Stromhold is the safest place in Nordur. No harm will come to you here.'

She met his gaze for a briefest of moments then dropped her head back to her bowl.

'Such unusual eyes,' my father said, stroking his chin. 'The girl is a mystery, I grant you that. Pray we learn more about her in the coming months.'

The girl fixed her eyes on mine and their startling shade mesmerised me again. There was something moving and shifting in their blue depths, evoking thoughts of lightning storms and rain. Time ceased to exist as I sank deeper into them, chasing shapes and patterns, trying to keep up as they danced and glimmered like stars in Nordur's midnight sky. My eyes grew heavy and my breath turned icy, the chill that spread through my body left me shivering and numbed my tongue. The girl dropped her eyes and I gasped, trying to steady my trembling hands and calm my racing heart. I caught her fleeting smile before hair concealed her face.

'Sven! Why do you have to be so heavy-handed?' Mother dabbed at her dress where a cup of mead, spilled by the serf, was turning into a yellow flower. He apologised and set to mop up the liquid dripping on the floor. They fussed over it and none of them had time to notice my curious interaction with the girl moments ago. I pushed my bowl aside, no longer hungry.

Mother smoothed her dress. 'We can't very well call her Girl.' She lowered her head and studied my face. 'How about you come up with a name for her until she has worked up the courage to speak?'

I looked at the girl again, but she showed no reaction.

'Lumi,' I said, remembering a tale about Nords who fought the great mage, Achr.

My father laughed. 'You have learned a great deal from your teachings. I must thank tutor Marco for managing to keep your interest in scrolls for so long. But I believe it's time for you to step away from the libraries and focus on your sword skills before he turns you into a scholar.' He drained the last of his mead and wiped his beard. 'Hyllus grows in power and we're the last remaining stronghold in Nordur.'

Mother's face went pale. 'He is too young for that. Leave the blood and the Varls for your men to deal with.'

'No, I'm not too young, Mother.' I sprung to my feet with a burning need to convince her that I was ready to become a warrior. 'I'm taller now, and even Father said I've grown. I want to learn how to handle a real sword so I'm able to protect you and the fort when he's away.'

Father laughed. 'That's the spirit. Fierce, like a true Nord.'

Mother placed her hand on mine. 'Time for that will come soon enough. For now, take Lumi, as you have named her, and show her around the fort. Perhaps she will be happy to talk to you. But before you go, thank the gods for the food they have placed on our table today.' She joined her hands together.

'The gods didn't give us food, Argil brought supplies from Hvitur,' I said. 'We should thank him instead.'

'Jarin,' my father said in a sharp voice, 'do as your mother says.'

I sighed and closed my eyes whilst Mother sent her thanks to Yldir in a sheepish voice. I cared little for the gods. How could they know what we ate? They've been sleeping for as long as I could remember. But defying Mother meant defying Father and I wasn't foolish enough to test his patience.

Once the prayer was over, I turned my attention to the girl. The way she made me feel earlier made me want to find out more about her. I took her hand and noticed how cool it was to the touch. 'Come, I'll show you the best places in the fort. You don't have to be afraid, I know Stromhold better than anyone,' I said, leading her away.

We walked to the library where the wooden shelves stretched all the way to the ceiling and weak light streamed through a set of windows high above them. The room was vast and the beams loomed above us, curving like an archer's bow. A distinctive smell lingered in the air, the smell of ancient scrolls and charcoal. Dust motes floated around Lumi when she made her way to a wooden table in the centre. It was covered in waxy patches and half-burned candles. She ran her fingers across it, tapping the uneven surface.

'Here, this is my place.' I pulled her to one of the scroll cases at the back. 'Sometimes, I hide here from Marco.' I looked over my shoulder, for my tutor had been known to spring up from nowhere when I was least expecting him.

The floor in this little corner was lined with pillows and blankets and a small box, filled with candles, was hidden in the gap between the shelves. 'My mother doesn't like me to light candles, so I have to keep it secret. Now you know, too, but you mustn't tell anyone.' I hesitated for a moment.

Lumi looked around and her blue eyes met mine. She nodded and a shy smile spread across her lips.

'This place is full of stories,' I said, pointing at one of the shelves. 'Scrolls talk of legendary battles and fierce warriors.' I picked one, bound in leather, with a female warrior etched on the cover holding a spear against a mage. 'This one is for you.' I handed her the scroll. 'Lumi was the greatest warrior in the North. She battled Achr and killed him with only her spear, despite fighting against the powers and magic the mage had at his disposal. Hers is my favourite tale.'

Lumi placed her hand on the cover, feeling the image with her fingers. She pointed towards the shelves then back to me.

I tried to guess the meaning behind her gestures. 'Do you mean have I read them all?'

She nodded.

'I've read many of them, but I haven't much time for reading now. I must train, you see. My father expects me to join his men and prepare myself. Nordur must be protected and I need to keep my mother safe from Varls.' I placed my hands on my hips. 'Now that you're here, I'll have to protect you too.

You're safe in Stromhold. My father leads the most powerful army in the North.'

Lumi cocked her head as if trying to ascertain if I was telling the truth. The conclusion must have been a positive one because she smiled again.

'So…is it difficult to be quiet all the time?'

She placed two fingers on her lips and shook her head.

'Did someone cut out your tongue?' I asked. I never saw anyone without a tongue before and I found it hard to imagine how it felt not having it in your mouth. I bit lightly on my own to check it was still there.

She shook her head again, looking around the library. Her eyes drifted to the scroll with the image of Lumi and Achr. She pointed at the mage and touched her lips.

'Magic?' I asked. 'Someone placed a spell on you?' This was becoming more and more interesting.

A nod was her reply.

We stood, looking at each other, in the great library that told tales of so many people through the ages. There was something hypnotic about Lumi and I stretched my hand to touch her black, silky hair. The mystery of her, and the fact that she was unable to tell me her story, was intriguing. Surrounded by the towering shelves, she looked fragile and alone, in need of protection—and who was better equipped for the role than the son of the great Nordern warrior? I felt a rush of excitement at the realisation that I could be the hero who would release her from the spell. To hear Lumi's voice became my purpose.

III

A few weeks had passed and it felt as if Lumi had always been here. Where before I pursued imaginary adventures, now I cast them aside in favour of her company. She was real and more fun than any illusive beings I conjured up.

'All you have to do is stand here and keep watch,' I said.

We lingered at the corner of the workshop where Einir, Stromhold's blacksmith, forged new weapons for the warriors. It was rare that he left the building unattended and I wanted the opportunity to try out the bellows. My mother forbade me to venture into the forge but I managed to convince Lumi to take part in this break-in.

I glanced one last time around the courtyard but the smith was nowhere to be seen. 'Clap twice if you see Einir,' I said.

Inside, the forge was hot and stuffy, stinking of warm brass and coals that tickled the back of my throat and brought on the urge to sneeze. A round stone oven graced the middle of the workshop, and when I came near, the heat radiating from it struck my cheeks and caused my eyes to water. Einir's tools lay scattered around the platform, the massive hammer among them, and I made an attempt to lift it, but it didn't even budge, so I turned my attention to the large bellows—the real reason for my visit. Hanging at the side of the oven, supported by chains, the leather contraption and its workings was a mystery, but even so, I wanted to try it out. I fumbled with the bag and its handles and it took me a while to get a grip on them when I realised a certain amount of physical strength was required to bring the bellows to life.

'What are you doing, little whelp?' Einir boomed in my ear. Busy, I didn't see him coming up behind me. I jumped and tripped over a bucket. 'You fancied yourself some mischief did you?' Einir dragged me up by the sleeve. 'Should we tell your mother about this little intrusion of yours?'

My heart pounded in my chest as I jerked away from Einir's grasp and ran for the door with his footsteps following close behind. Lumi was still outside, busy stroking a horse. So much for keeping watch. I should have known better than to trust a girl with a task of such a high importance.

'Run,' I urged her and we raced across the courtyard for the watchtower. We scrambled up the ladder and when Lumi was safely up, I closed the trapdoor behind her. 'You left your post,' I said, rasping for breath.

Lumi shrugged and sat on the floor.

'You can't wander off when you're on guard duty. It could get us killed.'

She frowned and picked up some charcoal, showing little regard for my near-death experience.

The room that served as our hideout was used for storing weapons before my father decided it was too cumbersome to climb the ladder with heavy weaponry. It had been abandoned ever since. Spiders infested its dusty corners, spinning webs that formed curious patterns on the walls. With no hearth to light the fire, the place was freezing. As breath passed my lips it formed into a mist, but Lumi wasn't affected by the chill and looked as comfortable as ever.

'We're safe for now. Let's hope Einir won't go to my mother.'

Lumi was hard at work, drawing on the parchment that we smuggled from the library when tutor Marco wasn't watching. I joined her, labouring over my own blank page.

After some time had passed, I turned my attention to her drawing. 'Is it a horse?'

She nodded and with a few additional strokes of charcoal drew a long, messy tail. She picked up the drawing with her blackened fingertips and showed it to me, her blue eyes gleaming. I examined it against my own picture of men engaged in battle—it was much better than Lumi's creature, but I didn't want to make her sad, so I acted impressed.

'You're getting better,' I said. Drawing pictures had become our game for the last couple of weeks and we tried hard to outdo each other.

She placed her right palm over her heart—a gesture for 'thank you' that we had worked out together. We created more gestures every day. Lumi tapped her palm with her finger—she wanted to know more about my drawing.

'This is my father's army slashing the Varls without mercy.' I swung my invisible sword from left to right. 'They're fighting in a snowstorm. Do you like it?' I asked, worried by the lack of reaction.

Lumi rested her hand on the empty surface depicting the sky and brushed her pale fingertips across the yellowy parchment. The room was still, the silence within disturbed only by the muffled sounds from the courtyard and a whistling wind trying to force its way in through the gaps in the shutters. Transfixed, I followed the movement of her fingers across the page where warriors and beasts remained locked in a struggle, swords piercing armour, arrows raining down in all directions. Our room in the watchtower ceased to exist and the drawing took on a life of its own as the battlefield came alive with the sounds of men urging their comrades forward or screaming for help in their final hours. The air around us grew colder and ice flowers spread across the page, little shards connecting the frozen petals that fell on the warriors, bringing winter into their world. I watched in amazement at Lumi's finger as it transformed the plain background into Nordur's wintery landscape.

She lifted her hand and looked at me, lips pressed together.

I drew the air in. This mysterious ability came as a surprise and I wasn't sure how she did it. The warriors in the drawing were still again, fighting their battle in the snow—blood smeared in black across the page and Lumi's frozen flakes falling on the battlefield. I wanted to try it, so I placed the tip of my finger in the exact spot she did earlier, but ice melted under it, leaving a wet patch.

'Who showed you this trick? Can you teach me, too?' I pushed my fingertip harder at the parchment, trying to mimic her.

Lumi frowned and shook her head.

It was unfair that she was able to create magic with her fingers whilst I still waited for my real sword. 'Never show it to my mother,' I warned her. 'Magic is forbidden by the gods and she'll be angry with you.'

Lumi pressed two hands upwards in agreement.

I wanted to ask her about her ability, where it came from and who taught her, but it was time for my study session with Marco and he would be looking for me if I didn't get to the library on time. Besides, without a voice, Lumi would never be able to explain things in a way that made sense.

This was another of her mysteries that needed solving. Breaking the spell and getting her voice back became even more urgent. The only question was how.

* * *

Days at Stromhold weren't as lonely as they had been before Lumi's arrival. My father went away again, but his absence was no longer so disheartening because I had Lumi to keep me company, and although she couldn't speak, she was great at acting out schemes I coined for us. I ran to her with my troubles or when I had something joyful to share, she joined me in my escapades around the fort, and we played games in which she pretended to be a princess captured by the enemy and imprisoned in one of the hallway rooms. In my search to save her, I scoured the dungeons of Stromhold, killing the ferocious Varls that crossed my path, and calling her name. I could never tell if she was pleased with the game, but she looked happy enough once released from her captivity.

Lumi's favourite game was when we took turns hiding from each other. Stromhold was littered with nooks and places where an eleven years old could easily disappear. On one such day, standing with my eyes closed and listening to Lumi's fading footsteps, I felt a pleasant tingling in my hands and feet at trying to guess where she would hide this time. When silence filled the corridor, I went forth, checking every corner in case she was concealed behind one of them, lifting drapes and inspecting storage rooms.

'I'm coming for you.' My voice echoed through the hallway as I ran to her room. The hinges made a sharp noise when I pushed the door open. Empty. 'Where did you go?' I asked, blinking away the shadows. 'Under the bed?' I checked the eerie space, but no sign of Lumi.

This part of the fort was far removed from the main living quarters and an uncomfortable silence hung in the air. A floorboard creaked somewhere in the corridor and my skin came alive with gooseflesh.

'I don't want to play anymore,' I said, hoping she would reveal herself. 'You can come out now.' My voice turned into a whisper in this empty space. The sense of fun from moments ago dissipated and I kicked a shoe across the room. My mother gave her shoes, but Lumi never wore them, she ran around barefoot as if she lived in the South.

It was snowing outside. Dark clouds rushed across the sky, swallowing the afternoon light and bringing the storm with them. I rubbed my arms at the chill emanating from the walls. Lumi didn't like fire, so the hearth in her room was always cold. I turned to leave when a clap cracked the silence, chasing my heart to my throat. I spun around to find Lumi with a hand over her mouth and body shaking with silent laughter.

'It's not funny,' I snapped, and stormed for the door.

She ran after me and grabbed my hand. She joined her palms together in front of her face and the creases on her forehead deepened as her eyes met mine in a silent apology. A slight twitching in the corners of her mouth told me she was still pleased with the way she managed to sneak up on me. I tried to hold on to my anger but my mouth betrayed me and I burst out laughing. Lumi's lips stretched in a grin.

'It's my turn to hide,' I said, taking her hand in mine and leading her back to the hallway. It wasn't possible to stay angry with her for long.

* * *

Despite the fun I had with Lumi, my mother still expected me to study under the guidance of my tutor, Marco. She wanted me to learn the language of Vester, and said that it would prove useful if I ever found myself on the wrong side of the border. Marco was a scholar that came here from Hvitur upon her request and spent most of his time buried in the scrolls in our library. He'd travelled far and wide and had many stories to tell, and I much preferred listening to his tales than learning the foreign tongue.

'You're distracting yourself again.' Marco looked at me from under his eyelids. Behind him the fire from the hearth wrapped his shadow in an orange glow.

I turned my attention back to the page in front of me. 'I'm tired.'

'It's not a question of fatigue, it's a question of focus. It's unlikely your father would stop in the midst of battle due to tiredness.'

'My father never feels tired, he's the Guardian of Stromhold, the strongest man in Nordur.'

'That he may be, but he's still just a man in the eyes of the gods. If you wish to follow his path you must learn persistence and that means doing things that aren't always pleasurable.'

'Have you been to Vester?' I asked, fully aware that he had.

He put the scroll he was studying aside. 'You possess an uncanny ability to divert our attention from the task at hand. Knowing the tongue of your enemies will give you a deeper understanding of who they are. Your mother insists upon it.'

'But I don't care who they are. All I need is a sword sharp enough to slice them up.'

Marco frowned, lowering his bushy eyebrows. 'True strength doesn't lie here—' he touched his right arm—'it comes from here.' His finger tapped the side of his head. 'This is where all answers lie.'

I yawned. This was becoming the most boring lesson ever. 'You must consider yourself the wisest man in Nordur.'

'Far from it. I have gained only a fraction of the knowledge available to us. There are others more powerful in their wisdom.'

'Others?' It was hard to imagine someone more adept than my tutor.

'Witches of Sur—old and powerful beings. Their skills are well known in the South, and not many people dare to stand before them. Some say they're capable of whispering curses that turn living men into ash.' He lowered his voice. 'Others claim they have the ability to speak with the dead.'

I felt a rush of excitement as an idea formed in my mind. 'Can they cast spells?'

'Spells and more. The witches can see into the future, a rare gift indeed. But enough of this idle talk, let us get back to the lesson.'

I ignored him as my mind filled with possibilities. If Marco was right and the witches could do all these things, lifting a spell should be easy. The parchment before me, covered in an unfamiliar script, became more interesting. If I was to travel to

Sur, I needed to learn the Vestern tongue. From this moment, my tutor had my full attention.

* * *

Months later my father was still away and Mother withdrew into solitude. Every day she emerged from her room with red eyes and a solemn look on her face. She scarcely ate, clothes hung off her thin body, her cheeks were sunken and touched by grey shadows, and I couldn't understand why she worried so much. My father was the greatest warrior in the North. There was no way that he could ever be defeated.

One day, when she hadn't come to the morning meal, I went to find her in her bedchamber.

'Mother?' I said, knocking on the door. When there was no reply, I stepped into the dim chamber, filled with a sweet scent of burning candles. My mother knelt, her lips moving in a silent prayer in front of the wooden statue of Yldir on the mantle. 'Are you unwell?'

She regarded me with her lifeless eyes, tears still fresh on her cheeks. 'I'm praying for your father's safe return,' she said in a flat voice, and pushed herself off the floor.

'Father doesn't need prayers, he needs warriors and sharp steel to defeat the Varls.' I didn't understand how worship could help him do that.

'Don't say things like that. The gods keep us safe—it's because of their sacrifice we're alive.'

'How can they keep us safe if they're asleep? They can't hear us.'

'Yldir have mercy on your soul. I should have devoted more time to teaching you the ways of our faith. Your father's beliefs have also dwindled. He'll bring the ire of Agtarr upon himself. The gods have the power to aid us in our fight with Hyllus, but they also have the power to destroy us. Our prayers and devotion are the only ways to tip the scales in our favour.'

'Father is busy fighting Varls. He has no time for prayers.' I waved at the statue of Yldir. 'When I join him, we'll be even stronger. You and Lumi will be proud of our achievements.'

'Lumi? I still can't understand her. There is something about this girl that eludes me.'

'I know what it is,' I said. 'And I'll cure her. She'll get her voice back and you can pray together when Father and I are away.'

'Cure her? What are you saying?' My mother's eyes narrowed.

'I know what to do. Lumi's voice was taken. A witch put a spell on her and I intend to break it.' I grinned. 'She'll be like us then.'

'That is madness. The girl has muddled your mind. It was reckless of your father to bring her here. I warned him, but he didn't listen.'

My mother was usually calm and thoughtful, but now she said foolish things.

'No, Mother, Lumi is one of us. All she wants is her voice, and the witches of Sur can aid us. I know what to do, and when I'm old enough, I'll travel south and find them. They know how to cast spells and they can help her.'

'Who told you this? I'll hear no more of this madness. You're a child and your place is here in Stromhold, not in the South.'

'I'm not a child! Lumi depends on me. All you do is sit here, pray, and worry. I can't wait for Father to come back. Unlike you, he likes Lumi.' My eyes filled with hot tears.

'Listen to me.' She took hold of my head, her eyes burning into mine. 'You don't know enough to make such decisions. You must stay in Stromhold where your father can keep you safe.'

'Safe from what? I don't need his help, I'm old enough to look after myself. I'm not scared of Hyllus and I'll soon ride with our warriors to fight him.'

'Her power is strong—it'll call out to you, it'll taunt you as the time draws near—but you must stay strong, you must resist. Come...' She grabbed my arm and pulled me towards the altar. 'Let us pray together. Yldir has the ability to change your fate. If you seek his guidance, he won't turn you down.'

I pulled free from her grip. 'Whose power? I don't want to pray and I don't want to listen to you. I don't care about the gods!' My scream echoed through the chamber and I stormed off into the hallway.

IV

On the day I turned fourteen, my father summoned me into the main hall. The stairs creaked as I walked down thinking of reasons why he'd asked for me, hoping he might acknowledge my readiness to take on more responsibilities around the fort.

I had shared my aspirations with Lumi now that we spent less time getting into mischief and more time talking about the future. We took long walks in the cold, braving snowdrifts, discovering parts of Nordur on foot. I thought more and more about Sur, and the idea of hearing Lumi talk about her own dreams strengthened my resolve to help her. I was now as tall as some of my father's men and my wooden sword was no longer fit for my purposes. I cast it away and spent most of my days eyeing the steel swords carried by the warriors. I watched with envy as Einir sweated over his anvil, the heat from his ovens melting the snow outside the workshop where he forged weapons fit for the warriors of Stromhold.

The central hall was empty. I waited, looking at the walls decorated with shields depicting the emblems of the past guardians of the fort. My father's sword rested on a plinth above the hearth. Ancient symbols were etched on its surface, running horizontally from the tip to the cross guard that sheltered a green jewel. I felt the rough surface of the hilt with my fingers and the blade reflected my distorted features, glistening and daring me to pick it up. It had claimed many lives and I needed to prove myself worthy before I could wield it. Even though I knew I shouldn't touch it, the longing to hold it was stronger than fear. I wrapped my hand around the hilt, feeling the coolness of the metal against my palm. With all my strength I lifted the sword from its holder. It was heavy, too heavy for me as it slid from the stand. The sound of its point hitting the floor echoed through the hall, leaving me with a sudden urge to flee.

'You need to grow your muscles before you're ready to swing that blade.' My father stood in the doorway. His voice made me flinch and I kept staring at the sword, unable to meet his gaze.

'I wasn't always able to hold it, you know,' he said, coming into the room. 'I had to work hard—it takes time.' He picked up the sword with ease and twisted it with minimal effort. 'It has brought me many victories and saved my life more than once.'

'Do you know what these symbols mean?' I asked.

'It's an ancient script, long forgotten. I doubt anyone alive is able to decipher it.' His fingers brushed against the symbols. 'Some say that Skaldir herself inscribed the words and sealed them with magic so that one day the powers within can wake her from her slumber.' He regarded me with a sharp eye.

Skaldir, the Goddess of Destruction, who came close to tearing down the world with her rage. 'Do you believe that's true?' I asked. It was hard to imagine that some script had the power to awaken a god.

'The urge to know drove your grandfather into madness. Some things are better left unanswered.' He placed the sword back on its holder. 'The time will come when you'll be the owner, but for that to happen there's much work to be done, and this is the reason why you're here. You have grown and your interest in our cause is clear. If you wish to be a part of our force, you need to learn how to fight. I believe that the time has come for you to start your training. It may help you focus your energies on something other than following Lumi around.'

He presented me with a sword.

I gasped and looked at him in disbelief. The sword was still wrapped in its black sheath, the leather decorated with criss-cross patterns. I brushed my fingers against the hilt, tracing the twisty lines etched into its surface. With one smooth motion, I pulled the sword out. The silver blade glinted in the light and I turned it over, marvelling at the skills of the sword-maker and trying to replicate my father's moves from before. I wanted him to see that I knew how to handle a sword and that I was ready to train.

'I asked Einir to forge it,' my father said. 'I hope it'll serve you well.'

We had the best blacksmith in Nordur. He followed my father when he left Hvitur, and his weapons were the most sought after in the North. 'I've spent hours watching Einir in his forge, dreaming that one day he would be making my sword,' I said. 'I won't disappoint you.'

'I have arranged your sword practice with Argil. You're to join him at noon in the practice yard. It's a chance for you to learn and prove yourself before joining the warriors.'

I straightened up. 'I'll make you proud, Father.'

'I know you will. We Norderners are not so easily beaten by our enemies. We'll show them what it means to fight and defend what is ours. Use your time with Argil well, and you'll play a part in Nordur's victory.'

* * *

I couldn't wait to share my excitement with Lumi and see her approving smile, so I ran for her bedroom, my new sword in hand.

In the hallway, I heard voices coming from her room and recognised my mother's unhappy tone. Her displeasure with Lumi upset me. It was as if she suspected her of some terrible deed that had yet to transpire. Lumi was special and had the ability to create snowflakes. Though there was no threat in simple magic, my mother was still so mistrustful of her. Mother's need to please the gods overshadowed reason, and she looked for opportunities to remind us of our duty to them.

Through the crack in the doorway, I saw Lumi sitting on the edge of her bed, looking down at her hands.

'This can't be happening here,' Mother said, pacing around the room. 'This thing that you do, there is a powerful magic within you, but you conceal it well. I have tried to ignore it but it's getting stronger and the evidence is here.' She made a sweeping motion with her hands. 'We welcomed you to Stromhold and took care of you. We taught you our ways, treated you like we would treat our Nordern children, and you repay us by bringing forbidden magic to this fort? My husband fights against Hyllus's sorcery and you practice it under his roof.'

Silence answered her.

'I don't want any of this near Jarin. Do you understand? You have filled his mind with enough foolishness as it is. His promises to cure you and his plans of travelling to Sur, towards danger… I won't allow it. If any harm comes to him, I'll have you cast out.' Clutching her skirts she whipped from the room.

I ducked away from the door and waited until my mother was out of earshot. When I stepped into the room, it was like stepping into the courtyard on the coldest of nights. The flowers on the window ledge were frozen and ice patterns decorated the thick glass from the inside. The room felt as if a snow storm had rushed through it, touching everything apart from Lumi, who sat still as before, no sign of frost on her dress.

'Lumi?' I walked to her, skin prickling on the back of my neck. It dawned on me that Lumi was the storm maker, and choosing what and who to freeze was the source of her power, and the danger that my mother feared. 'What did Mother say to you?' I wanted to ask her about the flowers and the cold but it meant disclosing my eavesdropping, so I decided against it. 'Did she upset you?' I studied her face, searching for signs of distress or regret, but it was frozen over much like the lakes of Nordur.

She waved her hand as if to chase away the conversation and smiled, melting away any suspicions I might have had. I didn't have any reason to distrust her. She shared her secret with me long before my mother knew of her abilities. The sword clunked against my hip, reminding me why I was here. 'Look at this.' I unsheathed the blade, unable to stop the grin of satisfaction. 'From this day forward, I'll take daily lessons from Argil. He's the best swordsman in Stromhold.'

Lumi touched her left arm, a silent question in her eyes.

'Despite the injury, he still is the best,' I said. 'When I'm skilled enough, I'll join my father's warriors and test myself against the Varls.'

Her eyes widened.

'You don't have to worry. I have a plan. Once I'm ready, I'll travel to Sur. I've learned of witches who dwell there that can break spells. Marco told me about them and I've made a lot of preparations. I've read scrolls that spoke of enchantments and the ways to break them. The witches of Sur will have the answer for us. They're versed in spells and use black magic, so lifting your curse should be easy. You'll have your voice back and a chance to wipe away my mother's suspicions by telling us your story.'

I didn't know how I would get to Sur, or if the witches would even answer my plea, but I wanted Lumi to believe in me. I wanted to be the hero who would lift the spell. Standing in her room with my new sword in hand it seemed an easy task to accomplish.

V

The next few years were filled with hard work in the practice yard as I put my efforts into mastering the way of the sword. I trained hard, learning as much as I could under Argil's guidance. He was a fierce swordsman and never held back, pushing me and testing my limits. Many a time I tasted dirt and cursed him, but he kept encouraging me and ignored any complaints on my part. Despite him being ten winters older than me, a friendship forged between us and I began to value his advice all the more over the years. He was one of the few men my father trusted to deliver messages and bring supplies from Hvitur where Nords guarded the seaport. I often asked Argil about our cousins, hopeful that someday I could accompany him on one of his journeys. My father was not so keen, holding on to a past that was a mystery to me. I once asked him about Torgal, wanting to understand the animosity between them.

'It does not concern you,' he said. 'The matter is between my brother and I.'

'But you said it yourself that Hyllus grows in power. Every time you return from hunting the Varls, the void in our ranks gets bigger, more men fall with each raid. Torgal doesn't know the full extent of the problem. He could aid us with his men and—'

'Don't lecture me on the strategies of war, boy.' The warning in his voice was clear, I was not to pursue this matter further.

'But what could be more important than saving your people?'

He sighed and waved me away. My fists clenched. More than anything, I wanted my father to trust me enough to share his burdens, so I could understand the reasons for his quarrel with Torgal, but today was not the day.

* * *

When I was able to mount a horse unaided, my father arranged to meet me at the stables. In the dim building, the sharp and musty smell of hay hit my nostrils and made me sneeze. The horses stirred and snorted within their stables as I walked past.

'This one is yours,' my father said pointing at a bay horse.

I approached the horse and stroked the white blaze running down his face. It resembled lightning and felt coarse beneath my fingers. 'Blixt,' I whispered, moving my hand down the side of his neck. His muscles twitched and quivered under my tentative touch.

'You can try him out,' Father encouraged me.

I took the reins and led Blixt out of the stable. Placing one foot into the stirrups, I pulled myself up with ease and settled into the saddle. The horse shifted, slightly shaking his head, and I patted his neck, trying to assure him that my intentions were pure.

'We'll get along just fine, Blixt.'

Across the courtyard, Lumi waved at us from her bedroom window.

'Will you ride with me?' I called.

She nodded and disappeared from view, and moments later ran down the steps towards me with an excited smile lighting her face, purple skirts dancing around her bare feet. Her hair mirrored black ice on the lake's surface, a stark contrast to her pale skin, and with her large, upturned eyes, she made the women of Nordur, with their red and golden locks, look plain in comparison. Even though we spent most of our time together, it struck me how much her body had changed. Her dress was wrapped around her slender frame with the curves of her breasts visible through the soft fabric. My face grew hot at the sight of her narrow waist, swaying in line with her light steps. Lumi was no longer the child my father brought home six years ago; she had turned into an alluring woman and watching her stirred something deep inside me.

I helped her up and she felt weightless in my grip. A sharp, cold smell, heavy with ice crystals, filled my nostrils as her soft hair brushed across my face. She settled in front of me and the familiar chill that I had grown so accustomed to emanated from her body. I increased my grip on the reins, feeling lightheaded. My knees weakened and to my horror, I felt a stirring in my loins. Shifting in the saddle, I spurred the horse forward and let the bitter wind take the edge off my desire to love her. We sped off towards the white landscape, bringing snow to life, and the ground thundered under Blixt's hooves. The wind whistled in my ears and I laughed at the sky with my heart singing in its chamber.

We rode on fast until the snow was too deep to gallop and I slowed Blixt down to a comfortable trot. Pine trees, in the livery of white, lined our way like an army of men marching to battle. The mountains in the distance were angry and unmoving. Their jagged peaks, pointing at the Nordern sky, resembled spear tips. Stromhold stood at the edge of Nordur with the Great Atlantic to the East and the Grand Isfjells further South, their icy walls guarding the dark waters. My face went numb as frost settled on my eyelashes and tangled the hair inside my nostrils. Pain stirred in my chest as cold stiffened my lungs, making it difficult to breathe.

'This is why I love Nordur,' I whispered in Lumi's ear. 'Only Nords can understand and enjoy the unforgiving and icy weather.'

She nodded and inhaled deeply. My lips brushed against her ear and the sensation of being so close to her sent a shower of hot sparks through me.

'We're Nords, Lumi. Fate brought us together and I wish nothing more than to break the spell that binds you.'

She looked over her shoulder, her lips parted as if trying to say something, but no sound escaped them.

'I'll set you free.' A thick pine towered ahead of us and I turned the horse around. We started back for Stromhold.

* * *

My days centred around sword practice with Argil as we faced each other on the training yard. It was a square area surrounded by wooden pillars with the doors to the fort in the eastern wall, sheltered by a roof running from one end to the other.

I cursed as the back of Argil's hilt crashed against the bridge of my nose. My sword lay two feet away and I was once again sprawled on the ground.

'Come on, up,' Argil said, tucking the sword beneath his gory stump and extending his right hand to help me up. 'You lack concentration today.'

I spat on the snow, turning it crimson.

'Is this something to do with the white princess over there?' he asked, looking towards the pillars.

Lumi leaned against one of the columns, watching me with intensity in her deep blue eyes. I shoved his hand aside, jumped to my feet, and retrieved my sword. I hated that Lumi witnessed my failure, but Argil was right, my concentration waned whenever she was near.

'Hey,' Argil said in a sharp voice. 'I'm here to teach you, so pay attention. Less anger, more focus.' He pointed his sword at me.

I took a deep breath, feeling Lumi's eyes on me.

We started our usual dance, footwork patterns and ripostes firmly ingrained in my muscle memory following the years of practice. I managed to attack and defend in quick succession, feeling the adrenaline rush as my senses heightened and beads of sweat tickled my forehead. My breathing quickened and the only sound came from the steady beat of my pulse, responding to the changes in my body. The metal hilt dug into my glove as I swung the sword with ease.

'This is good,' Argil said in between breaths. The way he worked his sword with just one hand amazed me.

I readjusted my body in preparation for the fight to resume, the taste of blood still present in my mouth, but a quick glance towards the columns stopped me in my tracks. Lumi was no longer watching me but chatting with another man. It was Modi, one of my father's scouts. He stood close to her with one hand resting on the pillar and Lumi leaned forward, listening. At the sight of him tucking a loose strand of hair behind her ear, my chest filled with fire and I tightened my grip on the hilt.

'Hey, are you still here?' Argil slapped my shoulder with his sword. 'What is the matter with you today? I could have taken your head off. There's no time for admiring pretty girls when fighting for your life. The enemy will not be so forgiving.'

I ignored him, my attention was on Modi as he grabbed Lumi's hand and urged her to follow him. She shook her head and tried to pull free of his grip, but he paid no heed. I forgot all about Argil and marched across the yard.

'Leave her alone,' I said and shoved Modi out of the way. He stumbled against the pillar. 'Are you all right?' I asked Lumi.

She clutched at her hand and nodded. Her chest rose and fell rapidly and my heart squeezed at the look in her eyes. She was frightened.

'There's nothing wrong with her,' Modi chuckled. 'We were just getting to know each other.'

I balled my hand into a fist. 'If you ever touch her again—'

'What then?' he asked and his hand found his sword. 'Is she yours to claim?'

I didn't answer but aimed the point of my blade at his face and charged. Modi deflected my blow and came back at me, but I no longer registered his presence. Something darker took over and I threw myself at him as if he were one of Hyllus's Varls. We fought until the world turned into a blaze, and in the fury of battle, I ran him down to the ground.

'Enough!' Argil's voice jerked me back to reality.

I stood, looking down at Modi, breathing fast and heavy with my sword at his neck. His face was scarlet and his eyes narrowed to slits. When I withdrew my blade, he pushed himself off the ground.

Argil snatched the sword from me. 'Enough training for today.'

Modi brushed the snow off his leggings and wiped his mouth on his sleeve. A trickle of blood ran down his chin. 'This isn't over,' he said. He stormed off without as much as a glance at Argil.

I looked around for Lumi, but she was gone.

'What came over you?' Argil said. 'You know the rules. We've plenty of enemies as it is without you trying to kill each other. If your father hears of—'

'Leave Father to me,' I said. Shadows fell across the training yard and the evening air became sharper with frost. The flames from the torches flickered with an inviting glow, illuminating the snow and driving away the darkness that lingered at the edge of the light.

I had to find Lumi.

'Jarin!' The snow crunched under heavy boots and Orri came into view, his silhouette blending with the impinging darkness. 'There you are,' he said, the air steaming around his mouth. 'Eyvar wants to see you both. There was an incident—one of our men was found dead outside the gates.'

'Who?' Argil asked. 'The Varls wouldn't dare come so close to the fort.'

'Rodolf. He was sent on patrol two days ago,' Orri said as we crossed the training ground. 'Whatever got him waited at the gates. This is where his body was found, frozen solid.'

Rodolf was an energetic, red-headed man that often disobeyed orders in favour of doing things his own way. He had a habit of winking at me whenever we met and the idea of his death was difficult to imagine.

'No man born in the North would freeze to death unless ambushed,' Argil agreed. 'Any signs of injury?'

'Your father is trying to ascertain what happened. He's questioning the scouts as we speak.'

We hurried to the room where Father was engaged in a heated discussion, with hands clasped behind him and the right half of his face distorted in the shadows cast by the fireplace. Three scouts with bows strapped to their backs surrounded him in a semi circle. Tall and jittering shadows, cast by the men, shifted around the room like invisible guardians watching over their mortal bodies.

'What do we know?' Father asked as we joined them.

'Not much.' This came from Thommas, a stocky man with a ginger beard. 'We didn't see anyone. The mountains and forests are clear. No signs of the Varls or otherwise.'

'Rodolf was an experienced scout,' I said. 'It's unlikely that he would succumb to the frost.'

'He was the most agile, but he had a tendency to venture into the wilds on his own,' a man known as Knell said. 'I warned him to stay within the area assigned to him but he was too curious. Every sound attracted his attention and he kept talking about a shadow that moved in the snowdrifts at night.'

'Shadow?' my father asked in a strained voice.

'We swept the area but couldn't find anyone.'

'Are you certain?'

Knell nodded. 'The wilds are clear, no footsteps in the snow, no evidence of life beyond wild animals.'

Father sighed, his heavy brows drawn close together.

'Did anyone examine his body?' Argil asked, looking around the room.

Bertel, the one-eyed archer, stepped forward. 'I did, but I couldn't see any wounds.'

'Where is he?' I asked.

'Outside,' Bertel motioned towards the window. 'The pyre preparation is underway.'

'I want to see him.' Stromhold's scout, frozen to death. It was hard to believe, and I needed to witness it for myself.

Orri and Thommas followed me out. My palms were clammy inside my gloves and I felt a mixture of fear and curiosity. We found Rodolf's body in the courtyard, ready for his final journey. The clouds raced across the face of the moon and the wind picked fights with the snowflakes, growing more powerful with each gust. Thommas lifted the lantern and I leaned in to examine the body. In the flicker of the flame, Rodolf's face was sunken, his closed eyes positioned deep in their sockets. I reached out to touch his skin and it felt like parchment under my fingers. His muscles were stiff and hard to the touch, and his mouth had twisted into a ghostly grimace. I shivered under my cloak. Imaginary battles were one thing, an actual dead body was quite another. Facing the death of someone I knew perturbed me, and all of a sudden I felt like a coward.

'He looks as if someone has sucked the life out of him,' Thommas whispered.

I lifted Rodolf's eyelids and his glassy stare gaped back, frozen and cracked like a mirror.

'Father needs to know about this,' I said to Orri. In the glow of the lantern, shadows moved across his scarred face. 'This is no work of winter. I hope he'll see we need to double Stromhold's guard.'

'I'll inform him at once,' Orri said and strode back into the fort.

'He was a good scout.' Thommas clenched his fists. 'His murderer must pay for this.'

Later that night, a funeral pyre was lit and we stood to watch Rodolf's body being devoured by flames. The air stank of charred flesh mixed with an acrid odour of a burned liver. The heat peeled his skin off, exposing flesh beneath and distorting his facial features until he started resembling the Varls Father spoke of. The fat leaked out from the body and angry flames hissed and gobbled up the liquid spreading around the pyre. I thought of Rodolf's final hours—alone in the dark, facing unknown horrors, he died at the gates, so close to safety. Would I meet the same fate? A sour taste filled my mouth and I looked about the courtyard. Every dark corner looked sinister, the perfect hiding place for someone that wished to do harm. As my time of joining Father's men neared, I questioned my readiness as a warrior. I had wanted to fight against our enemies for so long that I didn't have time to elaborate on what that meant. Would the hours I spent training with Argil be enough when I stand against the horrors dressed in flesh? I had a gnawing feeling that something was coming for us, disguised in the blizzard, its steps covered by the falling snow.

As the sparks flew into the sky, I caught the sight of Lumi, blended with the night's shadows, and relief filled me—she was unharmed. She kept away from the fire, wrapped in a thin cloak. The sight of her ushered my grim thoughts away and her presence filled me with courage. The day my father brought her home, my life altered and I bid farewell to loneliness. I wanted to prove that I was worthy of her, and if that meant facing the dangers to keep her safe, I was ready to do so. The wind howled and I imagined it to be Rodolf's soul travelling to the gates of Himinn.

VI

Stromhold stayed on the lookout for weeks following the death of Rodolf, but no more frozen bodies turned up at our gates and we abated the defences as the threat diminished. I focused all my efforts on honing my fighting skills while Lumi took my place in the library, tracing tales of the past. Tutor Marco taught her how to read and she was able to discover the story behind her name. Sometimes, I would sneak in and watch her over the scrolls as she traced letters with her slender fingers. I often imagined her reading the words aloud and it reminded me how much I wanted to hear her voice. On one such day, I found her sitting at the table with the scroll unfolded in front of her.

'You're just like her.' I pointed at the image of Lumi on the leather casing. 'With your magical ability and the skill to tangle my thoughts with your smile alone.'

Lumi's eyes lit up and her face brightened in response.

The familiar longing washed over me. The way she parted her bluish lips when she smiled caused my heart to bounce wildly and made me stammer over my words. Every time she was near me, my fingers yearned to touch her milky skin and erase any distance between us.

She was full of mystery, her skin always cool to the touch and unaffected by the winter cold, as if she were part of the Nordern ice. The way she used her hands to draw my attention to something delighted me, and I wanted to catch her fingers in mine and never let go. I enjoyed watching her from a distance as she walked through the snow barefoot, creating snowstorms with her hands. At such times, she would gaze longingly towards the frozen landscape as if her heart was buried in the Nordern wilderness.

'It's freezing in here.' Mother's voice cut through my thoughts. She entered the library and her eyes narrowed as she looked from me to Lumi. 'It seems the blizzard affects some of us more than others. Jarin, get the fire going before we turn into icicles.' She spoke to me, but her attention was on Lumi, who scooped up the scroll and moved to sit closer to the window.

Mother's intrusion broke the moment and I became aware of the chill. 'I was just leaving,' I said. Whenever Lumi and my mother found themselves in the same chamber, wariness followed them, infecting everyone around.

'Stay and help me with the fire.' Her request sounded more like an order, cutting short my attempts to get away.

When the fire came to life and the glow from it filled the library, Mother turned to Lumi. 'Don't just sit there on your own. Join us.'

Lumi sat with her eyes closed and forehead propped against the window, but the request made her look up. Her eyes caught the glow from the fire and she flinched.

'If you wish to live among us, you must adopt our ways,' Mother said, opening her palms to the warmth from the hearth. 'My son has a great affection for you. It's time you embraced Nordern ways and our gods.'

'Mother, please...' I wanted to grab Lumi and run away like we used to when we were children. Since the day she confronted Lumi about the storm she had created with her magic, Mother watched her every move like a raptor, waiting for any sign of disobedience.

'It's time you started teaching Lumi about our faith, so she understands the importance of the divine rules, which abhor magic in all of its forms.' She looked back at Lumi and all gentleness left her face. 'Those who disobey will be shunned in life and denied entry to Himinn.'

'If the gods ever wake, that is,' I said, trying to control my frustration with her constant disapproval of Lumi.

'Why is it that you and your father refuse to acknowledge what is for sure a test from Yldir to see how we fare against the evils of magic? There's a reason why it was forbidden. Have you forgotten what happened when mages called on Skaldir to aid them?'

'How could we with your constant reminders?' I said. 'Perhaps Father refuses to give in to your obsessions.'

She gasped and the colour drained from her face.

'Come, Lumi.' I extended my hand to her and when she took it, a shiver ran through my arm. Could one so cold accept the warmth of another? I may have fled the library and the fire, but the question followed me.

* * *

Despite my affections for Lumi, something troubled me, a feeling or sensation that caused unease to settle in the pit of my stomach, and as much as I tried to usher it away, it lingered like a seed reluctant to sprout but unwilling to die. Much to my displeasure, I found myself mimicking Mother's suspicions, questioning Lumi and her whereabouts in my mind whenever she was too long out of my sight. During one such instance, I gathered the courage to confront her. Lumi was absent for most of the day and when she walked through the gates, anger stirred in me at the sight of her light steps. I blocked her path. 'I've been looking for you. Where did you go?'

She regarded me with a questioning expression as if confused by my abruptness.

'You go as you please, alone, unafraid of the dangers lurking in the wilds,' I said. 'What's so important that requires hours of your time? Do you think your magic will save you when the Varls come crawling?' Words poured out of me and I despised the sound of my voice, judging and condemning her actions.

Lumi's eyes widened and a shadow crossed her blue pupils before they came alive with hurt, pulling me into a storm of emotions, a whirlpool of sorrow and disappointment. I felt everything she felt and it was like falling into an ice hole and clutching at the frozen edge with the current pulling you down.

She motioned towards the plains, placing her palm over her heart.

'I'm sorry, I know how much you love the wilds,' I said, choking on my guilt and resenting myself for causing her pain with my unfounded suspicions. 'I should take you there more often. It's just that I'm so busy with Argil and have so little time to devote to you.'

Lumi brushed my cheek with her cool fingers and her touch sent a jolt of pleasure through me. She smiled and all my doubts floated away with the wind.

* * *

On the day I turned eighteen, my father summoned me to his chambers. Mother called this room the Silence Chamber, a place where Father liked to indulge in his solitude. The interior was stripped of all official signs of his leadership: no swords, shields, or spears on the walls. From the large hearth, set in the middle wall, quivering flames gave life to the shadows, some shaped like elongated claws, scraping at the surface, others resembling raven's beaks, agape with a shrill cry. A leather map was laid out on the table, strategic points marked with charcoal.

'Jarin.' He motioned me to step closer. 'We had reports of Varl sightings near the village of Elizan. My scouts informed me that Hyllus's creatures were seen skulking around the perimeter, setting fires to the houses on the outskirts.'

I looked at the map, tracing the roads until they took me to Elizan. 'They crossed the border?'

'They have never ventured as far as Elizan. They're getting bolder.' He crossed his hands behind his back. 'Our progress is slow and we need more men.'

'Can we just strike Hyllus? This is his doing, so if we drive him out of Vester the war will be over.'

Father's hollow laugh filled the space between us. 'Very good. And how do you suppose we do that? We have no men, the Citadel of Vester is out of our reach, and Hyllus hides behind impenetrable walls, surrounded by his watchful Varls.'

I couldn't argue with my father's logic, he was Stromhold's Guardian after all, well versed in the art of war, and men trusted his wisdom. I wished to become as knowledgeable as he was, so I could lead warriors into battle when my time came.

'I watched you train with Argil on the grounds and I must admit, there is a skill that you possess that I never quite mastered. You command the sword with such conviction it appears effortless. You have a knack for it.'

It took considerable effort to stop my lips from grinning. I wanted to race outside and perform a victory dance, but my feet stayed glued to the rug, recognising the gravity of the moment.

'Witnessing your efforts and commitment to our cause, I believe you're ready to join us. I was only two winters older than you when I left Hvitur to command Stromhold, and not as accomplished with the blade.'

'Who trained you in the way of the sword? Had you fought in battle before then?'

'My father, Bodvar, taught me how to fight with a spear, but Torgal showed me how to wield a sword. It was against him I drew it for the first time.'

It was a risky subject, so I steered away. The moment between us was too precious to spoil with talks of family disputes. 'I'll give you no cause to doubt me.'

'I'm sure you won't, but there is a matter that concerns me greatly and which I feel we must discuss.' His eyes met mine with a piercing stare. 'The girl is a liability. You have grown too attached to her and your mother tells me you want to travel to Sur in search of witches.'

My muscles stiffened up in reaction to his disapproving tone. 'That has nothing to do with you or Mother.'

'It is if you're actually thinking of pursuing this quest of yours. I can understand your weakness towards her but it can't come between you and your duty as a warrior's son. I care for Lumi, but the helpless child I brought home is gone. I see that you're fond of her, but your destiny is to protect your people and watch over our land. Have her if you must, but stay focused on the task at hand. With you rests the future of Stromhold. This fortress—' he made a swooping hand gesture—'has been guarded for generations by the fathers and sons of Nordur.'

'I have to do this, Father,' I said. My breathing quickened and I felt heat crawling up my neck. 'I made a promise to recover what was stolen from her. You and Mother should stay out of this.'

'Watch your tongue with me, boy. You know nothing about this Lumi, and your mother has every right to interfere. You have grown too stubborn for your own good, too quick to disobey.'

'I know more about her than you or Mother. She would keep me company when you were gone for months at a time. There is a bond between us you could never understand.'

'Such foolishness!' He slammed his fists on the table. 'I didn't raise you to be a weakling. The blood of Nords flows in your veins and you should honour it. We weren't born to indulge in life's pleasures. We die with swords in our hands, so our families may live in peace.'

'If you were so worried about the people of Nordur, you would have asked for help from your brother long ago,' I said.

Veins in his neck grappled towards the surface, blood thumping in them like molten lead, ready to break out. The tender moment between us was lost and I turned away from him.

His voice chased after me as I left the room. 'I should have left her to die in that snowstorm!'

* * *

Two days later, preparations for our trip were complete and I went to see Lumi to say goodbye. I had mixed feelings. Part of me couldn't wait to mount Blixt and join my father's men so I could test my skills in a real fight and see how much of Argil's teachings stayed with me. The day I dreamed about as a child was here. But another part of me wanted to stay near Lumi and watch over her.

An unusual heaviness wrapped my body in a tight grip and I had a sinking feeling in my stomach as I crossed the threshold and saw her standing next to the dead hearth, one hand resting on the mantelpiece. She wore a blue dress and I could make out the shapely form of her body hidden under the light fabric. I wanted to pull her close and free my hands to experience every part of her, to feel the softness of her cool skin and bury my face in her midnight hair. The thought of touching her this way brought back the desire to make love to her and I had to breathe deeply to calm my longing. Lumi was made of dreams and I wanted nothing more than to spend eternity wrapped in her embrace.

'We leave for Elizan. It's a long ride to the border.' There was so much I wanted to say but my mouth betrayed me with small talk. I took her hand in mine. 'Once the Varls are defeated, I'll start my quest to free you.'

Lumi lowered her head.

'Aren't you excited? I promised I'd end this and I can finally fulfil my vow.' I lifted her chin so I might meet her eyes. 'I don't care how far the road will take me, the only thing that matters is your voice. I'll not rest until I hear it.'

She touched my cheek, letting the familiar chill spread through my body, and I was thrown into the vortex I had come to recognise as her magical force, swirling in the blue storm that lived in her pupils. She pulled me into the freezing depths where the light had no claim and the frost stretched its icy fingers, grasping at my flesh. Lumi stepped closer and her lips touched mine in our first kiss. My skull exploded from the hundreds of icy shards that pierced it and my heart slowed down, red cells turning into solid crystals as I lost all sensation.

I pulled away, gasping for air, my boots covered in frost that spread on the floor around us. Lumi's eyes widened and her hand flew to her parted lips as if she tried to stop something from escaping them. The memory of my mother standing in the frozen room brought her words about magic back to me and I realised that this was the first time I'd felt the true effects of Lumi's power. I perceived her abilities as harmless tricks, but standing here, half-frozen, made me realise they might be more destructive than I had first thought.

Before I left the room I said, 'I'll find a way to break the spell even if I have to drag those witches by the hair all the way from Sur.'

* * *

Father and his warriors waited in the courtyard. A bitter gust of wind tugged at my cloak but I welcomed it as a relief to the heat radiating inside me. The men tended their horses and weapons, ranging from swords and spears to axes and bows. Each man favoured one over another, but they all looked equally sharp and deadly and my sword felt like a trinket. Orri was busy adjusting the straps of his cape, tightening them around his chest, Argil concealed a knife in the folds of his leather jerkin and another one in the side of his brown boot, and Modi's booming laughter carried across the courtyard. Knell was filling his quiver with arrows, alone and silent. They were battle-hardened men preparing for another hunt, and I felt like an amateur among them. To hide my burning cheeks, I concentrated on adjusting the saddle straps on Blixt, hoping the warriors would ignore me.

My mother approached, wrapped in furs, her golden hair tangled by the wind. 'Look at you,' she said, 'all grown up. With your long, wavy hair...you remind me of your father when he was your age.'

Her face was drained of colour, the familiar red circles around her eyes, puffy skin beneath them—the face I grew so accustomed to during my father's absences. Despair clawed at my throat, holding back any words. I spent eighteen winters in this fort with my mother running to the rescue in cases of scraped knees, bruises, or strains. She would tell me to stay brave while applying stinging pastes and lotions to ease my childish aches. The image of her sitting by my bed, holding a cool cloth to my forehead when I suffered from the red fever, flashed in front of me and I hugged her tight, hiding my blurry eyes in her soft furs. I was heading out into the world to taste real pain, and she wouldn't be there.

'I love you. Stay safe, and may Yldir watch over you.'

'I will. We'll return home victorious in many ways.'

'Your father told me about your quarrel,' she said with a serious expression. 'I beg you to reconsider.'

'You know I can't do that, Mother.' I turned to Blixt. My mind was made up and I didn't want her to pursue this matter further.

She sighed, pulling her red cloak tighter.

I mounted Blixt and spurred him forward in the direction of the men gathered around the gates. One backward glance at the window assured me that Lumi was tracking my progress from her bedroom. I tugged at the reins, feeling more determined than ever to find the witch responsible for her plight. The mournful sound of a horn accompanied us as we set off, thirty strong men, ready to face the winter and the horrors awaiting us.

VII

Lengthening shadows of nightfall chased us into the first settlement where wattle and daub huts huddled together as if afraid of the darkness creeping around them. Nords wrapped in tunics made from animal skins and trimmed with fur clustered around smouldering fires where hefty iron pots hung over the flames, spreading a rich smell of roots and meat. The aroma reminded me of hearty broths prepared in Stromhold's kitchens and flavoured by my mother's secret spices, resourced by Argil during his trips to Hvitur. She stored them in wooden pots by the kitchen hearth where the damp couldn't spoil them, and knowing how much I enjoyed the warm, sweet taste of negull seeds, she would sneak some into my breakfast bowl. Children chased each other in the deep snow, their laughter resounding throughout the settlement, and it made me think of those happy times when Lumi and I ran and played in the fort. I had been away from Stromhold fewer than two nights but it felt like months and I already missed her.

Lanterns illuminated the entrance to the tavern and the creaking, weathered sign welcomed us to the Dancing Moon.

'We sleep here tonight,' Father said, dismounting.

'With your permission, Eyvar, we'll head to the Weeping Willow,' Modi said, already turning his horse around. 'We may as well have some fun tonight. It'll be in good spirit to find relief in the softness of Engla's bosom before we have to rip the guts out from Hyllus's Varls.' A group of warriors clustered around him nodded their assent.

Modi had a sharp tongue. His keen interest in Lumi and the way he watched her with that cunning smile clenched my fists. Despite the Stromhold's rules that forbid any form of violence between warriors, I challenged him once and wouldn't hesitate to do so again. Even now, he addressed my father in a casual, matter of fact tone, devoid of loyalty towards his guardian.

'Be sure to come back on time. We leave at first light,' Father said.

I snorted at the lack of a reprimand on his part—if I was a guardian and one of my warriors acted with such disobedience, I would not hesitate to make an example of him.

When the warriors made for the tavern located outside the village walls, I turned to follow, but Father grabbed Blixt's reins. 'We're staying at the Dancing Moon tonight,' he said in a voice that left little room for negotiation.

I have always admired my father, and his courage inspired me. I strove to be like him, strong and fearless, to have people follow me as they did him, to gain his approval and to make him proud, but now, with Argil, Orri, and others listening in, I felt like shoving him away from me. Instead, I returned his cold stare and spurred Blixt out of his reach where I dismounted and proceeded inside the tavern.

The smell of sweat and damp wafted across the threshold mixed with smoke from the hearth, and it took me a moment to adjust my eyes to the dimly lit room. The place was deserted apart from a few stragglers nestled in the far corner, blathering away, too drunk to move, watching us as we made our way towards the free tables.

'It's good to see you again, Eyvar,' said the inn keep girl, filling our mugs with mead. 'Shadow grows in Elizan. The Varls invaded the settlement, leaving many dead in their wake. They never dared to cross the border before.'

'We'll deal with the Varls,' Father assured her. 'The beasts should know better than to cross into our territory, but until then, keep your children indoors.' He drained his mug and she refilled it.

A cook with a stained apron tied around his waist served food on a sizable platter and my mouth watered at the sight of mutton ribs, hearts, and liver, swimming in thick roasting juices. I inhaled the smell and my stomach cried with hunger when another platter followed, laden with potatoes and roots basted in fat from the meat.

'Let us eat and rest tonight. We'll need our strength come tomorrow,' Orri said, and a hiccup escaped his lips.

Argil laughed and clapped Orri's shoulder. 'It looks like some of us have had their share of mead for tonight.'

In response, Orri snatched Argil's cup and gulped his mead down. 'In that case, those with empty cups can seek their beds.'

Their light-hearted banter widened the gap between us. If they worried about tomorrow's assault, they didn't show it, poking fun at each other and jesting with my father. The thoughts of the upcoming battle stole my appetite and I pushed my bowl away, feeling suddenly nauseous.

'What's the matter, son?' Father asked in a low voice.

I wanted to admit the doubts that consumed me since we left home, but his creased brow and the look of concern in his eyes made me reconsider. When he gifted me with a sword I promised I wouldn't let him down, and I intended to keep that vow. 'It was a long ride,' I lied. 'Best I get some sleep before tomorrow.'

I bid them good night and fled to my room.

***

Unsettling dreams haunted me through the night. A blizzard raged outside, my bed smelled of mould and sour milk, and nightmares thrust me into an icy storm. I desperately tried to find my way out, but every direction led me back to the centre where a blanket of snow erased my footsteps. My body was freezing and I could do nothing but scream into the whiteout. The dreams pushed me further until I stood face to face with Rodolf, his eyes empty, mouth twisted in a ghoulish sneer.

I woke, my hair drenched in sweat, teeth chattering. Dawn streamed through the gaps in the shutters, casting silver light into the room. The realisation that I wasn't ready to face death brought a sudden urge to run away from Elizan, from my father and the warriors, to ride Blixt back home in shame and defeat. I scrambled out of bed and vomited on the floor, sour bile burning my nostrils. My legs felt weak as I hustled in search of my clothes, strewn around the room.

Outside, my father walked amongst the warriors with his cloak sweeping the snow, he gestured orders, urging all to make haste. We faced a long road to Elizan and the snowfall in the night covered the only path towards the settlement. When the remaining warriors joined us from the Weeping Willow, everyone looked in good spirits, preparing for the ride and tossing jokes at each other about the events from the previous night. With no jests to share and no experience in battle, I felt like an outsider among them and even reassuring nods from Father couldn't ease the feeling that I didn't belong here.

I found Blixt among the horses and the familiar lightning blaze against the reddish-brown of his coat took the edge off the dizziness that settled behind my eyes. I adjusted his saddle bag, and all the while my stomach churned, insides drifting up and down like ocean waves.

Argil squeezed my shoulder. 'Are you all right?'

I shrugged, keeping my head down, not wanting him to see my face for fear it would betray me.

But he must have sensed my anxiety because he pressed on, 'You'll do well. Remember your training and stay focused.'

'We'll head for Elizan,' Father said, his voice loud and clear, with no sign of hesitation. 'This is where the Varls were last seen. We'll approach the village from the west and purge it clean.'

'Stay still,' I muttered, trying to stop Blixt from fidgeting, but he sensed my unease and tossed his head around, stomping his feet. I pulled myself into the saddle, groaning with the effort.

My father's warhorse betrayed no signs of agitation and stood calm and responsive to his master's directions.

I leaned towards Blixt's ear. 'One day, we'll be like them, nothing will get to us.'

He snorted and I patted his neck.

We set off under the orange glow of the eastern sky. Burdened with weapons and riders, the horses braced the knee-deep snow, pushing through the drifts and clearing the trail for their companions, and Blixt, too, struggled against the harness, shaking his head. Elizan lay three night's ride to the west—a stop for merchants and travellers who made their way from Vester to Nordur and back. The white landscape reminded me of my first horse ride with Lumi and the way she smelled of ice and snow. I wondered if she thought about me. Did she believe in me and my quest? I imagined her reaction upon my return and the tone of her voice, pure and clear like a chiming of crystal bells in the breeze.

The settlement soon faded away, replaced by the white plains of Nordur. We worked our way through the empty landscape, touched by an occasional paw print left by a wolf or some other animal that happened to cross our trail. Each day, the scouts went off to hunt, returning with provisions for supper, and we would make camp and set about skinning and filleting the meat for the fire.

Huddled around the crackling flames, warriors sang songs about Nordur and exchanged tales of past battles. I listened in awe about the lost city of Antaya where mages and humans broke their alliance and started a war, bringing the wrath of

Skaldir with it, and on such evenings I felt one with the men, my heart full of courage and free from doubt.

At night, the cold reached out for us, finding its way through the smallest gaps in our furs, and I would shudder in my sleeping hide, at the merciless chill that prickled the insides of my skull. In the morning, I would wake, my face and clothes stiff and eyelashes stuck together with frost and a body full of aches and pains from the time spent in the saddle, to endure another day on Blixt's back.

Each mile brought us closer to the Varls. As the pressure mounted, our horses became jumpy and so did I, shifting in the saddle, tightening and loosening my grip on the reins, until at last, with dusk draining away the last rays of daylight, we neared Elizan. The conversation between men died down and the only sounds came from the clanking of bridle bits and grunting of horses.

A harsh smell tainted the air around us and Argil cursed under his breath. 'They did this the last time.'

'Burned the village?' I asked, looking at the circles of melted snow. The heat from the fires reached all the way here.

'If only…we're too late.'

'You mean they killed everyone?'

'That and more,' he said. Deep wrinkles covered his forehead.

My nausea returned in waves and I ushered away the images conjured up by his words. 'Do you remember your first fight?'

'In Hvitur, we fought against the bandits who killed my wife.'

'I'm sorry. I didn't mean—'

'She was seventeen.' He slouched in the saddle and a heavy sigh escaped him. 'We moved to the outskirts because Hera wanted to live away from the hustle and bustle of Hvitur. I wanted to make her happy, but in the end she paid with her life.'

'What happened?' I saw Argil in a different light for the first time. The man who rode next to me was the opposite of the one I faced every day on the practice yard, his expression pained as if his spirit had flown back to meet horrors of the past.

'They broke in when I was away, seized Hera, and stole the little that we had from the house. When I returned, she was lying in a pool of blood.' He tightened his grip on the reins, jaw muscles twitching. 'She was pregnant.'

Argil shared his darkest moments, honouring me with his trust, and I wanted to tell him how sorry I was, but the right words eluded me. The horrors of losing a loved one were unknown to me. 'Did you find them?' I asked instead. 'The people who did this to your wife?'

'They paid for their crime,' he said, his voice colder than the air around us, 'but it didn't bring Hera back.'

'But surely she must be at peace knowing that you avenged her, that her murderers had been slain by your blade.' His words baffled me. If anyone dared to hurt Lumi, I would seek them out, no matter the cost, and my vengeance upon them would be ruthless. I was sure the retribution would fill my heart with joy and bring me peace, but Argil sounded anything but peaceful.

'That may be, but with vengeance comes emptiness and the ache in my heart will never cease until I see her again in the Fields of Life.'

I didn't know if it was Argil's story or my own fear that made me say the words, but regardless of the reason, I said, 'I'm scared.'

His expression turned serious. 'There is no shame in that. Fear is your ally in battle, and you'll be wise to listen to it. It'll guide your step and save your life in many unexpected ways.'

'But how will I know what to do?'

'Just remember your training. Let the battle take you in. Feel it, and move with the rhythm of your sword. Pay attention to your foe and anticipate his next step. Don't let him distract you. Focus is your best friend. Sharpen your senses and let your body guide you.'

The sinking feeling in my stomach didn't wane. 'What's a battle like?'

Argil opened his mouth as if to say something, but then shook his head. 'It's different for everyone.'

I suspected he held back the true answer. 'I need your honesty, so I know what to expect and prepare myself.'

'You can never prepare for your first real battle.' He hesitated. 'It's bloody, gory, and painful. There's no glory, just misery and grief.'

That was not how I'd imagined it. The fabled battles that I spent my childhood reading about were filled with victory and triumph, with brave warriors and defeated villains. It was my chance to prove my worth to Father and myself. I felt the hilt of my sword between the folds of my cloak, its weight gave me reassurance and filled me with confidence. My father brought me here because he believed in me. He said I was ready, and with warriors like Argil by my side, I had no reason to doubt my abilities. I had trained so long, the moment to showcase my skills was finally here, and I couldn't let fear control me.

We stopped at the edge of the woods, seeking shelter amongst the trees, under branches covered with a thick blanket of snow. Nestled between the clouds, the full moon glared through the gaps and the shadows grew longer under its sharp stare. The darkness that lingered in the forest was uninviting and I didn't trust the sounds of life that came from within. Blixt shared my unease, shifting and grinding on his bit.

Father chose his two best scouts to investigate the surroundings while we kept in the shadows, but they returned bearing bad news—we were outnumbered by at least fifteen. The Varls had overrun the settlement and most of the inhabitants had been skinned or burned alive.

'We must weaken their ranks before we can attack in full force.' Father looked to Argil and Orri. 'There is no one I trust more to carry out this task. Take three more with you and use the night as your ally.' He jabbed his finger at Elizan. 'Hyllus threatens us with his beasts and foul magic, thinking us feeble and incapable of defending our land and people. I say, let's show him how wrong he is.' His voice grew louder. 'He wants to break us by sending the Varls to plunder and kill on our very doorstep and I say, let him try, for we're the true sons of Nordur. This is our home, and none will threaten us here.'

The warriors cheered and rattled their weapons and I joined them, feeling bolder, stronger, and fiercer than ever.

He gave the horn to Orri. 'We'll wait for your signal.'

'Can I go with them?' Knell, the archer among the warriors, stepped forward. 'My bow can prove useful.'

'Take him with you,' Father ordered, patting Knell on the shoulder. 'Agtarr's Warrior of Death rides on his arrow tips.'

Orri motioned for Knell to join them and the five of them disappeared into the night.

'Are we just going to sit here?' I wanted to feel useful, but most of all I couldn't wait to try out my sword.

'We will. We have to be ready once they give the signal.' Father fixed his stare on the burning skyline.

'Shouldn't we follow them? You've always said warriors should attack in force, that we're more powerful together.'

'Not if you're outnumbered. You must learn the strategies of war if you want to be successful leading men into battle in the future. Here's your first lesson: patience. Don't be reckless when the lives of others depend on you. I told you before, you must control your impulses. Rushing ahead into the unknown will likely end in defeat.'

Of course he was right; he was always right. I looked towards Elizan—a fiery dot on the horizon. Night claimed the Nordern sky and swallowed the forest along with us, until we were no more than shadows across the snow. The wait was long and cold. Frost sank its icy teeth into my fingers and numbed the tips of my ears. My eyelids grew heavy as the restless night pressed down on them and I jerked my head each time sleep tried to lure me in. Tension tightened its noose about my neck, and around me the warriors adjusted their swords and armour while horses fidgeted and snorted as minutes stretched into hours. I tightened the grip on the hilt of my sword and focused on catching the signal. In the silence that filled the space between us, my heart pounded like a battle drum at the thought of the struggle ahead.

At last, the faint sound of Orri's horn reached us from far away and the air ripped with the excited cries of warriors drawing their swords and spears.

'Get ready,' my father said. His strong and assured hand squeezed my shoulder. 'Cast all doubts aside because you have no need for them. I wouldn't have brought you along if I thought otherwise. Trust your sword and tonight we'll celebrate our first victory together.'

The Varls assailed us and the stories I heard about them crumbled to dust. Horribly twisted faces took shape in front of me, covered in scars, with jaws harbouring razor-sharp teeth. Once human hands were replaced by claws, curled around maces and axes. Their bodies gave out a foul odour of rot and scorched flesh, and furious shrieking sounds escaped them as they lumbered our way. Terror stole over my hands and they trembled as I drew my sword. The air, thick with soot from the burning buildings, stung my eyes and I choked on the smoke, struggling to breathe from fear that took hold. The sounds of battle came at me from all directions—desperate screams and howls joined by the clashing of steel—as warriors and creatures merged together in fury.

A Varl waded towards me, swinging an axe and ripping the air with his claws, but before I could strike, he knocked the blade out of my hand with one stroke of his axe and his claw caught my face, setting my cheek on fire. I leaped to the side to avoid another blow and snatched up my sword, almost stabbing myself with it. The Varl thrust his chest forward and let out a challenging roar. Air swished and the axe fell, an inch short of my right leg, its deadly cutting edge sinking into the snow beside me. He pulled at it with force and lifted the weapon high over his head. I didn't know if it was panic or fear that guided my hand, but I stabbed him with all my strength, through the gut, pushing the blade all the way to the hilt. His howl echoed through the burning village. Rasping for air, I scrambled to my feet and stabbed him again and again, kicking his jerking body to the ground in a frenzy.

I gaped around the field, my heart close to exploding, and everywhere I looked scrunched up bodies oozed blood onto the snow. In the chaos, I glimpsed Thommas, with his beard tangled and clothes torn, sliding a spear into a Varl's chest. But the creature grabbed at the shaft and lifted it, taking the warrior up into the air with it. There was a high-pitched sound as

Thommas hit the ground, blood gushing from his mouth, and the Varl shoved him back deeper into the snow.

I leaped to his aid, but a crash to my head stopped me in my tracks. The world went blurry and the echo of my throbbing pulse drowned out the sounds of battle. Another blow to my back sent me to my knees. Vomit burned the back of my throat and I dug my fingers into snow that turned my gloves crimson. Groaning, I crawled towards an unknown destination, my thoughts fuzzy.

Where am I? Did Argil beat me again on the training grounds?

A warm trickle ran down my temple and I tasted iron on my lips.

A piercing scream and the sound of steel grating on steel split the air and it felt like Agtarr's Warrior of Death was closing in on me. I rolled onto my back to witness two figures locked in battle, sword against mace, and everything around me became loud at once as warriors and Varls wrestled with each other, hoping to deliver that final blow.

Argil was ahead. He struggled against a creature with swollen sinews and twisted muscles instead of feet. With a cry, I lunged for my sword and sliced at the Varl's legs until he crashed to the ground with an ear-splitting roar. Argil finished him off with another thrust into his bloated face.

'Are you hurt?' he asked with his breath coming ragged. 'Anything broken?'

'No, don't think so.' Despite the pounding in my head and back, I was still in one piece. 'I owe you my life.'

'Can you walk?'

I took a few steps. 'I'll live.'

'Good. We managed to kill a few of them before we were discovered. Let's move.'

The men fought around us and blood drew dark patterns in the snow. Spears jabbed and stabbed in all directions, swords clashed with axes, and arrows rained down from every angle. We neared the gate leading to the village centre when two Varls charged us and I lost sight of Argil in the commotion. With a battle-cry, I rushed at the one holding a scythe with blades at both ends, and the smell of decay washed over me. The Varl's brain, visible through strands of hair, looked twisted, like a multitude of worms piled together. I shoved him away from me, choking on my spit. He turned the scythe in a circular motion, blades slashing around me like vicious snakes, and stabbed at me, cutting through my leather and forcing me to vault back. I rolled away and sliced the knotted muscles of his spine.

I wiped away the sweat from my brow. My sword and gloves were sticky with blood, my back burned where the mace crashed into it, and the wound in my head throbbed in a steady rhythm as if someone worked a hammer against it. My strength was fading and my knees shook, refusing to take another step, but the bodies strewn around the village attested that the battleground didn't care for the weak, levelling beasts and warriors alike.

Illuminated by the flames, shadows pushed and stabbed, kicked and screamed, and I thought I recognised Orri, latching onto a Varl, jabbing a knife into his back. Another warrior crawled with his leg ripped off, a trail of blood behind him as he wailed into the night.

A Varl ran at me from the side and sent me flying into a pile of guts. An axe fell and I braced my sword against it. A foul spit sprayed my face, and the Varl's eye closed in on me. The air hissed and the creature fell dead at my feet, blood bubbling from the hole where an arrow struck his neck. Knell stood nearby, bow in hand. He nodded as if to acknowledge the significance of the moment then disappeared into the settlement.

Death had followed me since I set foot in Elizan, and the reality of it hit me all at once: the howling of Varls, the cries of the dying men, more vivid than any stories ever told. My heart worked hard to keep me from blacking out and the ringing in my ears grew louder. Around me, the ground was covered with dismembered limbs and smashed heads, and it was hard to distinguish between the creatures and our own.

I wiped my eyes and a face stared at me from the river of blood—Modi with his jaw ripped out. Seeing his dead body sparked the familiar loathing and a part of me felt like justice was served, but the feeling was quickly replaced by guilt. If not for Argil and Knell, I too would be lying in the snow with my bones shattered. I despised Modi's arrogance, but even so, he was one of us, one of Stromhold's warriors, and no Nord deserved to die this way.

I lurched to my feet.

Father.

I had to leave my fear behind and find him, stand by his side, and let his courage fill me.

With renewed energy, I sprinted towards the village gates, but out of the shadows of the archway, a Varl dropped down on all fours and blocked my path, his tongue black and covered in pustules. I charged, aiming at his head, but he dodged and rose on his hind legs. Standing tall, the Varl slashed at the air, his claws dancing around my face, close to gouging out my eyes. I sliced at the claws and delivered another slash to his throat.

My father's voice reached me from the clamour of battle, shouting orders and urging men to push hard. His silhouette stood dark against the fires, with the sword proudly in one hand and a flaming torch in another.

I started his way, excitement mounting with each step, his name on my lips. I was about to call him when a man emerged from the shadows, wrapped in a cloak, face hidden in the blackness of his hood. When Father turned to face him, the stranger pulled his hood back and in the light of the torch, I saw his face—skin pulled by the weight of time, eyes as black as the darkest night. His top lip was split in two, exposing teeth through the gap, and his left cheek was blistered as if someone held a hot iron against it for a long time, until the flesh melted to the bone. Father dropped his torch and the darkness swaddled them.

'Father!' I lunged forward, shoving the warriors and Varls out of the way, but it was like wading through a swamp—the harder I pushed, the more of them blocked my path.

My father's body started to shake violently and his head arched backwards. I kicked and stabbed in all directions, screaming and cursing. I struck a man with my elbow and he fell into the snow, a Varl flew at me and I drove my sword into his neck. Father slid to the ground and I broke into a run, jumping over the scattered corpses. The stranger laughed—a sound like madness descending on the battlefield—and it made my soul shiver. He cast one last look at the body crumpled at his feet before vanishing into the night.

I dropped beside my father and shook him by the shoulders, but his body remained still. 'You can't die here.' My tears spotted his lifeless face. 'You said we'll never fall. You said the warriors of Nordur could never be defeated. We were supposed to show them what it means to cross us. What of the victory you promised me tonight?'

I squeezed his hand, heaving. The Guardian of Stromhold had been killed by a twisted beast. I ripped at his leather and shirt, my hands trembling in a struggle against the laces. A black bruise spread across the left side of his chest, directly above the heart. Tiny marks surrounded it as if someone dug nails into the flesh.

''Hyllus!' I cried at the sky. 'You'll pay for this!'

My body shook with rage that filled every cell, and I sprang to my feet. With a roar, I threw myself at the first Varl in my way and stabbed through flesh, chopped at claws, and sliced limbs. As warm tears rolled off my chin and turned my lips salty, everything became a blur. My arm turned into a vengeful force and directed my sword, hacking through the bodies like a sickle through grass until my energy was spent and the Varls were dead.

Elizan lay in ruins and so did my heart.

VIII

We tended to the wounded and counted the fallen. More than half of our warriors were killed, including the greatest leader among them. Silence spread across the scorched landscape and the first ravens descended to claim their battle shares, cawing the final songs for the dead. My father's stiff body was quickly claimed by the frost that tinted his skin blue and wove ice crystals through his beard and hair. Even in death, he looked proud, his face strong and determined, as if he was about to stand up and demand an account for our losses.

But his lips remained silent.

His passing opened a void in my chest and I had to keep the emotional storm brewing inside at bay, conscious of the warriors who gathered around us to pay respects to the man who led them in battle through countless winters. My first battle at Father's side, my first lesson in blood, and it had ended in defeat. The physical pain from the cuts on my head and back returned with a vengeance.

I faced the men and their eyes full of pain and regret met mine. My throat felt like grit and every attempt at swallowing proved more difficult than the last. But I knew I had to live up to my father's expectations and demonstrate my worth to the warriors, even if I felt like a failure. 'Gather the bodies, we'll burn them before we leave here.'

Two men stepped forward and leaned over Father's body. I grabbed one of them by the arm. 'No,' I said. 'My father goes home.' I thought of Mother, looking towards the road and praying to Yldir for our safe return, unaware that her god had abandoned her.

'Orri has fallen,' Argil whispered in my ear.

I shut my eyes and the stone of regret sunk deep into the pit of my stomach. Another great warrior lost. First the Varls disfigured his face and now they took his life. The night felt like a cruel nightmare, filled with loss and grief.

Knell picked up my father's sword and handed it to me. 'It belongs to you now.'

I took the sword, the memory of trying to lift it as a child clear in my mind. The blade felt light in my grip, its weight no longer a factor. The ancient script, visible through the smears of blood, enticed me with its secrets. If the legends were true, I held the blade of Skaldir, but instead of my usual anger towards the gods, great calmness washed over me, as if a long-missing piece was finally returned.

The warriors formed a tight circle around me, the points of their swords facing the earth. Was I the one to lead them? A hoax who lacked the knowledge and skills to command the men whose lives were shaped by battle, who chose swords for company in their darkest hours. I felt like a child all of a sudden, scared and helpless, but my mother was not here to guide me and my father lay dead at my feet. Stromhold, Lumi, my childish dreams, all hazy and distant. The Jarin who left for Elizan seemed unreal, like the scenes from Stromhold's tapestries and the purpose of my life was no longer clear. Warrior? A notion, filled with promises and glory but wrapped in blood and decay.

'Jarin Olversson, son of Eyvar Olversson, the Guardian of Stromhold.' Argil's voice rang in the air, clear and confident.

I anticipated laughter and ridicule, but the warriors, *my* warriors, chanted my name, stabbing the frozen ground with their swords in a steady rhythm.

'Where you go, we follow. What you command, we heed. Luck be with you and may the gods be forever at your side to guide you on your path,' Argil said and one by one, the warriors who swore allegiance to my father when I was but a baby, approached me with respect, offering their swords and loyalty to their new guardian.

I stared at the sword, lightheaded, a multitude of thoughts pressing at me from all directions. If Mother and Lumi could see me now—the warrior, the Guardian of Stromhold. My dreams, so distant a few months ago, now in the palm of my hand, placed there by no other than Hyllus, our sworn enemy. The irony. I breathed in the crisp, morning air. Not all was lost. Not yet. I had a promise to fulfil and a spell to break. I refused to accept defeat and return home empty-handed.

We built pyres from the wood scattered around Elizan and started fires that consumed the bodies of the fallen. The flames burned high, reaching for the heavens, turning great men into ash. The glow created shadows on the faces surrounding them. Perhaps they considered the journey that faced the dead before they could reach the gates of Himinn. With the three gods wrapped in a deep slumber, the Passage of Trials stood silent and empty, and I wondered if Father would make it to the other side. His soul was hampered because his killer still walked amongst the living, and it was my duty to relieve him of this burden so he could rejoice in the Fields of Life with the past guardians. I sent a silent promise to him that he wouldn't have to wait for long.

* * *

Dawn rose to the east, throwing a pink veil across the sky. Stars shimmered with the last light of the night and the moon shrank back in the face of the arising day. The fires died down, leaving smouldering patches on the ground.

'It's time,' Argil said, rubbing his eyes.

'It is,' I said. 'You'll lead our men back to Stromhold. The Varls have been defeated for now and the roads should carry you back safely.'

His eyes widened. 'What about you?'

'I'll make for Sur.' In my heart, I knew that giving Lumi her voice back was a worthy quest to pursue and would make up for the losses we endured. It was the only thing I had left in the face of all that had happened, but I feared that Argil and my men would never understand my reasons.

'Sur? But you are injured and—'

'No matter, I'll head south regardless.'

The warriors gathered around us, filling the air with whispers of confusion. 'The men of Nordur have no business in the South,' said Ulrik, the oldest of the group. His words came in rasps, half of his grey beard was torn out exposing the wound on his chin. The battle had taken a toll on him and he leaned on his spear.

'You're right, we didn't belong in the South until now. I'll no longer stand idle and let Hyllus invade our land. You know too well my father demands vengeance, and the killer must pay with his life.'

'What are you talking about?,' Argil said. 'You can't march on Vester with a handful of men. That's madness.'

'I'm going alone. I must find the witches. Everyone speaks of their powers, and Hyllus is a mage, so they should know how to defeat his kind.'

Ulrik frowned. 'Only if you get there alive. What happens if you walk into an ambush? Alone, with no warriors to keep you safe?'

'I'll keep to the borders. No one will challenge a lone man on a horse and hardly anyone knows my face.'

'I'm going with you,' Argil said with urgency in his voice. 'I can't just let you go alone to risk your life in foreign lands. Your mother would never forgive me.'

I trusted Argil more than anyone else among the warriors, but knowing my mother would be grief-stricken at the news of Father's death, I wanted him to be with her until my safe return. 'I don't think swords and arrows will do any good on this journey. I don't want to draw attention to myself, and with armed warriors at my heels I'll be asking for trouble.' I regarded each one of them in turn. 'I trust you'll take care of Stromhold while I'm gone. Once I return, armed with the knowledge of how to kill Hyllus, we'll drive him and his Varls out of Nordur for good.'

Argil leaned over. 'Can we speak in private?'

When we were out of earshot he grabbed my arm. 'You are not thinking rationally. Losing your father must be tough, and believe me, I understand the pain too well, but this idea of yours is...'

The anger I was trying so desperately to control wrestled to escape, and I had to swallow hard to contain it. 'Do you have any idea how it feels when you are given responsibility you aren't prepared for? When everyone suddenly looks to you for answers you can't possibly give them? I act as if I know what I'm doing, but I don't, and with Father gone, I don't know if I ever will.'

'Nobody expects this of you. Eyvar's death was a shock to us all, but we'll stand by you no matter what.'

'What about the guardian's oath to defend Nordur and my people to the death? How could my warriors support me if I can't even avenge my father?'

'But you will.' Argil grabbed my shoulders. 'We will find a way to kill Hyllus, but wandering off and leaving your men behind is not the way to do it.'

His words were blunt and unforgiving and ignited rebellious fires within me. 'Did you see him? Did you see Hyllus in Elizan last night? He took my father's life with one hand—no swords and no blood—and then he vanished. The witches may be the only hope for Nordur.'

'How can you be sure it was him?'

'I know it. The way he looked at me...'

Argil snorted and shook his head. 'Is this really about vengeance or is it about the girl?'

'Lumi does not concern you.' I had a lot of respect for Argil and I was grateful for everything he taught me over the years, but I wasn't prepared to listen to his lectures. Not today.

'So that's it then? You're going to go and nothing I say will change your mind? What about your mother? What do you think she will say when she hears of this?'

The thought of Mother sent a sting of pain through me, but I knew that was Argil's intention. I let the silence extend long enough for me to find the answer. 'You know how much I love my mother, and I want you to be the one who gives her the news of Father.'

'I'm not her son. I can't console her. It's you who should be with her to ease her grief.' He fell quiet before my stare.

'My return to Stromhold won't change anything. Father is dead and I'd rather try to find a way to destroy Hyllus than sit and wail over his body.'

'Think of your mother. Return with us and at least let her see you alive.'

'If I go to Stromhold now, Mother would never let me go. I'd have to take over Father's responsibilities and forget Sur. Hyllus will return again and again until we fall. The witches may be the only ones who know how to stop him.'

Argil's frown grew deeper and I knew he wouldn't let this go.

'Look,' I said, 'I know where this is going but I won't let you question my decision.' I stood up straight. 'You'll take my warriors and my father's body home and tell my mother what happened here. I don't expect you to understand my reasons, but I do expect you to follow your guardian's orders.'

'As you wish,' Argil said through gritted teeth. He turned on his heel and stormed off.

From afar I watched him share the news with my men and the look of dismay on their faces. Ulrik attempted to get past him, maybe to reason with me, but Argil stopped him and his voice carried my way as he pleaded with them to respect my decision. Even though he himself didn't approve, he refused to turn on me in an attempt to drag me back to Stromhold. He was a loyal friend.

No more words were spoken until we reached the fork in the road. I dismounted and walked over to where my father's body lay on a wooden frame, assembled by the warriors to get him to Stromhold. I leaned close to him, so no one else could hear my words.

'Rest in peace, Father. Hyllus will die, I swear it.'

Then I bid farewell to the warriors and set off into the unknown.

IX

I guided Blixt through mud furrows hardened by the frost. A snowfall brought an icy gale and I huddled in my furs as Blixt's mane turned white, glad for the trees guiding us to Vester with their branches stretched like a vault above us.

Watching the warriors tending their charges in the stables, I wanted a horse of my own, to ride and be like them. Still, I never understood the bond that could be forged between a horse and his rider. But since my father entrusted Blixt into my care, all that changed. The more time I spent in his company, the more I came to regard him as my companion and my equal even if we couldn't share a thought. His presence alone filled me with warmth and feeling his firm muscles, alive and working through the snow, made this lone journey more bearable.

The wind whipped my face and stung my wounds, waking the pain from the cuts and bruises. Its howling echoed in my thoughts, bringing back images from Elizan and my father's death. In a few days, Argil would reach my mother and the thought of her face crushed by shock and sorrow at the news, made me want to turn around and race back home to comfort her.

I camped away from the main path, finding shelter among the trees. Using supplies assembled after the battle, I lit fires to warm my stiff fingers and chewed on strips of dried meat and salted fish while Blixt enjoyed his share from a bag of grain. At night I was at the mercy of the frost and ice and I warmed myself with images of Lumi's smiling face, reassuring and familiar in the emptiness of Nordur's plains. I wanted to see her running towards me with arms outstretched, laughing, her voice loud and clear.

Days came and went. Gradually, when I had begun to lose hope of ever reaching my destination, the snow started to melt and I entered the world of sun and heat with trees heavy with honey-scented fruit and grassy crops, shifting in the light breeze. Insects buzzed in the undergrowth. The breeze warmed my numb body and as I sucked in the air, there was no sharp prickling or shortness of breath associated with the winter clime of Nordur. If Lumi was here, her eyes would widen and blue lips part at the sight of this colourful landscape, but after witnessing the events in Elizan, I couldn't bring myself to admire it.

After weeks of eating dry foods and drinking melted snow, I was hungry for some fresh food and a tree of yellow fruits looked inviting, so I picked one. It had a nice, zesty smell to it and I sunk my teeth into its firm flesh. Saliva filled my mouth as the sourness curled my tongue and I spat to get rid of the acidic taste. Even the food here was unwelcoming and bitter.

In a small pond, my reflection shimmered on the surface and I could hardly recognise myself. Gone was the smooth face and curious eyes of the dreamer who raced around Stromhold in search of tales under the watchful gaze of his mother. Stubble covered my chin and the cut across my cheek scabbed over, showing no signs of infection. I splashed the cool water on my face, rubbing away the crusted dirt. My hair reached down to my shoulders, matted with dried blood where the Varl had hit my head. Seeing my eyes staring back at me filled my heart with doubts. Did I do the right thing? Maybe Argil was right and I should have returned with him to Stromhold to mourn Father and console my mother in her grief. Perhaps travelling to Sur was a mindless idea and I had made myself look a fool in the eyes of my warriors. If my father was alive, he would know what to do.

But he was dead and I sat in a foreign land with only loneliness for company. Tears burned my eyes and I clenched my hands to try to stop them, but they escaped, rippling the surface of the pond. When the water settled, another man stared back—Hyllus. The need to destroy him grew stronger each time I recalled his deformed face. I smashed his reflection with my fist and pounded the water again and again, screaming until my throat turned raw and my voice was a croak.

I rode on. A village came into view, white stone and red roofs gleaming in the haze of the morning sun. It looked peaceful and unthreatening, but I had never been to Vester and I didn't know what to expect, so I remained watchful. I tied Blixt to a wooden post near a tavern with blue doors and benches outside. I ran my fingers over the walls as I passed, but unlike the flat stones of Stromhold, they felt gritty and uneven.

The tavern was bright, with sun's rays streaming through the wide windows, but the air was stuffy and with each intake of breath it felt as though I was inhaling wool. Tapestries lined the walls, but instead of warriors and battles, they depicted fields of red flowers, green trees, and orange fruits. Pans, pots, and cups hung off the ceiling near the bench at the back where the innkeeper talked to a woman wearing yellow. A handful of people sat around the tables, slurping from their mugs and chattering in the Vestern tongue, wearing clothes that made them look like puppets wrapped in layer upon layer of skirts and rags.

When the innkeeper approached, I asked for food and drink, silently thanking my mother for her insistence that I learn how to speak Vestern. Then I walked out the back door to sit outside. Apart from two men in the far corner, the tables here were empty and I settled with my back to the tavern wall.

The food in Vester defied Nordern tastes and my platter contained green leaves, cured hams and fish, scattered with green and black pieces of local fruit that left a sharp taste on my tongue. But to my relief the tavern served mead and I gulped down the honeyed liquid and every drop tasted like home.

A man, whose skin was leathered and dark, approached my table. 'Do you mind company, traveller?' He held a jug of wine and wore a colourful garb. A bright red turban was wrapped around his head.

Not wanting to draw attention to myself, I met his question with silence. It would be unfortunate if I found myself in the wrong company in the land where Hyllus exercised his power, but my lack of response didn't deter him.

'You're not from here, are you?' he asked, slumping beside me on the bench.

I watched him over the rim of my cup.

'I guessed as much.' He took a sip of wine and smacked his lips. 'Sweet and cold. What is better than a jug of luscious wine?'

'Mead?'

He laughed. 'I'm Mirable—a humble merchant by trade. What brings you to these parts?' His deep-brown eyes looked sharp but soft at the same time, and his black beard harboured strands of silver.

Despite my resolve not to get acquainted I said, 'I intend to cross the Great Passage.'

He sucked his teeth and studied my face. 'Ha! Very brave endeavour, if not foolish. Sur is not a welcoming place.'

A serving girl brought a plateful of round chunks of meat wrapped in dark leaves, and Mirable drowned them in oil. 'It's good for you,' he said when I looked away in distaste. He took a swig from the bottle. 'It works wonders for your health and vitality.'

'I'm used to fat.' Nords chose animal fat for cooking and preserving meat and on cold winter nights I enjoyed the taste of sliced mutton served with melted lard. Everything was much simpler in Stromhold and my thoughts chased towards home with longing.

Mirable ate his food making grunting noises joined by a chirring of insects hiding in the grass. The heat shimmered above the surface of the road and in the distance, fields upon fields of trees lined the horizon, their trunks dry and twisted with evergreen branches reaching out towards the rainless sky. Sitting in the shade didn't help much, my skin burned and sweat trickled down my neck, soaking my clothes in damp patches.

'You're attracting attention,' Mirable said.

I followed his gaze to the two men I saw earlier. They watched us, whispering to each other.

I pushed my jug aside and reached for my cloak, but Mirable stopped me with his hand. 'Don't move,' he whispered. 'I know these parts of Vester well. You're safe with me as long as you remain calm.'

I jerked my hand free. 'Do you know these men? They weren't interested in me before you came.'

'I have nothing to do with it, but perhaps…' he paused and tailed his eyes over my thick and dirty clothes, 'you should have thought about a better disguise than your Nordern furs.'

He was right. Considering that most people here wore summer fabrics, my shirt and leather trousers were a giveaway I wasn't native to the South. 'I haven't much coin with me to afford a disguise.'

The two men got up and walked towards us. One was short, his gut stretching his shirt. The other was tall and bent like a blade of grass in the wind, with harsh stubble that failed to conceal deep pockmarks on his sour face.

I reached for my sword.

'Let me handle this,' said Mirable. 'One of the skills I had to master before becoming a merchant was the ability to negotiate, and I promise, you won't find a better negotiator in these parts.' He lifted his chin and cleared his throat. 'Welcome, fellows, care to join us?'

The large man puffed and spat near Mirable's foot. 'He's not one of us. He is a wolf from Nordur.'

The other man placed his hand on a curved knife at his belt.

'We don't want any trouble.' Mirable waved his palms. 'We should all enjoy the glorious sunshine and delicious food as friends, no?'

'Shut your mouth, merchant, and hand over your purse.' The big man sneered at him and Mirable sank back onto the bench.

'Negotiations, huh?' I said. 'Why did I bother listening to you…'

I stood to leave when a silver blade flashed at my throat. 'You're not going anywhere until we're done with you.' Yellow teeth drew close to my face and the sour breath of wine and garlic washed over me. 'The likes of you aren't welcome here. We'll take the sword and your horse—and don't make a sound if you value your life.'

The time for negotiations was over. I jerked my head away from the blade and grabbed the man's arm, twisting it. I smashed my knuckles into his nose, grabbed his shoulder, and kneed him in the stomach. He bent in half, blood from his nose splattering on the table, and I pointed my sword at his companion. He eyed his knife and his cursing friend and let the blade slide into the dirt.

'Get out of here if you want to keep your teeth,' Mirable said, pushing his chest out as if he was the one they feared.

'Come on, get up.' The bigger man pulled at his companion and they scrambled away in haste.

'That was close.' Mirable let out a sigh. 'Lucky for us that I know my way with words. My mother used to say the skill of speech is most useful to merchants, but I admit that you fought well. Even so, relying on violence to have your way won't get you far.'

'If we relied on your prized skills, it would be our blood on the table.' I walked in front of him, my hands still shaking. When Father first asked me to start my training with Argil I doubted it would do me any good when faced with real danger. I was afraid of my own fear when the day came and I was plunged into battle, but as always, Father knew better. Not only was I able to cut down the Varls in Elizan, with half of my body seized by shock, but moments ago, my muscles remembered every move I was ever taught and relied on that memory to save my life.

Outside the tavern, I found Blixt chomping on the grass in the shade of the stables, and I had to smile. My four-legged friend had no such worries and I wondered how it would feel to live only in the present moment, without the need for swords and violence, content with a measure of grain and fresh grass. For Blixt, Nordur, Vester, and the open oceans were just places and his lack of ties to them granted him eternal freedom, without moral obligations, where sky was just sky and earth was just earth.

But such luxuries were denied to humans.

'Wait.' Mirable's voice pulled me out of my thoughts. 'You can't be walking around in these.' He slapped my shirt with the back of his hand. 'We must do something about your attire unless you want more thugs to follow us.'

'Us?' I tried to make sense of his babble, but Mirable steered me towards the road, his sandals kicking at the dust.

'First, we find you an appropriate outfit.'

'I have no coins and—'

'My mother taught me to help those in need, and lucky for you, I make my living selling and purchasing goods.' He grinned and patted the purse swinging from his belt. 'Coins follow me wherever I go.'

'I have no time for this. I must get—'

'I know, I know, witches of Sur and all that. You're intent on going, but I advise you to keep away from Sur and the witches if you treasure your life.'

'Why do you say that?'

'Don't you know? The witches of Sur specialise in black arts, illusion, and trickery, and are highly skilled in witchcraft. I knew a man once who went to see them, seeking a cure for his daughter's illness.' He lowered his voice. 'When three days had passed and he didn't return, his wife went after him.' He paused and looked at me with eyes narrowed. 'Neither of them returned.'

'That's hardly proof of black arts.'

He let the air out in a poof as if offended by the lack of fear on my part. 'Perhaps you'll disrespect the witches also and learn of the man's fate.'

Truth be told, I didn't know the way to Sur and needed someone who knew their way around. 'You sound like you have knowledge of the witches—and of Sur.'

'I heard they can see into the future, and merchants take fortune telling seriously. Knowing my own would help greatly when investing coin and deciding on what choices to make for the best outcome.'

'How is that different to magic?'

He fixed me with a wide-eyed stare. 'Magic kills, boy.'

I shrugged at that. There was no denying that Mirable was becoming more interesting with each passing minute. 'Have you met them, then? Witches, I mean. What happened?'

He sighed. 'In truth, I'm a coward. I went to Sur twice, but each time I lacked the courage to cross the Great Passage. I walked in circles at the crossroads, trying to steady my nerves, but to no avail. My fear of witches overpowers my need to know the future, yet I have so many questions and no way of getting the answers. Do riches await me or am I going to succumb to poverty?'

'Shame. You could've used your artful negotiation skills to persuade them to tell you everything.'

'You can jest all you want, but I'll never set foot in Sur. I despise magic and those who exercise it. It's no wonder the gods damned this foul practice. From what I've heard on my journeys, the witches are loathsome creatures, truly terrifying.'

'Can they cast spells?' I asked, thinking of Lumi and her lost voice.

Mirable shuddered. 'They can do more than that. Their power is great and legends say that even Agtarr fears their magic.'

I doubted that. There could be nothing more terrifying than the God of Death. 'If that is so then why do people travel to consult with them?'

'Ah, but that's the thing. I heard that those who were courageous enough to face them were subjected to torture and pain out of this world, and when they returned, their minds were scarred forever.'

'Have you met any of those people?'

'No, but…'

'I suspected as much.'

We walked towards the village along a narrow dirt track laced with potholes. A cart pulled by two sagging-headed oxen passed by. The driver of the cart, an old man with his eyes closed, swayed in rhythm with the wagon. The slow squeaking of wheels reminded me of Argil coming back from Hvitur with supplies and how excited I always was to see him. He delivered messages to Father and Mother and food to the kitchens, and all the while I would pester him for stories about Nords and their ships. Hvitur seemed like a distant land full of wonder, but now, so far from home, even those stories paled in comparison to the distance I covered to get to Vester.

'Why such interest in me?' I asked when the sound of the wagon faded away. 'Aren't you afraid the witches will devour me, too?'

'Can I persuade you not to go?'

I shook my head and Mirable opened his palms at me. 'I thought so. Since you're intent on going and there's nothing I can do to stop you, the only thing I can do is wish you good luck and help you on your way.'

I laughed for the first time since Elizan. 'I see. You want me to ask your questions for you.'

Mirable adjusted his turban. 'This is not a laughing matter. The business of my future is most serious.'

'Well then, guide me to Sur and I promise to do what I can,' I said. 'If I survive that is.'

'Truly?' His eyes widened and a smile stretched his lips. 'It is as my mother said, I was born under the lucky star.'

* * *

The market square in the village was alive and bustling with people dressed in colourful tunics, engaged in trading with locals and fellow merchants. They haggled, laughed, and shouted from behind their stalls, under linen roofs that provided relief from the piercing sun. Peddlers bit on coins to check their value, arguing over the price of fresh meat and fish and pickled vegetables stocked in jars and wooden barrels. We waded through the waves of people and animals, the commotion making me queasy. I tightened my grip on Blixt's reins to steady myself. A mixture of smells I never knew existed assaulted me and the earthy, sharp aromas of spices made me sneeze. My eyes watered just from looking at the long, green pods kept in wicker baskets.

'What are we looking for?' I asked, pushing past a merchant with a basketful of yellow flowers and orange fruits.

'Something to fit your broad shoulders…' Mirable's words drowned in the sea of voices.

A large, horse-like creature with two humps rising out of its back towered above one of the stalls, making sounds akin to someone being strangled.

'It's a camel,' Mirable said at my incredulous stare. 'Foul creature, but necessary if you plan to cross the Eydimork Sands.'

I gave the creature a wide berth. Crossing the endless desert on its back didn't feel like a safe thing to do. 'Have you done it?'

'Me? No. I treasure my life. The desert is a forgotten land, hostile and unforgiving. A scholar I knew ventured off seeking knowledge. Ales was his name and he was hungry to discover what laid at the edge of the Eydimork Sands. That was the last time I heard from him.'

A woman with a red flower in her hair crossed our path. Her face was covered in the folds of a colourful shawl adorned with golden tinsels that chimed as she moved. 'Are you seeking pleasure, stranger?' she whispered, setting her deep brown eyes on mine and sliding her slender fingers across my arm.

Mirable pushed her. 'Go away, thief.'

She hissed and her eyes narrowed to slits. Like a snake, she weaved into the crowd and disappeared from view.

'Damn Willbenders. They sneak up on you with offers of pleasure and before you know it you're caught in their webs and robbed clean. Best stay sharp and keep your eyes open.'

It was difficult to remain watchful in the loud sea of people where everyone pushed at each other, trying to draw your attention and steal your gold.

Mirable stopped at a stall containing clothes and materials in all shades of blues, reds, whites, and greens. 'This is perfect.'

'The best garments in the market,' bellowed the trader. He grinned at us, showing his teeth.

Mirable went through rack upon rack of colourful fabrics and pulled out one of the garments. 'This will do,' he said, handing me the robe. 'Get to it. The sooner you change, the better.'

There was no point in arguing, Mirable was on a mission, adamant to turn me into one of the locals. Resigning to my fate, I slipped behind a wooden screen and dropped my clothes in favour of the southern fashion, which allowed men to walk around resembling women. Despite that, it felt good to drop my tattered garments and relieve my sunburned skin from the constant rubbing of the furs and leather. The tunic consisted of two pieces draped about the body and secured with a pin that allowed for a greater flow of air in Vester's hot clime. But what would Lumi make of me? I was glad that my warriors weren't here to witness this, seeing their guardian dressed like a woman would no doubt bring up smirks and sarcastic remarks. Guilt snatched my thoughts, and instead, I heard their voices full of accusations and disappointment at the guardian who abandoned them when they needed him the most.

'It suits you.' Mirable looked delighted with the result. 'Shame we can't do much about your sunburnt face. Well, no matter, let us move on.'

Before I could ask, he was off, his turban bobbing up and down as he navigated his way through the masses. I followed, afraid that without him I would never find my way out. We stopped at another stall and Mirable bought a horse—an old and rundown nag that nipped at his turban as soon as he got too close. I watched with curiosity as he negotiated every bit of silver in his palm until he persuaded the exasperated owner of the horse to hand him the reins.

'Isn't she a beauty?' he asked, snatching the fabric away before the horse had a chance to devour it. His satisfied smile assured me that he found immense pleasure in this exchange, but I had seen enough ailing horses in my father's stables to disapprove of this purchase.

'Waste of coin if you ask me. You'll be lucky if it lives to see another year.'

'Looks can be deceiving... But let's not linger, you have a passage to cross. Pray that the Volkans stay asleep during your intrusion.'

'The Volkans?' I asked as we mounted our horses.

'The fiery mountains of the South. The Great Passage to Sur lies at the western edge of Vester and the Volkans guard the trail. They've slept for centuries with their fires dim and seething inside, but who knows, if the fancy takes them they may explode and burn everything to the ground.'

* * *

We rode together, keeping as near to the border as we could without falling into the ocean. The smell of dust in the air intensified as we neared the Volkans. With each passing mile, I felt less sure of myself. The path to Sur, so simple when reading about it in Stromhold's library, seemed more uncertain. But worst of all, I couldn't know I would come out of this experience alive. Even Mirable—a well travelled merchant—was too afraid to cross the Great Passage.

'What's the capital like?' I asked. Talking was better than wallowing in my doubts.

'It's large and busy, and it used to be a great place for merchants, but since Hyllus built his tower in the city, people live in constant fear.'

I clenched my fists. Everywhere I went, my adversary followed, even if only in name. 'Have you met him?'

Mirable's eyes opened wide. 'By the gods, no. To meet him would mean death, but he's more of a ruler to Vester that the archeon himself. The old man is weak and feeble and Hyllus controls him with his magic.' He shuddered. 'Nothing good ever came from magic.'

'Don't people want to fight back? Nords would never bow to a leader out of fear.' I thought of Stromhold's warriors—strong and daring—and was proud to be one of them.

'They're busy trying to stay alive. Hyllus's hunters come unannounced and seize people.' Mirable curled his lips. 'I'd rather die than end up like one of his creatures.'

I needed to know more about my enemy. 'With Antaya destroyed close to two hundred years ago, where does his power come from?'

'Antaya may be gone, but not all mages died with it. I have no doubt that some still skulk at the edges of the world, waiting for their goddess to wake. But Hyllus wasn't always this powerful.'

Hyllus's name was forever on my father's lips and he was a threat to Nordur for as long as I could remember. No one revealed to me his exact intentions but with the Varls assaulting our land, it wasn't hard to guess that Hyllus wanted to take over Nordur and turn Nords into slaves or worse.

'He was born to a Vestern family,' Mirable carried on, 'but because of his deformities he was laughed at, ridiculed, and shunned. Years later, he returned to Vester a changed man, obsessed with transforming flesh using magic. It was harmless at first, an odd animal here and there, but it all changed when the archeon summoned him.' He slapped at a fly buzzing around his neck.

I imagined Hyllus as a disadvantaged child, forsaken by the very people who brought him into this world, but instead of sympathy I felt only rage towards the man who killed my father. 'Having a misfortunate childhood doesn't give you the right to inflict pain on others. How could any of the hardships he's wrought justify his acts? He does to people what the gods did to him, except he's no god and never will be.'

'Agreed, but until we bear his scars we'll never know how it feels to be tainted this way. One could assume your heart would reflect the pain of such disfigurements. Some of us would rise above it and do good, but others, with blackness in them, would cast away the light and choose a darker path. Who knows... But enough of Hyllus. I wish to learn about you. Aside from the obvious, that you're a Nord, why are you here, so far away from your lands?'

I had to choose my words carefully so as not to upset him, without revealing too much of myself or my purpose. 'My loved one needs help and I'm here to find answers to her affliction.'

'Why don't you try a healer instead? You won't have to risk your life and he may be able to aid you. I know a man—'

'Her illness is not of this world and can't be cured with physical means.'

'How can you be sure?'

I couldn't tell him without revealing details about Lumi and the cause of her muteness. Given Mirable's fear of magic it was best if I remained just a man with a sick family member. 'I can't be sure, but I hope the witches can help me understand.'

* * *

At last, we reached the crossroads. Mirable dismounted and tied his horse to a lone tree. Fields stretched far and wide in all directions and the afternoon sun lost some of its heat.

He pointed at the valley ahead. 'Once you cross the Great Passage, the land will become a mirage. The road ahead will look never-ending and the landscape will stay the same. Don't stray from the path. You'll reach a bog surrounded by a forest.

Wait at the edge. If you go further, the bog will claim your life. That's as far as my knowledge goes. What awaits you there, I cannot tell.'

The road ahead looked desolate and I wanted to delay my farewell. Since my lonely weeks on horseback through the plains of Nordur, having Mirable as a companion made me realise how much I missed human contact. I wasn't much of a talker, but he had enough words for both of us and listening to his chatter kept me from thinking about my father's death and worrying about Stromhold. At times I regretted refusing to allow Argil to join me.

'Are you sure you don't want to come?' I asked.

'For this journey, my friend, you're on your own.' He grabbed my hand and squeezed it tight. 'When you get to the bog, sit and wait. The witches choose who to listen to and who to ignore. Pray they don't take your life, and instead provide you with the answers you seek.'

'My thanks. You've been a great help to me and I won't forget it.'

'If you ask the witches about my future, I'll consider the debt repaid.'

'Jarin,' I said, steering Blixt towards the Passage. 'My name's Jarin.'

'Well, Jarin, I'll await your return in this very spot. May Yldir guide you.'

X

I rode further into the Great Passage. The answers I sought awaited me there, and yet my stomach felt like stone. As a young boy playing with Lumi, I had imagined this journey so many times, excited about the idea of travelling to Sur and unravelling the mystery surrounding the witches. I wanted to return to Stromhold a hero, bearing the gift of voice for Lumi, and win her affections for all winters to come.

I laughed—a grim and sorry sound in the surrounding emptiness. Others attempted the challenge I set myself and it didn't end well, but here I was, riding Blixt into the witches' nest, foolish enough to disregard Mirable's warnings.

But how could I not? Father's death changed everything. Even if I managed to stay alive and break Lumi's curse, my return home would be far from victorious. I would have to take the guardian's oath, lead the warriors of Stromhold, and defeat Hyllus. What chance had I to succeed where my father, the strongest man I knew, had failed.

Nearing the Volkans, the air grew heavy with grey specks and the foul stench of spoiled eggs. My mouth was dry and throbbed with a dull ache. When I touched my lips, my fingertips came away bloody from the cracks caused by the heat from the mountain walls. Blixt snorted and flinched at the rumble emanating from the depths of the Volkans, which stood tall and proud, their vapours turning daylight into an overcast. Vibrations travelled under the surface of the earth as we moved cautiously forward. I patted Blixt's neck with soothing words to calm him, but he jerked and stepped erratically with every tremble. The fog of ash intensified as we headed deeper into the valley and I rubbed the soot off my face and covered my mouth and nose in the pit of my arm, praying we wouldn't get lost.

The ground turned to rock shaped like smooth waves with layers of grey and brown, and it felt as if we were wading through the ocean, gliding up and down, except it was solid stone under Blixt's hooves. This valley was like no other, and even with the danger from the Volkans and the offensive odour, I had to admire nature's creation.

When the path curved, I spied white shards poking through the coat of ash, and when we got closer, I recognised human bones. Like a bad omen, a skull stared at me through hollow eye sockets, as if foretelling that I too would become one with this barren landscape. Nearby, a rusty axe and a saddle lay abandoned—a testimony that not all managed to cross the threshold to Sur. I saw myself and Blixt in their place, our bones withering away in this valley of death. I looked away before fear had a chance to engulf me.

A blast of fresh air came our way and Blixt surged forward, leaving the heart of the Volkans behind. We both welcomed a change of scenery. The road ahead was as straight as an arrow and overgrown in places, which confirmed my suspicions that not many travellers came this way. To my left and right, mist shrouded bare fields and I couldn't hear any animals or birds in the silence that enveloped us. The only sound came from the gravel flicking from under Blixt's hooves. The air was sticky and still, as if the wind was too afraid to venture this far. We passed a dead tree, bare, its lifeless branches reaching out our way, and moments later, the same tree came into view. I picked up speed.

A movement caught my eye—a silhouette, wrapped in white fluttering robes, danced in the field, making shapes and figures with her hands. My mind was playing tricks on me. For an instant, I thought it was Lumi and my heart fluttered. I wanted to call out to her, but the merchant's words rang in my ears, warning me not to stray from the path.

The mysterious figure dispersed into the mist, leaving me alone again. A sudden longing for company came over me and I wished Mirable was here to take the edge off with his cheery voice, though he would no doubt be quivering with fear and rebuke me for dragging him through this silent wasteland.

The world grew darker and more ominous as we drew closer to the bog that Mirable spoke of, and I let out a sigh of relief. Thanks to his guidance, I was able to stay the course. I stopped at the edge of the woods and it was as he said, naked trees thronged together, the swamp stretching beneath them with the smell of decaying peat in the air. The midges buzzed around, dancing in self-formed spheres, attracted by the odour of our sweat. I sat on the grassy bank with my stomach sealed tight by nerves. The aura of foreboding hung thick above this deserted corner of the world and a voice in my head urged me to abandon this place.

I was about to risk my life to obtain answers to my questions, but why would witches listen to me? I may be a Guardian of Stromhold in the North, but in Sur, I meant less than a grain of salt. Like a ribbon of smoke, a whisper slinked into my ear, speaking words in a tongue I couldn't decipher, but it sounded like an ancient curse and when I searched for the source, only silence answered. I sprang to my feet, grabbed Blixt's reins, and placed my foot in the stirrup, ready to gallop back.

But then I heard it—a faint, ringing sound. Startled, I looked around. All was still, but the feeling I was no longer alone intensified and dread crawled over me like a multitude of earwigs. Silence fell over the forest and even the buzzing of the midges faded away.

Something was coming.

The forest parted, making way for the witch as she rang her silver bells. My compulsion to flee returned with force. It was as if her presence stripped every part of me until I stood naked, rooted to the spot and wrapped only in fear. The witch was ancient, seemingly older than the Volkans themselves, with folds and deep lines in her arid face. Her skin stretched thin over the veins on her fingers and gaps in her hair revealed withered patches of scalp. Her left eye was missing and the socket was filled with a dark, gelatinous substance that pulsated with life. A white raven perched on her shoulder, plunging its beak into the blackness and ripping at the tangled mass. I gagged.

'You come before us, Jarin Olversson, hungry for answers to things which are better left unanswered.' Her voice was a whisper and I wasn't sure if she spoke the words or if something rustled in the trees.

'How do you know my name?'

'We know all about you. I read your name in the stars, the desert sand whispered it to my sister long ago. We traced your life in ripples of water and the flicker of flames.' She swayed as the raven plunged its beak into her socket.

I took a step back and the witch sniffed the air as if sensing my disgust. 'Do you fear Hrafn? He means no harm; his wisdom is greater than the world itself and we are his vessels. He takes a piece of us and in return grants us the power to see into the future. Wouldn't you trade your feeble body for such a gift?'

The raven shifted on her shoulder, black dripping from his beak, and he trained his eyes on me as if sensing we spoke of him. I tried to hold his stare, but those glistening eyes cut into me like sacrificial daggers, forcing me to look away or be stabbed to death.

'Hrafn is no ordinary raven. He speaks to me from the depths of time, but to comprehend such matters, you would have to be one of us.'

This encounter with the witch couldn't end well for me, but even so, I pushed away my fear and took a deep breath. 'I've come before you to break the spell that cursed someone dear to me, and to obtain magic strong enough to defeat Hyllus.'

She focused her other eye on me. The pupil was clouded and something shifted beneath the cataract. 'Such confidence! You think the girl is bound by a spell, do you?'

'Magic sealed her voice. My father found her wandering in a blizzard years ago. She was mute when he brought her home.'

The witch sniffed the air again. Everything about her terrified me, but I held on to the last strands of courage.

'Only your kind could be so foolish as to let the evil inside your walls,' said the witch. 'There is no curse. The girl is not bound by magic of any kind.'

'What do you mean? Is this some kind of a trick, a riddle for me to solve?'

'It's not a trick, boy.' Her tone lifted the hair on my skin. 'The woman you call Lumi is not from here. Her heart belongs to the wintery slopes of Shinpi. She manipulated your mind and has taken away your home.' The witch's laugh carried through the misty woods.

I couldn't understand the meaning of her words. 'Stromhold stands firm against invaders, stronger than ever. We defeated the Varls sent by Hyllus in Elizan and my warriors returned to the fort with my father's body.'

'Your trust in the girl is ill placed. But that's not what you wanted to hear, is it? You filled your witless heart with her image, hoping to charm her with your dreams, but by choosing to come here, you unleashed a storm. It will consume all you ever loved, including yourself. We expected better from you, but your lesson is on its way, and it will be a dark one.'

Nothing she said made sense, but I was afraid to demand clarity, so instead I asked, 'What of Hyllus?' I was ashamed at the sound of my sheepish voice. 'He killed my father in Elizan and I must avenge his death. Agtarr demands it.'

'Hyllus is a mere pawn, indulging in transformation magic, broken by the very people who brought him into this world. Madness drove him to the citadel where he brings his creatures to life. You are too weak to stand against him and your body too hollow to sustain any kind of magical powers. With magic comes darkness and your soul is too meek to welcome it.'

'But I need your help!'

'Your father, Eyvar, was a great warrior, but his sacrifice was in vain, and it seems his son is heading down the same path.'

'Sacrifice? He died defending Nordur.'

She laughed. 'There is much you don't understand. Your father and mother died protecting you, hoping destiny could be altered, but you wouldn't know that, being shrouded in the lies they wove for you.'

'My mother is safe at home. She wasn't in Elizan.' The old crone had it all wrong and I grew angry. 'Your predictions are false. Can you help me or was my journey for nothing?'

She waved me off and turned back to the forest, ringing her bells.

'Wait!' I tried to stop her in a final, desperate attempt. 'I met a man… a merchant. He calls himself Mirable. Do you know him?'

She twisted her head my way. 'Mirable… His fate is sealed.'

'What is it that awaits him?'

The witch regarded me with her unseeing eye. 'I feel pain… great pain. I smell freedom and I see transformation. Challenge lies in his way and he shall follow his path until he will be no more.

'What about me? Of my future?'

'Return to Stromhold and you will find the answers you so eagerly seek. Time will reveal all.'

I caught her arm, but it turned to mist in my hand and the witch was gone.

XI

With a heavy heart and grim thoughts thundering in my head, I took the reins and led Blixt back the way we came, treading through the empire of angry Volkans until we reached the fork where I parted with Mirable. He promised to wait for me here, but the crossroads were empty and I couldn't see the merchant anywhere. I resolved to wait for him, but when the hours passed and Mirable didn't show, I cast one last look at the Great Passage and steered Blixt back onto the road leading north.

My efforts were in vain, and coming to Sur was a mistake. My limbs felt heavy as if the whole journey had settled on them—my wounds, the miles spent on Blixt's back, the heat and the fear pressing me down. The witch didn't harm me, but she didn't help me either, and now I had to go home, face the warriors, and tell them of my second defeat.

The journey to Stromhold was a blur. The witch's words lurked in my subconscious like an assailant waiting for an opportunity to strike, and no matter how hard I tried to ignore them, they wouldn't go away. She implied that Lumi was from Shinpi—a distant land that no one had ever set a foot on. Some said it did not exist, others spun tales of its people praying to the Laughing Gods who had the ability to shift forms and change faces, feeding on the souls of their worshippers. How could it be that Lumi came from such a mystical place when my father found her alone in the wilds? A little girl would have no means to cross the Great Atlantic, and she was mute.

That's what she had led me to understand, at least, and I had no reason to disbelieve her. I realised how little I knew about Lumi. Although we grew up together, due to her ailment I could never question how she came to be in the wilds. But what did it matter? There was no one who knew her better than me, so why should I even consider the words of the witch, a creature known for her cunning tricks? If anyone was to be mistrusted, it should be the old crone with her foul mouth and that disgusting raven.

I stopped at the tavern where I met Mirable and searched the place, hoping to see his red turban and cheery smile, but my chest tightened with disappointment and I berated myself for growing so attached to a stranger. Perhaps because I grew up surrounded with disciplined warriors, Mirable's merry and light-hearted nature drew me in.

I ate and drank alone, but the food tasted sour in my mouth and worry for what waited for me in Stromhold grew with each passing day. A deeper, darker thought followed me home, planted by the witch when she spoke of my mother's death. I didn't understand much of what the withered crone said, but even as I refused it, some part of me knew the legends of Sur held true and the witch's powers couldn't be denied.

Forever faithful, Blixt carried me forward until we left the Vestern sun far behind us. As we edged closer to the cool winds of Nordur, the nights grew colder and colder, and soon, the snowy slopes welcomed us home. I missed the familiar chill and so did my skin, flaking from the constant exposure to the heat, and I enjoyed the cool wind as it embraced me, easing the burning on my cheeks. Wrapped in my Nordern cloak, I looked forward to seeing Argil and Mother, but still, the unshakable feeling that something was amiss intensified.

I complained about the deep snow and took my irritation out on Blixt, pushing him harder through the drifts until, gripped by frustration, I dismounted and followed the path to Stromhold's gates on foot. It wasn't any faster, and for the first time I cursed the snow that clung to my boots as if determined to thwart me from reaching my destination. Father's scouts would have approached me with orders to halt, but no one came to question me and I pushed myself harder.

The gates were ajar—another worrying sign.

In the courtyard, a shape was buried in the snow and I brushed the white crust away, revealing Knell's frozen face, glassy eyes staring at the sky. I remembered him nodding at me in the midst of battle and the shock at seeing him dead shoved me backwards into the snow. I rubbed my eyes in a foolish hope that I was seeing things. Knell saved my life, so how could this be? The sky hung low and the darkness gathered, pressing the angry-looking clouds together. The wind howled louder, more forceful, as it rushed around the courtyard picking fights with my cloak and hair. In a window above, a shutter crashed open and closed, sending my heart into quivering spasms. I felt exposed in this sea of whiteness and Stromhold, with its walls that once offered security and shelter, loomed above, grey and impenetrable, leering down at me through the multitude of windows. For the first time I saw the fort through the eyes of our enemies. It looked harsh and merciless. The outbuildings that I scoured as a boy and knew so well, offered many crevices for someone who wished to remain unseen.

I unsheathed my sword and crept to the entrance, though my heart was hammering and I barely had the strength to hold the blade. Dread crawled under my skin at the thought that someone was inside, and despite the icy wind, rivulets of sweat damped my forehead. If someone was still within the walls, I stood little chance on my own. There were more bodies: Ulrik, who opposed my journey to Sur. Sven, who laughed at his own jokes in the kitchens. Bertel, who was with my father when he found Lumi. And others whose names escaped me as I tried to make sense of the death around me. The scouts, servants, and warriors who fought beside me in Elizan with their sunken eyes like broken mirrors...

I had to stop at the door to steady my shaking hands. It was as if the ice from the Grand Isfjells swept through Stromhold, freezing everything in its wake.

Snow swirled into the hall when I crossed the threshold and crept up the steps. The foreboding silence lingered within the walls and every step I made seemed ridiculously loud. I stumbled across the body of Selma, with skin dry as a husk, limbs stiff, and mouth gaping. She held a bundle tight to her chest as if she was running away from someone or something, but her assailant caught up with her here and dealt her the same hand of death. Seeing someone who was so close to my mother in such a state turned my fear into terror and I whispered into the shadows, 'Mother? Lumi?'

I inched for the stairs, my back to the wall. Wood creaked under my feet and I stopped, certain that ambush was inevitable, but the silence persisted. The door to my mother's bedchamber was wide open and I saw the body of Argil sprawled across the threshold, hand frozen around the hilt of his sword. His mouth was stretched in a silent scream and it looked as if he fell attempting to protect the entrance to the chamber. I knelt beside him.

'What happened…?' Argil was like a brother to me and the shock strangled my words. He was one of the best swordsmen in Stromhold. Who had managed to overpower him?

Through tears, I recalled my boyhood and our sword practice. Argil shaped me into a warrior and never let me down. Even during the battle in Elizan, he found me and saved my life, but I wasn't here to do the same for him. I failed him, I failed everybody. Against all advice, I insisted on travelling to Sur and sent my warriors to their deaths. I betrayed my father's legacy and because of me Stromhold was no more. I wanted to apologise, to ask forgiveness, but what good would the words do to a dead man? Argil didn't need my apology, he needed my loyalty and friendship and I refused him both when I ordered him to return home.

The chamber spun around me as I got to my feet and crossed over Argil's body. Mother laid on the bed, frozen like the rest of them, mouth twisted in a ghostly grimace, unseeing eyes staring at the ceiling. I forgot about the threat and rushed to her bed. 'Mother?' Panic tightened its grip on my throat. 'Mother!' I shook her in a foolish hope she would come back to life. 'No…this can't be happening. Not here, not like this. You told me this was our safe place.'

I lifted her body and it felt rigid in my arms, her spirit was long gone. I buried my face in the folds of her frozen dress and

I wept, rocking her back and forth, my body numb and weak all over. Without her, my life was broken, and a great flood spilled across the world I knew, drowning me, pushing me further and further away from the familiar shores, my meagre dreams shattered like a raft against the Grand Isfjells. And for the first time, I prayed. I pleaded with Yldir to allow her safe passage, to keep her from harm and grant her a place in the Fields of Life, next to my father, until I was ready to join them.

I was beginning to understand the witch's words. Mother, always upset with Lumi about her little magic tricks, Lumi's attraction to snow and ice, our first kiss that almost killed me, Rodolf's unexplained death. Holding my mother's body in my arms, I could no longer deny the truth. The witch warned me about this moment, about Lumi; she sent me back home with the words that time will reveal all, knowing my questions were already answered. What a fool I had been for denying her warnings. If I hadn't, perhaps she would have shown me the way or advised how to save my mother, but instead I berated her, calling her predictions false, and now it was too late. My foolish dreams and fascination with Lumi led to this tragedy and there was no one left to blame but me. My mother died in grief, knowing that her husband was dead and her son abandoned her when she needed him the most. I wasn't here to protect her and my ignorance and stubbornness killed her in the end. I gently placed her body back on the bed and strode for Lumi's chamber.

I pushed the door open. 'Lumi?' I bellowed. The fireplace was a gaping, dark hole. Her bed sheets neatly folded, blue dress hanging off the footboard, and the wind banging the shutters against the wall. No sign of her.

I returned to the courtyard where snow fell in thick and large flakes, the storm breaking from the sky.

'Lumi!'

I strode towards the gates.

I started to run with Father's sword weighing me down like guilt. My eyes burned and I couldn't think clearly, my thoughts scattered like hearth embers in a draught. Stumbling over the snow dunes, I screamed her name into the blizzard, but only the wind howled back. Everything turned fuzzy, but I pushed forward with no sense of direction when I tripped over a branch. With half of my face buried in the snow, I thought of death. Freezing in the storm was a fit way to go for someone like me and I would know what my warriors and Mother felt when the ice consumed them. Jarin Olversson, the son of Guardian Eyvar Olversson, the biggest fool in Nordur, tricked by a girl from Shinpi, the land that didn't even exist.

Then, there she was.

She came at me in a haze, bare feet leaving delicate footprints in the snow with her white gown fluttering in the wind, the blackness of her hair a startling contrast against the icy landscape. Her narrow eyes looked down on me piteously. I scrambled to my feet and met her gaze, feeling the chill of her breath on my face, colder than the blizzard. From the day my father brought her home, my life had revolved around her and the ways I could please her. I travelled miles in search of a way to break her curse, lost my father and mother, everyone I knew, and now Stromhold was an empty shell. Everything I held dear had vanished without a trace. In this moment, looking into her frozen eyes, my heart could take no more and it shattered into a thousand pieces. I felt an urge to throttle her, to see life slipping out of her nimble, beautiful body.

'Jarin,' she said, her words ringing in the air like a sharp peel of crystal cups coming together. 'The hero returns to Stromhold.'

The shock snatched my voice and I stared at her.

She laughed. 'My magic grants me control over every part of my body, but you were too busy to notice, dreaming about being my saviour, breaking spells... How foolish. Your mother knew...'

I stumbled backwards, shaking with humiliation. 'You killed her. You killed everybody. Why? Why kill people who showed you nothing but love?'

She pouted her lips. 'Love…I don't know the meaning of the word.' She shook her head. 'Your ignorance cost you dearly. Let it be a lesson for your kind, never to defy Goro-Khan.'

'Who is Goro-Khan?' Everyone, it seemed, had secrets, and I was the only person left in the dark.

'My master, of course. The Laughing God.'

'The Laughing God? But Shinpi is just a legend. It doesn't exist.'

'If it doesn't exist, how do I stand here? Shinpi is my home and your people are right not to travel there. We don't take well to strangers.'

Her every word sounded like a tale recited from the scrolls we read as children, ancient and mystical, but never real. 'Why now? Why wait all these years? Why not slay us all when you first came here?'

'My power grows with maturity, so patience is the key. Goro-Khan gave me a task and there's too much at stake for me to fail.'

'What about me? You left me till last so you can shame me, see me broken?'

'You must live, Jarin Olversson. You have to play your part and fulfil the prophecy. There is a much greater power at work and you'd do best to stay out of the way until your destiny calls on you. The storm is coming and when it's here, you'll be the heart of it.'

Lumi's voice, every word, ripped and burned everything inside and I wanted to see her dead. Rage wiped out every trace of shame and I drew my sword.

'You can't kill me with steel,' she said. 'The essence of my being is out of reach, hidden in a place where none can enter, even me.'

I didn't care. Her betrayal rocked my very core and I could take no more. I slashed at her with all my might, but the blade went right through as if she were made of air. Her laugh vibrated around me and she disappeared into the storm.

* * *

I rode Blixt into the forest and axed branches for the funeral pyres. I carted them back and stacked them together, so everyone had their own bed of twigs to lay on. Dragging the frozen bodies on top of each one, I begged for forgiveness, thankful for the frost that preserved them until I could bring myself to bid my final farewells.

In the days that followed, I walked through Stromhold like a ghost, paying little attention to the world around me. I heated fresh water from the well and cleaned the dirt and grime off my body, and with my father's razor I shaved off my beard, but only when blood dripped into the basin did I realise I had cut my cheek. The fog of hurt that wrapped my heart drowned any physical pain, leaving me numb to all sensation. I replaced my worn clothes with new ones and spent the afternoon repairing and treating my leather boots. Stromhold kitchens were well stocked and I had ample food, but I couldn't recall what any of it tasted like.

At first I decided to sleep in my chamber, but after a night of tossing and turning, I fled, finding refuge in Blixt's stable where I sank into the straw beside him and lay, with my eyes wide open, staring into the blackness. Tutor Marco once told me a tale of a man who couldn't cry. No matter how hard he tried, the tears weren't there and people started calling him the tearless one. I didn't remember the full story, but eventually the man died of silent grief and I was just like him. No matter how hard I tried to force tears, my eyes remained dry as dust. On some nights, I prayed to Agtarr to send his Warrior and take my life, but even the God of Death closed his ears to me. I was alone in my suffering, forsaken by all and unable to change the past. Even having Blixt to keep me company couldn't ease my grief and loneliness.

On the nights when I drifted off to sleep, nightmares filled with Hyllus, Lumi, and my dead warriors chased me around until I woke, trembling and soaked in sweat. Even Mother paid me a visit. She stood frozen, pointing her finger at me, with Father's body at her feet, and her scream would thrust me back into wakefulness. And all the while, Lumi's laughter echoed inside my skull like the voice of a spirit trapped in an eternal loop.

When I couldn't put it off any longer, I lit the pyres. With flashing of flames, the time had come to send my people to their final resting place. Standing beside my mother's burning body, I welcomed darkness into my soul, letting hatred wrap her claws around my heart. I had only one purpose now. Hyllus, Lumi, Goro-Khan—the three of them would pay for this destruction.

I raised my father's sword to the sky. 'I'm coming for you all.'

XII

The walls of Stromhold faded away to a grey outline on the horizon. Once brimming with warriors and the sound of chiming swords, the last fort in Nordur stood empty, its halls silent but for the wind, roaming free in the abandoned chambers. My home was now full of ghosts and memories and I was at the heart of its demise. Turning my back on the past, I spurred my horse forward in the direction of Hvitur where I hoped to find refuge among my fellow Nords and meet my father's brother, Torgal. Two things drove me forward—Blixt with his unwavering strength as he tread the deep snow, and the fire that ignited in my heart on the night my mother's body turned to ash. I swore vengeance and I would not rest until my family was avenged and Lumi's betrayal punished.

The day was bright, with sun poking through the clouds. The surface of the snow mocked me, glittering like a multitude of scattered gemstones. Everything was light—unlike my thoughts, which swam in a sea of anguish of my own making. Numbing pain settled in my muscles and no matter how much I shifted in the saddle, I struggled to get comfortable. I should be grieving my mother and my friends, wallowing in my loneliness and hurt, but instead I thought of her.

Lumi—the name tasted bitter on my tongue. After so many years of longing to hear her voice, now its reproachful sound rang in my ears, the voice of a silent killer, strengthening my resolve to hunt her down, and no measure of time would soften the disappointment and hurt she left in her wake. Her betrayal was like a cheek stuck to an icicle; the instinct is to free it and as the pain rips your skin away, you are left with no choice but to feel it, moment by moment. I offered her my life and in return she took the lives of everyone I loved. Once I considered her to be the most beautiful girl alive, but now, all I saw was the pale face of a murderer. And still, I couldn't think of anything else and despised myself for my weakness towards her. She was the first woman I opened myself to and she would be the last. And whatever game she and Goro-Khan played, they would pay for every life lost.

Hours stretched into days as I followed the path to Hvitur with only bitter cold and grim misery for company. On the snowy nights, I didn't light fires to keep warm, instead I huddled in the dark, shivering and listening to the chatter of my teeth, daring Agtarr to come for me. Some days I pleaded with him, on others I demanded relief, but my treacherous body and soul remained in a tight embrace, withstanding the harsh conditions of our journey. The little food I had lasted for five days and when my saddlebag ran empty, I didn't hunt to refill my supplies, allowing hunger to be a constant reminder that I was to blame for everything that befell me. I wanted to remember every stretch of this journey, the pain and hardship, so I could go back to these moments if I ever thought of steering away from my chosen path.

Days later, the road narrowed and in the distance, where the mountain peaks dipped, thatched roofs embraced a settlement. The path was no longer buried under the white drifts and the snow covered the ground in patches, freeing yellow strands of grass to spike the surface. The wind lost its bite and the air smelled of sea grass and salt, a sign that the Great Atlantic must be near. Blixt picked up the pace and the wooden palisades surrounding the settlement came into view.

Two men rode my way, wrapped in heavy animal furs, their horses small and nimble. One of them, his head shaved clean, raised his hand. 'Halt,' he said. A serpent chasing its tail was inked into his right temple. 'State your business.'

Perhaps it was his ear-piercing voice or maybe because of the way he stared me down, I took an instant dislike to him. 'I'm Jarin Olversson. My father, Eyvar Olversson is, or rather was, the Guardian of Stromhold.'

The men exchanged glances.

'You're far from home,' his companion said. He had the longest beard I've ever seen. It fell to his stomach and was tied in knots with leather bands. A scar, jagged and deep, tainted the left side of his face, catching the eyelid and causing it to sag. 'Why isn't Argil with you?'

I responded with silence, long enough for him to realise I wasn't planning on answering his question.

The serpent man stretched out his hand. 'Your sword.'

I didn't want to part with my father's sword. It was the last relic to remind me of him and giving it away felt like another betrayal, but I had no choice. When I released the blade from its sheath, the symbols glinted in the afternoon light and the two men raised their eyebrows. A sudden urge to refuse them came over me. 'Would you give away your only means of protection? What sort of warriors are you to demand this of me?'

'If you are who you say you are, you should know our customs,' the longbeard said. 'None can cross Hvitur's threshold with a weapon.'

The blade was mine by right, and against reason my fingers tightened around the hilt. With steady hands, the men reached for their weapons, but I could sense their readiness to strike at speed if the situation called for it. Two against one—the odds weren't in my favour, considering I was wearied by the long journey and lack of food. It wasn't wise to taunt my fate at a time like this. 'How do I know you won't overpower me the moment I surrender my sword?'

'We're asking the questions,' the serpent said with a smirk. 'Eyvar would never let his son come here.'

'What if I told you that Eyvar was dead?'

They looked at each other with dismay. 'That's impossible,' the longbeard said.

'Just take me to my uncle and then you can judge what is possible and what's not.'

They whispered to one another and from the tone of their voices I guessed they disagreed. At last the longbeard said, 'Come with us.'

We rode in silence. I couldn't tell if they believed my story and I was impatient to see my uncle, hoping he would give me a better welcome. Two Nords guarded the gates to Hvitur with their spears. They exchanged greetings with my escorts and parted to let us through.

Hvitur was much larger than it looked from the outside, with multiple paths forking in all directions, lined with huts built of timber and stone. Some of them resembled burrows with archways made of wattle and clay, others were round with gaping fissures in their roofs through which smoke escaped in thick, grey clouds, turning the air misty. Wells dotted the settlement and people carried water using shoulder poles, balancing buckets like scales on either side. We rode past fields where men and women worked the ground with hefty tools, and past them, the smith's workshops. The rhythmic sound of the hammer beating iron into shape made me think of home, and the heavy chains of grief tightened around my chest.

My companions said nothing during the ride, apart from the occasional greetings uttered to passers-by. Growing up in Stromhold, I was used to seeing armoured men with swords, but Hvitur had all manner of people walking the streets, and hardly anyone wielded a weapon. Women wearing plain skirts clustered around the doorways, rubbing linens on rough stones, their laughter and chatter mixed with that of children playing with sticks. A baby cried behind a closed door and someone hollered within. A stout man emerged with a bucket full of rotten scraps and tossed them on the path. I held my breath at the foul smell and watched a pack of dogs that appeared out of nowhere, their hackles raised, bearing teeth at anyone who approached the stinking mess. The business and bustle of Hvitur lacked order and it reminded me of the chaos in Elizan, with noise and people running in all directions, and I was surprised to find that I longed for the structured life under my father's command. The life I could never lead again.

We rode further into the settlement and through a market where a strong smell of raw fish lingered in the air and stalls sagged under all manner of seafood.

'Where's Torgal?' I asked.

'You'll meet him soon enough,' the longbeard answered.

'How soon?' I asked, but he did not reply.

A man in a bloodied apron gutted a sea creature with tentacles as long as my arm, while his assistant cracked shells with a blunt tool. Further on, a woman with a colourful scarf wrapped around her head plucked a chicken, feathers flying around her stall as her fingers moved with practiced speed. More birds hung by their necks from hooks, clean and ready, waiting to be exchanged for silver or skills. Seeing a wagon full of supplies arriving at Stromhold every month, I often wondered where the supplies came from, and Hvitur's market had the answer. Still, it was unusual seeing Nords leading such simple lives.

The smell of salt intensified and the choking cries of seagulls grew louder, their outstretched wings like white banners in the wind. An oval structure, resembling an upturned boat, was set in the centre of Hvitur. Wide steps led to double doors with unfamiliar runes carved into them. More symbols ran along the front of the building and two timber snakes with exposed fangs eyed each other across the roof. We dismounted and climbed to the entrance. The sound of crashing waves grew louder, and when we reached the top, the view stalled my breath.

Many times I had imagined Hvitur's shores as a boy, but nothing prepared me for this. Dark and angry waters rolled into the bank, waves standing tall like snowy mountain peaks, swelling and growing more powerful in their advance, smashing against the docks and spitting white foam in all directions. A long and graceful vessel with black sails decorated the shoreline, the entire length of the boat lined with ports holding powerful-looking oars. The shore was filled with men, hard at work cutting, shaping, and planing wood, and towering above them was a half-built hull, its stern curved like a crescent moon.

The two men urged me inside and I sighed. This wasn't how I imagined my first time in Hvitur and being ordered around tested my patience. We stepped into a small hallway with a linen curtain at the far end. Apart from a couple of worn benches, the room was bare. I was close to expressing my opinion of the manner of my reception when heightened voices interrupted me.

'I won't do it!' A female voice rang across the hallway. 'I'd rather die than agree to this.'

'The matter is settled and the promise made. You will obey.' The man's voice was strong and sharp, not a voice to oppose.

'I didn't spend my years training so you can lock me up and do as you please. I'm a warrior, not some—'

'Enough! Do not provoke me, Fjola.' The warning in the man's voice reminded me of my father when we disagreed.

The curtain brushed open and a girl emerged. Her long hair fell in soft waves down her back, rusty like autumn leaves, with some strands woven into braids, and there was a touch of red to her high cheeks. She pushed past us and her green eyes met mine for a brief moment. If looks could stab, I would have a knife sticking out of my chest.

'Fjola.' The serpent caught her elbow, but she hissed and shook him off. Before he could say more, she stormed outside.

He looked at me and snorted. 'Wait here.'

'I will not.' My control was wearing thin. 'I'm the son of a guardian and I don't need your permission to see my uncle.'

When I tried to walk past him, he blocked the doorway. We stared at each other, neither of us willing to back down.

'It's all right, Skari' the voice called out. 'Let him through.'

I pushed past the curtain, Skari and the longbeard at my heels, and halted with breath caught in my throat. 'It can't be...'

A fire pit in the middle of the room cast soft shadows on the timber walls and smoke curled towards the hole in the ceiling, enticed by the whistling wind. There was a smell of spice and meat; a meal had recently been eaten and greasy wooden plates were stacked in a pile. A man sat in an elevated chair at the back of the chamber. His palms rested on the arms adorned with two-headed serpents writhing around like the twisted branches of dead trees. Carved into shape by skilful hands, the serpents, with their forked tongues, looked real and ready to strike. The man himself was a living image of my father. Apart from his hair, which was cut short, their features were identical: nose, broad with large nostrils; grey eyes, cool and confident; the sharp outline of his jaw...Everything about him screamed Eyvar.

'You're not...You can't be...' I stumbled over my words. Part of me wanted to believe the lie that it was indeed Father sitting in the high chair, and everything that happened in Stromhold was but a dream. I wanted to run and embrace him, tell him how much I missed him and how glad I was he was unharmed, but the part of me that suffered his loss wasn't fooled.

'My blood-brother was a tough warrior and we didn't see eye to eye, but it pains me to learn of his demise.' He got up from the chair, exposing ancient runes, similar to those outside, carved into the backrest. 'Are you truly my nephew?'

I nodded, my voice trapped in shock.

'You didn't know we were twins? It must come as a surprise, then. Our mother died at birth, her body too frail to withstand such forces as my brother and I. We were bound from the start.'

'He has the blade,' the longbeard said.

'Show me.' Torgal stretched out his hand and I didn't dare refuse him. He turned the steel in his hands, frowning. 'It's true then, Eyvar is dead.'

'Elizan…' My mind was that of a drunkard, trying to form words from strands of confusion. How could two people look so alike? 'He died…Hyllus killed him. In Elizan.' A sound like a bark escaped from my lips.

'Hyllus…Where is he now?' Torgal shot me a sharp look that cleared some of the fog. 'Speak.'

'Fled before I could get to him,' I admitted with a sudden pang of shame.

'What of your mother, Aliya?'

Mother's name was a live iron against my skin. 'D-dead,' I choked on the word.

'Dead?' Torgal let the sword slip and the point struck the ground at his feet. The look in his eyes reminded me of that in my father's when he heard my younger sister had succumbed to the red fever.

'We had a traitor in Stromhold.' To speak Lumi's name was too much of a task. 'A woman from Shinpi.'

'Shinpi? Are you certain?'

'Father took her in. We didn't know what she was until it was too late.'

Torgal exchanged glances with Skari and the longbeard. 'We knew this would happen, but I thought Eyvar would be more cautious. I see that you came alone.'

'It was just him and the horse,' the longbeard said.

'Everyone's dead.' I pushed my fist against my chest. I wanted this interrogation to end. Each question ripped the hole inside me wider.

'What is it you're not telling me, boy?'

I couldn't admit how badly I misjudged Lumi, how I fell for her charms and how my foolishness led to this tragedy, but now was not the time for regrets. I pulled my sword from his grip and placed it back in the sheath. 'There's nothing more to tell, but a lot to do. I won't rest until my parents are avenged. Will you aid me, Uncle?' I had to squash the traces of shame for not telling him the truth, but I needed help and couldn't risk his refusal.

From the wide fire, cracking flames released a surge of sparks. I met Torgal's gaze and again the feeling I was looking at my father returned. I didn't know how to act around these men. Back in Stromhold, everything was simple. I was the son of the guardian and the warriors treated me as such, but here I felt like a stranger who had to be questioned. Maybe coming to Hvitur was a mistake and this was why Father didn't want me to in the first place.

But I had nowhere else to go.

Torgal joined his fingertips together and pointed them my way. 'Your heart is hot with vengeance, and Agtarr demands it, but there is much you don't know—'

'I'm tired of hearing how much I don't know. My father died at the hands of that madman, Hyllus, and an ice demon killed my mother. That's enough knowledge for me.'

'Hot-headed, just like your father. You want revenge? Then learn how to control your temper. You would do well to heed the advice of someone who has fought more battles than you lived winters and who understands the reasons behind this war.'

I seized hold of my anger and set it against him; it was better than sharing the insides of my heart. 'Hyllus hides in his citadel and laughs at our efforts. The more Varls we kill, the more he sends our way. This will never end and now that Stromhold has fallen, he'll come for you. Nordur will never be free until we take a stand.'

'And what is your plan? Have you seen the Citadel of Vester?' He turned to the longbeard. 'Njall, tell Jarin what you saw.'

'The walls are made of marble, smooth and impenetrable,' Njall said in a low voice, hands folded across his chest. 'The circular structure has one entrance guarded by the Varls, who stay motionless for days. I couldn't see any windows, so ropes are no use. The citadel stands at the edge of the city, clear of buildings and surrounded by a scorched wasteland.'

'And what do you make of that?' Torgal asked me.

'I'll worry about it when I get there.'

Skari's quiet laughter drifted across the room. 'And this is a destined man. More like a stubborn child. We're wasting our time.'

I took a step forward, hand on my sword, ready to strike Skari's smirking face.

'Quiet!' Torgal's voice stopped me in my tracks. 'Whatever grievances you have, this isn't a place for them. We have much to talk about and you must be tired from the road.' He clapped his hands and a girl in a linen tunic appeared from the side door. Her skin had a Vestern tan to it and her left cheek was smeared with soot. She reminded me of Lumi, small and fragile, surrounded by warriors, and even though I knew this was irrational, I felt immediate distrust towards her.

'Nola,' Torgal said, and the girl's braids bounced about as she stepped forward, 'show Jarin to Eyvar's chamber. Take him to the baths and give him fresh clothes.' He squeezed my arm. 'We'll speak tomorrow.'

I was glad for an excuse to get out of the hall and away from Torgal's questioning. 'Tomorrow,' I said.

I followed Nola down a narrow staircase and along a woven rug in the corridor. At the far end, three statues of the gods formed a semicircle, their features chiselled with masterful precision. 'You have some skilful carpenters in Hvitur,' I said and she nodded.

The gods lowered their heads around a stone altar dotted by stumped candles, and I imagined my mother praying at its feet. The statues stood unmoving, as dead as the wood they were made from, every crease well-defined. Yldir, the God of Life, the one my mother favoured, held a sphere with a ribbon of smoke carved on its top—a human soul leaving her mortal body. Where was Yldir when my mother needed him? She rebuked me for not praying and for my lack of respect for the gods, but in the end, despite her devotion, she died and I lived.

I brushed my hand across the wood and a splinter stabbed my fingertip.

'The God of Life is prickly tonight,' I said. 'Who do you pray to?'

Nola's eyes locked on Yldir.

I turned to Skaldir. The Goddess of Destruction had an angry scowl on her face, wrinkles scored with uncanny detail, hands resting on the hilt of a sword with its point facing down. In Stromhold's library, I listened intently to Marco's stories about the release of Skaldir's wrath upon the world, how she crashed and burned everything until her brothers lured her to sleep and spent their powers to keep her dreaming. At least now, I had something in common with the Goddess of Destruction and my angry soul called out to her. To her left, with a cowl covering his face, stood the God of Death, the most cunning of them all, the one who demanded revenge for wrongdoing and murder.

'When I was your age, I was desperate to know what Agtarr looked like. But until you face him in the afterlife, he remains a mystery.'

His cloak was painted in black and sculpted to look like feathers. A three-headed raven sat on his shoulder and each head spoke of a different destiny: one for eternal flames, another for eternal cold, and the third for eternal darkness. The life choices and their consequences. My mother wanted me to fear him, to pray and beg for his mercy, his understanding, but now I knew why I never could. Prayers didn't offer justice. Prayers couldn't save you from hurt and betrayal.

I turned away from them. The gods weren't there when Hyllus killed my father or when Lumi froze my family to death, and so I had little regard for their powers. My heart was empty and there was no place for worship within its dark walls.

I stepped through the low arch into my father's room and it felt like stepping through time. Apart from a single bed in the corner and a lone chair facing the hearth, the room contained little else, so different from the one my father had in Stromhold. I placed my hand on the backrest and imagined Father sitting in it, watching the flames. Was he anything like me at that age? A worn iron shield, dented in places and spiked with rusty metal studs, hung on the wall. Perhaps he too dreamed about becoming a warrior, joining Stromhold's men and fighting the ceaseless wars. I never asked how he met my mother. There were so many things I never asked them, and now, I never will.

Nola laid out a set of cloths on the bed: a grey linen shirt, a jerkin made from animal skins, a pair of leather trousers, and heavy boots with straps and buckles. She motioned me to take them and made for the door, but I caught her hand.

'Can you speak?' I asked.

She nodded.

'Say something then.' I'd had enough of mute people to last me a lifetime.

She dropped her dark eyes to the floor. 'We mustn't speak with outsiders.'

'I'm not an outsider. These are my people.'

She didn't respond, looking as if she thought talking to me would bring some unseen wrath upon her.

'How did you get here?'

'Sold,' she whispered.

'By your parents?'

She blinked and wiped her nose with the back of her hand, smearing grime across her other cheek. In a way, she reminded me of my loneliness before Lumi's arrival and I pitied her. 'My parents left me too… sort of. But I hope to meet them soon,' I said. 'One day you'll be a strong and powerful woman, and travel home to find yours.' I touched my heart. 'But for now you must keep them here.'

A shy smile lifted her lips and I said, 'Let's go. Torgal promised me a bath, remember?'

Outside, the sea wind buffeted our clothes, Nola's hair, and the rubbish strewn around the village. A rusted bucket rolled by with a clatter. Trapped between the bare tree branches, a piece of colourful cloth flapped to the gusty tunes.

Nola led me away from the settlement and into the forest lining the perimeter. Twigs cracked under our boots and the wind died down as we moved deeper into the woods, leaving the smell of the sea behind and welcoming another, more familiar scent. It intensified with each step and soon my nostrils tickled with a stench of sulphur. The trees parted, revealing a vast space surrounded by hills and spotted with patches of snow and withered vegetation. Gentle peaks rose and fell like camel's humps, and clouds swollen with rain hovered above them, spreading grey mist. The air was heavy with steam floating from the many springs scattered around the place. Some were populated by people and others empty, with nothing but a veil of fog around them. They made the valley look like some otherworldly place, painted in various shades of green and blue.

'Hot water? In the middle of winter?' I never imagined such things existed.

Nola made her way through the mist and I followed, unable to keep my eyes off the water that bubbled gently in places. She led me to a smaller, more remote spring occupied by Fjola, the angry girl I met back in Torgal's hall. Nola placed my clothes on the ground, but before I could thank her, she turned and ran back the way we came, her plaits bouncing in the steamy air.

'How long are you going to stand there?' Fjola asked. She sat in the spring with the water sloshing around her neck, hair wet with moisture, and the rustiness of her locks a stark contrast to the green-blue waters.

I glanced about where men and women shared the springs. 'Is it a custom in Hvitur to bathe with strangers?' I picked up my clothes. 'It's best if I return later.'

'The springs are the only place where everyone is equal. There's no distinction here between a common man and a warrior. Besides, I wouldn't advise coming back here in the black of the night.'

I wasn't convinced, but Fjola looked at ease, so with tense fingers, I undid the laces of my jerkin and stripped off my shirt. The pain from the bruises shot up through my back and caught my breath. She watched my struggles with a slow smile as if enjoying my discomfort.

'Have you ever been to wild springs?' she asked when I stepped into the warm waters. The change in temperature set goosebumps racing in all directions, but the sensation was a pleasant one and I lowered myself deeper into the spring. Following days on Blixt's back, my tense muscles relaxed and I wriggled my toes, encouraging the blood to flow.

'Never. I'm used to snowdrifts and ice.' I certainly wasn't used to sharing a bath with a naked woman. Unlike Lumi, Fjola had a typical Nordic face—sharp with prominent cheekbones, fair but not ghostly pale skin, and a straight-edged nose. Her presence made me giddy and I was glad the deep-green water concealed my body.

She fixed her eyes on mine. 'I saw you with Skari. What brings you to Hvitur?'

'Passing through on my way south,' I didn't feel like sharing my quest with Fjola, but she pressed on.

'South? Dangerous place for a Nord. You must have a good reason to risk it.'

'I have.' I took a lungful of sharp air. The smell from the springs wasn't as offensive as when I first got here. 'I found Vester to be less dangerous than my home.'

'Where is home?'

'Stromhold.'

'Stromhold? Argil told me a lot about the fort during his visits. Is he with you?'

'No,' I said, rubbing my eyes. Argil, my dear friend, frozen at the entrance to my mother's chamber. How I wished he was here to answer everyone's questions for me.

'He trained me, taught me how to handle my daggers, so one day I could join the warriors.'

'Join them? You?' I asked.

She glared at me with a green storm in her irises. 'What of it? Do you think only men know how to fight?'

'It doesn't matter what I think, but no woman was ever allowed to join the warriors.'

She splashed the water with her fingers as if flicking an annoying insect. 'I planned to be the first.'

Her words brought on an uncomfortable silence. The sky swam in a range of colours from various shades of crimson to glowing oranges as the sun made its way down towards the mountain peaks. People started shifting from the springs; mothers urged children to abandon their frolics, men conversed in deep voices, young women chattered with their naked bodies smoking from the chill that sucked the warmth out of them.

'You're too late,' I said. 'The warriors of Stromhold are gone. The fort has fallen.'

She snapped her head my way. 'Fallen? Nonsense. Argil only ever brought news of your victories. Eyvar is the strongest guardian to ever lead the warriors.'

'Eyvar is dead. The fort is empty. There is nothing for you there.' I got up from the spring and stepped onto the cool grass. My clothes clung to my wet skin when I rushed to force them on.

'We had no news of Stromhold's defeat. Does Torgal know about this?'

'He does now.'

'Wait!' Fjola sprang from the water and grabbed my hand. Her hair brushed the surface of her firm breasts. 'How do you know this?'

Fjola's body, absorbed by the night shadows, steamed in the evening air and I marvelled at her shapely outline. A scar snaked from her left thigh and across her stomach. My face turned hot at seeing her naked body and I was no longer sure if it was fog from the springs or heat of desire that wrapped me. I had to turn away before my impulses got the better of me. I let my guard down with Lumi and paid a heavy price for trusting her. I wasn't about to make the same mistake twice. 'I'm the Guardian of Stromhold—or what's left of it. Eyvar was my father.'

I walked back to the settlement. Maybe Fjola had the same dream, perhaps she wanted to follow that taunting voice, whispering in her ear about battles and glory, the same voice that ushered me to pick up my sword. When I did, I couldn't even use it to save my father. Nords believed that our destiny is written in the stars, which guide us along the right path. If it was true then my star fell from the sky the day I was born, leaving me to scramble in the darkness.

XIII

I woke up to the sound of rain. Back in Stromhold, closer to the Grand Isfjells, snow was the only thing that ever fell from the sky, but here, the ocean softened the air, bringing hail and rainstorms that melted the ice.

'Nephew.' Torgal sat at the table in the company of three other men and Fjola. He placed his hand on the chair next to him. 'Join us. I trust you slept well?'

'I did,' I lied. Lumi's voice had haunted my restless dreams; she had mocked me every night since I left Stromhold and each nightmare strengthened my resolve to hunt her down. I knew that only her death could free me and bring back my peaceful nights.

'You remember Skari and Njall,' he said.

Skari looked at me from under his eyelids, clenching his jaws as if my presence offended him. Njall stayed silent, scooping the contents of his bowl with a wooden spoon, flakes of oats stuck in his long beard. There was an aura of calm about him that made me feel at ease.

'This is Marus, our very own scholar and keeper of history.'

Marus pushed his bowl of oats aside. 'Welcome to Hvitur, Jarin,' he said, peering into the mead flagon.

He was an old man, bent by age and withered by years of study. A bald patch on the top of his head, ringed by a thin strip of grey hair, resembled a chicken's nest. Red veins poked through the skin on his nose and his beard was thin and unkempt.

'Have you met Fjola?' Torgal asked, jamming a fork into a slab of meat on his plate. 'This damn mutton gets tougher each day.'

Fjola sat next to Marus with a scowl on her face, drumming the table with her fingertips, the oats in her bowl untouched. Two daggers with hafts wrapped in leather jutted out from under her armpits. Unlike women I saw on the way through Hvitur, Fjola was dressed in trousers, boots, and leather gloves that concealed her arms all the way to her elbows.

'We have met,' she said.

'Good. We've much to discuss,' Torgal said, chewing on a piece of gristle.

I broke off a hunk of bread. The soggy oats had bits of meat floating in them and it tasted of sea salt. 'I won't stay long in Hvitur. I need supplies and new shoes for my horse.'

'Surely you aren't leaving us already?' Marus asked. He had a coughing fit and wiped his lips with a cloth. 'This cough will be the death of me,' he croaked.

'I can't linger. My father's soul won't know peace with Hyllus hiding in his tower, unpunished.'

Fjola's head came up sharply, thick eyebrows drawn close together. 'You plan to kill Hyllus? How?'

'I'll find a way or face Agtarr. We waited long enough, waged countless battles to drive the Varls away, achieving nothing. My father died fighting them, and no help came from Hvitur. Instead you sat idle while our men laid down their lives.'

Skari leaped to his feet, sending the chair crashing across the floor. 'How dare you question our efforts? You know nothing of the war.' He leaned towards me, eyes gleaming.

I shoved the bowl aside and stood up to face him, my nerve endings tingling with a need to confront him. 'I faced the horrors. I saw our people ripped to shreds by beasts. I know what's coming.'

'Enough!' Torgal bashed his fists on the table, sending plates clattering. 'I have ruled this land for almost twenty winters and I'll decide what we are going to do. Stromhold was our last stand in the North. We all made sacrifices.' He looked me in the eye. 'Skari is right, you don't understand the stakes.

My brother hid you away for too long, but I never approved of his choice. It's time you knew the truth.'

There was power in Torgal's voice, strength similar to that of my father but it lacked spirit, as if my uncle spent his energy years ago. Despite that, he commanded authority and I felt a hint of pride.

Njall put his hand on Skari's shoulder. 'Stand down. This is bigger than us.'

Marus wriggled out from his chair with the support of his cane. 'I'll get the horses ready.'

* * *

Outside, the sky took on a shade of steel and the rain eased to a drizzle. The erratic wind pushed at the clouds, blowing them apart and herding them together again as if trying to find the right shape for each one. An earlier downpour had overfilled the puddles and created rivers in the fields.

I was glad to see Blixt. 'Here you are.' I patted him. 'Did they treat you well?' He nuzzled me and snorted warmth into my neck.

It felt good to be back in the saddle. The world seemed less complicated when faced from above. Others followed suit, mounting their own horses, with the exception of Marus. He climbed onto a much smaller animal with pointy ears and a greyish muzzle. It made strange and painful sounds as he urged it forward.

'This cursed donkey grows more stubborn every year,' Marus said, puffing in the saddle and slapping the animal with his cane. 'The merchant assured me that it's a placid and obedient breed. Far from it—it's a demon in disguise.'

As if on cue, the donkey showed its front teeth and screamed.

'You don't treat it right,' Fjola said with a laugh.

'Donkey?' I asked. 'I don't remember seeing horses this small in Vester.'

'We don't breed them here,' she said. 'They come from beyond the Eydimork Sands. A dark-skinned merchant visited years ago on the very same donkey that Marus is tormenting now. These animals are a rare gift indeed.'

The scholar managed to persuade the donkey to move, but the animal wasn't in any rush, stomping lazily through the mud, swishing its tail and shrieking.

'Ready?' Torgal waved his hand at us. He headed the column on his black horse with Njall at his side. His gesture took me back to the day I left Stromhold at Father's side. Whilst before I doubted myself and lacked courage and experience, now I had both. Touched by curiosity about our destination, I spurred Blixt after him.

We followed the path towards the mountains. The rain stabbed at my clothes, leeching through the fabric, finding its way into my sleeves. My neck itched from the droplets that slithered down my skin and under the collar.

Fjola levelled her horse with mine. 'I take it you don't like the rain?'

'It never rains in Stromhold.'

'I always wanted to see the fort and the Grand Isfjells,' she said with longing.

'Everything is white. Horses can get stranded in the snowdrifts, that's how deep they are. Incessant gales crash the walls at night and stars spark the sky. We keep the fires burning to chase away colds capable of freezing a man to death.' I swallowed hard, the memories of everything that was lost to me filled me with regret. I wanted to go home, turn back time, sit by the fire and listen to my mother's soft laughter, to spar with Argil and laugh with Orri, but those moments were lost to me forever.

'The Great Atlantic claimed my father's life,' she said, pulling the hood tighter around her face. 'He loved the ocean and spent most of his time fishing. He used to talk about freedom, but had no love for fighting. I say, you have to fight and take what's yours with steel.' Fjola's hands tightened on the reins and she looked towards the stormy horizon. 'My father taught me that anything is possible if I wanted it hard enough. He was just a simple fisherman, but he understood me better than anyone. If he was alive, he would never want to see me wasting away as a village wife.'

'What of your mother?'

'Torgal took me and Njall under his care and kept our mother out of harm's way. Her sight is all but gone. Her mind wanders and she spends her time on the shore, waiting for Father to return. She believes he's alive, but lost at sea, struggling to find his way home, so she sings to him hoping that waves will carry her voice and lead him back.' Fjola waved her hand. 'It seems love and loss are entwined.'

Her final words sounded like something my mother would say and they touched some deeper part of me. I had loved and I had lost, and worst of all, I couldn't tell if I would ever stop grieving.

'At least you have your brother to look out for you,' I said.

'His devotion to Torgal is greater than family bonds.' She pursued her lips. 'He'd rather see me married and burdened with children than wielding daggers.'

Skari inched his horse closer, his face twisted in a grimace more sour than spoiled mead. Hooves clattered on the rocks. The rain and wind became one, lashing our faces in waves and filling the air with whistling tunes, occasionally interrupted by

Marus's curses as he tried to bend his donkey's will. The carcasses of wild animals were scattered on the hills and high above them crows flapped their wings against the wind like black sails, cawing mournful songs.

'The Ulfur Valley,' Marus said, and took a swig out of his flask. 'Wolves come to feed here. Savage beasts snatched my goat that grazed in the hills.'

'You should have kept her home,' Skari said.

Marus turned in his saddle. 'She had a wild spirit and belonged in the hills.'

The valley narrowed and fog rose between the peaks, snaking through the damp grass like an eel through the weeds. Further on, the path disappeared into a gorge.

Torgal dismounted at the foot of the tallest ridge. 'Leave the horses. We'll cover the rest of the way on foot.'

I tied Blixt to a nearby tree and scratched his blaze. 'Watch out for the wolves. You know I could never go on without you.' He was more than a horse, he was the closest thing I had to family and the only tie to my old life and the memory of my father.

Skari fastened his horse next to Fjola's. He leaned towards her and whispered something. She replied in an agitated voice. They exchanged words, but I was too far to hear them and Fjola stalked away from him. There was a connection between them, and from the look on her face, a challenging one, but I wasn't privy to it. Whatever it was, Fjola seemed to share my dislike for the man and I was glad I wasn't the only one to find his attitude testing.

We entered the blackness of the cave with its musty smell of soil and wet rock. The chill from the walls settled on me and I shivered. Njall lit a torch and the flame illuminated the tunnel ahead. Stones crunched under our boots, sending echoes through the cavern, joined by a faint sound of dripping water. When the opening was swallowed by darkness, a feeling came over me that we may never find our way out. Something rushed past my ear and I slammed my hand at the empty space.

'Bats,' Fjola said.

'What is this place?' I asked, feeling the rough and jagged stones with my fingers.

'The Heilagt Passage.' Marus's arched shadow rose and fell as the light shifted on the walls. 'Nords came this way to worship the gods.' He slipped and almost fell, but Skari caught him in time. 'Blasted stones. I say the best way to honour the gods is from the safety of your own bedchamber.'

Fjola's laughter bounced off the walls. 'Have you no regard for the gods?'

'Wait until you get to my age,' Marus complained. 'Remind me, why is it I'm stumbling in the darkness with you?'

'You know the secrets of this place.' Njall's voice drifted from up ahead.

'Well then, wouldn't hurt to show some respect, would it?'

Ahead, the light pushed its way through a small crack that grew wider as we neared the tunnel's opening. I welcomed the daylight and the steps cut into the mountain.

'Incredible,' I said, looking at the ridges.

The hills were on fire, touched by all manner of colours from rich browns to burned umbers and russet reds, putting Stromhold's white peaks to shame. The obsidian rocks spiked from the mountains as if trying to break away from the glorious inferno, and hanging above them, green moss sank its roots into the cliffs. We climbed the steps, skirting the lichen encrusted boulders that sank deep into the soil and under the overhanging rocks that appeared ready to crush us.

'How many are there?' I asked, shielding my eyes from the sun rays that jabbed their fingers through the gaps in the sky. The ash coloured clouds moved away, gathering their forces far on the horizon.

'Three hundred,' Marus said, panting. 'It seems our ancestors didn't have much to do, so they spent their energy building steps.'

'Respect, Marus.' Torgal's voice didn't betray any signs of exhaustion. He was strong and fit, the way my father used to be, and the similarity between them struck me again. Did Father know of this place? Perhaps he scaled the very same steps. 'Nords climbed here to worship Skaldir.' He turned my way. 'They hoped to pacify her and stop the upcoming doom.'

'That didn't work out so well,' Marus grumbled.

Torgal cast him a scornful look. 'The mages summoned Skaldir to tip the war scales in their favour, but even they weren't prepared for the wrath she unleashed.'

'I know the story.' I didn't care about the gods and their deeds. Whilst I wasted my time climbing hills and listening to the old tales, Hyllus walked free. 'Where are we going?'

'We're almost there,' Torgal said.

A rock arch loomed above the final step like a doorway to another realm, the narrow fins thinned and polished by the forces of nature. Beyond it, a bow formed in the sky, glimmering with a multitude of colours as if created by the stroke of a magical brush.

'Beautiful, isn't it?' Fjola said. 'It's a sign from the gods that we're not forsaken. The day after Skaldir was forced into a dream a rainbow appeared in the sky. The legends say that it's made out of souls, rushing towards the gates of Himinn to seek peace in the afterlife.'

'Rainbow,' I whispered, enchanted by the colours. Did my mother and father travel across this shimmering bridge to find each other? Although I didn't keep the gods in high regard, I wished for my family to rejoice in the Fields of Life. Mother's beliefs were strong and I hoped that Yldir took her under his protection.

The mountaintop was flat and bare and weeds found their way up here, thriving in the absence of other vegetation. A stone platform akin to a crumbling coffin perched in the middle and situated on its top was a slit-like opening with stale moss growing through the cracks. Ancient symbols were etched on the four corners and they looked familiar.

'The magic of Skaldir,' Torgal said, running his hand over the markings. 'The key to her awakening.'

'This?' I held up my father's sword. The symbols on the blade resembled those on the platform. 'I thought it was just a legend.'

'There's a grain of truth in every legend,' Marus said, shuffling closer to the platform. 'Each life is a story, passed on through the ages, to help us remember those who lived before.' He read the words on the platform:

'When my soul spills across the sky,
'Heed my call and seek out the blade,
'The power is yours to take,
'The judgement is mine to make,
'The end of mortal vanity
'The beginning of divine eternity.'

'You can read the script?' I asked. Even Marco, my old tutor, didn't have such knowledge.

'Yes, but there aren't many left of us who can.'

I looked from my sword to Torgal. 'Did my father know?'

His eyebrows knitted in a thoughtful frown. 'Eyvar insisted we must take the sword as far away from the mountain as possible. He wanted to keep it hidden from the world. The blade has the power to awaken the gods and many lust for it.'

I wanted to drop the sword, let it clatter down the mountain. The weight of it, so reassuring during my journey to Hvitur, felt like a burden all of a sudden, too heavy to carry.

I offered the blade to Torgal. 'If that's the case then take it, keep it safe.'

He didn't move. 'There is more.'

'More? We hold the world's destruction in our hands. How could there be more?'

Marus rummaged in the fold of his cloak and pulled out a withered scroll. The parchment was cracked and torn in places from years of folding and unfolding. The scholar cleared his throat. 'On the Night of Norrsken, heeding the goddess's call, a child will come into the world, Valgsi, marked by Skaldir herself. She will bestow upon him the greatest power, the magic to pull her from her dreams. Together, the god and the mortal, will face her brothers in battle and bring the Day of Judgement upon the world.'

'What is this?' I asked. 'You can't honestly believe this to be true?' The only person I knew who would was my mother.

Torgal took the scroll from Marus. 'Every twenty winters, on the Night of Norrsken, magic appears in the sky. It's a sign from the goddess, a call to Valgsi. The heavens cast a green glow over the mountain and you can see it for miles, shifting and shimmering. We guard this place from those who want this magic and the power it holds.'

None of this made sense. 'But you said only Valgsi can wield it.'

'That's true, but you're a mortal and powerful forces are hunting you,' Marus said.

'Hunting me?'

Torgal let out a deep sigh. 'Your mother and father knew this day would come. They couldn't keep you locked away forever. Dark forces want to wake the goddess and you're the key. They won't stop until the prophecy is fulfilled.'

'Who are *they*?'

'When Antaya fell, the mages who survived fled to the east,' Marus said. 'Led by the priest from Shinpi, they plan to restore their power and bring back the days of magic.'

Skari snorted. 'More like days of destruction. I say we find them and cut them down.'

'It's not that simple. The mages are far too powerful for your axe.'

'Hyllus, and whomever he bows to, seek the blade,' Torgal said. 'They worked hard to flush you out of Stromhold. When you mentioned Shinpi and the girl's betrayal, it became clear that forces are gathering in the East. The Night of Norrsken is upon us and—'

I burst out laughing and the sound tore through the valley like the shriek of a madman. 'You spin the most marvellous tales,' I said, astonished they even considered such things, but nobody answered.

I looked at each of them in turn. Torgal had a serious frown on his face and Njall looked thoughtful and sad at the same time. Fjola shifted her gaze down to her boots. Skari stood next to her, smirking. 'You can't truly believe this,' I said. 'I'm not Valgsi. Mother and Father said nothing of this to me.' I clung to the faint string of hope, wanting to believe they would have told me the truth.

'How could they?' Torgal asked. 'They feared for you. Tried to shield you from your fate. This is the reason why Hyllus's Varls attacked in such numbers. They needed you to leave Stromhold and come to the top of this mountain, to answer Skaldir's call.'

'Are you saying that everyone's dead because of me and some foolish riddle?' The thought alone was unbearable.

'What can we do?' Fjola asked. 'Is there a way—'

'I'll leave,' I said, dropping the sword on the cobbles. 'I'll travel far away from this place until the time has passed. We'll hide the blade and keep it safe.'

'If only it were that simple,' Marus said. 'It doesn't matter how far you run, the call will be too strong to resist. The force of it will steer you back.'

'How can you be sure I'm the right man?'

'The writings don't lie. Have you a mark on your temple?' Marus took a step towards me.

'Get away from me!' It was difficult to breathe all of a sudden and I leaned over, hands on my knees, gulping the air into my burning lungs.

The rainbow faded away, taking hope with it and leaving the sky bare and open to a new assault from the storm. Rain pattered on the stones. I didn't even care about the gods and they chose me of all people. To what purpose? To punish my defiance? To teach me a lesson?

'Your path is set and it's unlikely you can change the course.' Torgal's voice mixed with the rumble of a distant thunder. 'You're the key, the sword is useless without you.' He placed his hand on my shoulder. 'Jarin—'

I jerked away. 'It seems Valgsi's fate has been decided and the man himself left out. All of you planned my future and made choices on my behalf without asking my opinion on the matter.' I pushed passed them, under the archway, down the three hundred steps, and I broke into a run. Was this the reason Lumi spared my life? Because I was the key to unlocking Skaldir's power?

Lightning split the sky and the thunder answered with a low growl.

When I left Stromhold I hoped to find relief among the people of Hvitur. I considered them to be my family—all of us fighting for our land, but in truth I didn't belong with them. My fight wasn't theirs and I was destined to bring doom upon them. A black hand, the hand that everyone feared, marked me and threatened not only Nordur, but the world. I stumbled through the cave, feeling my way along the stones in the blackness. I slipped and fell, scraping my hands and knees on the rocks, but I was past the pain, the need to get away from the hill and the people I left at the top, stronger than any physical discomfort.

Blixt had waited where I left him and his presence calmed my trembling hands. I placed my boot into the stirrup, ready to mount.

'Jarin,' Torgal called after me, stumbling from the cavern.

'Let me be,' I said, pulling myself into the saddle.

He gripped my boot. 'Fate chose you and no matter how far you run, you can't escape it. Believe me, I know. You can't change what's written in the stars.'

'I would never follow a path I didn't choose for myself.' I spurred Blixt into a gallop. The clouds ripped open and flooded the world. Lumi said that storm was coming, but she was wrong. The storm was already here.

XIV

The hut smelled of damp and moss and its timber walls let the wind in through the rotten gaps. Rain fell in drops from holes in the roof, adding to the puddles on the floor. A shelf with one of its planks broken sagged under the weight of rubble, and a lone crib sat in the corner with a mouldy blanket poking through the gaps, waiting for a child who never came. The flames bounced erratically in a rundown fireplace, hissing and blowing sparks through the roof into the night. Beyond the walls, the ocean waves crashed against the shore with fury, pushed back and forth by the wind.

    I sat with hands wrapped around my legs, watching the glowing embers. This was a dark place, tainted by sorrow and grief, but I felt more at home in this hut than in my father's room. Perhaps Argil sat here, next to his pregnant wife, dreaming of the future. He said that Hera wanted to be closer to the sea, away from the clamour of Hvitur's streets, and so he granted her wish, but darkness soon followed the light, enticed by the innocence of her brighter sister. The shadows fell and swallowed all traces of joy, turning Hera's laughter into tears and Argil's hope into misery. They joined each other in the afterlife and a part of me envied them. My life, my dreams, and everything I believed in turned out to be a lie conjured up by my parents, the very people I trusted. They knew my purpose and destiny, but they chose to conceal it. How pitiful my childhood ambitions must have sounded to them, my foolish hopes of becoming a famed warrior worthy to take my father's place.

The door screeched on its rusty hinges and Fjola stepped through with my father's sword in hand. 'I looked all over for you.' She glanced around. 'Sad things happened here. Bloody things.'

'Fitting place for the likes of me.'

She hunkered down on the floor beside me. 'There's nothing for you here. You've been assigned an important task.'

I laughed bitterly. 'To be Skaldir's puppet. My family's dead. Everyone I knew is gone, and for what? So I could be hunted like an animal, with her sword in my hand until the Night of Norrsken.'

'If you wish to see it that way, but I'd rather think of you as the one with the power to save us from her wrath.'

The blade glinted in the firelight. 'Why did you bring it here?'

'It's yours and you must decide what to use it for. It drove your grandfather mad, split his sons, and started this chaos.'

'My grandfather?'

Fjola edged closer to the fire. Her wet hair clung to her face and shadows crept across her cheeks. She tossed a log into the flames. 'The elder folk in Hvitur know the story. Your grandfather, Bodvar, was enchanted by the sword. He sent for Marus to help him unravel the mystery of the symbols etched on it. He was desperate to know if the legends were true, and he spent all his time up the mountain seeking connection with the gods.' She drew her legs together and rested her chin in the space between her knees. 'They say that in the end he refused to talk to anyone but your father.'

A strong gust of wind crashed against the wall of the hut and something howled in the night. Fjola shuddered. 'This place brings out my deepest fears.'

'Where did he find the sword?'

'No one knows. He returned with the blade from one of his raids.'

'Did Torgal kill my grandfather?' It would explain Father's hatred towards him.

'Everyone thinks he did. On the Night of Norrsken, Torgal fought Bodvar at the top of the hill. By the time your father reached them it was too late. Your grandfather was gone, struck through the heart. Eyvar grabbed Skaldir's sword and came at his brother. He would have killed him if not for Aliya.

Swollen with child, she followed suit and stopped them, but the ordeal forced her to deliver on the mountaintop.'

'How could this be? She never told me any of this.'

Another betrayal, I thought, but this time by my mother. How could she keep the circumstances of my birth a secret?

'Eyvar took the sword and left, with you and Aliya, to command Stromhold,' Fjola went on. 'Torgal became the ruler of Nordur. I don't know much else.'

'I wanted none of this.'

'We seldom get to choose. We've to take what's given.' Her voice was quiet and soothing.

Before I could respond, a dark form shifted from the corner of the hut. Fjola pulled her dagger and threw it. I ducked on instinct, scraping my cheek against the grit on the floor. I caught my tongue and my mouth filled with the taste of iron. Fjola drew her second dagger and aimed. A shadow writhed on the spot where her first blade had hit its black flesh. Screeching, it shaped into a new form.

Fjola kicked the sword my way. The creature advanced and I sprang to my feet.

In its new form it seemed half-bird, wings broken on either side, and half-human, eye sockets filled with nothing but blackness.

Fjola threw her second dagger and it wedged in the creature's forehead. The shadow melted around it and her dagger clattered to the floor.

The dark entity shifted its form again, pieces of bone twisting together like roots. With a scream, it came at me, talons aimed at my face.

I sliced through the black fog.

Fjola grabbed her daggers from the floor and launched at the creature's back, stabbing. With a scream, it turned on her and wrapped her in the blackness of its cloak.

I cut at the tightly woven smoke and the point of my sword disappeared into the darkness. The creature released its grip and Fjola fell free.

I backed to the door where I stumbled into something soft and sticky—a giant web weaved around the entrance. I pulled my arm in a frantic attempt to free myself, but it was useless. Thrashing like an insect before an approaching spider, I watched the creature float towards me, claws forming into hooks. I strained against the bonds, helpless.

Fjola's roar filled the hut and she ran at the creature with her arms outstretched. They collided and the impact cut her battle cry short. She pushed the shadow towards the flames. It writhed in her grip, screeching, claws entangled with her hair, and all I could do was watch the struggle and fight against the web. Fjola stabbed the creature's face again and again and drove it into the hearth with her body. A shriek filled the hut as the shadow caught fire, merging into different forms and releasing a puff of black smoke through the chimney into the night.

The screams faded and the web holding me fell away and dissipated.

'What was that?' I asked, sagging against the wall. The existence of the Varls was known to all, but I didn't consider there may be other creatures lurking outside the walls of Stromhold.

Fjola slid beside me. 'Skygga. It's drawn to places with a dark past. Our presence enticed it, the smell of fresh blood led it to the hut, but it's just a demon. More malevolent spirits roam these lands. We should keep the fire going.'

'Why are you here?'

'I thought you may be in trouble, and look at that… I came just in time.'

'The question wasn't meant as a jest.'

Her face tightened and the last traces of a smile fell away. 'I'm promised,' she whispered. 'I'm to marry Skari in a fortnight.' She pulled away from the wall. 'I'm a warrior. If I marry Skari, I'll have to bear children, wash pots, and squawk about nothing with other women.'

The situation was heavy with irony. Fjola yearned for greater things and I wanted to be forgotten.

'I can't marry him,' she said. 'It'll be the end of me.'

'That bad?' I struggled to empathise with her. After all, what was an unwanted union in the face of being chosen as Valgsi by the Goddess of Destruction?

'Worse.' She dropped to her knees and gripped my hand. Being so used to Lumi's cold skin, the warmth of Fjola's fingertips was strange. I forgot how it felt to be touched by someone who was like me—not a demon but a living being, a human. 'You have to help me.' Her voice grew urgent. 'Take me with you to Vester. I can fight and I promise to stay out of your way.'

'What? Impossible. It's too dangerous, and besides, it's unlikely I'll return to Hvitur. Skari doesn't hold me in high regard as it is. And what about Torgal?'

'I don't know and I don't care. I can't stay here.'

'Is this why you wanted to join Stromhold's men? To escape your fate?'

'I trained hard because I didn't want to end up like my mother, sitting at the seashore, waiting for her husband to return. Hopeless. I want to be free, to decide who to love and who to hate. I don't want to marry just for the sake of tradition. I want to find my own reasons to live for.'

The wind still raged outside, singing songs in contrasting tunes, some heated and wistful, others sullen and mournful, and I listened for the sound of skygga's return. Fjola unfolded a blanket she'd brought with her and wrapped it around her shoulders. She passed another one my way.

'Can you do something for me?' I ran my fingers through my damp hair. 'Marus spoke of a mark, and I have no one else to ask.'

'Are you sure?'

I nodded, my throat as dry as ash.

We moved to the fire and as she edged closer I caught a faint smell of lavender. A memory of my mother wrenched my chest. She used to sprinkle lavender on my pillow to scare away bad dreams.

Fjola parted my hair, searching for the sign between the follicles, and the touch of her fingers stirred the goosebumps. I imagined what it would feel like to have someone in my life I could trust, a relationship without fear of betrayal, but I doubted it was possible. Even my parents had managed to keep secrets from me. I held my breath, wishing against odds that she found nothing. Her hand stopped, crushing my hopes.

'What does it look like?' I asked.

'Like stars.' She brushed her fingers against my left temple. 'An alignment of some kind. Marus might be able to decipher it.'

'I don't want him near it. Can it be removed?'

'It's embedded in your skin like a faint scar. It's part of you.'

Any hope of escaping my fate diminished. The mark confirmed Marus's words. It was an invisible chain, holding me hostage. I didn't have any power over the present or future. I was bound by this unknown force, imprisoned. Would I be able to withstand this magic, resist the call? Or would I play my part at the goddess's hand and destroy the world? It felt like having one foot trapped in a snare and hearing hunters from afar—I had a choice to stay where I was and let them come, or sacrifice my leg. If I chose the latter I might escape the hunters, but with a torn off limb I would bleed to death.

I would die either way. From this moment, nothing would ever be the same. I knew that.

'What will you do now?' Fjola asked.

'Before any of this, all I wanted was to join my father's men, fight, taste victories, and protect the people I cared about, but the boy who wanted those things is gone forever.' Lumi's face flashed before me with her lips twisted in a sweet smile and the memory made me sick. 'I've lost all of that and more.

My only reason for staying alive is to avenge them. Hyllus killed my father and he'll be the first to die. And the demon who took my mother's life will be next. Valgsi or not, I swore an oath and I won't rest until it's fulfilled.'

'Marus said there are bigger forces at work. With the Night of Norrsken fast approaching, you'll be hunted.'

I thought of Lumi on the day she left me in the storm. 'Let them come. And when they do, I'll be ready.'

XV

I woke to the sting of cold. It crawled under the blanket, leaked through my clothes, and sealed my veins. My breath hovered over the fabric, pierced with frost that spread through the hut turning everything white. I flexed my numb fingers and toes, wincing at the pain. Fjola's head rested on my shoulder, her cheeks pale, mouth tinged with blue, and hair stiff under the touch of frost. Her breath was slow and shallow and having her so close made me want to pull away. I didn't know why she chose to be here, but my experiences with Lumi taught me to keep a safe distance.

I shook her gently. 'Fjola.' As her name left my lips, my lungs coughed in protest. 'We have to move.'

She opened her eyes, parting tiny crystals on the tips of her eyelashes. 'It's freezing.'

'The fire must have died during the night,' I said, rubbing my jaw.

She pushed the stiff blanket away. 'I'm sure you're used to worse.'

'It doesn't mean I enjoy turning into an icicle.' I got up and shook out my arms and legs.

Fjola shoved the door open with her shoulder. A sudden transition from dimness to morning sunlight infused my vision with an array of black spots and I had to blink multiple times to diffuse them.

She took a deep breath and stretched her arms towards the sky. 'Is there a better sound than the crashing of waves?'

We started along the shoreline. 'We're both Nords and yet we're so different,' I said. 'You with your love of the ocean and me with my snowy home, it's hard to imagine we share the same ancestors.'

The longer I stayed in Hvitur, the more differences I discovered. As a boy, I dreamed of sailing across the Great Atlantic, but now, looking at the vast waters, I wondered how anyone could survive out there without solid ground beneath them.

Pebbles crunched under our feet and the waves reached for us, eager to wet our boots. The weight of yesterday's events pressed down upon my shoulders like a giant boulder. I touched the side of my head, glad that my hair disguised the mark. If not for the pain, I would cut into my skin to get rid of it.

'Look.' Fjola pointed into the distance where the Great Atlantic merged with the horizon and waves brushed the sky. 'Don't you long to sail and discover new lands? It would be such an adventure. Marus used to tell stories about an island perched on the edge of the world.'

I followed her finger. 'You mean Shinpi? Do you think it's real?'

'I don't know. No Nord has ever sailed that far.'

'If the legends are true, Skaldir was created there. Inside an icy mountain. Giants forged her from steel and her brothers shaped her into a woman to keep balance between life and death.'

'How do you know so much?' Fjola asked. 'I thought the warriors of Stromhold spent their days training.'

'It's true, we train a lot, but there's always time for pleasure, and mine was scrolls. I read every scroll in my mother's library and sometimes I wonder what's more real—the legends or life itself.' Before Lumi's betrayal, I looked upon life as an exciting adventure, full of promise and discovery. I even travelled to Sur to face the witches and with that act I failed everyone, including myself. It seemed so long ago, but if I could make those choices again, Stromhold would be my priority. I would never have let my warriors ride home without me and I wouldn't have been so quick to ignore Argil's counsel.

'I'd give anything to be clear of my marriage bonds. To sail the Great Atlantic and cross the Eydimork Sands. To mark every corner of the world.' She wrapped her hands around her waist. 'Instead, I'll lead an unremarkable existence until envy and despair consume me.'

I didn't have words to comfort her. Fjola yearned to travel, to discover new places, and I would be content with staying in Stromhold and following in my father's footsteps, but life had other plans.

The gates of Hvitur loomed ahead and I recognised Skari. He strode along the well-beaten track with a deep frown on his face, hand wound around the head of his axe. He looked ready for a confrontation and was the last person I wished to see.

Fjola snorted. 'My betrothed.'

Skari grabbed her elbow and kissed her lips with force that made me feel uncomfortable. My father treated Mother with a mixture of respect and gentleness and Skari's behaviour lacked both.

'Your mother worried about you wandering alone after dark,' he said.

Fjola wiped her lips with the back of her palm. 'You should know better than to agitate her. Besides, she needn't have worried. I wasn't alone.'

'I can see that.' His eyes challenged mine before he trained them back on Fjola. 'Don't forget where your place is.'

'Have we exchanged vows?' she asked with a scorn. 'I haven't pledged myself before the gods. Until I do, I'm free to choose my company.'

He took a step closer to her, but I grabbed his shoulder. 'Let her be.'

The vein on Skari's temple throbbed, bringing his serpent tattoo to life and his mouth twisted into a one-sided smile. 'Jarin Olversson—the protector who couldn't even safeguard his own people.'

There was a challenge in his words, and even though I had no wish to fight, I held his stare. Father wouldn't stand for such squabbles. His family and his warriors were important to him. 'We are Nords, we stand as one,' he used to say. His bonds with Torgal were broken, but he cared for Mother and I and his men followed him without question. If Father saw Skari questioning Fjola in such a manner, he would intervene.

Skari shoved my hand aside. 'I'll wait for you at home,' he said to Fjola.

I watched his back as he headed for the gates.

'Thank you,' she said.

'Don't thank me. You should find a common ground. Who'll break up your quarrels when he's your husband?'

'I wish I had more time.'

'Maybe time isn't what you need.'

'What do you mean?'

'Ask your heart. It may have the answers.'

Fjola was silent, but the force with which she kicked a stone told me that my words held truth. I could advise her to trust her heart and yet my own betrayed me in every way possible. There was nothing else I could do for her and I knew I couldn't let her troubles distract me from my path. My parents' souls demanded revenge, and Hyllus was my focus now.

* * *

I sneaked into Torgal's hall, hoping it would be empty. I wanted to get to my room and make preparations for the journey to Vester. Blixt could do with new shoes and my supplies needed replenishing, but as soon as I crossed the threshold, my uncle appeared.

'Walk with me, Nephew,' he said, heading for the door.

The last thing I needed was a lesson about my destiny, which I didn't care about, and it surprised me that a man such as Torgal would consider ancient texts over logic.

'I plan to make for Vester without delay,' I said.

Torgal didn't even turn to acknowledge my attempts to slip away. He was so much like my father, his presence alone demanded obedience. I cursed under my breath and followed him out and around the building, down the steps leading to the shore where shipwrights assembled Nordern vessels.

'I wish I could spend more days out here,' said Torgal, taking a lungful of air, 'listening to the songs of the Great Atlantic and watching my men shape the boats of the future.'

'You rule these lands. You can do as you please. What's stopping you?'

'Duty. I wanted to train as a shipwright, but I had to give up that dream.' The wind caught his words and carried them towards the blue waters.

'I wished to succeed my father as the Guardian of Stromhold, but now I can't think of anything I want less.'

'To be a guardian is your duty, in the same way that my duty is to lead the people of Nordur. There's very little choice given to us when it comes to such matters. I never felt ready for the task, but when you assume responsibility for the people, there's no time to question your merits.'

If I closed my eyes and cleared my mind, I could imagine it was Father walking by my side. Torgal's words were like an echo of something my father would say to me when I tried to evade my responsibilities. I didn't know how to feel about these similarities between them. Before Lumi's betrayal, I would bow my head and try to live up to Father's expectations, but now all I wanted was to follow my own path and accept the consequences. Life as the Guardian of Stromhold was no longer fit for someone like me.

A Nord with two oars under his armpits passed us by and Torgal raised his hand in greeting.

'It's difficult to lose people you care about,' he said. 'I should know.'

'Was it your wife?' I dared to ask. I hadn't seen Torgal's family during my short time in Hvitur.

'I wish she was, but Aliya chose your father instead.'

His words stunned me. My face must have betrayed my confusion because Torgal hastened to add, 'You're the only family I have left and I don't want any secrets between us. I wished for a son of my own, but it wasn't meant to be. When your mother went away with Eyvar, I was left like a castaway on a deserted island. She took a piece of my heart and I couldn't bring myself to offer what remained to any other woman.'

My mother seldom mentioned Torgal and when she did, it was always when Father wasn't around. Once, when I asked her why we never visited Hvitur, she said that deep wounds need time to heal and that I was too young to understand. Listening to my uncle's confession lifted the mystery behind the dispute between brothers, but knowing the truth made me uneasy and I struggled to find words for him, so I focused my mind on Fjola's story. 'Is it true about you and Bodvar?'

I anticipated anger, fury even, but instead, he slumped his shoulders and heaved a sigh. 'What have you heard?'

I patted the scabbard at my hip. 'That you killed him with this sword.' I was glad we moved away from the topic of my mother, but surprised he didn't rebuke me for asking such personal questions. 'I need to know what happened to understand how I came to be and the reasons behind my parent's fears about my future.'

'Eyvar was like you in a way, stubborn and hot-headed, but his anger was long-lasting. He refused to listen to me. Come,' he motioned to the docks, 'let's get closer to the waves.'

The sun splattered the Great Atlantic with gold and I welcomed its warmth on my skin. Sharp pebbles and scraps of iron, washed ashore by the ocean, stabbed at the soles of my boots and among them I spotted unusual-looking shells. Close up, they resembled mountain rocks with black scores on the surface.

'Osturs are of great value and some hide pieces of the Atlantic's heart.' Torgal took the shell from me. He drew a small knife and pried it open, revealing a creature. At first, it looked like a shapeless blob, but under a closer inspection I caught movement between the folds. Torgal worked his fingers, separating its white flesh until they divulged a black orb. He laughed. 'Gods favour you today—a piece of the ocean itself, created in the depths where the heart of the Great Atlantic lies.'

I turned the orb in my hand. 'It doesn't look like much.'

'To the untrained eye, but before the Nordern traditions changed, our ancestors used these black orbs as a form of promise. With it you offered your heart.' Torgal hurled the shell into the sea. 'This tradition died out when fewer and fewer osturs washed ashore. After a time, we replaced them with bands of silver. It's considered good luck to find one.'

The orb glinted in my palm, seemingly unremarkable, but now that I knew it held timeless mysteries of the past, it felt precious in my grasp. My mother wore one around her neck, but I never thought to ask of its significance. It was unlikely I would offer it to anyone, but I needed luck in my life, so I put the orb in my pocket.

The docks creaked and the waves lapped beneath them as we made our way to the edge where the ocean stretched in its glory. The Great Atlantic called out to the hearts of people like Fjola who sought adventure, filling them with longing to set sail and discover unknown lands. How much I wanted to do the same before Lumi took my dreams away and replaced them with dark and lonely thoughts of vengeance.

'It wasn't me who drove the blade through Bodvar's heart,' Torgal said in a tired voice. 'But the blame will be mine until I die.'

'If you didn't kill him who did?'

'The sword drove my father mad. It took his sanity and in the end he was no longer the man we knew. The magic changed him and we failed to save him.'

The gulls cried out in the distance, diving at the waves and daring the ocean to catch them by swooping away at the last moment.

'Father pleaded with me to end his life, saying it was the only way. But I was too weak, so he forced the sword into his chest. When Eyvar reached the top of the hill, he saw me standing over Father's body.'

The story sounded too simple. 'Why didn't you say anything?'

'I tried, but Eyvar wouldn't listen. He grabbed Bodvar's blade and challenged me. I didn't want to fight him. If not for your mother, one of us would have died that night.' He looked to the horizon with a thoughtful frown on his face. Eighteen winters had passed, but Torgal seemed to remember every detail. 'It was the Night of Norrsken and Skaldir's magic turned the sky green. The sight captivated us.'

A group of men levelled a serpent-shaped figurehead similar to the tattoo on Skari's temple. They exchanged words and called out to their companions waiting at the top of the hull, ready to lift the head with the help of ropes.

'Why serpents?' I asked. Everything in Hvitur was decorated with snakes of one kind or another.

'Our ancestors chose them as a symbol of mortality and rebirth. When we build ships we want serpents to lead us through the ocean storms and keep us from harm.'

'How far did you take your ships? Have you managed to cross the Great Atlantic?'

'Two of our boats set off to the east, but none returned. We had no news, and we can't afford to lose more men.'

'Don't you wonder what's beyond?' I asked, thinking of Shinpi. Did Lumi flee there to seek refuge among her people? Did she know that even despite her warnings, I would come for her?

'I do. Perhaps one day our fortunes will change and we'll set sail and explore.'

'Was I born on the hill that night?' Although I knew the answer, deep down I wanted Torgal to disprove Fjola's accounts.

'Your mother climbed to the top and stood between us. She begged us to lower our blades. Eyvar asked her to step away, but she wouldn't listen. When he pushed her, she fell to her knees with a piercing scream. And so she gave birth under the shimmering sky and your fate was sealed that night.'

'I don't believe it. Maybe if I was a child, but not now. I walk my own path. My mind is set and I challenge my fate to change it.'

Torgal stomped the rusty nail back into the deck with his boot. 'I wish we could choose our destinies, but our lives belong to those who created us. They wield the power over life and death.'

It seemed that everybody regarded what happened on the hill as fate, but to me it was a misunderstanding of two brothers. Their Nordern tempers caused this event and destiny had nothing to do with it. My mother risked her life to stop her loved one from dying and if I wasn't born that night, then perhaps my parents would still be alive. 'I'll prove you wrong, Uncle, and no call will sway me. But if I fail, you're free to cut me down when the time comes.'

'Let's hope it won't come to that. I have lost my brother and I'm not about to lose his son. I know you're set on Vester and I understand your need for revenge, but I urge you to reconsider. There is more at stake than vengeance on Hyllus.'

'If I don't slay him, how will I face Father in the afterlife? His soul will never enter the Fields of Life and Mother too will wander aimlessly in Agtarr's shadow.' There was more to my quest than I was willing to admit. The emptiness inside me spread and the only way to find peace was to kill Hyllus. If I claimed his life, I would set myself free.

'I know what Agtarr demands of you, but your quest is suicide. The mage is too powerful.'

'I have a plan.'

He pursed his lips. 'A plan... Let's hope it's a good one. I'm sending Njall with you. He knows the Citadel of Vester and can help you find your way around the city.'

'I can't promise his safe return.'

'I'm certain he'll welcome the challenge.'

'So be it.'

XVI

I spent the next three days visiting various merchant stalls and bartering for supplies: a new blanket, flint, strips of dried meat and salted fish, a bag of oats. Seeing dark-skinned traders in Hvitur took me back to the market I visited with Mirable. With his guidance, buying and selling looked easy, but walking from stall to stall and persuading merchants to lower their prices showed how little I knew about trading. I was glad to leave the bustling square.

'We'll get you new shoes for the journey,' I said and Blixt nudged his head at me. I enjoyed leading him down the narrow street to the blacksmith's workshop. His reddish-brown coat turned eyes and I felt proud to have him by my side in this settlement full of strangers.

The workshop was more spacious than Stromhold's but not as well organised. Rust ate deep into hammers and tongs, and from the look of them they served little purpose in their current state, but the smith kept them near the forge for reasons best known to himself. The odours of sweat and smoke mingled with those of dust and molten iron. I offered three silver coins in exchange for his services to which the blacksmith scratched his bald head, mumbled, and rummaged through the benches at the back. He found the shoes, placed them into the furnace, and set to work on Blixt. He trimmed the frog and each hoof with a pair of sizable pliers. He retrieved the shoes and shaped them with a hammer. The ringing sound took me back home, to times when Lumi and I played in Einir's forge. How we ran from the smith when he saw we were up to mischief. The once sweet memories turned into ugly scraps of lies and deceit. My heart changed shape with each physical strike of the smith's hammer, shrinking with the hurt of Lumi's betrayal.

'Want me to look at your sword?'

The blacksmith's question pulled me out of the past. I declined, fearing he would recognise the blade and connect it to Skaldir.

Soon enough, the preparations were complete and I was ready to leave Hvitur.

* * *

Back in the saddle, my spirits lifted, and Blixt, with his new-shod hooves, gained sureness to his step. Following the events of past week, he was the one thing left that was familiar and comforting.

I didn't want to linger in Hvitur and endure the pitying looks of my kin. The loss of my family still throbbed like an open wound, but I dulled the pain with thoughts of revenge. I hoped my father and mother knew I hadn't forgotten them, and that they followed my progress from Himinn.

Njall tied the saddlebags to his horse, fastening each strap with care. His long hair was tightened with a leather band. He had a calm and thoughtful aura about him and one could think we planned nothing more than a trip to the market. When Torgal announced that he wanted him to join me, Njall hadn't said a word, didn't argue or inquire. He nodded and set about making preparations for the road. I couldn't tell how he would react when he found out about our destination, but I was glad for his company. In a way he was a replacement for Mirable albeit not a cheerful one, but having someone to talk to would disperse the loneliness of a long road. I often wondered what had happened to the merchant. He was so eager to hear what the witch had to say about his future, promised to wait for my return from Sur, and then he disappeared.

Skari leaned against a nearby post, watching us prepare with his mouth twisted into a half-smile. Njall came up to him, grabbed his hand and pulled him closer. How he could accept such a man marrying his sister was beyond me.

'Look after Fjola,' Njall said. 'I won't be here for the ceremony, but I hope to see you both when I'm back.'

'You know I will,' Skari said.

'She can be difficult at times, but stand by her.'

'Fjola has my heart, Brother.'

To my surprise, the smirk on Skari's face faded and his voice softened when he said her name. Maybe there was more to him than his confrontational ways, but I doubted I would ever see enough of Skari to find out. I looked around the settlement, but Fjola was nowhere to be seen and I felt a sting of disappointment. She didn't want to say goodbye. Perhaps she was angry with me, but turning her down when she asked to join me in Argil's hut was the right thing to do. Like me, she had to find her own path, and if it was freedom she wanted, running away from Skari wasn't the way to attain it. I suspected that her betrothed would simply chase her down.

Marus shuffled down the steps holding a water skin. His beard looked more tangled than the last time I saw him. 'Jarin, you can't leave without some spirit.' He handed me the flask. 'It's more potent than that diluted stuff you drink. One sip is enough to take worry off your chest.'

'Is that so?'

He gave me a look that was one of pity. 'Remember what you are. Never forg—'

'Ready?' I asked, steering my horse away from the scholar. I didn't know why my uncle trusted such a drunkard.

'Until I see you again,' Torgal said in a low voice. 'May the gods watch over you.'

'I'd rather they didn't.' All they granted so far was bad luck. I cast one last look around Hvitur and spurred Blixt onto the western road.

* * *

The road to Vester was very different from the one I followed during my first journey there. I had to fight my way through snowdrifts and endure the unforgiving cold, but now I had the ocean to my right and a forest to my left, with Blixt bracing the mud. The sun that graced the sky in the morning shied away behind the clouds and the world took on the colour of a mouse's fur.

'Does it ever snow here?' I asked, looking back at the white peaks of the high mountains to the east.

'Rarely. Snow in these parts doesn't linger.' Njall's low voice matched the drab landscape.

The forest stood in silence, tightly knit trees guarding its ancient secrets, and I didn't look forward to camp among those pines. In Stromhold, snow made for bright nights, diffusing darkness in the forests, so anyone could see an upcoming threat, but here there would be no warning of ambush, animal or otherwise. The confrontation with the skygga in Argil's hut made me weary of other creatures haunting these lands, which I knew little about.

'Why did you come with me?' I asked.

'Why not?'

'You'll miss your sister's wedding.'

'Few will enjoy it, and least of all Fjola.'

'Why not stop it? Why let Skari wed her?'

'It's not my place to question the gods.'

Njall sounded like my mother. Would she have been so devoted to the gods if she knew my fate couldn't be altered? In one of our heated exchanges, she hinted that Yldir had the power to alter destinies. I tightened my fingers on the reins. I'd rather die than ask them for help. 'Perhaps we should question them. Who decides that their words are final?'

Njall stroked the left side of his face. 'Your beliefs are your own.'

From where I rode next to him on the right, he looked like a different man. His eye was narrow and a mixture of steel and blue, cheekbone strong and sharp beneath his beard. When you faced him from the left, you got a different face entirely. 'How did you get the scar?'

'It's a long story.'

'And you don't want to share it with a stranger.' Njall's lack of engagement was exasperating. 'What about our journey?' I tried again. 'Aren't you going to ask me about my plan?'

'Have you got one?'

'I know someone who may be able to aid us. If we're lucky. You said it yourself, defeating Hyllus with a sword is impossible. Warriors in the legends used their wit and cunning as often as their blades. We must seek answers from more powerful sources.'

'I can't read.'

'But I can. We're going to Sur.' The witch with her crystal bell brushed me off with riddles, but I wouldn't be making it easy for her this time.

'Are you mad?' Njall jerked his head my way. This was the biggest reaction he gave me since we left Hvitur. 'You won't leave Sur alive.'

'I did the last time. I don't fear the witches. I've faced horrors far greater than their magic.' Seeing my family dead was enough to uproot everything I believed in and gave new meaning to fear.

Njall's eye went wide. 'You saw them?'

'The witches hold the wisdom of the world in their grasp and they would know how to defeat Hyllus.' And this time I was adamant to get my answers.

Njall shook his head as if unable to comprehend. He reminded me of Mirable, fearful and curious at the same time.

'During my first journey to Sur, I was scared, but the death blow didn't come from the witches. It came from someone dear to my heart.'

'Who?'

It was my turn to avoid the question, so I stepped Blixt up to a faster pace.

Njall's whisper reached me with the wind. 'Yldir help us.'

You can't help anyone if you're asleep, and I wasn't about to place my fate into the hands of those who dreamed the eternal dream.

* * *

Njall wasn't fond of talking, so for most of the day we rode in silence, apart from occasional comments about the weather or the horses. The most pressing subjects, those of Sur and Hyllus, were left untouched as if speaking about them would hinder our chances of success. Infrequent sunrays poked through the clouds, but the jealous sky claimed them just as fast, sending intermittent showers in their place. Dusk crept in from the shadows of the pines, bringing mist and the scent of damp earth.

'We'll make the camp here,' I said, guiding Blixt into the trees.

As we walked deeper into the forest, the rustling of foliage and snapping of twigs sent echoes through the woods. Our horses swivelled their ears at different sounds.

'We need a clearing to light a fire,' Njall said. His voice sounded unnatural in the enclosed space. A bird screeched in response as if the presence of strangers offended it.

'What are these woods?' I had a pressing sensation that someone watched our progress from behind the pine trunks and the feeling intensified the deeper we went. My ears prickled with every sound.

'Who knows? Nature sets her own rules here. Even animals don't venture too deep.'

'You must have come here…'

'Our land is full of places people don't dare to enter. This forest is such a place.'

Asking Njall questions never led to clear answers. A faint splintering sound drifted our way, but I couldn't tell if it was my imagination or creatures lurking in the shadows. Still, I heightened my guard.

Finally, we stepped into a clearing big enough to accommodate two men and their horses with room for a small fire. 'This will do,' Njall said.

I tied Blixt to a tree and we set off to gather wood. The forest was thick with fallen, moss-covered branches, shed by the trees and left to rot like the old roots in Stromhold's cellars. I scanned the ground for kindling while Njall sauntered in the opposite direction. I soon lost sight of him. When a shrub rustled nearby, the noise made me jump, but only a rat skipped past and I cursed my foolishness for letting the furry rodent startle me so. The daylight that accompanied us here dissolved and nightfall's shadows spread through the woods. With an armful of branches, I started back to camp, but another sound stopped me in my tracks.

'Njall?'

In a fraught silence the question hung in the air like a false accusation and I had a distinct feeling that I wasn't alone. I dropped the wood and half-drew my sword, ready to confront the unseen attacker, but the forest was silent once more. I walked to the clearing with my back to the camp, looking from left to right, every inch of my skin crawling, but nothing rushed at me.

'Where's the wood?'

I spun around to face Njall. 'I couldn't find any.'

He pursed his lips and turned to the fire.

I glanced at the blackness behind the trees. 'It'll be a long night.'

We unpacked our knapsacks and Njall went about cooking oats. The bubbling woke my stomach and I pacified its rumblings with strips of dry meat.

'Do you know much about Valgsi?' I asked, propping myself on Blixt's saddle. 'Do you believe it possible to wake the Goddess of Destruction?'

Njall took a while to respond, scraping the bottom of the pan with a wooden spoon. The smell of wheat spread around the clearing as he divided the contents between us. 'I believe the teachings. The sacrifices our gods made to save us can't be denied. They sleep so we can live. As for the prophecy, it's ancient.'

'Just because something survived for two centuries doesn't make it true.'

'It doesn't make it false.'

The oats lacked salt, but warmed my stomach. 'My parents died with sorrow in their hearts, and if I fail to kill Hyllus and cut down the demon who killed my mother, they'll never find peace. They'll wander aimlessly in the afterlife, bound by their grief.'

Njall blew on his spoon and slurped the food. 'It's not for us to know. We can't speak for the dead.'

'Don't you worry about your father?'

'If he died at the hands of humans, I'd seek vengeance, but I can't wage war against the Great Atlantic. We'll all face Agtarr someday, but until then, we ride towards our destiny.'

It was easy to say, and I envied him because his destiny wasn't as twisted as mine. I touched the side of my head where Skaldir's mark lived. It was becoming a habit. With some effort, I could imagine that it wasn't there. Njall put his empty bowl aside and ran his fingers through his long hair. The scarred part of his face was shielded by the shadows. It reminded me of Orri and his scars when he returned from the raid on that fateful day when Father brought Lumi to our home. So much had changed, so many people lost their lives. I didn't know how painful memories could be.

'I'll take the first watch,' I offered, knowing that the sounds of the forest wouldn't offer any sleep.

* * *

Thanks to Njall, I had wood to keep the fire going and plenty of thoughts and memories to keep me awake. While the night reigned over the world, the pine trees guarded the forest against the moon, absorbing its silver light into their thick crowns. A chill settled on the clearing. I prodded the fire with a stick and the flames came to life, licking the damper branches with reluctance. Njall snored under his blanket with one hand on the shaft of his spear, and our horses followed suit with their closed eyes and drooping heads. My thoughts turned to Sur.

I acted confident around Njall, dismissing his fear of the witches, but inside I felt less than sure. My last trip to Sur ended in disaster, so why should it be different this time? Part of me wanted to believe that witches would share their wisdom, but another part was like fertile soil where doubt took root. But I had no choice. I didn't know anyone powerful enough to aid me and I was prepared to do anything to find a way to defeat Hyllus. I tried hard to focus my energies on my quest, but Skaldir's prophecy gnawed at me.

Blixt snorted and stomped his hooves, dragging me away from my unsettling thoughts. His companion shifted uneasily, pitching his ears forward, and I too turned my attention to the sounds of the forest. Apart from the chirping of insects and the occasional hooting of a lone owl, another sound disturbed the night and I strained my hearing to guess its direction. Something crept at the edge of the clearing, shrouded in darkness.

Slowly, I reached for my sword, keeping my eyes on the perimeter. When I drew the blade, the symbols caught the firelight and even though I deplored their purpose, the feel of it in my hand offered reassurance.

I rose, ready to confront whatever lied in wait. Step by step, I edged towards the pines, careful as not to disturb the ground, adjusting my eyes to the blackness that thickened away from the fire. Leaving the camp behind, I headed deeper into the woods.

Something rustled in the trees and I half-expected an ambush, but instead, a bird rattled its wings with a scream, sending jolts of adrenaline through my body. I cursed, trying to steady my frantic heart. A twig snapped to my right and the sound of footsteps followed as something darted through the shrubbery. I leaped in pursuit.

I ran, feeling my way through the trees and stumbling over branches and uneven ground with stems lashing my face. Muffled cries and tumbling from up ahead assured me that the stranger struggled just as I against the shadows of the night.

Ignoring the painful spasms in my lungs, I pushed myself harder, urging my feet to take wider strides until I chased the dark, quick figure down. With a forward jump, I grabbed an ankle, causing the stranger to lose their balance and we crashed into the carpet of pine needles. Their sharp ends stabbed my face and eyelids without mercy. My bottom lip split and the cut filled my mouth with the taste of blood. The stranger kicked my head, thrashing to get free, but I held on tight.

'Let go of me,' the stranger yelled, and the voice sounded familiar.

'Fjola?' I asked, loosening my grip.

She scrambled to her feet—a black shape against the trees, gulping the air in deep mouthfuls.

'What on Agtarr? Why are you skulking around our camp?' I yelled, wiping blood off my lips.

'I wasn't. You chased me.'

'Why did you run?'

But before she had a chance to respond, a scream echoed from the direction of the camp.

'Njall!' I called, and we broke into a run.

The light from the campfire flickered between the trees, growing brighter as we closed the distance. We rushed into the clearing to find Njall brushing dirt off his coat, with Skari splayed on his back next to him.

'What is this?' I looked at each of them in turn.

Fjola cast me a sullen look. 'Don't ask me. I don't know why he's here.'

Skari scrambled to his feet. 'Did you think I'll let you disappear without a word?'

A headache from the tension pressed the spot between my eyes. 'So it was you creeping around the clearing? Explain yourself.'

Skari grunted and looked away from me.

'Why are you here?' Njall asked his sister.

Fjola pressed her lips together.

'Very well,' Njall said. 'Regardless of the reason, you can't stay. You must return to Hvitur.' He looked at Skari. 'Both of you.'

'I can't go back,' Fjola said in a strained voice. 'I won't.'

'I'm not leaving you,' Skari said. 'We go back together.'

'I don't intend to give up my freedom for you.'

'It's too late for that.'

She kicked a branch into the flames and the bits of burning wood scattered around the fire ring.

'Enough. The both of you.' Njall stepped in between them. 'Our task is difficult enough without having to handle your disputes.'

'I have no time for this,' I said. 'I'm responsible for the outcome of this journey and I don't need the pair of you to complicate this further for me. Camp here tonight, but you must be on your way at first light.' I sat down on my blanket and adjusted Blixt's saddle.

Fjola crouched in front of me, her green eyes gleaming in the firelight. 'I want to be part of your journey. Unlike some, you're pursuing a noble cause. You intend to confront Hyllus and I'd rather be by your side than back home playing wife.'

'We may not survive this,' Njall said.

'I don't care.'

Skari looked as if thunder struck his face. 'It's your doing,' he hissed at me. 'Why don't we settle this like men, Nord to Nord?'

My fingertips tingled with an urge to grab my sword and accept his challenge, but the anxious look on Fjola's face and Njall's slight head shake forced me to resist. 'You're nothing to me,' I said, forcing calm into my voice.

'At least I'm not the one who will bring the Day of Judgement upon us.'

'I took no oath to serve Skaldir. My actions are my own.'

Skari spat into the flames. 'We'll see about that.'

Njall asked about their horses and Skari joined him to retrieve the animals left at the edge of the forest. It was settled. Our party expanded from two to four and I wondered how long before we jumped at each other's throats.

Fjola sat across from me, poking the embers with her boot, forehead creased in thought. With her rusty hair and lips pinched in a stubborn resolve, she looked nothing like Lumi, but her being here scratched the wound, still fresh from the events at Stromhold. Her presence unsettled me and invited questions I was unwilling to answer. I wasn't ready to have another woman close so soon and I doubted I ever would, but

Fjola was self-assured and confident about what she wanted from life, so much so that she decided to flee Hvitur to choose her path for herself. It was difficult to deny that I was drawn to her qualities, and it was a good enough reason to create some distance between us. To trust a woman was to gamble your life away and I had little left to gamble with. I wished she would return home with Skari and take the doubts that plagued me away with her.

XVII

'I never knew such heat,' Fjola said, flapping the front of her shirt. 'This is the farthest I've ever been from home. Even the air seems sweeter.'

'I don't share your enthusiasm,' Skari said. He cursed, slapping at the flies buzzing around his neck.

'Nobody forced you to come with us,' Njall said, keeping his eyes on the road. He had travelled this path before, and I suspected that his thoughts were fixed on Sur.

The borders of Nordur were far behind us, replaced by the Vestern sun. We stripped off our cloaks and jerkins, but even peeling off the excess clothing didn't ease the heat and our linen shirts were soon soaked in sweat. Clouds dissolved, making way for the birds that swept above the green country that stretched for miles on both sides of the beaten track, with tiny farmhouses scattered far apart.

Skari avoided me for most of our journey, and burdened by my own worries, his disregard suited me fine. I didn't feel like laughing at the jokes he exchanged with Njall and I was happy to lose myself in hunting animals for the meals we shared around the campfire. One evening, with Njall's help, I even managed to bring down a deer.

Skari behaved strangely around Fjola. With everyone watching, he acted brash around her, but on the nights when everyone slept, he checked she was wrapped up warm and shared his own blanket if it got too cold. He was a difficult man to fathom, but it was clear he cared for her in his own way.

Since I mentioned my plans to see the witches, Njall withdrew and scarcely engaged in speculations about our journey. Perhaps, like I had, he thought death awaited us once we crossed the Volkans, or maybe he feared for his sister. Whatever his thoughts, he kept them hidden.

'Sur is half a day away,' I said, slowing Blixt down to a trot. 'We'll make camp here. It's best to stay clear of the taverns.'

'Why should we?' Skari asked. 'We came so far to cower before our enemies? I say, let's kill a few Vesterners.' He swung at the air with his axe.

'We kill no one,' I said. 'Our quarrel is not with them. We keep to ourselves until we reach Sur.'

'It seems the Guardian of Stromhold favours the language of weaklings.' He looked at Fjola. 'Is this the man you're so eager to follow?'

'I'd rather follow a coward than a fool,' she snapped back.

'Choose your words carefully, my bride. We've many years ahead of us.'

Njall levelled his horse with Skari and snatched the axe from his hand. 'I thought of you as a warrior, keen to earn the love of my sister, but jealousy loosened your tongue and I see you find it difficult to control it. Was I wrong to trust you?' He threw the axe into the grass.

I waited for Skari to lash out or dispense insults, but he said nothing. His face twisted in a grimace and he dismounted. 'Nothing's changed, Brother,' he said. 'Your trust is well placed.' He retrieved the axe.

'Then prove it.'

My lips twitched with satisfaction at seeing Skari scolded like a spoiled child. He deserved to be put in his place, and who was better suited to the task than his future law-brother, but Njall's slack face betrayed only disappointment. Even though I knew Njall for only a matter of weeks, I held him in high regard. He was calm and practical, and from our short conversations he'd shown himself to be a man of patience. By rebuking Skari this way, he displayed his devotion to Fjola. She was lucky to have such a brother.

We led the horses away from the main path, towards a shack crumbling under the weight of time. Inside, a willow tree poked through the gaps in the walls. The smell of moss and decay lingered within the ruins and the floor was a tangle of weeds and black earth. Half of the roof had collapsed into a pile of rubble in the corner, but another half held on, letting a waterfall of willow-whips through the fissures. A faint sound of rushing water indicated the presence of a river nearby.

'What happened to the people who lived here?' Fjola's voice echoed in the empty space.

'Could be any number of things,' I said, thinking of Elizan and the destruction caused by the horde of Varls.

'Most likely they left in search of a better life in the city.' Njall swept the debris off the floor with his boots. 'This spot will do for a fire.'

I stepped over the crumbling wall and went to find Blixt. Like a second shadow, Fjola was on my heels. 'Do you do that on purpose?' I asked when we were out of earshot. 'Skari doesn't want you near me. Why anger him?'

She patted her horse. 'I prefer your company to that of my betrothed.'

'I thought you wanted to be a warrior, to travel.'

'I still do.'

'In that case, you shouldn't seek my company. My quest is personal and I want to avoid unnecessary fighting. I'm not a man to be admired.'

A few months ago, I'd had a very different dream and it was strange to admit that I no longer desired glory and fame. I had no one to share it with, but Fjola was surrounded by people who cared about her. Why would she want to forsake all that in pursuit of a cause she knew nothing about just weeks before was beyond me.

'Like you, I wish to see Hyllus dead,' she said. 'If you fulfil your oath, Nordur will be free of his beasts. I want to help in any way I can.'

'It's likely we'll end up dead.'

'Don't lose heart. Stranger things have happened.'

'How can you be so carefree? Don't you fear death?'

'I do, but I have faith in the gods. They have plans for us all.'

We reached the riverbank and let the horses go free. I splashed the cool water on my face and neck, washing off the dust from the past few days.

Fjola took off her boots and walked into the stream. 'There's something to be said about the feel of water rushing through your toes,' she marvelled, stirring the river with her feet. 'Njall told me we're heading to Sur.'

'We are.' I unbuckled my sword and sat on the grass. It felt good to stretch my legs. I loved being on horseback, but too long in the saddle gave you sores in places you would rather not mention.

'Aren't you afraid? Who's to say the witches won't harm you?'

'If they want me dead, so be it.' I picked a stone and threw it across the river. It made patterns on the water's surface and sank into the depths.

'Do you think they have the power to change your destiny? To defy Skaldir's will?'

My father's sword lay on the grass between us. A stranger would look upon it with indifference, but to those who knew its purpose, the blade represented a force powerful enough to destroy the world. 'I don't need them to. The gods and Valgsi are no concern of mine. I have more pressing arrangements.'

'I don't believe you,' she said.

'I don't care what you believe.'

She sprung from the stream like a cat with eyes narrowed and grabbed the sword. 'Let's see how honest you are.'

I was on my feet even before my brain comprehended her words. 'Give it back.'

'I intend to throw it in the river,' she said, swinging her arm.

I tightened my fists. 'What are you trying to do?' I was ready to jostle her for the sword if it came to it.

'I want to show you the truth, Jarin Olversson. Torgal said the bond that forges between Valgsi and his blade is most powerful. You wish to escape your fate. You ignore the prophecy, but it changes nothing. Because of your ignorance, our people will pay the price.'

I leaped at her and snatched the sword away from her. 'It belonged to my father.'

A dry and bitter laugh escaped her. 'I wish it was the only reason.' She gathered her boots. 'Instead of avoiding the truth, face it and find a way to save the world.' She headed back to the shack.

I ran my fingers across the sheath, feeling the criss-crossed patterns on the leather. 'She is wrong. You hold no power over me,' I whispered, but my voice was weak. Fjola's words about the bond between the blade and Valgsi hovered in the air. Was it even possible to get so attached to a thing of steel? I knew warriors of Stromhold cared for their weapons, but was it with such intensity as I had experienced moments ago? Whatever was happening to me was caused by something greater. Skaldir dreamed against her will and her rage grew more powerful with each passing winter. Could anyone withstand such magical forces? I shuddered despite the heat. Maybe I was a fool trying to escape the inevitable.

'No.' I looked up at the sky where clouds fought each other in waves of red and yellow. 'You chose the wrong man to do your deeds.'

* * *

Once again, I faced the crossroads, the path to the Volkans stretching before me with the familiar odour of rotten eggs in the air. Same place, different time and different Jarin from the one that bid farewell to Mirable in this very spot. Despite myself, I looked around, hoping that by some miracle the merchant would show up.

'Are you sure this is the way?' Skari asked. He sniffed and his face twisted as he smelled the stink of sulphur. 'What's this stench?'

'The only way to Sur is through the fiery mountains,' I said. 'Keep the horses calm and pay no attention to the rumblings of the earth. The fire inside the Volkans keeps them alive.'

Njall glanced around, trying to steady his horse. 'How alive?'

'Mirable…a merchant who led me here said the Volkans can wake, but no telling when, so let's not linger.'

Reluctantly, they followed me. Even Skari didn't bother with any sarcastic or threatening remarks.

We rode into the valley; it was hotter than I recalled and I winced at the idea of crossing the Great Passage again in this heat.

'The air burns,' Fjola said and followed with a dry cough.

The flakes of ash floated in the air, finding their way up my nostrils and into my ears and eyes. 'Cover your mouth with your sleeves,' I said.

The stinging heat of the Volkans reminded me of fires in Einir's forge. I'd stood behind the blacksmith when he opened one of his ovens and the force of heat pushed at me like a roaring beast.

'It's Agtarr's Valley of Death on earth,' Njall mumbled, burying his mouth with his arm.

A low growl carried across the Great Passage, unleashing a rumble that shook the ground and sent gravel tumbling down the Volkans' walls in a haze of dust and hot air. Skari's horse buckled and skidded sideways, sending him crashing down. Free of his passenger, the mare galloped forward and disappeared into the cloud of ash. Skari was on his back, spitting and cursing, his face covered in soot. I leaped from the saddle and offered my hand to help him up, but he pushed it away.

'My horse is gone,' he said, getting to his feet and brushing dust off his coat. The ground beneath us trembled. 'This place is cursed and it's you who brought us here.'

Fjola turned her horse. 'Stop wallowing. You can share my saddle until we catch up with your horse. Let's hope it was just startled.'

Skari hesitated for a moment. 'I'll take the reins.'

She dug her heels into the grey mare. 'No, you won't.'

Skari looked darker than the valley's ash, but he didn't argue. He mounted the horse and wrapped his hands around Fjola's waist. 'My bride has the spirit of a true warrior. Our children will be known for their strong wills.'

'Try not to fall this time,' she said and there was a visible tension in her body.

The ground shook and trembled and I was glad for Blixt's calm. We had faced this treacherous journey before, and even though the fiery mountains stirred and grumbled like giants disturbed from their slumber, Blixt made me proud by showing no fear. At the valley's edge, we found Skari's horse chomping grass and swishing its tail. It betrayed no emotion at seeing his master in one piece.

Skari jerked the reins. 'Foolish animal. What possessed you to take off like that? If you prove to be of no use to me, I know merchants who would pay a good price for a useless horse.'

'Shame we don't know any merchants who would pay good money for a useless man,' Fjola said. 'If you treat it better, it may be less inclined to ride without you.'

'Don't lecture me about my own horse—'

'The witches may taunt you with illusions,' I said before their squabble grew in force. 'Regardless of what you see, stay on the path.' There was no telling how I would react if Lumi's dancing ghost appeared again.

'Illusions?' Njall followed my gaze, but the fields were empty.

'Witches play tricks on those who venture here. Keep your eyes on the road.'

Fjola lifted her palm into the air. 'There's no wind...'

'Nothing lives in Sur,' I said. 'The witches alone rule these lands.'

'How can you be sure they'll help us?' Njall asked.

'They had a chance to take my life, but they didn't. No...they knew I'd be coming back and they better have answers this time.'

We rode the horses along the track. Everything seemed out of place in Sur, as if the forces of nature had given up on this part of the world. The familiar tree came into view with its lifeless branches. I remembered the trick and refused to fall into the trap of surprise, but the dead branches didn't appear again. Something was different this time. Riding through Sur felt like sitting in an empty house, straining to catch the quietest of sounds and giving life to creaking floorboards and every rustle in the walls. Whatever magic reigned here, it shrouded the land in dread.

I caught a movement to my right—a form in the distance that soon took the shape of a man. I was about to warn my companions to ignore the apparition, recalling too well my own vision of Lumi when I first set foot in Sur, when Fjola pulled on her reins and halted her horse. She squinted at the man who walked towards the road. He wore a tattered coat and rubber boots, his face shielded under an oilskin hat typical to that of the fisher folk. The man's beard stuck to his face like sea grass to a rock and his skin was pale, almost transparent, but the closer he got, the wider Fjola's eyes opened until she made a yelping sound, jumped off her horse, and ran to meet him.

'Fjola!' I screamed, but she didn't look back, didn't stop.

Njall raced after her and I followed.

Ground that looked solid from the road turned to sludge and pulled at my boots in an attempt to sink them. Njall faced the same challenges, but he caught Fjola before she reached the stranger.

'Father,' she cried out and looked at Njall, her eyes wild. 'It's Father. Can't you see?'

I caught up with them. 'It's not your father. It's an illusion created to lure you into the wilds.'

Njall's face slacked at her words and he loosened his grip. Fjola ripped free of him. I cursed and sprinted after her, but she was too fast, closing the distance between us and the apparition. I drew my sword and flung myself at her, desperate to push her out of the way.

Pain rippled through my shoulder as I crashed into Fjola's ribs, but I had no time to indulge it. Instead, I slid the blade through the ghost. It yelped like a dog, with ribbons of blood spraying in all directions, and it was gone in a puff of grey smoke.

'Father! You killed him!' Fjola scrambled to her feet and came at me with fists, throwing punches at my chest.

I caught her hands. 'Your father is dead, remember? He drowned. This isn't real. It's a trick.'

'Liar!' Sobbing, she buried her face in my chest and I wrapped my arms around her, feeling her loss as if it were my own.

In Elizan, I too wept over my father's body. Fjola and I shared the same pain and no words were powerful enough to ease that grief. All I could do was to rock her gently and let my shirt absorb the sorrows flooding her heart. When Njall approached us, his eyes were as haunted as her cries and he covered his face with his hands. Holding Fjola and witnessing Njall's pain brought me closer to them in ways no other experience ever could, and in our sadness we knew each other as intimately as if we grew up behind the same walls.

'What magic is this?' Skari yelled. His boots sunk into the black soil as he staggered across the field. 'Who was that man?'

Fjola pulled away from me, wiping tears in haste. 'No one.' With her head lowered, she pushed past him.

He turned to follow her, but Njall blocked him with his body. 'Leave her alone. She's in no mood for your questions.'

Skari snorted. 'Was she ever? Tell me, Brother, how long are we going to follow this madman?'

'As long as it takes. I made a promise to Torgal, but you have no such obligations. You're free to go back.'

'You think Fjola would agree to that?'

'I said nothing about Fjola.'

'Why would you? You're too busy following this coward.' He pointed his thumb my way and made a mocking bow. 'All hail to Stromhold's Guardian.'

'What is it with you?' Njall pulled him up by the collar. 'Be the man my sister was promised to.'

Skari shrugged him off and strode to the horses. It was a strange thing, for reasons best known to himself Skari wanted Njall's approval above all else.

'Pay no mind to him,' Njall said. 'He had a soft spot for Fjola since she offered him a scrap of cotton to wipe the blood off his face following his father's beatings.'

'Beatings?' It was hard to imagine Skari letting anyone abuse him, least of all his father.

'Maybe another time. We best be off.'

No more ghosts appeared to mock and terrify us and we reached the forest just as the sun crested the ridge far on the horizon. The evening shadows grew deeper with the approaching nightfall, turning trees into elongated phantoms. A veil of fog as thick as smoke hovered over the bog, and when I stepped closer to the edge, my mouth filled with the taste of putrid roots. I had no doubt the rot spreading across Sur was caused by the foul occupants and the ancient magic they practiced to keep people away from their land. I too wanted to get away from here—as soon as I got what I came for.

'What now?' Fjola asked.

'We wait,' I said. 'The witch will come in her own time.'

We sat on the grassy bank in grim silence. Skari polished his axe and Fjola pulled at the yellow grasses poking between her feet. Njall had his eyes fixed on the forest, face as still as the air around us, and apart from the buzzing of insects, no other sound stirred the evening. In the hush that settled, even my own breath died as soon as it passed my lips.

I heard the bell long before they did. When I sat here weeks ago, fear fought against hope in my heart, but now, each ring tapped at my most painful memories, mocking, like Lumi's laughter in the storm. I covered my ears, but the ringing didn't cease.

Fjola touched my hand. 'What's wrong?' she said.

The forest whispered and the branches parted to clear the way for the crone who shuffled from the gloom, with Hrafn perched on her shoulder. The odour of decay followed them.

Skari dropped his axe and Fjola gasped.

'Agtarr have mercy,' Njall whispered.

I didn't think it possible, but the witch had aged even more since our last meeting. Her face was blotched with yellow stains, the few strands of hair were gone, and her scalp peeled like burned skin.

'You have returned sooner than we anticipated,' the witch said.

My stomach felt as hard as a rock, but despite the fear, I met her eye. 'And this time I won't be so easily swayed by your riddles.'

She spoke a word so quiet that at first I thought I'd imagined it, but the pain that followed soon after assured me the witch didn't like to be opposed. It felt as if a giant hook tore into my chest and ripped open my rib cage.

It lasted only for a moment, but it was enough to choke me and bring me crashing to my knees. Fjola's scream tore the air and she leaped to my side, but I stopped her with my palm.

'I'm all right,' I said, and to demonstrate, I got to my feet. A burning bile rose at the back of my throat and I fought for breath. 'I chose to come here and I'm ready to accept the consequences.'

The witch rang her bell. 'Trofn... the Guardian of Stromhold has returned to seek our wisdom.'

A second witch emerged from the shadows with her gaunt fingers wrapped around a wooden staff and her crooked frame concealed in a black cloak. Her face was lost in the folds of her hood and the thought that she may not have one sent the deepest of chills through my bones.

'Is he the one, Kylfa?' Trofn asked. Her voice rustled like a dead leaf.

'Indeed. And he brought his companions.'

Trofn sniffed the air in the same fashion as her fellow witch and turned her head upwards. 'A brother... a sister... and a lover.'

'I seek answers,' I said, trying to keep my voice from breaking.

'He seeks answers, Sister.' Trofn's voice echoed my own.

'He always does. He is full of questions…What do you want to know, son of Eyvar?'

'You warned me about Lumi. You said she was from Shinpi. Where is she now?'

'He speaks of the demon, Sister,' Trofn said, scratching at the air with her curled fingers. Dark veins ran up her arm, fading into the folds of her cloak. 'Lumi, he calls her.'

Kylfa's laugh stirred the forest. 'Have you courage to pursue her?'

'She killed my family and I won't rest until she's punished.'

'Your sword can't kill her,' Kylfa said and Hrafn stabbed her black eye with his beak.

Fjola dropped to her knees and gagged.

The witch fixed her milky eye on her. 'She is fragile… too fragile to chase demons.'

'It's not her fight,' I said.

Like lightning during a storm, the old witch appeared next to us, grabbed Fjola's face, and dug her dirty nails into her chin. Njall sprang at them, but with one chime of her bell, Kylfa froze him onto the spot. His lips opened in a scream, but he made no sound. She turned Fjola's face in her hands. 'Green... too much green. The eye of a serpent, passionate but selfish...'

Fjola's eyes fixed on the witch and her body jerked. Her breathing came quick and ragged and drool frothed at the corners of her mouth.

'Let her go,' I said, reaching for the sword.

Kylfa loosened her grip and Fjola slipped onto the grass. Her eyes rolled up and her body shook in an uncontrollable fit. Njall, released from his state, crawled to her and tried to still her trembling.

'What did you do to her?' Skari screamed, aiming his axe at the witch.

Kylfa ignored him and her face twitched. 'She is fighting time. Her brain is too fragile to absorb the events she wanted me to show her.'

'Leave her alone,' I said, horrified. 'She has no part in this. None of them have. It's me you want to torture, not them.' My heart went out to Fjola and I cursed myself for bringing her here. What was I thinking? It was bad enough I ruined my own life and now I put my friends through pain. 'Please, just tell me how to find and kill Lumi and we'll leave.'

'The heart of the demon lies under the ocean, in the lost city of Antaya. Find the heart and shatter it.'

I looked at Fjola, still fitting in Njall's embrace. All I wanted was to get them out of here alive, but I needed answers and this was my only chance to obtain them. I felt like a traitor when I asked, 'How do I get to this city?'

'He wants to find the city, Sister,' Trofn echoed.

'The entrance lies hidden on the southern shores of Vester. Hyllus has the key.'

'Hyllus…You told me what he was. I need the power to defeat him.'

Trofn jerked her head my way, but the blackness within the hood betrayed nothing. 'He wants the power, Sister…'

Kylfa fixed her eyes on mine. The black mass moved and shifted in her right socket and the cataract clouded her left. 'How much are you willing to sacrifice to get it?'

'I'll stop at nothing to avenge my father.'

'If we give, we must take in return. A life for a life.' Trofn's whisper rippled the silence.

'As you wish, Jarin Olversson. We will grant you the power to kill Hyllus, but in return we want your soul.' Kylfa's words rang through the bog and Hrafn cried out in response.

'Why?'

'Our master demands it. You carry Skaldir's mark. Your soul can absorb her magic. Her power is the greatest force.

Magic is energy and your soul is the concentration of your being.'

Fjola's body calmed and was no longer shaking. Strands of her hair tangled around her face and her eyelids twitched as if she were in a dream, seeing things not of this world.

Njall got to his feet. 'Forget them. No vengeance is worth such sacrifice. You'll find the way and I'll stay by your side until Hyllus is dead.'

Njall knew nothing about the pain eating away at my heart, and only Hyllus's death could relieve me of it. I looked into the shadows of Trofn's hood. 'Have it.'

'Very well.' Kylfa motioned at Trofn with her cane.

The black witch hissed and murmured to herself. 'Your hand, Guardian.'

She shuffled closer and grabbed my right arm, her fingers leaving white impressions on my skin. Her strength surprised me and I fought the instinct to tear away from her grip. She whispered ancient words, making patterns on my forearm with her nails. With no warning, she pulled my hand to her face and sank her teeth into my wrist. The agony was like a vice with its jaws tightening around my arm until my skin was ready to burst under the pressure of blood gathering in the spot. I howled as the pain rippled through me and intensified. My senses filled with images: me as a child, running around

Stromhold with my wooden sword; watching Lumi by the fire on the night of Rodolf's death; fighting the Varls in Elizan; weeping over my mother's body in her chamber in Stromhold—the life I had lived from moment to moment, until the visions faded with the image of Hyllus staring at me across the burning village.

I ripped my arm free. It burned and throbbed and a symbol formed on my wrist, where Trofn had bitten me. It resembled a circle with multiple lines running inside it and a black eye in its centre.

'The pain is a reminder of your oath,' Kylfa said. 'When the time comes, it will guide you back.'

'What if I don't return?'

'He thinks to cheat us, Sister,' Trofn said.

'Oh, you will return,' Kylfa said.

'What of your promise?' I asked through clenched teeth.

Trofn reached into the folds of her robe and retrieved a black box. 'Take this.'

I turned it in my hand. Its surface was scored with symbols I have never seen in any scroll. 'What's this?'

'Our gift to you. The power to kill the mage.'

'A box? Is it one of your tricks?'

'The best things are often made to look small and insignificant. A wave that brings the storm powerful enough to swallow almighty ships. A spark that breeds a fire capable of burning cities to the ground. A seed that turns into a newborn. Open it when the time is right and the deed will be done.'

I pushed my finger into the gap between the bottom and the lid to pry it open. Kylfa rushed to my side and grabbed my fingers. 'When the time is right. Open it before and you will perish.'

'How do I know you're telling the truth?'

'You asked for a life and you offered one,' Trofn said. 'We take what is ours and we give what is promised.'

They turned to the forest, back into the bog. Before trees swallowed them, Kylfa's voice echoed from the gloom, 'once Skaldir's prophecy comes to pass, we will wait for you in Sur.'

Before I could respond, the witches were gone, claimed by the mist that bore them.

XVIII

We left Sur under the watchful eye of the full moon. With the absence of wind, the air was still and odourless, smothering our lungs in a sultry embrace. The horses churned up the gravel with their hooves and stirred the night with the chiming of their bridle bits. Njall rode at the fore, swaying with the rhythm of his horse, and Fjola followed with Skari at her side. Since the encounter with the witch, Skari watched her closely as if afraid another fit was imminent, but she paid no attention, face concealed in the rusty storm of her hair. Kylfa's visions turned Fjola's passion for the journey into apathy and left her hunched in the saddle with shoulders drawn close together. I tamed my curiosity, remembering well how difficult it was to answer questions you weren't ready for.

The black box pressed against my chest in the pocket of my jerkin—a constant reminder of the pact I had made. My soul was no longer mine.

How could I exist, knowing the essence of my being belonged to someone else?

I had lost too much to care. My family had been massacred, my dreams of becoming Stromhold's guardian were gone, and the woman I loved had betrayed me. Men sought weaknesses in others, and if given the opportunity they would use them to mislead and betray the way Lumi broke faith with me. If the witch told the truth, the power trapped inside the box would kill Hyllus, and my oath to avenge my father would be fulfilled.

I touched its sharp edge. What if Kylfa had tricked me and I surrendered my soul for an empty trinket? It wouldn't be the first time someone played me false, and my sacrifice would be for nothing. Nausea stirred my gut and blood rushed to my head. The temptation to open the box was hard to resist, but I had to ignore the voice inside me that was challenging me to see what I had given up my life for.

Without warning, Njall spun his horse around and levelled with me. 'Why did you do it?' The question was sharp with disapproval.

'I had no choice.'

'There's always a choice.'

'Not for me.'

'You didn't even bargain. You gave away your soul without a fight and for what? Is vengeance more important than your life?' A scowl darkened his face. 'It was reckless.'

'Say what you will, but don't lecture me about my soul. I did what I had to do.'

'How can you trust them, with their tricks and foul magic?'

'I don't trust anyone.'

We entered the Great Passage, the Volkans withheld their anger and kept the earth still, letting us ride under the shower of ash in relative peace. By the time we reached the crossroads, my mouth was a desert and my tongue a dry bark. Skari brushed the grey specks from Fjola's shoulders, but when he tried to pick some off her hair, she pulled away.

'Aren't you afraid?' Njall asked. 'Himinn is closed to you. Without a soul, you can't enter the Fields of Life. You'll never rejoice with your family.'

I laughed him off. 'Himinn isn't for me. Nothing gives me more satisfaction than knowing the gods have no claim on my soul.' How I wished I could believe my brave words and match the courage of my retort.

Njall shifted in the saddle. 'Weigh your words carefully.'

'Why? Mother prayed to Yldir all her life, but he wasn't there to save her. Where were the gods when Hyllus struck my father down?' I looked at the sky where stars glimmered against the blackness like embers in a fire pit. 'They demand loyalty, worship, and what do they give in return? Skaldir threatens us with the Day of Judgement and her brothers do nothing.'

'Their power locks her in a dream.'

'Like the rest of us. It's easier to dream than act. People fear the prophecy instead of confronting it.'

'We pray——'

I let my breath out with a rattle. 'Prayer. An excuse for inaction.'

Njall's face sagged. 'Grief speaks through you. The Great Atlantic snatched my father. My mother ambles along the shore hoping he'll come back. I know the pain of losing someone dear to your heart…'

I pulled on the reins and brought Blixt to a halt. 'My father was the greatest warrior, the Guardian of Stromhold, admired by all. If he lived to see his family betrayed, he'd stop at nothing to avenge them. I'm his son and I won't let the traitors get away.'

'I don't know if it's courage or foolishness that drives you.' He rubbed at his forehead. 'The witch spoke of Lumi.'

Her name disturbed the night and rocked my heart. 'She was a girl my father saved from death on the plains. The demon I seek has no name.'

'Antaya had been locked away since the War of Mages, but some say their magic still lingers in her depths.'

I pushed back my shoulders. 'The demon's heart is there and I have to destroy it. If I must travel alone, so be it. You faced enough dangers and the greatest of them awaits in Vester. I couldn't ask more of you.'

Njall drew his spear and the moonlight bounced off its tip. 'You made a powerful sacrifice. I'll stand with you till the end.'

My chest expanded with gratitude. I couldn't wish for a better and more loyal companion. 'And what of your sister?' I asked with a stab of guilt. 'I led Fjola to Sur and because of me she was exposed to Kylfa's magic.'

'Fjola is strong and Skari is watching over her. She'll speak when she's ready.'

I rolled my eyes. 'Skari…I wouldn't trust him with my saddlebag.'

'He didn't have it easy. Broken bones, humiliation…'

'Do his ordeals give him any right to Fjola?'

'Torgal gave permission to their union, and it's not for me to question his reasons.'

I closed my eyes, allowing the night breeze to wash away my tiredness. Sur was far behind us and nature resumed her reign over the world. 'Your blind faith in my uncle is formidable,' I said.

'The man saved my life—a debt I can never repay.'

Skari began humming and his voice merged with the droning of insects. The song used to be a favourite among

Stromhold's warriors as it spoke of the great victory of the Nordern king over the tribes populating the southern shores. I sang it many times, sitting at my father's feet, with fire crackling in the hearth, but I knew nothing of the true sacrifices made to keep Nordur's freedom. To me, it was just a song then, like many others, but hearing it now, so far from home, brought back a longing for those evenings when Father watched over us, exchanging smiles with my mother, her cheeks rosy from the heat and fingers busy mending his shirts.

'His father,' Njall motioned to Skari, 'brought shame to Nords in Hvitur. Drunkard, unable to provide for his family… I was ten winters old when his wife died giving birth to Skari, and the boy suffered for it. Between beatings, he used to sneak away to watch me practice with my spear. Fjola, being his age, used to hold his hand when he came bruised or bleeding.'

I couldn't imagine having a father like that. 'My misbehaviour met with my father's disapproval plenty of times,' I said, 'and I still recall being unable to sit down for a week, but each punishment was just and well deserved.'

'Skari wasn't so fortunate. No child of ten should face such ordeals.' Muscles rippled under the skin of his throat. 'I had to put an end to his misery.'

'Turning on another Nord is punishable by death,' I said, more to myself than to Njall.

'If not for Torgal, my bones would be rotting in the ground somewhere, or worse, scattered by the wild beasts.'

I looked at Skari. He hadn't had access to a shaving blade since we left Hvitur and his head was covered with spikes of fresh hair. The tattoo on his right temple all but disappeared, like my own mark. Knowing about his past made it easier to understand his need for conflict and connection to Njall and Fjola. Each of us carried a story in our heart and I was fortunate to have such companions joining me in pursuit of justice.

* * *

At dawn we reached the outskirts of the city where stone houses with rounded walls and square windows occupied both sides of the cobbled path. Our horses' hooves echoed through the street as we led them to a tavern under a canopy of overhanging trees. A sign depicting a pair of blue fish leaping from the water pointed to a set of steps and a green door.

'The innkeeper is a Nord. He won't ask questions,' Njall assured us.

'Traitor,' Skari mumbled. 'Vester is no place for a Nord.'

'You opened Hvitur's gates to the southern merchants,' I reminded him.

'If I had a say in the matter, the gates would stay shut.'

A candle flickered on the window of an outbuilding from which a stable hand came out to greet us, yawning and rubbing his eyes. The youth took the reins with a pinched expression and led the horses into the stables. Through an archway was a room with gnarled beams and rectangular tables that reminded me of Nordur's taverns. I much preferred the dimness inside to the colours of the street. They were too happy for a place harbouring an evil such as Hyllus.

The innkeeper lumbered from behind the counter, tying back the straps of his apron. 'Welcome.'

'We need food and rooms,' I said in Vestern.

He appraised us and cleared his throat. 'I have beds,' he replied in Nordern, 'but we won't be cooking yet. Cold meats are all I can offer.'

I thanked him and paid five silver coins for his hospitality. Judging by the odour of burned mutton in the air, we wouldn't be missing much. He showed us to a table in the far corner where he lit a candle stump. Skari propped himself against the wall, stretching his feet on the bench.

'You speak Vestern?' Njall asked, making room for Fjola. She slipped between us without a word and leaned back with her eyes closed.

'My mother insisted on it, and now I'm glad she did.' The hours I spent with Marco, labouring over the scrolls with unfamiliar letters hadn't gone to waste. The innkeeper brought a jug of mead and another filled with wine. To my surprise, Fjola reached for the wine, poured some into her cup, and gulped it in one go. I gave her a questioning look.

'Marus stocks wine in Hvitur's cellars,' Njall explained with a slow smile. 'Fjola raided the place many times while I watched the entrance.'

'Vesterners should be cut down and not admired for their wines,' Skari said. He raised the mug of mead to his lips.

I anticipated a prickly remark from Fjola, but she said nothing. Not a full day had passed since we left Sur and I already missed her voice. The thought made me uncomfortable and I turned my attention to the innkeeper.

He served plates of cold meat and fish strips scattered with olives and green leaves. A ceramic bowl full of pickled cabbage appeared soon after, with hunks of cheese, bread, and lard.

Skari spread the fat over a piece of bread. 'What's our intent?' he asked with his mouth full. 'The citadel is the only thing standing between us and Hyllus.'

At the sound of Hyllus's name, the innkeeper stopped polishing his mug and looked at us from under his eyelids.

'Keep your voice down,' I hissed.

Njall filled his plate to the brim and Fjola followed. She proceeded to taste every bit and when she tried the olives, her lips twisted and she spat. I chuckled; we had similar tastes. My past experience told me to exercise caution, so I chose bread and cheese.

'I spent months watching the Citadel of Vester and could see no way in,' Njall said, scooping meat and fish with green leaves.

'It's not a case of storming the tower. We need a subtler approach,' I said. 'Back in Hvitur you mentioned two Varls guarding the entrance.'

'I never saw them shift. It's as if they're statues. However, at feeding time, an old man opens the gate and throws meat and bone on the ground. The Varls launch at the scraps and one thing is for certain, I've never seen creatures as vicious as these.'

'Even so, they're humans, transformed by Hyllus's magic. They feel pain like us, they bleed and die. There must be a way…'

'Then we should kill them,' Skari said and burped. The mead loosened his tongue and his voice went up a notch. 'Nords carve their way with steel.' He slapped his palm on the table. 'Instead of sitting idle let us teach them a lesson and show Hyllus our true strength.'

'Quiet,' Njall said in his ear and glanced at the innkeeper, who abandoned his place behind the counter and moved about the tavern, cleaning tables and rearranging chairs. I was sure he listened in on our exchange, and considering we were in Hyllus's territory, it wasn't wise to make our intentions towards the mage known.

'Your debates and best forged plans would turn to dust the moment your presence is discovered,' Skari said, lowering his voice under the scrutinising eye of his future law-brother. 'We were born to fight, so let us use the skills to our advantage. Shame we didn't cut down the old crones in Sur when we had the chance.'

To Skari everything was simple, and with his axe he would happily barge ahead, cutting down everyone who crossed his path. Charging Hyllus's citadel in such a manner would be foolish. And if the Varls were as keen as Njall described, they would catch our scent before we got near the gates and turn us into a pile of meat and bones for feeding.

'Poison,' Fjola said.

Her voice caught me unawares. 'Poison? I know nothing of herbs and we have no alchemist in our party.'

'Besides,' Njall interjected, 'we wouldn't get close enough to poison the meat. The Varls have a powerful sense of smell.'

'There must be an alchemist in Vester,' she said. 'Every big city has them.'

Skari raised his brow. 'And how do you suppose we find this alchemist?'

'We can ask someone in the city.'

Njall frowned at her. 'Even if we got the poison, we wouldn't be able to come close enough to use it, and—'

'We'll set up a watch,' I said, looking into Fjola's eyes. Now that she was back, I wanted to keep her engaged and away from what was bothering her. I knew she had Skari and her brother to lean on, but despite that, this was my quest and she willingly became a part of it. I felt a need to protect her from future harm. I only felt like this once before with Lumi and the thought scared me. 'We'll scout the area, and between the four of us we may be able to find a way inside.' The corners of her mouth twitched in a smile. 'Tomorrow, we head into the city. We need somewhere with a clear view of the citadel, but away from the crowds.'

'Worry not, I know such a place,' Njall said. 'I spent my share of nights scouting for Torgal.'

'It's settled then,' I said. 'Let's get some rest.'

Skari and Njall headed up the stairs and I whispered in Fjola's ear. 'Good to have you back.'

Her face turned serious. 'The witch showed me things. My father's death…in her vision, I saw his final hours and never felt so much pain.' Her voice caught. 'Watching him through the veil of time, unable to help…the past felt like the present to me.'

'I'm sorry. I should have never let you come along.'

She clutched my arm. 'What? No. I'd rather know what happened to him than spend the rest of my life wondering.'

'What will you do now?'

'We have both felt loss. You know my pain better than anyone. You've lost your father, your mother, your friends…Hyllus deserves to die at your hand and I want to help.'

'It'll be dangerous.' From the short time I spent with Fjola, I knew that telling her what to do was useless. She didn't take well to being ordered around.

'Danger is everywhere. Hvitur isn't safe. The Varls are still a threat and the only way to stop this madness is to kill Hyllus.' She raised her chin. 'I'm coming.' Her confidence left little room for dispute.

I started up the stairs.

'Why sacrifice your soul?' she said, bringing me to a halt, but before I could respond, she grabbed my wrist and ran her slender fingers across Trofn's mark. 'Please, Jarin. Help me understand.'

I hardly understood myself. My life was like an empty shell, washed away by the ocean to be abandoned among the pebbles, hoping for the tide to take it back. After the loss of my family, the void inside me refused to shrink and I had to keep moving forward for if I stopped, it would consume me.

'It's the only way to—'

'You're a guardian,' she interrupted me. 'When this is over you must restore Stromhold, assemble new warriors, and protect Nordur like the guardians of the past. You can't just walk away from your responsibilities.'

'I'm no guardian. Just because my father is dead and I'm next in line doesn't make me one. I failed my parents and my warriors. I couldn't even save my mother.'

She frowned. 'So this is it? You want to give up and walk away? Take the easy road?'

Disappointment hidden in her words stung like nettles. 'There's nothing easy about this,' I said.

'When Skaldir awakens, you'll walk away and leave the world to fall into chaos,' she said. 'The goddess won't have mercy. She'll judge us as it's written in the scrolls. Humanity will perish. Is this what you want?'

'My soul is promised, but it doesn't mean I stopped being myself. I'll find a way to resist Skaldir's call. No god has the power to decide my fate, no matter how many scrolls they leave behind. I decide my own destiny.'

'The gods hold power over humanity. They created us and watch our lives until we stand at the threshold to Himinn. You speak as if they don't exist and defy them at every turn. You'll bring their wrath upon yourself. Why be so stubborn? Why not seek their help?'

'Never. I walk my own path and don't fear their judgement.'

With a last scornful look, she raced up the stairs.

* * *

Later that night, my hand found the hilt of my sword. Since Fjola's attempt to throw the blade into the river, I was suspicious of anyone showing interest in it. The blade filled me with courage and it was like having Father at my shoulder.

Kylfa spoke of a heart under the ocean, hinting that Hyllus knew of its location. I didn't know how a heart could survive outside the body and I had no idea where the mage kept the key, but my purpose was clear—to find the heart and crush it.

I retrieved Trofn's box and placed it on my chest, impatient to reveal the magic and witness its effects. It fell and rose with the rhythm of my chest and my eyes grew heavy. The end was so close I could hear my heart singing a song of vengeance.

XIX

When I woke, the world was a haze of dawn and shadows. A silhouette hunched over me, breathing heavily with a rancid odour, and in the faint light streaming through the window, I glimpsed the edge of a blade.

My senses sharpened in an instant and I rolled to the side, avoiding the scythe that ripped through the bed. I grabbed my sword, but before I could draw it another blow fell on me. I parried and the scythe glanced off the scabbard.

A scream echoed from somewhere in the tavern, followed by a roar as something heavy crashed against the wall. I kicked the intruder in the chest and sprang to my feet when a fist caught my rib and the impact sent me sprawling into a cupboard. A familiar shriek filled the room as the Varl hurled the bed out of his way. I regained my balance and pulled the cupboard away from the wall just in time for the Varl's scythe to wedge into the wood. I charged, slashing downward at his claws. He let go of the scythe with a howl.

I jumped onto the cupboard and aimed my sword at his neck, but he evaded it and I only caught his shoulder. I leaped forward and crashed into him. The impact knocked him down and I found myself looking into a face full of tumours and the smell of rotten blood filled my throat with bile. I smashed the pommel of my sword into the Varl's forehead, but he knocked my sword away and grabbed my neck. I struggled against his arm, desperate to loosen the grip, but he held on. My temples throbbed louder and louder as I fought for air, clawing at the putrid flesh.

The door flew open. 'He betrayed us!' Njall yelled. He ran up and with one swift move sunk his spear into the Varl's face. I ripped free, gasping for air; my throat was raw and each swallow a fresh agony.

I grabbed my sword and we ran down the corridor, past the bodies of two Varls sprawled dead against the wall. In the main area of the tavern, Skari stood behind the counter with his axe drawn and the innkeeper at his feet. The man cowered, hands over his head, babbling in Vestern.

We kicked the door outside to find Fjola atop a Varl. She'd made swift work of him and the skill with which she handled the daggers impressed me. Argil's training paid off for both of us and it was a testament to how great a warrior he was. How I wished he was here to guide us.

I ran to the stables and released the horses from their pens. Blixt was unharmed and I buried my head in his neck, relieved that the Varls didn't get to him.

Skari emerged from the tavern with blood dripping off his axe. A billow of grey smoke rose behind him—the tavern was on fire. From his cocky smile, I guessed the fate of the innkeeper and the thought stabbed at me. There was a difference between taking the life of a human being with all his senses intact and killing a Varl intent on ripping you apart. I found the pleasure on Skari's face sickening.

'Follow me,' Njall called and spurred his horse away from the main track.

* * *

We halted the horses at the edge of a thicket and sought shelter under a cluster of low trees where the smell of a stagnant pond, coated by a layer of green scum, tainted the air. Morning dew settled on the grass, glowing in the light of the rising sun like beads of silver. The path to the city curved ahead and disappeared among the houses.

'What now?' I asked, but the question came out as a croak. My throat was still raw.

'We need to get into the city and blend with the crowd,' Njall said. 'If anyone's following, it'd be harder for them to find us.'

'Why would a Nord do that?' Fjola asked. 'Betray one of his kin…'

Skari spat. 'He was no Nord and he won't be betraying anyone anymore.'

'How do you know it was him?' I asked.

'Who else? His tavern was the first we visited.' He curled his lip. 'I warned you not to trust him.'

'Maybe if you kept your voice down, he wouldn't have found out about our plans in the first place,' Fjola said.

'Oh, so now it's my fault?' Skari opened his arms wide. 'I see...*He* sent for the Varls to ambush us in our sleep, but *I am* on trial here?'

She waved her hand at him and faced her horse.

'It doesn't matter,' I said. 'We must stay focused.' I turned to Njall. 'What do you suggest?' He knew these parts better than any of us and I trusted his judgement.

'Town square. It's the busiest place in Vester.'

I caught Skari's eye. 'Stay out of trouble.'

* * *

All manner of people crowded the streets of Vester, from leather-skinned desert trawlers to merchants wrapped in turbans, and elders with their feeble bodies supported by canes. Women pulled vegetable carts and rebuked their squabbling children who ran around, throwing sticks and stones at passers-by. Multiple paths jutted out from the main street to form alleyways between the mud-brick houses, with trees and flowers lining each corner.

Skari shoved the masses with his shoulders, spitting and cursing, his face scarlet from the heat. 'Out of my way,' he screamed in Nordern at an old woman. She screeched back in Vestern, jabbing bony fingers at him.

Njall caught his elbow. 'You're drawing too much attention.'

'She'll taste my axe if she doesn't stop wailing,' Skari growled, but the woman followed him to the corner of the street, waving her arms and screaming curses.

'You're such a fool,' Fjola said, tightening the hood around her face. 'Can't you control your impulses once in a while? You're no longer a boy of ten.'

He gave her a sour look.

Fortunately for us, people appeared too busy going about their business to pay heed to our scrawny group. We led the horses along the pebbled street where each wooden door was painted in shades of green, blue, and red. Fjola peered inside one of the windows. 'No hearth?' she asked.

'Who needs fire in this heat?' Skari said, wiping sweat off his forehead.

She peered into another building. 'Such colourful tapestries…'

Skari looked over her shoulder. 'Useless junk. I see no weapons of any kind. How do they fight? With their pots and pans?'

'Varls fight for them, and people pay a heavy price for such protection,' Njall said, stepping over an overturned cart. Apples rolled in all directions and a man rushed to pick them up. 'Many fear Hyllus, but can do nothing. Even the Archeon of Vester allows him to practice his foul arts.'

Fjola picked one of the apples from the ground, wiped it on her sleeve, and sunk teeth into it. 'Juicy,' she said, licking the corner of her mouth.

A large square opened up in front of us with a giant fountain in the middle in which water cascaded down three shallow plates. A statue of a woman, carved from stone and wrapped in traditional Vestern clothes with her hands outstretched in a greeting, stood erect on the top of the highest bowl. Four Varls, with their faces partially concealed by hoods, paced the area, and a cluster of merchants spoke in hushed voices in the shade of a great pillar.

Fjola looked at the statue. 'Who is she?'

'Before Skaldir unleashed her wrath upon the world, Vester was ruled by women,' Njall said. 'She must be one of them.'

'We best move on,' I said, conscious of the Varls' presence.

'This way.' Njall ducked into a less crowded alley. 'The citadel isn't far from here. Stay on your guard.'

The crowded streets turned into a maze of remote alleyways lined with sagging hovels and broken fences, where the scent of urine, faeces, and rot pervaded the air. It seemed the protection of Varls didn't stretch as far as the poor districts of Vester. A man wearing only a tunic sat against the wall with a metal bowl between his crossed legs. When we levelled with him, he started chanting and shaking the bowl at us. Further up the path, a boy shied away behind a broken doorway, watching our progress with one eye, his face hardly visible through the layers of dirt.

'Where's your father, boy?' Skari asked him, but the boy ran back inside. 'He should be teaching him how to fight instead of letting him rot in this hole.'

'Since when do you care about Vestern children?' I asked.

Skari shrugged and said nothing.

'Exercise caution,' Njall warned. 'Although in lesser numbers, the Varls still patrol these streets.' He leaned on the wall of a decrepit building and peered around the corner. 'Looks clear.'

'Where exactly are we going?' I asked, following Njall into the shadows of another narrow alleyway.

'It's not far. You too could do with some patience.'

We passed a warehouse with gaping holes in the planks and doors hanging off their hinges. Visible through the cracks were old barrels and shards of iron.

'Even the poorest of Nords enjoy a better life,' Fjola said with a harried look in her eyes.

'No wonder Vesterners want a piece of Nordur,' Skari said with a scorn.

'You mean Hyllus,' I corrected him. 'He's our concern.'

'They're all and the same to me.' Skari dismissed anyone who had the misfortune to be born anywhere other than Nordur. If I learned anything about him during the short time I spent in his company, it was his fierce love for Nords, despite his childhood misfortunes. But his contempt for people from foreign parts of the world matched it in intensity.

In my heart, I too was a Nord, but my travels through Sur and the kindness that Mirable showed me altered my beliefs about Vester. Where Skari saw only enemies waiting for an opportunity to take the Nordur away from him, I saw people, some kinder than others, but people nevertheless, with their own burdens and worries to bear. Nords didn't live in constant dread that Hyllus would snatch our men and women to turn them into beasts, but all of us shared a fear of the Day of Judgement, and I hoped I was strong enough to prevent it.

Fjola frowned at Skari. 'It must pain you to have to—'

A dark shape sprung from the shadows of the adjacent alleyway and slammed her against the wall. Before I could react, a knife flashed at her throat. More men emerged: two from the same street as the man that held Fjola, one from the rundown warehouse and another from the window of the house further up, all gripping knives and hatchets. I grabbed my sword.

'Move and she's dead,' the man warned. A round patch of dark hide covered his right eye and a greasy stubble daubed his cheeks.

His companions formed a circle around us and each had a deformity of some kind. One's right arm was puffy, with muscles twisted like a pack of venomous snakes, another's bald head was badly scarred. The third man was bent under a heavy swelling on his back, and the fourth had an ugly grin, exposing a set of gaps between his teeth as if someone purposefully pulled them out to create this hideous expression.

'Vestern vermin,' Skari growled.

'Let her go.' I showed my empty palms to the assailant.

The knife pressed harder against Fjola's throat and her chin started to tremble. I wanted to throw myself at her captive and cut him down for causing her so much distress.

'Silver.' The man with a twisted arm took a step closer, hands shaking. 'Give us. All.' He eyed Njall's spear. 'Weapons too.'

His companion pulled his lips back, exposing more of his broken smile. 'And horses,' he said, slurping the words and patting Blixt's saddle.

'What do they want?' Skari asked.

Njall pulled out his empty pockets. 'We don't have silver.' He gestured to his mouth. 'I know who you are. The broken Varls who failed the transformation. Your scars betray you.'

'He knows about us,' said the man with the swelling.

If what Njall said was true, these men suffered unimaginable horrors at the hands of Hyllus. I looked at each of them in turn. Varls or not, no human being deserved to suffer such tortures.

'You live in the shadows,' Njall carried on, 'away from people and with no help from the gods. No hope.'

'Hope?' The man holding a knife to Fjola's throat spat. 'We cut and kill,' he said.

Blixt shifted and neighed uncomfortably and the man holding Fjola jerked his head at him. Fjola seized the moment of distraction, pushed the hand with the knife away from her throat, and smashed her fist into the man's nose. She grabbed him by the shirt and rammed her knee into his crotch. The man fell to the ground and yelped as her boot crushed his fingers. Everyone dived for their weapons.

The hatchet was inches from my face when I raised my sword to meet the assailant's steel with my own. His arm was surprisingly strong and I struggled against the deformed muscles that sprung to life, blood throbbing through bulging veins. He hissed and saliva splattered my face. I slammed my head into his forehead and the impact sent him staggering back, earning me a precious moment to thrust the blade into his chest. He looked down at it, eyes wide as if unable to comprehend how it got there, then he tried to pull it out but lost his balance and fell backwards. I pulled the sword free, releasing a dark patch of blood that spread around the body.

Fjola danced with her daggers, delivering skilful slashes. The man with the broken mouth tried to match her with his own knife, but she was too nimble and evaded his efforts with ease. With one swift move, she pushed past him and cut his neck open. There was a glow to her when she put her daggers to work. Watching her using the skills that Argil taught her made me realise why she didn't want to be a wife. She had energy and prowess to match those of the young warriors under my father's command, and even though having a woman join Stromhold was untraditional, I found myself wanting to break the custom. But of course, I had no warriors and there was no one left to command.

Skari stood over the body of the man with a scarred head, wiping the blood off his axe, and Njall pinned the man with the swelling with his spear.

'It's easy to see why Hyllus shunned you,' Skari said. 'Kill him and be done with it.'

'First, we question him,' I said. 'Get up.' I dragged the man to his feet. 'What's your name?'

He cowered. 'Before this,' he touched his deformed back, 'they called me Alkaios.'

'What do you want with us?'

'We broken, left for dead. Hunted. Hiding and stealing to survive.' Saliva dribbled from the corner of his mouth and down his chin. The magic-induced tumours grew inside his mouth, which altered his speech and prevented him from swallowing and forming the words fully.

'Any more of your companions?' Njall asked.

Alkaios swept his hand towards the dead bodies. 'The men I walked with, you killed. No others.'

'What should we do with him?' Fjola asked once I translated.

Alkaios grabbed her hand as if he understood her question. 'Kill me. My endless pain. Body burning. Inside. Outside. Wish to face Agtarr. His judgement brings peace.'

Skari rammed his boot into Alkaios's chest and sent him toppling to his knees. 'Don't touch her with your filthy hands.' He swung his axe.

'Wait!' I stopped him. 'He can be of use.'

Skari's face hardened. 'Must you always stand in my way?'

I hunkered down and placed my hand on Alkaios's shoulder. 'I can do better. I can offer you a chance at revenge.'

Alkaios's eyes met mine and the left side of his mouth twitched uncontrollably. He smelled of sweat and grime and his nails were curling over. His swelling prevented him from standing straight and as a result, the left side of his body was bent. When he walked, his hand brushed the ground. He was broken in more ways than just his name. His sorry state brought back Hyllus and the way he looked at me in Elizan, mockingly, as if he knew that I could never catch or punish him. The memory was like acid, corroding my innards.

'Vengeance?' Alkaios asked, wiping his chin on his tattered sleeve. 'I'm good for nothing. Weak.'

I looked around. Apart from the flies drawn by blood decomposing in the heat of the afternoon, the alley was empty.

'We aim to strike at the citadel and we could use your help.' I turned to my companions. 'He's coming with us.'

Skari pursed his lips. 'He's one of them, and he'll betray us at the first opportunity.'

Alkaios met my gaze. 'What help you need?'

'Poison,' I said. 'Strong enough to kill the Varls at the gates.'

'Alchemist. Need nightcup, root of akar, snakeweed.' He found it difficult to form the words.

'He knows of an alchemist,' Njall said to Fjola.

'Can he take us there?'

The broken Varl shook his head when Njall asked the question. 'Slow. My back full of pain.'

'He can ride my horse,' Fjola said.

'You can't be serious.' Skari looked from Njall to his sister. 'We can't trust him. It's a trap.'

'I'll go with them,' Njall said. 'But first, the house.'

'Walk!' Skari pushed Alkaios in front of him. The broken Varl winced and a wet sound escaped his throat as if drool suffocated him from the inside, but he hobbled on.

We traversed more abandoned alleyways where decay marked every corner. The houses spied on us through the gaps in their shutters, aching for life that once filled their sagging walls. The muffled sound of a dog's bark echoed through the streets then turned into a sharp yelp. Alkaios matched our pace with difficulty, muttering under his breath like a captured animal. His presence made the horses skittish and I sensed Blixt's anxiety through the reins. None of us knew if we could trust the Varl, but I had a feeling that a chance at revenge on those who scarred him beyond recognition would win over treachery. Fjola and Njall settled on going with him to obtain poison, but we still didn't have any idea how to administer it to the Varls without raising an alarm.

Njall stopped before one of the deserted houses. 'We're here,' he said.

It was a tall building with arched windows through which vines tangled their way inside. Plaster crumbled away from the walls in places where thick bush and roots gouged the stonework. The ancient carvings of the gods adorned the apex with their faces fractured by years of neglect. At the back, cast in shadow by a tree, was a fenced yard where we tied the horses.

'It's a tomb,' Skari said, pushing the wooden boards away to reveal a doorway. 'We'll be lucky if it doesn't crash in on our heads.'

Fjola squeezed through the opening, waking white dust with her boots.

'Up those stairs,' Njall said. 'The people of Vester think this place is haunted. According to the locals, spirits roam the house on the nights of the full moon.'

I followed Alkaios up the broken staircase. 'Ghosts are the least of our worries,' I said.

The room Njall led us to had the largest windows, with shutters hanging limp at each side. 'And here she is,' he said.

The Citadel of Vester loomed on the horizon, her marbled, cylindrical walls smooth and shiny in the setting sun. The tower had no windows and no doors other than the main gates guarded by two shapes, standing motionless like the wooden gods in Torgal's hall.

'And so our watch begins,' I said.

The room that would serve as our home was bare. In one dusty corner, pushed against the wall, was a crooked table on which sat a bowl and a cup. Inside it, spiders nestled safely in their webs. A sleeping hide lay folded under it, wrapped in layers of thick dust.

'The night is closing in. We should go,' Fjola said, pulling her hood back on.

'How far is the alchemist's place?' Njall asked.

'Edge of the city. Beyond river.' Alkaios leaned against the wall. He struggled to breathe and looked in no shape for a lengthy trip, but we had little choice.

'It's a trap,' Skari said. 'I don't trust this weakling. Let me come instead.'

'You don't know Vestern,' Njall said. 'How will you communicate?'

Skari shrugged and put his arm around Fjola. 'Don't let this cripple out of your sight.'

'We'll return with the supplies.' Njall looked at the citadel. 'Keep watch. We've yet to find her weak spot.'

'And watch out for the Varls,' I said. 'We still don't know who sent them. They may be following our trail.'

'I know these streets better than any of you—' Njall smiled at Fjola— 'and I have my sister's daggers to keep me safe.'

She returned his smile with her own and headed out into the evening with Alkaios shuffling at her feet.

Skari and I unbridled and untacked the horses before settling down in front of the windows. A cooling breeze breathed life into the night and made the trees in the yard sway. Shadows cast by the branches reminded me of a painting brought by a merchant who travelled to Stromhold with a supply of herbs for my mother: a set of graves on a linen canvas, with the dead climbing their way out, clutching the earth with their skeletal fingers. The image terrified me but my father laughed and said that I shouldn't fear the dead as they were already damned, empty shells clinging to a force of life that wasn't meant for them. Treachery of the living posed a much bigger threat.

Skari sat in the corner with his back propped against the wall, hands resting on his knees, and eyes trained on the dark outline of the citadel.

'I can take the first watch,' I offered. It was unlikely I could sleep with Hyllus so close and so far at the same time.

'I'd rather stay and wait for their return.'

A fly buzzed in, circling frantically around the room as if confused by unfamiliar walls. It swooped up and down until it found its way back into the night, leaving the room still again.

'She admires you.'

Skari's words caught me off guard. After weeks of nothing but hostility, his even tone surprised me.

'Fjola?'

He snorted. 'Don't take me for a fool. Who else? Her eyes follow your every move. She left Hvitur to chase after your enemies.'

'Hyllus is *our* enemy. As long as he lives Nordur will never be free.'

'Fjola is promised to me and I'll never have her.'

An uncomfortable silence settled between us and I didn't know how to break it. I much preferred the other Skari—defiant, brash, the one that challenged my every word.

'Once Hyllus is dead, you'll return home and join with her. You'll get a chance to prove yourself.' It was odd to talk to Skari this way and even stranger to offer advice.

'She doesn't want to be a wife. My wife. I despised Argil's visits.' He made a fist with his hand as if he wanted to punch the air and the memory of Argil with it. 'He spent hours training her how to fight and then she'd practice for days, waiting for his return.'

'Fjola isn't like any woman I know.' Not that I knew many. 'She can be promised, but you can't claim her heart. That you must win.'

'Easier said than done.' There was bitterness to his words. 'She'll never look at me the way she looks at you.'

'I'm a dead man.' Visible through the linen was Trofn's mark, stinging with pain as if the witch herself stared at me through the black goo of her eye. 'Even my soul doesn't belong to me. I sacrificed everything and my time is running short. I'm not a man to be admired.'

'And yet she does.' He picked up a handful of loose stones and weighed them in his hand. 'Since you came to Hvitur, I wanted to hate you. The prophecy and your disregard for the gods are good enough reasons.'

'It's not by choice that—'

'But then I found myself travelling with you and witnessed your exchange with the witch. I consider myself to be a strong man, a warrior worthy of Nordur, but even I couldn't go as far as to give away my soul.'

A light flickered on the roof of the citadel. Was Hyllus out there, laughing at my efforts? I found Kylfa's box with my fingertips. I had been given the power to destroy the mage and I didn't like to think further than that.

'When this is over,' Skari said, 'I'm taking Fjola back to Hvitur. I'll fight for her.'

'And so you should.'

'What will you do?'

'I'll travel east, to Shinpi.'

'It's a long way. Some say the place is nothing but an illusion.' Skari released the stones from his palm and they scattered over his boots. He shook them off.

'I swore an oath to find my mother's killer.'

'You swore many oaths, Guardian of Stromhold. Pray you keep them all.'

* * *

The morning sun licked the eastern sky when Njall returned with the rest of the party. Skari sprang to his feet at the sound of footsteps and Fjola's voice. His usual angry frown was back and he betrayed no signs of our conversation. Last night, I got a glimpse of the Skari that Njall talked about, proud and protective of the woman he loved, but I suspected that the bold and confrontational part of him would never admit to having shared his fears with me. Strangely, I was relieved to see his old self back. It was easier to carry on as if nothing happened than to try to understand feelings festering inside each of us.

Fjola stepped through the doorway and pulled her hood off. Her hair, freed from constraints, spilled in tangled waves down her shoulders, dark shadows nested beneath her eyes and she tried to stifle a yawn. I found myself glued to her face, comparing it to Lumi's. In contrast with her soft and fragile features, Fjola, with her sharp cheekbones and a slight lift to her brow when she was displeased, looked strong and confident. Despite my experiences with Lumi, she drew me in.

Skari leaned close and whispered in her ear. She smiled and something pinched my heart. I forced myself to look away. 'Did you find it?' I asked.

'Here.' Njall showed me the vial with a cloudy liquid. 'The broken Varl led us to the alchemist.' He patted Alkaios on the shoulder. 'He's a skilled thief and knew what to look for.'

'He did well,' Fjola said, taking the vial. She examined the content. 'Let's hope it works.'

'Will work,' Alkaios said. 'Varl's transformed body is less immune to poison.' He slumped into the chair and it creaked under his weight. 'How you use it?'

'We'll poison the meat,' I said, taking in the citadel with a gesture. One side of it gleamed in the rising sun while the other had shadows clinging to the marble and the ground around it.

'How?' Alkaios caught the drool with his tongue.

Njall walked up to the window. 'The keeper delivers meat once a day. It's the same routine. He comes, throws the scraps, and goes back inside. That's our chance to plant the poison. Before they feed.'

'We'll need to find a way to get close enough to the meat,' Skari said. 'Without a distraction it's hopeless.'

'Your smell too strong,' Alkaios said. 'Varl's nose powerful. Weak eyes, but sharp smell sense.' He got to his feet, and grumbling with effort hobbled to the window. 'Hyllus knows no human can pass.'

'What is he saying?' Skari asked in a sharp tone. 'I wouldn't trust him. He may be broken, but these filthy creatures are still his brothers, created with the same magic.'

Fjola rolled her eyes. 'Will you ever stop? If you have nothing useful to say, be quiet. Thanks to Alkaios we have the poison and with it a chance to infiltrate the tower. All you do is curse him.'

'I didn't know we came here to side with cripples. His body and mind was corrupted by the same foul arts. That's enough for me.'

Scarlet tinged Fjola's cheekbones and she turned away from him. Listening to Skari, it was hard to imagine that our conversation last night took place.

'There must be a way to get in,' I said. 'If there is a door, there is a way to walk through… and we'll find it.'

* * *

For the next three days we spied on the citadel, following the keeper's routine. Our initial plan of poisoning the meat quickly fell apart when, to our dismay, he used a whistle as a signal to the Varls that they were free to feed. Only when he blew it, they abandoned their post and lunged for the scraps. The marble structure guarded Hyllus like a jealous maiden, and apart from the shadows sliding around the sleek walls, everything was still.

I missed my father's confidence and wisdom and wished for his guidance. I imagined him scrutinising the citadel with deep lines creasing his forehead and tried to think the way he might have done and see what he would have seen.

The circular building was surrounded by a wasteland of scorched earth, and according to Alkaios, Hyllus burned all vegetation to deter animals and warn off humans foolish enough to venture into his domain. The two Varls would catch the scent of anyone who dared to cross the open ground and the intruder would meet a grisly end, torn to pieces by their powerful jaws. In his deformed tongue, Alkaios explained how the guardians of the citadel were the best of his kind, created for one purpose only—to stop anyone from getting in.

The gates opened and a man came out, heaving under the weight of the cart and the Varls watched him emptying meat and bones, but they didn't shift.

'Human meat.' Alkaios said, and droplets of spit fell from his lips. 'Broken Varls. People who failed transformation.'

'Why let you and your friends go free?' Njall asked.

'Hyllus wants perfect warriors. His likeness. Captures people to use them. To test his magic.' Alkaios shook his head. 'You enter the citadel. No escape. The walls will be your tomb. He released me. Other Varls too. Broken. To wander the city. Example to people who think to disobey.'

In the afternoon light, shadows around the citadel grew longer, spiking the creatures with dark spears. I couldn't imagine the horrors Hyllus set free within its marble walls.

'And no one tries to stop him?' I asked.

'Fear. People say more powerful man speaks orders to Hyllus.'

'I saw Hyllus's face,' I said. 'He too is deformed.'

'Yes. Born with contortions. Tormented. His mother called him Monster. Shunned him.'

The shadow moved further away, like the hand of a sundial, and I followed with my eyes as it shortened on its journey around the citadel. 'The man *is* a monster, and he'll face Agtarr's judgement soon enough.'

'Hyllus is no man,' Alkaios said. 'You watched his tower for days. Still no plan to breach the gates.'

'Not enough time.' Njall slammed his palm on the wall when the whistle sounded and the Varls dived in for the meat. 'The keeper is too quick with the signal. We'd never poison the meat in time.'

Fjola's shoulders sagged. 'It's useless.'

'We're not giving up,' I said. 'One way or another, I'm getting into that citadel.'

'We'd have to fight, and Hyllus would be alerted by our presence,' she said.

'We can't let that happen. I can use shadows to cross the yard. Alkaios said that the Varls have poor sight and I'm ready to test this.'

Njall squinted at the sun and I put my arm around him. 'At different times of the day, the citadel blocks the sun, and shadows form over the yard. I'll follow their trail and plant the poison.'

"It's a high risk. You'd never escape if they smelled you,' Fjola said. 'Besides, you have the box. Who would use it if you die?'

'It's our only chance.'

'To get killed,' Skari said from the other corner of the room where he sat polishing his axe. 'The cripple said those Varls will smell you before they see you. They'll be onto you before you get anywhere near the gates. Besides, these aren't your regular creatures. You heard him. He said they're the best of his kind.'

'I'll find a way to disguise my smell.'

Skari laughed. 'Good luck with that.'

'Please, don't hold back,' Fjola snapped at him. 'Illuminate us with your ideas.'

Alkaios wiped his mouth. 'You could never fool them. I go. I carry the scent of magic. It'll confuse them.'

Fjola looked at me questioningly and I translated his words. She shook her head. 'Even if he gets there, he'd never make it back. We're fit enough to fight them if need be, but not him. He'd be ripped to shreds.'

'And why should we care?' Skari asked.

Alkaios looked me in the eye. 'Death, remember? You promised me vengeance.'

Skari chuckled from the corner. 'How daring. Self-sacrifice. He volunteers because he knows his brothers would never harm him.'

I glanced at Njall and bit the inside of my cheek. Sending Alkaios into the yard meant certain death.

'Let's not be hasty,' I said. 'There may be another way. Let us think.'

XX

'It's gone!' Fjola's panicked voice jerked me from my restless sleep. 'The poison. It's gone.'

Dawn streamed through the windows and the softening sky promised another hot day. I yawned and rubbed my forehead to ease the ache that latched on to it.

Njall pushed aside the blanket and stretched. 'Where's Alkaios?' he asked, reaching for his boots.

Fjola opened her arms wide. 'I searched every room, but there's no sign of him.'

'I knew it,' Skari said. 'We shouldn't have trusted that wretch.'

'If you didn't fall asleep on your watch—'

A dark silhouette hobbled through the trees in the direction of the tower and my heart sprang in my chest. 'He's heading for the citadel,' I said.

'Damned cripple will alert the Varls!' Skari cursed and rushed outside.

Down the stairs that wobbled under the pressure of our boots, we raced after Alkaios with little hope of catching him before he reached the wastelands.

The world awakened, birds crying out into the morning silence, as we hurried to the ring of woods surrounding the Citadel of Vester. Our footsteps sent echoes through the deserted streets. No one dared to live so close to Hyllus's tower, and most of the houses had fallen into ruin.

Alkaios's intentions were unclear, but I had a suspicion he wasn't out there to betray us. The broken Varl was eager to help us in our cause, and he'd insisted that none of us could ever make it to the meat without being noticed.

What would he gain by giving us away?

We clustered on the edge of the forest, taking advantage of the few living trees that had survived Hyllus's fires. Further on, the stumps and dead branches, scorched and twisted into knots, offered little protection from the creatures guarding the gates. Though they were once human, the Varls showed no signs of it now. Exposed through layers of thick skin, their faces changed beyond recognition with fangs like saws stretched over their shapeless jaws, and ribs prominent through their chests.

Skari squinted at the broken Varl who limped his way into the open.

'Alkaios,' Njall hissed after him, but the Varl didn't turn.

'Aren't you going to do something?' Fjola looked at each of us in turn and when no one answered, she leaped forward.

I seized her arm. 'We can't do anything for him. If he wants to betray us, it's too late.'

The air turned brittle and I clenched and unclenched my fists to get rid of the tension cramps that settled in my fingers. Fjola squeezed my arm and her nails dug into my skin, her eyes following Alkaios's advance as he left the last remnants of the seared forest. Only a stretch of black earth remained between him and the Varls. Njall reached for the spear and Skari drew his axe while Alkaios hobbled onward, hunched and silent like a thief, his hand brushing against the ash that covered the ground. He was halfway through the wasteland when he tripped on a branch and fell to his knees. The Varls jerked their heads, snuffing up the air. Alkaios scrambled to his feet and I stopped breathing in anticipation of a signal or a scream divulging our presence, but no sound came. Instead, he opened his arms wide and waited.

'The fool wants to be torn to shreds by his kin,' Skari said. 'That or it's a greeting of some kind.'

The Varls pulled back their lips and with their fangs exposed moved towards Alkaios. Fjola's grip on my arm tightened and I wished I could do more to ease her anxiety, but the unfolding events were out of my control and by intervening, I would risk her life and those of my companions.

Her body stilled when a blood-curdling roar split the air and the creatures lurched at the broken Varl.

'They caught his scent,' Fjola said. ''We can't leave him.'

When I said nothing, she turned to Njall, but he too shook his head. Her face went slack and she turned away from us with a scowl. The Varls descended upon Alkaios, howling and ripping at his body in a frenzy until it was impossible to make out who was who in the tumble of blood and flesh.

'He's gone,' Njall whispered.

Tears made tracks down Fjola's cheeks. 'It's our fault. We sent him to his death.' She rushed back through the trees and Skari followed.

The creatures, done with Alkaios's body, paced the grounds, breathing in loud snorts. Nothing remained of the broken Varl.

'She's right,' I said, turning my back on the tower. 'Whatever his intent, Alkaios failed and the poison too is lost to us.'

'We'll find another way,' Njall said.

I spun my head. 'What other way? The only way is to challenge them, and if we do, who knows what will be unleashed from those cursed walls.' We walked back to the hideout under the rising sun. The sky burned orange and so did my desire to see Hyllus dead. He had to pay for every life he deformed and destroyed.

Back in the house, I sank in the corner. No one spoke. Outside, Fjola slumped against a tree, crisscrossing the ground with her dagger.

Alkaios wasn't one of us and yet he'd managed to keep his humanity. Despite being broken and in an abiding pain, he was willing to aid us in our quest and I failed to even keep my promise to him.

Perhaps Torgal was right and I was a fool trying my luck against forces that far outweighed my own skills and that of my companions. I traced the outline of the witch's box and the mark on my wrist prickled as if pinched by hot tongs. Would I ever get close enough to make use of it? I couldn't let my sacrifice be for nothing and I would rather die fighting Hyllus than surrender in the shadows of his citadel. I had to find a way.

As the morning wore on, I became more restless, pacing from one corner of the room to another. Fjola busied herself with the horses; she brushed them and fed them with the last of the grain.

I suspected all of them waited for me to decide our next move, but I hesitated. To assault the citadel with Skari's methods would pit us against the unknown, and most likely

Hyllus would send more Varls to challenge us. We wouldn't stand a chance against his beasts, and I couldn't risk the lives of people I had come to regard as friends.

'Jarin!' Skari's urgent voice severed my thoughts. He scaled the garden wall and rushed up the stairs with Njall and Fjola at his heels. 'They're dead.'

His words stopped me midstride. 'Dead?'

'The Varls,' Skari said. 'I wanted to be alone for a while, so I went into the forest. When I reached the clearing, their bodies were there, in the ash. Dead.'

I leaned out the window. The Citadel of Vester loomed as before—still and impenetrable, with sun brushing against the marble walls. Two shapes laid in the shadows, motionless.

'How can it be?' Njall asked. 'Are you certain?'

'Check for yourself,' Skari said.

I rubbed my eyes, afraid that light was playing tricks on me, but it wasn't so. The Varls guarding the gates were no more.

'What did he do?' I asked.

'Sacrificed himself,' Fjola said, staring down at her boots. 'And we let him. We're no better than those heartless creatures.'

'He drank the poison...' Njall's words hung in the air, thick with guilt.

'Alkaios knew the price,' I said. 'His life had little value to him. He said as much.'

'Is this what we're going to tell ourselves to make his death acceptable?' Fjola said. 'Who are we to decide the worth of someone's life?' Her voice went quiet. 'The line between us and them is a fine one. Can the unjust serve justice?'

'At least he did something useful during his wretched life,' Skari said. 'Your daggers took more than one life, so how can you speak of justice?'

She glared at him. 'With each life I take, my heart darkens more. Just because I say nothing to you, it doesn't mean I feel at peace with myself.'

'Right or wrong. You have the gods' favour,' Njall said to me.

'The only favour granted here is Alkaios's,' I said, 'and it mustn't be in vain. When the keeper opens the gates at nightfall, we must be ready for him.'

* * *

When the evening deepened, we stepped out of the woods and sneaked across the yard, passing the bodies of the dead Varls. Despite the others urging me to make haste, I crouched over one of the creatures, noticing how the skin took on a strange shade of cyan. Thousands of tiny veins in his hand looked like lines on a map of an unknown world, blackened by the workings of the poison. The ground where Alkaios fell was stained with blood and only scraps of clothing remained to tell the story of his final moments.

A heavy latch secured the gates of the citadel and Njall gave them a tug. 'Shut.'

Fjola, with her knives at the ready, pressed her back to the wall and Skari gave her a warning glance, but she refused to move.

'As much as it pains me, it's work for my daggers,' she said, and none of us argued. She was quick and agile—all that was needed to silence the keeper's dying breath.

Njall and I took up positions on the opposite side with our weapons drawn. The smell of ash and scorched earth warred with the coolness of the evening air and an unusual silence settled here, with no sound of insects or night critters. It was as if Agtarr himself descended upon the citadel and the surrounding grounds, touching everything with his hand of death. I wetted my lips, again and again, listening for any signs of the keeper.

At last, there came the muffled din of something heavy being rolled and I stilled my breath. The bolts crashed, one by one, and with each my fingers tightened around the hilt of my sword. When the gates creaked, I half-expected an attack, but the first thing that ambushed us was the reek of rotting flesh. I stifled a gag.

An old man appeared soon after, pushing a cart full of dismembered limbs with flesh falling off the human bones.

Fjola darted from the wall like a snake at its prey. Her hand covered the keeper's mouth and with one swift move, she slashed his throat with her dagger. He jerked in her grip, but she held him tight until the convulsions ceased. She let his limp body slide to the ground.

'Fast work for someone filled with regrets,' Skari said as he crossed the threshold.

Fjola's face stiffened and the girl who clung to my arm watching Alkaios was gone, replaced by a hardened warrior who took a life without remorse. My heart swelled with regret at the sight. Only this morning she fretted about Alkaios's sacrifice and wanted to risk her life to save him and now she killed a man without as much as a sigh. Her willingness to act with no hesitation and readiness to put aside her own feelings for the good of our cause left me heavy with grief and I wanted to go back in time and forbid her to follow me in the hope that she would remain Fjola, a girl hungry for travelling the world. But my hopes were just that, hopes. In truth, I had little control over someone's destiny, I barely controlled my own, so I turned my attention to Skari.

'Wait,' I said. 'Someone needs to stay and keep watch in place of the dead Varls. Our presence must stay a secret for as long as possible, and with the night upon us, it'll be hard to distinguish who you are. Just two silhouettes guarding the gates.'

'I'm going with you,' Fjola said.

Skari's face softened. 'Let me do this.' He brushed her cheek with his fingertips. 'Despite our squabbles, I want you to see me as a man, so let me aid Jarin and bring you this victory.'

Since Hvitur, Skari complained about this quest, voicing his disapproval, but now he wanted to walk with me into the bowels of the Citadel of Vester. The man was full of contradictions, but surprisingly, I felt relieved that he insisted on coming with me. I didn't want Fjola to witness whatever horrors lied ahead and for them to take away another piece of her.

'I wish to be a part of it,' she said in a stern voice. 'To see Hyllus in his defeat for the grief he caused our people, for the fear he spread across Nordur.'

'Fjola—' Njall started, but Skari cut him off.

'Give me this chance to prove I'm worthy of your love. It's the only way I know. You make no secret of how you feel. You disapprove of me, but I'm ready to chase your heart until it welcomes mine.' He kissed her on the lips and disappeared inside the gates.

Fjola's fingers flew to her mouth and she took a step towards the door as if to stop him.

'Let him go,' Njall said.

She looked at me with dazed eyes as if wanting me to take sides. I shrugged. Her relationship with Skari was complicated enough without my intrusions. I couldn't figure the man out or what drove him, but it was clear he cared for Fjola. He didn't show it in ways people expected him too, but his heart was in her hands. I left them with a nod and followed Skari into the darkness. Njall shut the gates and the blackness swallowed us. Alkaios's words hummed in my ears: Once you enter the citadel, there's no escape.

Despite the heat, chill touched my fingers, partly from the excitement that we had managed to breach the walls and partly from fear of what awaited us at the top of the tower.

'I can't see a thing in this forsaken place.' Skari's voice echoed off the walls.

'Keep quiet,' I hissed, feeling the ground with my boots. It was made of marble like the outside walls and sloped upwards where a faint flicker beckoned us.

We crept along a wide, circular corridor where a sharp odour of burning hair failed to mask the stench of decaying flesh. I cupped my palm over my mouth and nose to block out some of the stink.

The flicker of light grew stronger—a lantern that illuminated a room beyond a set of steps. I took each one, listening for any signs of presence, but the walls were silent and only my breath disturbed the darkness.

Skari edged closer to the door, but I grabbed his shoulder and whispered, 'Let me.'

There was no telling who occupied the room and I knew Hyllus hid out somewhere in the citadel. If danger lurked inside, it was only just for me to take the fall. Licking the cold sweat off my lips, I pushed the door open.

The musty, dry scent of scrolls washed over me, taking me back to Stromhold and the library of my childhood. A dimly lit room was filled with scrolls of various shapes and sizes; some rolled tightly and secured inside traditional tubes, others yellowed by age and cut into squares, with pages upon pages stacked together and bound with ropes, their vellum covered in thick layers of dust.

I removed a lantern from the wall and shined its light upon the shelves. I read the inscription on the leather casings: '*The Forbidden Arts, The History of Eastern Lands, Shifting Matter.*' I ran my hand over one in a language I wasn't familiar with. The chamber contained so much knowledge and I longed to find a quiet corner and read each scroll the way I used to back in Stromhold.

Skari regarded the shelves with hard eyes. 'What of it? We aren't here to admire Hyllus's collection of scrolls. Waste of parchment if you ask me.'

I unrolled one of the scrolls and dust motes sprung to life as I blew them off the pages. The inscription read: *The Power of Transformation.*

'We've lingered long enough,' Skari said and crossed the chamber towards a doorway at the back.

'Wait—' A piercing scream cut me off. It was filled with agony and died on the highest note as if cut clean by a razorblade.

I dropped the scroll and blew out the lantern. Skari's breath sounded loud in the tension filled silence and despite his usual contempt for things, I sensed his wariness. The cry came from deep within the citadel, conveying panic and torture. It reminded me that the Citadel of Vester was the home to an evil we knew little about, and the sooner we found Hyllus the sooner we could leave this place.

I fumbled for the door handle at the back and we stepped into a cold room with a cove-like ceiling that reeked of sour mead and mould. Rusty iron tubes piled up in the far corner, next to a fire pit made of clay and shaped like a wide bottle. In the middle was a table with a multitude of cylindrical vials covered by a thin film of dust. Skari overturned a crate with his boot and withered herbs and roots spilled on the floor. Whatever its purpose was in the past, the room looked abandoned, so we retraced our steps and climbed further along the corridor.

The citadel was cylindrical, with alcoves in the solid walls on either side, and I suspected they led to other chambers similar to the one we found the scrolls in. We would see anyone coming, but equally there would be no escape, and having Skari as a companion—next to the feel of my trusted sword—reassured me. The only source of light came from torches mounted on the walls at regular intervals, with blackness lurking in-between. I found the witch's box with my fingers—it served as a reminder of what had to be done and heartened my spirit. I wasn't chasing after Hyllus alone.

Our steps sent faint echoes through the marble walls and our shadows stretched forward as if trying to escape. Another stink weaved through the stale air, bringing back memories of Elizan with all the blood and fallen bodies. The smell grew stronger and another agonising scream tore through the air. Dread came alive in the pit of my stomach, urging me to take flight, and if not for the oath I swore over my father's body, I would have heeded it.

'Yldir help us all...' Skari whispered.

I halted at the base of the final step. From here, the incline widened and the walls on each side turned into prison cells. The darkness stretched ahead of us with no source of light of any kind and the occupants in the cages stirred, rattling their chains.

'The Varls,' I said. A stench of rot hung thick in the air, mixed with the odours of sweat and blood.

'There must be another way,' Skari said.

Hyllus reigned somewhere in the citadel and the only way up was through the spiral corridor, with the cages full of Varls. The risk was great, but our cause greater still. My mind called out to my father and his memory filled me with courage. He would've told me to be patient, to plan ahead, but I was certain that no matter the risks, he too would go forth. 'Keep to the middle and make no sound.'

'Useless. They don't need eyes to know we're here.'

'Can you see another way?' Skari's newfound caution began to irritate me. 'We go.'

He sent a quiet prayer to Yldir and followed me. The gods could do little to protect us from the Varls shifting in their cages, so asking them for aid was a waste of time.

We inched down the middle of the walkway in the blackness, guided only by a glimmer of a torch at the far end. I buried my nose into my sleeve to shield it from the foul odours and to silence my breath, but the beasts were not so easily swayed. Their sharp nostrils caught our scent and one by one a growl rose from each cage, low and careful at first, but growing deeper and more vicious. The cages rattled and the shrieking grew louder and louder. I imagined their warped faces poking through the bars with bared teeth, ready to tear us apart if released from their bonds. My compulsion to flee returned in waves and I couldn't see how we could survive this.

'Silence, you foul creatures!' a voice yelled. A loud bang followed as something smashed against the metal bars. 'Master is not to be disturbed.' Another bang reverberated off the cages, but the Varls didn't show any intention of quietening.

At the sound of the voice, I dropped to the ground, smashing my chin on the cool marble. It felt as if my teeth had been crushed by the impact. Pain spiked up my jaw but I stilled against it, hoping that the keeper wouldn't descend our way.

The man waved his torch and took a few steps down the corridor. 'Who's there?' He shone his light upon the cells, but the Varls continued to shriek.

As if goaded by them, he walked further, slow at first, but then more assured. I drew my sword, wincing at the loud sound. My body tensed, ready to pounce at the keeper if he got within the range of my blade, but a heavy boot pressed against my back. As swift as a winter wolf, Skari sprang towards him and sunk his axe into the man's skull. There was a gasp and a thud as the body hit the ground. I leaped to my feet and ran, chased by the howling and rattling of bars.

The path took us higher and higher until we left the Varls behind and the cages became walls again. My heart rattled against my rib cage, filling my chest with sharp pangs of pain.

'You were close to breaking my back,' I said between breaths. 'A little warning would have been nice.'

'There was no time for such luxuries. He'd have stumbled upon us within moments.'

'I was ready.'

'But not fast enough.' He wiped his palms on his trousers.

'Do you always charge into danger without a thought?'

'It's the only way to snatch victory, however small.'

The echoes of the Varl's howling carried across the citadel and I cursed. 'The beasts will alert Hyllus, and we left the keeper's body in plain view. An invitation to come after us.'

'Let them come. My axe is ready for a challenge,' Skari said.

To reason with Skari was useless. 'More doors,' I said.

The torches cast a weak light upon the three doorways in the left wall, with chains wound around them. What secrets did Hyllus keep inside?

Judging by the rusty bolts, they hadn't been opened for years.

We climbed higher, and another set of doors came into view.

'No chains,' Skari said.

We stood at each side with weapons drawn. I nodded at him and shouldered the first doorway ajar but only darkness glared back. Skari grabbed the torch off the wall and illuminated the chamber.

'For such a mighty place, this citadel is full of empty chambers,' he said. 'Apart from the keeper we didn't come across any guards. Doesn't it strike you as odd?'

'If you wielded the power of ancient magic, would you have need for protection? And what of the Varls we just passed? If released, they would have been a swift end of us.'

I took the torch from him and stepped into the chamber. Inside, I scraped the dark blotches on the walls with my fingers and examined my nails. One whiff assured me it was blood.

'They must have kept bodies here, but not recently. The blood is dry.'

Skari spat and pulled the door shut, but as we came up to the next one, the stink of rot returned. He held his ear against the door and shook his head. 'It's quiet.' He pried it open with his axe and stumbled backwards, retching.

I braced myself against the stench that filled my mouth with spit and made my eyes water. The cylindrical chamber was filled with corpses, twisted in ways that put the Varls I faced in Elizan to shame.

'Now we know where the meat comes from.' I coughed up bile, barring the door. 'Bodies that didn't transform. Like Alkaios.'

Skari's face looked pale in the torchlight. 'They don't deserve any better for letting such a monstrosity as Hyllus walk among them.'

Even at a time like this, Skari had to voice his hatred towards Vesterners, but I couldn't shake off the anguish that filled me at the sight of so much cruelty. It didn't matter who the people in this chamber once were, what mattered was the torture that befell them at the hands of Hyllus. The tide of my anguish retreated, replaced by a seething anger. How could the gods remain asleep through such cruelty? Surely, the screams of those who died in so much pain would reach Himinn itself.

We walked on, up the marbled stairs winding around and around. My calves burned with effort as we climbed higher into the unknown and it seemed the tower had no end. I wondered how one could build a place from such a rare stone and then fill it with nothing but horrors.

All knew Hyllus was an unfortunate child, born with deformities of his own, but even so, how much hatred did it take to destroy the lives of others by inflicting the same pain upon them? The answer eluded me.

The ground levelled and we stopped at the base of another corridor. No torches illuminated the way, but a small strip of light cast a spear-like shadow from the doorway on the end. I motioned towards it and we crept along the hallway, feeling the right wall with our hands. A murmur could be heard from the chamber, followed by a high-pitched laugh and more voices.

I caught Skari's sleeve in the darkness. 'Wait here.'

He nodded and crouched, hands on his axe.

I closed my eyes and took a calming breath before proceeding to the door. With my back against the wall, I peered into the chamber. Unlike other places in the citadel, it was well lit, with torches and lanterns mounted at every corner. The air was tainted with odours I didn't recognise. Most of them drifted from vials and jars filled with liquids in shades of grey and blue. Some were thick as glue, and some more watery, bubbling away over tiny fires.

The shelves were stacked full of yellow-looking shapes and it took me a moment to realise these were body parts. A disembodied eye stared back at me from one jar, a pair of twisted fingers curled inside another, and something akin to a human brain filled the next—jars upon jars of contorted tissue drowned in clear liquid, and I couldn't tell if they belong to animals or humans.

My throat burned and I felt a sudden urge to be sick.

A large table occupied the middle of the room with a body shackled to it. A man leaned over it, rubbing his hands together and whispering words in a foreign tongue. The flame from the torch cast a light on the left side of his face, but even without it, I recognised my father's killer. The same blistered cheek, the yawning gap in his lips, the black eye with the haggard look of a madman…

I clenched my teeth.

Hyllus.

It was because of him my father was lost to me forever and now I found myself in the very heart of his forsaken lair.

'You're going to be the best of them all,' Hyllus said, and his mad laughter filled the chamber. 'My greatest creation.'

I shrunk back and terror swept over me, chilling my very bones. The man strapped to the table moaned and it took me a moment to realise Hyllus wasn't talking to me. A silent breath of relief escaped my lips and I peered back into the room.

'Shhh...' Hyllus stroked the captive's head. 'If only you knew how important you are. How extraordinary.' He giggled to himself and poked the muscles on the man's arms. 'I worked so hard, endured countless failures, but now...this...you.'

I squinted to see the captive's face, but his head was turned away from the door. Hyllus began chanting again. The words were in an ancient tongue, filling the chamber with dark and powerful energy, and each sent a wave of quivers through my muscles. The prisoner screamed, straining against the bonds that held him, and his body arched over the table.

'Such strength and resilience. Who would have known? Good. Good...' Hyllus lifted the man's face and examined it under the light and in that instant I recognised him.

'Mirable...' I whispered into the darkness.

XXI

I withdrew from the door and re-joined Skari at the end of the corridor. 'We have to help him,' I said.

'What we *have* to do is kill Hyllus. We didn't come here to rescue—'

'Dark magic surrounds him and the chamber is filled with abhorrent objects. We have to draw him out before we strike.'

'To where?' He looked over his shoulder. 'The only way is up and we don't know how many Varls he keeps there. Now is the time to strike, before someone discovers our presence.'

Another scream tore the air. 'He suffers while we skulk in the shadows and do nothing.'

'You have the box, so use it,' Skari snapped.

My hand trembled as I pulled it out of my pocket. 'Let's finish this.'

We charged into the room.

'Hyllus!' I shouted—but aside from Mirable still tied to the table, the chamber was empty.

'Where is he?' Skari yanked Mirable's shoulder. 'Where did he go?'

The merchant groaned, but his eyes remained shut. His rib cage and right arm were swollen and covered in deep purple bruises.

'Hyllus knows we're here.' Skari kicked a stool out of the way. 'So much for sneaking up on him.'

'Help me free him,' I said, looking for something to pry the shackles open. 'There.' I motioned towards the table with the cooking jars and a metal hook. 'This'll do.'

Skari forced the hook between the table and the metal bonds, and using the weight of his body, pried them apart. Freed from the restraints, Mirable's arms fell limp. He had angry lacerations on his wrists where the metal had cut into the skin.

'How did you end up here?' I asked. The last time I saw Mirable was at the crossroads. I was full of hope then, looking to break Lumi's spell. Seeing him imprisoned, under the influence of Hyllus's magic, added another drop to the pool of hatred that filled my soul. 'Mirable?' I slapped his face and he groaned again. 'It's me, Jarin. Remember?'

'We should go, before Hyllus sends his Varls after us,' Skari said, pacing across the room. 'There's no time for heartfelt reunions.'

'Jarin...?' Mirable croaked through swollen lips, and a trickle of blood appeared at the corner of his mouth. I sat him on the table and propped his body on my shoulder, wrapping his arm around my neck. But when I tried to help him up, his legs buckled from underneath him.

'Don't waste your time,' Skari said. 'Look at him... he'll never make it. He's too weak and will slow us down. We should concentrate on the reason we are here.'

'He's coming with us,' I said. 'With or without your help.'

Skari grumbled, but offered Mirable his shoulder and together we managed to drag him to the door at the back of the chamber. 'Hyllus must have gone through here,' I said. 'It's the only way out.'

Skari kicked the door open, revealing a metal staircase. 'It's too narrow for the three of us.'

Even though it pained me, I had to agree. We eased Mirable onto the floor. 'I'll come back for you.'

His head flopped back, but he gripped my arm. 'Don't leave me. This place is worse than Agtarr's Chamber of Torments.'

I squeezed his hand. 'I won't. I promise.'

I led the climb, warming the metal railing with my sweating palms. This passage lacked marble walls and appeared older than the rest of the citadel, except for the staircase that, in the torchlight, looked polished and free of rust.

I turned to Skari. His lips were drawn into a tight line and he gave me a hesitant nod. I lingered for a few moments, trying to steel my nerves. This was what I had lived for since I left Stromhold, the day when my father would be avenged and the archenemy of Nordur put to death. With my head on Blixt's saddle, looking up at the stars, I imagined this moment countless times, feeling the flood of dark joy at the chance to take Hyllus's life. But now, standing in his tower with Skari breathing down my neck, the excitement vanished, leaving numbness in its wake.

'What are you waiting for?' Skari asked.

I wasn't sure, so I braced myself and shoved the door open. It screeched on its hinges and a stream of cool air washed over us. I took a step back, almost pushing Skari down the staircase. The floor of the roof was made of crystal, so thin and fragile that I could see through and down to the lowest levels of the citadel, where torches flickered like sparks in a fireplace until blackness consumed them. Night draped over Vester, illuminated only by stars that joined together to form magical constellations. I recognised one of them from Marco's teachings—the Giant Snake—its body twisted into shape by stars.

'Ah… here you are. My uninvited guests.' Hyllus's voice struck us from the darkness.

I took a hesitant step across the crystal floor, fearing it would shatter under the burden of my weight.

'And not just any guests.' Hyllus laughed his mad laughter. 'Jarin Olversson, Skaldir's Valgsi graces my humble citadel with his presence.'

'Come out, you piece of filth,' Skari demanded, training his axe on the shadows. 'Your time is up. Show your face and feel the blade of my Nordern axe.'

'Fool, you can't kill me with your pitiful weapons.'

I scanned the shadows for any movement. Hearing the voice of my father's killer reignited the blaze that had burned my heart for so long. I curled my fingers around the box. 'Your reign of terror has come to an end. After tonight there'll be no more Varls and disfiguring of innocent people. My father's soul demands yours.'

'Ha! He seeks revenge. How woeful. Embrace your fate, Guardian. The goddess herself chose your wretched body as a vessel for her powers. Your vengeance is but a drop of water in the Great Atlantic.'

The darkness stirred and Hyllus appeared on the other side of the crystal floor, wearing scarlet robes. His hand rested on a cane that emanated weak light. Carefully, he removed his hood, revealing his blistered face, and it was as if time itself went backwards to the burning walls of Elizan. I met the blackness in his eyes and the image of my father's dying body manifested before me. Whatever magic was at work, I could hear Father's heart, thrashing in panic, faster and faster until it could take no more and all blood vessels ruptured, flooding his own chest. The screams of dying warriors and the clashing of steel filled my ears and I could almost taste blood on my tongue. The vision ended as abruptly as it began and I was back under the Vestern sky.

'Your Varls are caged. No help is coming, old man,' Skari said.

Hyllus tightened his grip on the cane. 'Old man? Do you think I need the Varls to deal with Nordern rats? I command this city.' His shriek of solitary laughter wasn't that different from the sounds his creatures made. 'I bestowed on its citizens the greatest gift. The gift of transformation and the power that comes with it.'

'Gift?' I asked. 'You deform people, turn them into beasts stripped of their humanity—'

'Silence! What would you know about power? Hiding behind your mother's skirts... No wonder the demon deceived you so easily. Goro-Khan was right. You're weak. Once you've outlived your usefulness, you'll savour my magic. I'll transform Vester *and* Nordur, and every land beyond the Great

Atlantic. *My* Varls will walk the earth while Skaldir purges it clean of wretches like you.'

'You sick monster,' I said—and Skari lunged forward, swinging his axe, but Hyllus flicked his wrist and the axe was twisted away with a snapping jolt. Skari tumbled to the floor, clutching his hand to his chest and wincing in pain.

'Did you think you could worm your way into my tower and I wouldn't know?' He trained his staff on Skari. '*I* rule here! My magic can transform every muscle of yours and shape it into any form I want. The arcane ability to control living cells is mine.' His staff shone brighter and Skari gripped his head with a cry.

'Enough!' The witch's box clicked. 'The only one who dies tonight is you. It ends here.'

Hyllus lowered the staff. 'And so it shall.'

Skari fell silent and all I could hear was my pulse flogging the insides of my skull. My hands shook as I pried the lid open and held my breath, anticipating a flash of light or the unleashing of power that would strike the mage dead—but nothing happened.

I peered inside. Apart from a few grains of black charcoal, the box that cost me my soul was empty. Another betrayal…

A cold, stark fear like I'd never experienced before struck me. I threw the box aside and it clattered on the crystal floor.

Hyllus laughed, all traces of madness gone from his voice. He advanced on me. 'You thought you could confront me with your little axes and trinkets and come away unscathed?' He reached for me with his open palm. Pain jolted my chest as if someone wrenched my insides. 'You'll taste the agony just like your father did during his final moments.'

Skari crawled towards his axe but Hyllus struck the crystal floor with his cane. A split zigzagged across the surface, branching off in multiple directions and Skari was flung away by an invisible force. My veins felt as if they were about to explode from the pressure and blood that whooshed in my ears.

'I can break you in ways even the goddess won't be able to heal. Your body is hers, but I can twist it in whichever way I please.'

Hyllus's power pressed me down until my legs gave way and I collapsed onto the shattered crystal. With my cheek against the floor I watched the box through tears as my body struggled against the magic. I thought of Mother and Father, facing Agtarr with their final breaths and for the first time I understood what they felt in their dying moments.

Skari's warrior scream split the air and the force tormenting my body eased. I rolled on my side with a groan. Every breath sent a stab of pain through my ribs. Skari latched onto Hyllus, his axe embedded in the mage's back. Hyllus roared, struggling to shake him off. I grabbed my sword but I couldn't grip it properly and my hand went limp. All I could do was lay there, wheezing and watching Hyllus as he overpowered Skari.

From the corner of my eye, I caught a string of black smoke forming at the edge of Trofn's box. My right arm began throbbing, the witch's symbol burning my skin with intensity and I didn't know how much more my body could endure. I ripped the sleeve with my teeth, exposing the ancient mark and it pulsed and writhed with life.

Hyllus tortured Skari's body with magic in the way he did mine moments before. Knowing that Skari wouldn't last long, I shouted, hoping to draw the mage's attention and focus his wrath back on me, but all that came out was a croak. The smoke danced over the crystal floor, growing darker and denser in its blackness and the burning inside my arm answered with a stabbing agony. Skari cried out when another snap split the air followed by a sharp pop and he let the axe clatter to the floor.

The smoke crawled towards the spot where Skari struggled against Hyllus's magic. Near the box itself, more smoke formed, taking on multiple shapes and changing back again into a formless fog. The mage threw Skari against the wall using the force of his open palm and blood splattered where his head hit the stones.

The thought of Skari dead jolted life back into my muscles and I struggled to my knees just as the string of blackness reached Hyllus's ankles. It wrapped around them, silent and sinister in its purpose.

'Enough of these games.' Hyllus walked up to Skari. The smoke slithered after him.

A hand, black as tar, emerged from inside the box and its claws dug at the trail of smoke, pulling a head and body out of the swell of darkness towards Hyllus. As a boy, I saw a drawing in one of Marco's scrolls in which Haamu dragged a living soul to Agtarr's Chamber of Torments. The image terrified me and when I asked my tutor about it, he said that only those who are beyond salvation would be subjected to Haamu's tortures. He hastened to add that it was only a story and there was no truth to it, that Agtarr was the one who judged the unworthy and it was his punishment that people should fear. But I was sure it was Haamu creeping after Hyllus like a black spider.

Dread crawled across the back of my neck and the patch of skin where the witch made her mark felt as if wild beasts tore into it from the inside. I let out a cry and Haamu halted and turned my way. In it, I saw faces of men and women, dead and rotten, warping and morphing into one another and I forgot my pain as panic overtook me. I scrambled away on my elbows, my boots scraping the crystal floor until my back hit the wall.

Hyllus curled his fist. 'You won't slip away that easily, worm.'

With an agonising scream, Skari's body jerked from unconsciousness.

The smoke rose behind the mage and Haamu with it, billowing in a dense cloud, until it matched the man in size. Torches mounted on the walls dimmed and their flames shied away from the presence that filled the roof. A black claw pierced Hyllus's back and the smoke seeped into him like poison into an open wound. His eyes bulged and he raised his hand as if to ward off some invisible entity.

Before today, I thought there was nothing that could scare this mage with his infinite power, but now, looking into his face, rippled by shock, I knew it wasn't so.

Blackness oozed from the corners of his mouth and another claw ripped into the folds of his cloak. He stumbled and dropped his staff, body jerking and twitching as the Haamu's essence filled his being, but no sound passed his lips. It was as if they were locked in a nightmare. The magic, more powerful and terrifying that any Hyllus could ever wield, devoured the mage's body inch by inch and he was powerless to stop it.

Using the wall for support, I pushed myself up, my hand clasped around my wrist where the witch's symbol burned deep inside my skin. I stumbled towards Skari, hoping that life still lingered within his body. When I crouched beside him and shook his shoulder, to my relief he groaned and opened his eyes. Blood trickled from his left eye and his right was swollen shut.

'Hang in there, Skari,' I said. 'Let's get you out of here.'

He attempted to get up and I supported his body despite the pain wrenching my ribs.

'My hand must be broken,' he said, cradling the limp arm to his chest. It was his right hand, the one he fought with and the one that made him a warrior. 'I'm not leaving without my axe.' He freed himself from my grip and hobbled after his weapon.

The black smoke pulled back into the box and vanished, taking Haamu into the abyss from which it sprung.

Skari collected the axe and walked up to the crimson cloak enshrouding Hyllus's body. He leaned over the corpse. With the edge of his axe he separated the folds and stumbled backwards with a sharp gasp.

I pinched the cloak and lifted it. Hyllus's body was gone.

I stared at the empty rags and my thoughts scrambled to make sense of what was in front of me, unwilling to accept that his demise was so swift. Vengeance—the powerful need to destroy the man who killed my father—was complete, and I waited for relief to embrace me and take away the pain and loss that haunted me since Elizan.

But there was nothing but emptiness inside me.

My heart didn't swell with satisfaction or solace, instead, it ached all the same. Hyllus was dead and my father avenged, but the thought didn't fill me with pride because of the way he was annihilated. Witnessing his flesh consumed in such a sinister manner tainted our victory and I couldn't help but wonder if my soul would be dragged free from my body in the same way. I was damned and I could do little to change it.

A key on a chain glimmered at me from amidst Hyllus's clothing, and I picked it up. It was made of crystal with a handle shaped like a teardrop, holding a blue jewel. I put it around my neck and hastened back to the door, shuddering at the memory of Haamu, the creature that wasn't supposed to be real, brought forth with my bargain, awoken by the black magic of Sur.

I wanted to leave this forsaken citadel without delay so I waved at Skari, who still stared at what remained of Hyllus. 'Come.'

With a final glance at the crimson cloak, Skari hobbled after me.

The air split with a sharp crack.

Beneath his boots, rugged lines shot in all directions, forming new paths on the floor as the crystal, weakened by the impact of Hyllus's cane, fractured under Skari's weight. Skari looked down into the gulf under his feet, where torches flickered mockingly back at him.

'The crystal took too much damage,' I said. 'It won't hold long.' I looked into his eyes and for the first time I found fear in them. 'Focus. Take it step by step.'

He clutched the axe in his left hand and took a careful step forward. A faint crack escaped from under his foot.

'You're almost here.' I reached out to him.

He took one more step, but the crystal gave way, shattering into a multitude of pieces that plummeted into the bowels of the citadel.

We leaped for each other and I grabbed his broken arm. He cried out, his body suspended over the pit. The shards protruding from the edges cut into my skin, but I ignored the pain, putting all my strength into pulling him up.

'I got you,' I said through gritted teeth.

Shards dug into Skari's wrist and blood filled the gaps between my fingers, but I tightened my grip and held his gaze. His breath came in rasps.

'Use your axe.'

He swung his left arm towards the edge, but the axe slipped and gravity dragged his body down.

'Again,' I encouraged him. Blood slithered down his arm and I was losing my grip. 'Do it!'

He swung again and the force ripped his hand from my grasp. The axe caught on the crystal and I grabbed his shoulder and pulled him up. His stomach raked against the edge, leaving thick droplets of blood on the sharp tips, but I didn't let go until he was safely beside me. We laid for a while, filling the night's air with our labouring breaths.

I sat up and wiped blood off my palms. 'Let's find Mirable and get back to the others.'

Skari propped himself on his axe and got to his feet. Long and angry lacerations cut through his shirt and stomach. His face was pale, his eyes sunken, and just by looking at him I could tell that his most dangerous wounds festered on the inside. Hyllus let me sample the power of his magic for a few moments, but Skari endured his cruelty for much longer. I could only hope the damage done to him was reversible.

'Can you walk?' I asked.

He nodded, and descended the staircase back to Hyllus's torture chamber.

Mirable sat where we left him. 'You came back,' he said. The bruises on his arm and chest blackened and his skin burned with fever. 'How long was I here?'

'Long enough,' I said, searching the chamber for something to cover his body. 'It's time to leave this place. Hyllus is dead.'

Mirable's eyes widened. 'Impossible. He's immortal.'

'The forces that snatched his life cared little for his immortality. Here…' I threw him a dirty shirt I found crumpled in the corner. 'It'll have to do for now.'

'You're hurt,' he said, struggling into the sleeves.

I cast a worried glance at Skari. He leaned against the wall with his eyes closed. 'There's no time to dwell on our wounds. We must make haste. When Hyllus's disappearance is discovered, we have to be as far from Vester as possible.'

Mirable took a few steps and staggered. 'He did things to me,' he whispered. 'Things I can't explain…'

'Later. It's a long way down.' I wrapped his arm over my shoulder. 'At least you're still human.'

Every inch of my body ached, but the worst of it was fading and I was in much better shape than the merchant. I held the door open with my foot.

'Skari?'

He wiped his face with his hand and must have sensed the concern in my voice because he swung his axe. 'There's enough strength left in me to take on any Varls who dare to cross our path.' Despite his defiant grin, I wasn't fooled. He could never fight as well with his left hand.

We proceeded along the corridor and down the steps that led us here. I listened for any sounds of the Varls, but the Citadel of Vester was silent, as if unaware that her master had crossed into the afterlife. I wished to Agtarr that Hyllus's punishment would be merciless.

Skari stopped when we reached the prison cells at the bottom of the stairs. 'It's too quiet,' he said.

Further down, the body of the keeper laid crumpled in the darkness the way we left it, illuminated only by the weak flames from the torch. A deep growl came from the cage to our left. It echoed like a signal and was picked up by the other Varls who shifted in their enclosures and rattled the bars.

'The Varls,' Mirable said. His voice shook with panic and he attempted to go back. 'They'll kill us.'

'We can't turn back,' I said, forcing him down the spiral corridor. 'They're caged and can't get to us.'

Skari was a few steps ahead, and as he passed the cages, one by one the Varls began howling like rabid dogs. I struggled behind with Mirable attached to my shoulder and whispering prayers, his muscles jumping at every high-pitched shriek. Half way down, a loud bang filled the corridor and I spun around to find a metal gate barring the way we came. It was released from the side wall and controlled by some hidden mechanism. Another bang rang from up ahead, followed by clicking sounds.

'By Yldir—the cages!' Mirable cried out.

'It's a trap,' Skari said. 'Hurry, before we're cut off.'

The same gate that barred the way back was closing and the locks that kept the Varls in snapped open. I quickened the pace, but with Mirable's weight on my shoulder, it was more of a hobble than a run. Without warning, a Varl leaped out from a cage in front and Skari met him with his axe, sinking its edge deep into the creature's skull. It must have taken an enormous effort for him because he swayed on his feet and yanked the axe back weakly. He waved at us to hurry. More Varls crawled out, their beastly forms casting shadows on the marbled walls.

Six cages separated us from the half-closed gate. Skari took another swing, cutting the claws off a second Varl, and the creature howled into the darkness. His companions answered with more shrieks and Skari's axe engaged again, but his aim was unsteady and he stumbled on his feet. I wanted to draw my sword to aid him, but letting Mirable go would mean his death.

The Varls surrounded us now as more and more cages opened, and I knew we could never fight them off. Skari reached the gate and jammed his axe between it and the floor, slowing down the mechanism enough for me to get myself and Mirable through. I let the merchant go and drew my sword, but the gap was growing narrower with each passing moment. A Varl rushed at Skari, but before he could turn, claws ripped through his back and he lost his balance. The gate made a crunching sound and the axe slipped from its position.

I pushed myself into the gap between the gate and the wall. 'Give me your hand,' I called.

Skari grabbed his axe, rolled onto his back, and chopped into the Varl's knees. The gate was inches from my ribs and Mirable yanked me back to his side. Skari leaped to his feet and grabbed the bars, but they snapped shut with a final bang. Frantically, I examined the gate and the walls for any kind of switch, panic spreading through me faster than a snow slide.

The Varls formed a semicircle around Skari and he caught my hand through the bars. 'Forget it. Save yourself and the merchant. Leave them to me. It's the least I can do.'

'No—I'll find a way. I'm not leaving you.' I tried to pull my hand free, but he tightened his grip.

'There's no time. Let me do this one thing right.'

'And what of Fjola? What would she say if I returned without you?' I asked.

'She was never meant for me. I'm no use to her now.' He looked me in the eye. 'I'm dying. Even if I made it out of here alive, my body would never recover. If I can't wield my axe, what kind of a warrior am I?' He turned away and faced the Varls. 'Tell her…' His voice caught.

'I know,' I said and didn't try to stop the tears of despair that came alive under my eyelids.

With this final sacrifice, Skari proved himself a warrior I could only dream of becoming. He didn't falter in the face of his own death, and in that moment I would have done anything to take his place. I brought him here, so why was he the one standing on the wrong side of the gate?

'Come on, beasts,' he called, swinging his axe. 'It's time for me to have my share!'

With that he lunged at the closest Varl, but his swing was weak from the injuries sustained on the roof and the creature slammed his fist, catching him off balance. I clutched the bars, unable to move, watching in horror as the Varls descended upon him. I lost sight of Skari in the tumult of contorted limbs and deadly blows.

'We must go,' Mirable urged me. 'There's nothing we can do for him now.'

His words echoed those I used when Alkaios was heading to his death, but now they sounded like an accusation. I may not have shared a close bond with Skari, but he was a Nord, a warrior fighting my cause. I choked on a terrible sorrow that surged through me, like water surging through a sinking ship, and my first reaction was to give in to it and let it drag me down into the black depths, but Mirable was tugging at me.

He was too weak to manage the stairs without support, so he leaned on me and we made our way down, through the corridors and past the library, until we reached the main gates.

Outside, the morning light sent the moon on its way, inviting the first touches of sunrise to the sky. Following the rotten stink of the citadel, I welcomed the fresh air. Hyllus was dead, but we paid a heavy price for this victory. The witch's symbol on my wrist turned into a lifeless mark and the pain was gone, but in its place another ache put down roots as my heart grieved the loss of a fallen warrior.

XXII

Njall and Fjola were waiting for us outside the gates and judging by their deep frowns, they expected the worst. When I stepped out with Mirable, Fjola looked at me questioningly, then she rushed to the door and peered into the darkness.

'He isn't coming back,' I said. Guilt ate away at me like an earthworm at the raw soil.

'What do you mean he isn't coming back?'

'Hyllus set a trap for us and Skari got caught in it. He died with his axe in his hand.'

She staggered back and pressed her palm to her chest. 'This cannot be…'

'He was a strong man and fought bravely,' Mirable said. 'We escaped thanks to his quick thinking.' Mirable looked worse than before, body trembling, ravaged by fever, and it took Njall's strong grip to stop him from crashing to the ground.

In Fjola's ashen face I read emotions not that different from my own. None of us held Skari in high regard, his contempt for people and blunt remarks curled my fists many a time during our journey together, but now he was gone and I felt like a petty child. Njall was the only one who looked past his shortcomings and saw the real Skari: brave, loyal to the people he loved, a warrior unafraid to sacrifice his own life. I wrapped my hands around Fjola and she clutched at my shirt. Her eyes were full of questions, but this wasn't the place to answer them.

'Morning will be here soon. We best return to the house,' Njall said. He too looked pale and tired.

Fjola didn't let go of me and together we walked back to the hideout.

Inside, we lay Mirable on the sleeping hide and wrapped him in blankets. His skin was on fire and he entered a state of delirium, calling out to his mother and saying words that made little sense. Even his dark skin couldn't conceal angry and inflamed bruises on his right arm and chest. When I examined his wounds, they resembled those we saw on the broken Varls. I didn't know if Mirable was strong enough to resist Hyllus's magic, but I hoped we got him out of the citadel in time and all he needed to reclaim his body was rest.

* * *

Despite the danger, we stayed in the house for three days tending to Mirable. Njall couldn't understand what was so special about the merchant to put our lives at risk, but he agreed to stay until Mirable was capable of walking on his own. I spent my time sitting in the corner where Mirable slept and aided him every time he struggled with a nightmare or was in need of a drink. To me, he carried memories of my past. He was there when I travelled to Sur, full of childish hopes, and helped me find my way in an unfamiliar land. To abandon him now would be to abandon myself.

On the second day of our hiding, Njall spoke of Skari for the first time. Since the day we'd fled the citadel, we skirted around the subject of his death, as if speaking about it was to acknowledge that he was truly gone.

'Was there any other way?' Njall asked when I recalled the events from the tower.

'Believe me, leaving him behind was worse than surrendering my soul. It was Hyllus's trap, his final trick. I wanted to look for a way to free Skari, but the Varls were closing in on him and he wanted to stay and fight them.'

'But why?' Fjola asked. 'Why choose death?'

She couldn't possibly understand the effects of Hyllus's power. Nobody could unless they tasted the pain. 'Skari was tortured and exposed to the same magic as Mirable.'

'But you didn't abandon the merchant because of his injuries.'

'Fjola,' Njall interrupted her in a sharp voice. 'Blame won't bring him back.'

She left the room without looking at me.

'Don't mind my sister,' Njall said. 'We knew Skari a long time. Despite their differences, she cared for him in her own way.'

'You understood Skari better than any of us. I wish I had a chance to know him the same way.'

'Just because he's gone, doesn't make him a different person. Skari was stubborn and difficult. He was set in his own ways and cared little for those who disagreed with him, but he wouldn't want you to burden yourself with guilt on his account.' Njall stroked the disfigured side of his face and continued, 'His father's blade left me permanently marked, but Skari didn't blame himself for my scars. Instead of holding yourself responsible for his death, find a way to honour his memory in a way that he would understand.'

We sat in silence for a while, each enslaved by our thoughts. Njall was eight winters older than me, but I'd come to regard him as the brother I never had, and I respected his counsel.

'How are your injuries?' he asked.

'I'm lucky that Hyllus's magic didn't leave any lasting damage.' With rest, the pain in my body eased off and I was able to move and breathe more easily. 'I wish I could say the same for Mirable.'

'How do you know this man?'

'He's the merchant I met during my first visit to Sur. He showed me nothing but kindness and it's my turn to do the same for him.'

'His injuries are bad and the fever shows no signs of abating.'

'I have hope.'

Mirable groaned in his dreams and I wondered how far he stood from the gates of Himinn. Since Elizan, Agtarr's Warrior of Death stalked me and I feared he'd snatch another life from me.

'You had your revenge and your father's soul can rest in peace. What will you do now?'

'I found this.' I showed him the key I took from Hyllus's body. 'The witch mentioned Antaya. If I'm to destroy the demon that killed my mother, I must go there.'

'The lost city. Marus spoke of it on the winter nights when we huddled around the hearth.' Njall stared at the ground, his chin cupped in his hand. 'The entrance is said to be concealed somewhere on the southern shores of Vester, but even he couldn't say where exactly. How can you hope to find it?'

'Mirable's trading duties took him far and wide. Maybe he would have an idea where the entrance is. But I worry about his injuries. I have a feeling his fever and bruises are just superficial, that deep inside there is more damage. When we found Hyllus, he was exercising a magical spell over Mirable.'

'Do you think he would have become like Alkaios?'

'Hard to tell, but I wish I could do more for him. Ease his pain somehow.'

'He has a good friend in you,' Njall said. 'Despite his injuries, you didn't leave him behind. You saved his life.' He hesitated then said, 'Maybe we should return to Hvitur and seek Torgal's counsel. If the legends are true, Antaya's walls are protected by magic that is not of this world. In ages past, the mages who lived there practiced the art freely. Who knows what they sealed inside after Skaldir released her wrath upon the world?'

I traced Skaldir's mark on my left temple. 'Time is against me. The Night of Norrsken is getting closer and my bargain with the witches binds me. If Antaya holds the way to destroy the demon, I must go there.' I remembered my mother's frozen face and the feel of her lifeless body in my arms. 'When Hyllus was dragged into the abyss, I thought his death would extinguish the pain brought by the loss of my father, but it wasn't so. The void in me is as deep as it ever was.'

Njall picked up his spear and examined the handle. 'It's often the way with things. No matter how many lives we take, no matter how many wrongs we avenge, nothing can bring back our loved ones.' He set to polishing the tip.

Despite his words, I still had hope. If I could bring peace to my mother's soul, this alone would make my pursuit worthwhile. I didn't care what happened after that.

* * *

Fjola sat in the shade of the tree in the garden, legs crossed and head resting on the back of the trunk, the rusty strands of her hair tangled in the grooves of its bark. I settled down next to her. The afternoon light played with the shadows cast by leaves moving in the light breeze and an insect, hidden between the blades of grass, sang a high-pitched tune.

'I can't believe he's gone,' Fjola said. 'I keep thinking what I could have said or done differently… Maybe if I'd gone with you he'd still be alive.'

'Or maybe someone else would have died,' I said, careful not to further stir her grief.

She lifted her chin. 'I don't fear death.'

'People say they don't fear death until they're left with no choice but to face it.' I thought of Hyllus and the way Haamu dragged his soul away into the abyss.

'His last memory of me was my anger. He died thinking I hated him.'

'That isn't what he thought. He loved you and wanted nothing more than to spend his life with you by his side.'

'So why give up and walk towards death?'

She spoke as if Skari had a choice. 'He was trapped and his pride urged him to face Agtarr like a warrior. I always thought my father was the most fearless man, until I met Skari. The fire in him was something I envied.' I took her hand in mine. 'Let your heart grieve, but remember him the way he'd want you to. With pride.'

She wiped a tear from her cheek. 'You fulfilled your oath and Hyllus is dead. His Varls will no longer threaten us and you can return to Stromhold to take your father's place as a guardian. Nordur will always need protection, now more than ever with the Night of Norrsken so close. You're the only one who can save us… or destroy us. The choice is yours.'

'I must travel south, to the lost city of Antaya, to find the lock for Hyllus's key.'

Fjola regarded me with weary eyes. 'Is finding her heart worth more than saving your own people?'

I let go of her hand. 'She took everything from me, and it's the only way to destroy her.'

'Are you sure it's about revenge?' Her cheeks turned wine red.

'There was a time when Lumi meant more to me than life itself, but she's lost to me now.' Deep inside, her name tugged at the threads of my heart where she was still the same girl, standing barefoot among the warriors, with her enchanted eyes and silent lips. The image was soon shattered by the demon I faced in the snowstorm with her mocking laughter. The need to end her life returned with force. 'I called her Lumi, but she was a mere shadow of the female warrior who killed Achr in the legend. She betrayed me, betrayed all of us. She repaid my family's kindness with death, and for that I can never forgive her.'

'I wish to travel with you.'

'This quest is personal. You and Njall have no reason to risk your lives for a cause that isn't yours.'

'Oh, but we have a reason.' Njall leaned against the half crumbled wall. I didn't know how long he'd stood there and how much he'd heard of our exchange. 'We've followed you this far, witnessed the sacrifices you made... lost Skari. He may have been a hot-headed fool at times, but he walked willingly into the citadel to face Hyllus with you because he learned to believe your cause was worthy.'

'He was a true warrior,' I said. 'I wish I had his courage.'

'You gave up your soul to defeat Hyllus,' Fjola said. 'None of us, not even Skari, would be brave enough to make such a sacrifice.'

'We know nothing of Antaya,' I said.

'Even so, we have come this far, we can't abandon you now,' Njall said.

Fjola's eyes shone like the emeralds in my mother's jewellery box. 'Don't you see? My brother and I are here because we want to be. Your cause is ours now.'

Njall put his hand on my shoulder. 'She's right. Wherever you go we go, and I'm certain Torgal would approve.'

My voice died on my lips as I sought words of gratitude. I had not been blessed with many friends in my life and those who called on me had their life snatched away. Argil, Orri, my parents…Perhaps the time had come to open my heart again and test the truths of others. It was the only way to know if loyalty still had a place in this world, and so I searched Fjola's eyes and nodded my approval, bracing myself for what was to come.

* * *

I spent the next three nights keeping vigil by Mirable's side, doing all I could under the circumstances to ease his suffering. When he cried in delirium, I wetted his cracked lips with water and whispered to him about the time we met and how his advice saved me on my way through Sur. I urged him to stay strong and refuse to give in to the magic.

When his condition worsened, I prayed to Yldir to spare him, but even as I did, I doubted he would pay any attention to my pleas. My mother was a devoted worshipper and it didn't save her life. But when we started losing hope, morning welcomed us with good news—Mirable's fever was gone.

He stopped hallucinating and the tremors tormenting him ceased. His body, although still weak from the strain of Hyllus's magic, began healing, bruises lost their angry look and his spirits returned. This miraculous recovery was unusual, but I pushed my doubts aside, glad that the worst was behind him.

'You saved my life,' he said, hugging me. 'I won't forget it.'

'You were lucky to be in the right place at the right time.'

He scowled. 'Don't jest about such things. Fate brought us together for the second time and merchants pay their debts.'

'How did you find yourself in Hyllus's prisons?' I asked.

'When I bid you farewell on the crossroads, I fully intended to await your return. I feared you would come back with injuries, if not physical, mental. After all, it was me who directed you to your doom. It seems the Varls were prowling the area and the next thing I knew, I was being strapped to the table with that madman chanting over my body. I suspect they were hunting for new flesh. Vesterners call these hunts purges.'

'Yldir knows how you managed to pull through,' Njall said. 'You were in such a state, and could barely move, remember?'

'That abomination of a mage caused me pain I never knew existed. If not for Jarin and Skari, I'd be dead for sure.'

'I did ask the witch about your future.' I studied his face. 'Don't you want to know what she said?'

'Keep the secrets of my destiny to yourself. The experience at the citadel taught me that it's better to leave your future where it belongs—in the future.'

'You have changed,' I said.

'Perhaps. Or perhaps I'm just glad to be alive. My possessions are gone, taken by those savage creatures, so, regretfully, I have no coin to pay you with.'

'It's not coin I want. Your knowledge of the south will be of more use to me than silver.

'Speak plainly and I promise to offer my best.'

'I wish to enter Antaya.' I let my words sink in for a moment.

'The lost city beneath the ocean…' He trailed off and tapped his head. 'My turban! It's gone. Damn you, Hyllus.'

'It's the least of our concerns,' I said. 'Do you know where it is?'

'I had it on when the Varls apprehended me—'

I waved my hand at him. 'Not your turban. I'm speaking of Antaya.'

'Oh.' His face went slack as if finding the doorway to the ancient city was nothing compared to his loss.

'Do you know how to find it?' I pressed.

'Yes, yes…the mythical city.' He hobbled around the room. 'The old maps I acquired many summers ago spoke of the way, but none should venture there without protection.'

'What sort of protection?' Njall asked. He listened to our exchange with a sullen look, and I didn't blame him. When I first encountered Mirable, I too found his cheerful ways a bit odd until I got to know his heart. He was a good man, willing to help those in need and I knew that sooner or later, Njall would come to recognise that.

'Wards, spells, magic formulas…I'm no expert on the matter, but Antaya is lost for a reason. Humans stay away from it.'

'Can you even enter the city that stands on the ocean floor?' Fjola asked.

'Antaya was once regarded as the greatest city in the world. Her walls were made of crystal and surrounded by mountains, and her gates opened to those who wished to settle there. Merchants from around the world traded in her rich market streets.' He peered longingly through the window. 'The war between mages and humans brought Antaya to ruin. When the mages fled, they sealed the walls with magic, and so the city was swallowed by the Great Atlantic.' He looked down at his legs as if he saw them for the first time. 'My trousers!'

'You were naked when we found you, strapped to the table and barely alive. Besides, I had more pressing matters to attend to than looking for your clothing.'

'You can't expect me to enter the greatest city that ever was half naked.' He sniffed his shirt and winced. 'This simply won't do. We must find proper clothes before I can go any further.'

I counted silver pieces in my pouch. 'I haven't got much coin left.'

'Fear not, wise merchants don't carry all their silver with them. We'll go to my house in Vester, which I use for doing business.'

'What kind of business?'

'The kind you don't speak of lightly.'

'Let us go then,' I said. 'And seeing as you have no horse, you can ride with me, but only if you promise to sit still.'

Mirable rubbed his hands together. 'I remember Blixt. He is a fine horse and it would be a privilege to share your saddle.'

And with that, the four of us left the ruins and the Citadel of Vester. I was glad that Mirable seemed his old self, but noticed something else that made me wonder if Hyllus's magic affected him more than he let on. Despite his fragile condition, his movements were assured when he descended the stairs, two at a time, and he was able to mount Blixt without aid. I decided to keep my concerns to myself for now and resolved to watch him for any signs of change.

XXIII

Mirable guided us through the streets, choosing the less travelled paths, where people weren't as interested in challenging a merchant with three drab-looking Nords. I was happy to follow for a change, freeing my mind to deal with the events of the past few weeks. Stromhold was nothing but a fog and sometimes I found it hard to believe I spent my life behind those walls, in the company of Father's warriors. At times, I felt like my daily training with Argil and my attempts to impress my father were things done by someone else, another boy who I struggled to remember. His heart was full of curiosity and hope as he rode for Sur with a strange merchant by his side, but traces of him were long gone, wiped away by the evils of this world.

Even Mirable seemed different without his turban and beard. His curly black hair tangled with blood and sweat, full lips dry and cracked, and the whites of his brown eyes were bloodshot and he rubbed them vigorously.

I scratched my cheeks. Stubble had softened into a full-grown beard that put me in mind of my father. He never shaved and I wondered if I looked anything like him. With a sudden pang, I came to the realisation that none of my companions had ever met Father, and apart from Torgal, no one would be able to confirm my resemblance to him.

Is this what would happen to all of us? When we and those who knew us are gone, our memory would be gone with them, until nobody could recall who we were. My hair had grown past my shoulders and I had to tie it back to stop it falling over my face. This was another thing my father and I had in common.

Last time I saw my mother alive she said my hair grew the way his did when he was my age, and the thought brought me a strange comfort. Anything I shared with my father, however small, granted me an extra drop of his courage. The sword, with its curse, also belonged to my past life and so did Blixt, and they were my most precious things. I stroked Blixt's ear, hoping he could sense my love and gratitude and he whinnied quietly as if to acknowledge the bond we shared.

We reached Mirable's place when the sun was at its hottest and I couldn't wait to be out of its scorching gaze. The house, concealed by a cluster of unkempt trees and shrubbery, resembled a typical Vestern building, made of white stone with a timber roof. Panels nailed to the clay frames barred the front windows. Judging by the frowns on Njall and Fjola's faces, I wasn't on my own in thinking that Vester was the most unforgiving place in the world.

Mirable fumbled with a rock in the back wall until it came loose and he retrieved a key. 'Even my mother had no admission to these quarters. Come to think of it, she'd rebuke me for keeping a secret from her.'

Inside was soothing coolness. A stream of sunlight squeezed through the gaps in the panels and I spied bare rooms and a large kitchen with a table, a long bench beside it, and a couple of stools. A large and empty hearth occupied the wall, but I didn't see any cooking pots or pans. Woven rugs that had seen better days lined the floors, and a sorry looking plant had died from lack of water in the corner of the main room.

Mirable laughed. 'Excellent. You should think it's empty.'

He trudged to the vacant room at the back of the kitchen area where he pushed a heavy-looking chest out of the way and brushed aside the rug with his foot, revealing a hatch in the floor. He opened the lock secured around the ring handle, motioned us to follow him, and disappeared down a ladder. I stifled a laugh. Mirable never failed to surprise.

I descended to see him scrabbling around for a lantern. Njall and Fjola joined us and soon a weak light ushered out the gloom, revealing a round room stocked with clothing—from the Vestern kilts and tunics to leather jerkins—and food supplies and grain.

'Unbelievable,' Njall said, dipping his fingers into a sack full of gold and silver coins. 'You must be the richest merchant in Vester.'

Mirable smiled. 'If that was so, I wouldn't be walking around without my trousers on. Merchants aren't just traders and vagabonds. We secure our present and our future, knowing too well how quickly times can change.' He picked up a long length of red cloth. 'In truth, it's my mother who instilled in me this need for security. She wanted me to become a scribe, but my love of travel wasn't suited to a life behind a lectern, surrounded by wise men, so we both settled for a merchant. I never got a chance to thank her for this.'

'You so often speak of your mother. Where is she?' Fjola asked.

'The fever took her when I was away on my first trading assignment.' His voice turned tearful. 'Nothing was ever the same since then. Gold or no gold, some things could never be replaced.' He shook his head as if trying to chase away the memories and clapped his hands. 'Now, I welcome you to my home. Let us dress, eat, and prepare for our journey.'

Mirable dressed in the light of the flickering lantern and I watched him wince and suck in air as if the pain Hyllus inflicted on him never eased. When he raised his hands to pull a shirt over his head, I glimpsed his right arm where red and swollen lumps formed on his skin.

'Are you sure you're well enough to travel?' I asked.

He cradled his arm and evaded my gaze. 'It's nothing. A full recovery will take a while, but I'm glad to be alive.'

Somehow, I found it hard to believe him. The way he acted told me that the damage he had sustained was more extensive than he let on, but I didn't want to press him for answers just yet. He'd offered to help me and invited us to share his home. The Mirable I knew would do the same, and that thought calmed my suspicions.

I dressed, relishing the soft touch of clean linen against my skin. Following the stench of Hyllus's tower, the smell of fresh leather made me feel like a new man. Mirable didn't have any female clothing, but he managed to find a pine-coloured shirt that fitted Fjola's small frame and deepened the green in her pupils. She tugged the excess material inside her trousers and fastened the belt. Her shapely outline woke the memory of seeing her naked in Hvitur's springs. A wild heat spread through my body, forcing me to look away out of fear she would sight my weakness.

Perhaps if I were a free man and my heart wasn't full of darkness I could welcome Fjola's touch on my skin, but I was just a shell, a soulless being with a grim task ahead and Skaldir's mark on my temple.

Njall went back outside to see to the horses before we settled around the table. Mirable brought out dried fruit, cured meats, a slab of cheese, and a jug of wine.

'Tell us about Antaya,' I said.

Mirable had a fresh turban wrapped around his head and he looked more like himself. Every so often, he patted the fabric as if to check it was still in place. He filled his mug with wine and said, 'The road south of here leads to the city, through the forest and along the ocean shore, but few travel it. People tend to stay away from magic. Because of fear or revulsion, I cannot say.'

'The gods condemn magic. That's a good enough reason for people to be wary of it,' Njall said as he cut himself a large piece of cheese. 'But not you?'

'Oh, but I am,' Mirable replied. 'I despise magic as much as anyone, but when I was a youth, my friend dared me to walk up to Antaya's gates and bring back a stone as proof. I managed to travel as far as the shore before fear got the better of me and I ran back home.' He shuddered. 'I can still recall the foreboding in the air when I reached the path leading to the main gates.'

'Why fear it so much if it was sealed two centuries ago?' Fjola asked.

'The legends say that an icy tunnel, built by mages with the help of the ancient magic, leads down from the shore to the bottom of the ocean. Whoever dares to enter will be swallowed by the Great Atlantic itself. But I think they sealed something inside the city to keep it from spilling into our world.'

'Hyllus entered the city, and before his soul was ripped from him, he looked very much alive,' I remarked. 'If he managed to get in and out safely, so can we.'

'Hyllus was a mage, with the means to secure himself a safe passage, but let me remind you that we have no such powers. No one knows what magic lingers within the tunnel.'

'We're going,' I said. 'I'm not asking you to follow us inside, but we need your help to find the entrance.'

Mirable wiped the wine from his lips. 'Alone, I'd never undertake such a journey, but with you, I'm ready to face Antaya. I must admit, when you ventured into Sur I was certain you were lost forever. But here you are, alive and well.' He regarded me with a critical eye. 'Maybe not well, but it's to be expected after your ordeals. I dare to think we're friends and shouldn't friends help each other?'

Fjola exchanged glances with Njall. With Skari gone, they were the only two people who knew about my pact with the witches. I planned to tell Mirable the truth, but with the important task of retrieving Lumi's heart ahead of me, I needed his guidance and who could tell how he would react if he learned about my fate.

'Besides, there's something else,' Mirable said. 'Something far more important.'

'Which is?'

'Treasure, of course! I'm a merchant after all, and we never throw away an opportunity to make coin.'

'This isn't a trip to visit the lost city,' I said, mildly annoyed with his lack of care for the danger. 'We won't have time to walk the streets at your leisure.'

'I wouldn't expect you to. I'll keep my eyes open for anything of value and I shall know the treasure when I see it. It's in my blood.'

'You would risk your life for trinkets?' Njall asked with a scowl.

'It matters not what you need from the city,' I said. 'If you show me the way, I'd consider your debt repaid.'

'Very well. We go at first light, but for now, find yourself a place to rest. Regretfully, there's only one bed in the under floor chamber and I suggest Fjola be the one to claim it. She's a lady and my mother always insisted I respect women above all other creatures.'

'Do you class men as creatures then?' I asked, winking at Fjola. 'Are you suggesting we walk on three legs, groan, and dribble?'

Mirable scratched his forehead. 'I suppose I do. We're less pleasant to look at and our bodily odours can get quite unpleasant at times. Besides, the Varls are men transformed, are they not?'

Njall mumbled something about strange merchants and set to spreading the blankets and leather hides around the main room. I settled mine in a corner where I had a good view of the entrance.

Since we left Nordur, I had grown more cautious, my sleep wasn't as sound and each unfamiliar noise jolted me back into wakefulness. It was no different tonight. No matter how hard I tried to squeeze my eyes shut, they remained wide open and my mind was restless.

Soon, my companions fell asleep and their calm breaths filled the room. I didn't understand how they could be so unperturbed, knowing the dangers we were about to face. One doesn't enter Antaya lightly—Mirable said as much—but none of them showed any signs of fear or uneasiness about the journey ahead. The thought made me angry. This wasn't some trip on a dare, we were risking our lives by attempting to take on the ancient magic of the city we knew nothing about, the effects of which remained a mystery to us. My thoughts refused to still, growing darker and more impatient as the night progressed. I tossed and turned until sunrise.

* * *

We mounted our horses at dawn, keen to leave Vester and its citadel behind. Mirable had no horse, so I offered to share my saddle with him and he happily climbed into it. When we rode through the city streets, I felt building uneasiness among the people and whispers of Hyllus's unexpected disappearance. Skari's absence weighed heavily on us and I caught myself waiting for a sarcastic remark when Mirable said something that would have met with Skari's disapproval, but apart from the merchant's voice, telling stories of his journeys around the continent and answering occasional question from Fjola, it was quiet.

One thing remained the same—Mirable's ordeal in the citadel did not dampened his love of talking and I found his jests increasingly annoying. An impatient sigh escaped me. Part of me wished I was travelling alone, without Mirable and the others to slow me down, but instead I had to endure him harking back about the past—stories I didn't care to hear.

Guided by the afternoon light, we entered the forest and followed an old path towards the ocean shore. Trees, so different from Nordur's pines, grew wide with their branches outspread and crowns of brown and orange leaves casting large shadows onto the ground. A rat skittered into the undergrowth and Blixt snorted from time to time at the sound of other critters and small animals rustling in the bushes. Everything seemed so slow and Mirable kept fidgeting in the saddle behind me, but the road was narrow and I could do little to make headway.

The smell of seagrass wafted from the Great Atlantic, joined by the sound of waves raking the shore. Sandy dunes, shaped like Stromhold's snowdrifts, rose and fell to our left. The last time I looked at the ocean was with Torgal, on the day I found the black orb that still lived in my pocket. My uncle said the gods favoured me, but nothing was further from the truth. As much as Mother and my companions loved them, I regarded the gods with contempt and when Skaldir's curse was revealed to me, I swore that I would never answer the call and bow my head before her. Kylfa said I would return and satisfy my soul contract once the prophecy came to pass, but how could a witch command the Goddess of Destruction? If I succumbed to Skaldir's will, I would become her equal, a mortal god with the power to judge the world and bring about fire, ash, and devastation.

Out of the two, I much preferred to surrender myself to the witches than see the Day of Judgement realised. All of it sounded fantastical, like a story captured in a scroll, and at times all I wanted to do was to laugh it off.

When dusk turned the ocean into a rumbling black mass, Mirable tapped me on the shoulder. 'I suggest we camp here. It wouldn't be wise to stumble ahead in the dark and I'd rather see where I'm going.'

'And I would rather complete our task without delays,' I snapped at him and immediately felt guilty. Mirable meant well and despite his aversion to all things magical, he agreed to guide me to Antaya. It was difficult to accept another holdup, and with the lost city so close I wanted to press on, find the heart, and get it over with. 'But the horses do need rest,' I added to smooth my outburst.

We halted in a groove formed by sand and rock that provided shelter from the wind. With the forest so close, we found ample fuel to start a fire and Mirable set the oats bubbling in a copper pan. Fjola and I watered and fed the horses. When the food was ready, Mirable divided it between the four of us and topped each bowl with slices of dried meat. 'I like cooking,' he said to no one in particular.

'What did your father say when you joined the Merchant's Circle?' Fjola asked, settling down beside me. Her thigh touched mine and a pleasant shiver ran down my leg.

'My father wasn't around much. As an owner of an olive farm, he was busy growing trees and making pickles. I remember helping him as a child, but he was never satisfied with my efforts, so I trusted my mother's wisdom and relied on her guidance when choosing my own path, and for that I am grateful.'

Mirable's relationship with his parents was so unlike mine. My father, although often away chasing after the Varls, was there for me and he knew what was in my heart. The day he presented me with a sword of my own was the happiest day of my life. He realised how much I wanted to train to become a warrior like him and encouraged my pursuits. When he entrusted Blixt to me, he must have known the strong bonds that would forge between the rider and his horse and I would be forever grateful for this gift. My mother too did the best she could when Father was away and her love for me couldn't be denied.

I added wood to the campfire and the flames dimmed for a moment just to spring back to life with renewed energy. The wind stirred Fjola's hair and tugged at the edges of Mirable's tunic.

'What are you hoping to find in the city?' Mirable asked me.

'A heart,' I said, staring into the fire.

'Um...You don't mean an actual human heart?'

'I have longed for it for as long as I can remember and now the time has come for me to claim it.'

XXIV

At daybreak we folded our camp and continued along the shore, where sharp pebbles replaced the sand. The closer we got to Antaya, the barer the landscape had become. The forest lost its colour and the trees stood naked, their stripped branches tangled like the strands of an intricate web. High on the embankment, the grass grew in yellow clumps, flattened by the wind that tormented the landscape with its salty gusts yet unable to disperse the mist obscuring the face of the sun. Further on, the ocean and sand dunes were replaced by cliffs from which rocks protruded like a warning to whomever dared set foot on this ancient path.

'Are these the mages?' Fjola asked, pointing at the sculptures that towered on both sides of the road. 'They're huge.'

The carved figures scrutinised our progress. Some of them had scrolls folded under their armpits and others, with their heads crumbled at the base of their giant feet, gripped staffs similar to the one in Hyllus's possession. But despite their mighty appearance, time wasn't kind to the stone work. It was chipped and heavily damaged in places. Following my ordeal in the citadel I had developed a strong distaste for mages and couldn't bring myself to admire the work of the sculptor. Under their scrutinising gaze, a peculiar uneasiness settled on me as if the air thickened to try to prevent us from riding any further. Blixt, too, must have sensed the change in the atmosphere. His breathing quickened and the muscles in his neck stiffened.

'I wish we could see this place as it once was,' Fjola said. 'Imagine coming here to learn the arts and not having to fear the wrath of the gods. It's hard to believe Antaya came to such destruction.'

'Hardly,' Mirable said. 'In those days, the gods approved the gift of magic and the arts were used for good. To heal, calm the storms, bring criminals to justice… but in time, the mages started using magic for darker purposes and humans took a stand against their misuse of power. The war broke out and the mages sealed the gates to Antaya.'

'Surely not all of them were as corrupt as described in the scrolls,' Fjola said. 'With such gifts, they could have done so much good.'

'And so much evil,' Mirable pointed out. 'However, it's true, some mages sided with humans, but others, loyal to the cause, remained trapped in the city. They resorted to performing a ritual, during which they called Skaldir to aid them.'

'And she answered,' Njall said. 'With dire consequences.'

The road widened and three statues of scrolls came into view, set deep into the ground. Carved from stone and immense in size, the statues lined up the right side of the path, one slightly off centre from the next, with writing etched on the face of each in a language I couldn't decipher. There was a large, circular hole on the surface of the first scroll and smaller ones running vertically alongside its edge, with similar openings carved into the remaining two.

Fjola jumped off her horse and approached the middle scroll. The statue was twice as tall as her and she had to raise her head in order to admire the elaborate design on its top. It resembled a vault with a spike. 'Do you know what it says?' she asked Mirable.

'The language used in Sirili— the school of magic— is long forgotten and from what I know, all scrolls from those days were burned and the knowledge turned to ash to prevent another war.'

The closer we came to Antaya, the more anxious I felt, and Mirable's never-ending prattle stirred my nerves. I wished for him to be quiet and let us focus on finding our way into the city and to Lumi's heart. But instead, I had to listen to his musings about the past.

'You're very familiar with the histories,' I said. 'If I didn't know you were a merchant, I'd take you for a scholar.'

Mirable snorted at my back. 'Do you think us merchants are uneducated? We learn a lot more during our trading journeys than you could ever do sitting in your fancy libraries.'

I brought Blixt to a halt in front of a vast wall, running from one side of the path to another and blocking further passage.

'The gate to the city,' Mirable said.

The stone gate, twice the size of the scrolls, hung upon two pillars. Unlike the statues of mages it was untouched by decay or lichen. Two blocks on either side of it sat on top of one another, the lower one supporting the higher, and above them a stone tablet inscribed with letters similar to those on the scrolls. Smaller symbols ran along the surface of the two pillars. I dismounted and with the flat of my palm, examined the wall for any gaps in the stone, but it appeared solid.

'A gate with no doors,' Njall said with a puzzled look.

Mirable paced from one pillar to the other, inspecting every inch of the gate and tapping the stone with his knuckles. He placed his ear against the wall and listened with eyes closed. He shook his head.

'Hyllus had to get in somehow,' I said. 'There must be a way.'

'Hyllus was a mage and this gate is sealed by magical powers,' he reminded me.

Anger burned black inside me. 'Keep looking. I'll force this gate even if I have to tear my fingernails from my hands. I swore an oath over my mother's dead body that nothing of Lumi would remain and it will take more than a block of stone to keep me from her savage heart.'

Njall and Fjola exchanged glances, but said nothing and went on to inspect the east side of the wall while Mirable and I focused on the western half. We searched for signs of hidden passageways or any gaps that could serve as the means of entry, but the gate and the stones surrounding it were as smooth as the underside of a seashell.

'Nothing,' Fjola said.

Her cheek was smeared with dirt where she had pressed it to the stone and I felt a sudden urge to be close to her and brush it off. I pushed it out of my mind, irritated with myself for indulging in such thoughts when failure was looming large.

Mirable slumped to the ground in front of the gates. The scroll statues mingled with the evening sun, casting shadows on his back and with his eyes transfixed, he looked like a sculpture himself.

'What now?' Njall asked.

Defeat drained my energy and awoke the pain from Hyllus's injuries. Sometimes I wondered if, when he pinned me and used his magic to torment me, the damage he inflicted on my insides was permanent. I felt as if I were drowning in my own weariness.

'Antaya is closed to us,' I said.

'What about the heart?' Fjola asked. 'If you ever hope to kill the demon, you need to find it. We have come so far, you can't give up now.'

'Without a mage who can break the seal we'll never open the gates, and the only mage I knew is dead. Dragged into the abyss.' I kicked a stone and it bounced off the wall, leaving not a scratch, as if the force from years past shielded it from even the slightest damage. Lumi had eluded me again.

'We'll find a way and return here,' Njall said. 'It's not the end. You'll fulfil your oath.'

'I'm tired. Tired of living in the past and chasing after ghosts. Nothing I do could ever bring my family back. No matter how many mages I kill and how many demons I chase down, my father and mother will still be dead, lost forever.'

Fjola ran up to me and grabbed my shoulders. 'Don't say that. You killed Hyllus and saved Nordur from his Varls. That's more than we ever hoped for.'

'And for what? So it can be destroyed by Skaldir's fires? Where I go, Agtarr's Warrior of Death follows, taking everyone who walks with me. My family, my friends, Skari…Mirable too came close to losing his life because he was waiting for my return from Sur. If you both value your life, return to Hvitur before the same fate befalls you.'

'You must think so little of us,' Njall said, his voice low. 'I joined you on your quest as a Nord sent by his better to watch over you and offer aid, but that was many nights ago. With your courage and sacrifice, you have earned my loyalty and that of my sister. I could never abandon you now, Brother, and my wish is to accompany you on your final journey to Sur—if we both live to see that day.'

'And it's my wish also,' Fjola whispered, and a soft look stole over her eyes.

The force of their words crashed against a wall surrounding my heart, the wall I built and maintained since the day I left Stromhold, and now, the emotions I stuffed behind it spilled through the cracks, rushing to my throat and eyes. In that moment I knew I could no longer hide from them.

'There's no one I'd rather walk to Sur with.' My treacherous voice cracked as I said the words, and I turned my focus to Mirable in the hope to regain control. He still sat, staring at the gate, transfixed. 'Come, there's nothing for us here. Let's be on our way.' He didn't move. 'We're heading back,' I said louder. 'You don't want to be left here alone in the dark.'

He didn't appear to hear me, and when I reached for his shoulder he got to his feet and without a word walked through the gate and disappeared as if it was made of nothing but air. My mouth dropped open and Fjola and Njall gasped in unison. The archway was still solid stone and Mirable was nowhere in sight.

'Mirable!' I shouted, but only silence answered. Panic surged in me.

'He went right through,' Fjola said. She rushed to the gate and pushed her palms against the stone. They disappeared inside and she pulled them back with a cry.

'What is this?' Njall said.

But before anyone could answer, Mirable reappeared with a sly grin on his dark lips. 'I may be a mere merchant, but the ancient illusions are no match for my wit.' He smoothed his turban and pushed his chest out. 'Hurry, before we lose the sun.'

'But how?' I asked in astonishment. I knew Mirable had no hidden powers—no man feared and despised magic more than him—and yet here he was, transcending the walls.

'While you were busy baring your hearts, I challenged the tricks. Look—' he gestured to the gate—'can't you see?'

I followed his gaze, but apart from the smooth stone and deepening shadows, I couldn't see anything.

'An opening,' Fjola said, taking a careful step towards the gate. 'My hands…This is how they disappeared.'

'Indeed.' Mirable clapped. 'When the sun and shadows of the three scrolls blend together, they create an opening. The magic here is that of illusion. If we could decipher the writings on the scrolls, they'd no doubt provide the answers to this riddle, but lucky for you, you have me.'

'I see it,' Njall whispered.

And now I could see it too.

The sunlight shining on the scroll statues formed a shadow on the face of the stone that looked like a half-opened doorway with the circular carvings shaped into a handle. I closed my eyes and with my heart pounding in my chest, stepped through the opening.

Icy air washed over me, raising goosebumps on my arms, but apart from the cold, I was whole. It was like stepping through a normal doorway, only this wasn't a door created by a human.

Njall appeared next to me and inspected his hands as if they held the answers to this secret. 'We walked through stone. It cannot be...'

My insides trembled with anticipation, and when Fjola ran up to me, her face gleaming with excitement, I lifted her off the ground and without thinking, buried my face in her neck. Her skin was warm to the touch and for a brief moment I wanted to close the door on the past, forget Lumi and all that came before and stay here, with Fjola. I pulled away, with heat creeping up my cheeks, and when my eyes met hers, hope ignited in them. I cleared my throat to regain calm, but this small victory filled me with courage. I would succeed in finding and destroying Lumi's heart and fulfil my oath to my mother. Now that the possibilities opened again to me, my energy was back and I wanted to hurry forth without delay.

'We have braced the first seal, but there's still a long journey ahead and no way of knowing what awaits us,' Mirable said, trying to look serious, but in his voice I sensed pride. He had managed to best the ancient magic. With his love of talking, I was sure he would recite this story for years to come to whomever would listen.

The tunnel the mages had created was wide and transparent, with walls shimmering blue like the frozen waves of a waterfall. The floor was made from solid ice through which I could glimpse sand and sea. My breath left my lips in a mist as the temperature in the cave dropped to what I'd once felt in a deep underground cellar in Stromhold. Trapped in icy form, the ocean on either side of us cast a greenish light into the tunnel and I struggled to see how such a thing was even possible. Assuming that Mirable was correct, we entered the depths of the Great Atlantic but this wasn't how I remembered the world under water.

When I was a boy, I ventured too close to the edge of the rock on which Stromhold stood. Careless of the ice, I slipped and fell into the water where blackness and cold engulfed me. I couldn't see a thing and the pain was such I thought my skull and eyes would shatter like an icicle crushed underfoot. There was no light of any kind in those depths and the only sensations came from panic and terror that straddled me like a savage beast until Argil, who was ordered by Father to watch over me, pulled me back to the world of the living.

'How could this be?' Fjola brushed the walls with her fingertips and her voice reverberated like magic chimes. 'I've never seen anything as beautiful as this.'

'For all we know, it's another mirage,' Mirable said, wrapping his arms around his chest. 'Where's a spare tunic when I need it? Let's find that heart of yours and leave this place. I can't help but feel that something bad is waiting to punish us for our intrusion.'

'If magic has the ability to create such wonders, how could it be forbidden?' Fjola wondered, pressing her palms against her chest.

'Maybe because in the wrong hands it can destroy the whole world?' Mirable asked.

'What is the matter with you?' I asked him. Since we left Vester, Mirable had been full of bad omens and warnings. I understood his unease about Antaya. I too felt weary treading grounds no other was willing to tread, but so far luck was on our side. I lowered my voice, so only he could hear me and asked, 'Would you rather stay here and wait for us?'

He shook his head. 'I trust you would defend me if something bad happens.'

'With my life,' I said.

XXV

'The goddess who seeks only to destroy was very generous with her powers,' Fjola said, 'to give them freely to the common people.'

We walked through the tunnel, the icy floor crunching under our boots, and all the way she marvelled at the wonders surrounding us. Her amazement brought a smile to my lips. The girl I met in Hvitur was all about fighting and freedom, with a dream of breaking rules and joining Stromhold's warriors. I admired her for that, but here, in these caves, she looked innocent and full of awe like the enchanted ocean around her.

As for me, I was less fascinated with having to rely on the walls of water to keep me safe. The power suspended here tamed the spirits of water and stilled the waves in the very heart of the Great Atlantic. The thought of it crashing down on us deepened the cold in my chest.

'Mages worshipped Skaldir, and their sacrifices pacified the anger forever burning in her heart. The increase in followers meant more devotion and glory.' Mirable took a swig from the water skin and eyed Fjola. 'With your thirst for knowledge, you'd be better suited to a scholar's apprentice.'

'Perhaps, but like you, I'd struggle to find peace being surrounded by walls. I yearn for freedom and the world calls to me with its vast oceans and undiscovered lands.'

'What about a merchant then? My travels took me to the very edges of the Eydimork Sands, and some of my friends even went beyond.'

Fjola laughed and I found pleasure in listening to her ringing voice. 'Me?' she replied. 'I can't read or write well enough to be a merchant. The only things I'm confident in are my daggers.'

'Oh, but those are only details, and insignificant at that. As my apprentice you'd learn all there is to know about trade.'

'If I were you,' Njall said, 'I'd be more concerned with getting out of here alive. I don't trust these tunnels, it's unnatural.' His knuckles turned white from gripping the spear, and he jerked his head at the slightest of sounds.

'Are there any worshippers of Skaldir left?' Fjola asked, seemingly unconcerned by her brother's fears.

'You could say that. When I was a child, my mother used to say that if I misbehaved, the mages would come and snatch me in my sleep.'

'My tutor said that mages who survived fled Antaya to seek refuge in foreign lands,' I said.

'No doubt they lay in wait for the Day of Judgement, when their beloved goddess returns,' Mirable said. 'They're as foul as those creatures from Sur.'

Fjola looked at me from beneath lowered eyes. My father's sword weighed heavily at my hip—a burden and a reminder of my fate, which I refused to give in to. 'I wonder what Skari would make of this,' I said, refusing to indulge my grim thoughts.

'He would despise it,' Njall said. 'He had no interest in history.'

'The tunnel would shake with his complaints,' Fjola said and her laugh travelled down the walls just to return, broken up into a multitude of smaller laughs. The effect was mesmerising.

We fell silent and I wondered if she missed him. There was a time when she resisted Skari in every way, but I knew too well how easy it is to fail to appreciate people you love until they are gone, leaving you with nothing but regret.

'He was a warrior,' Njall said. 'This journey wasn't what he had chosen for himself, but he followed his heart.' He looked at Fjola and I knew he wasn't talking about Skari's heart.

'Our hearts often play their own tunes,' Mirable said. 'Pity that more often than not, the people we choose to love are deaf to their melody.'

My own only ever called out to one, the heart I was about to destroy.

Ahead, the tunnel opened up and the path ended abruptly at the foot of a large archway. Like the floor on the top of Hyllus's citadel, it too was made of pure crystal, clear of cracks or blemishes as if assembled yesterday instead of centuries ago. Its shape reminded me of the pillars that bolstered my bed in Stromhold. They had carvings of ivy leaves on them, which my mother touched with green dye for a better effect. Mirable walked under it and spread his arms wide. 'Antaya. The greatest city that ever was.'

For all our distaste for magic, we stared in wonder, awed by the beauty which unfolded before us. A crystal wall, marred with deep cracks, surrounded Antaya—a testimony to the siege. The houses and streets were separated from one another by rows of crystal trees with pellucid and leafless branches. Further on rose towers and spires, and unlike the insides of the tunnel, their walls glimmered with a silver light as if adorned by little gems. In the middle of the city, and twice the size of those surrounding them, four towers soared towards the crystal dome that enfolded Antaya like a shell. The dark ocean hummed and sloshed on the outside of the magical barrier, hungry for the smallest crack to penetrate and flood the streets denied to it for so long. For a time, I stood stricken and unable to peel my eyes off the view, witnessing for the first time what I had heard of so often, until amazement was replaced by a dread that touched my very bones.

Above this wonder, some ungodly aura hovered.

'How is it even possible?' Fjola asked. 'A city with the ocean for a sky. Is it another mirage? Like the door that led us here?'

'I can assure you the magic here is more powerful than any mirage,' Mirable said.

'Mirage or magic, can we find the heart and leave?' Njall looked as uncomfortable as I felt.

I curled my fingers around Hyllus's key, hoping it would guide my steps.

Past the city gates the signs of decay were more evident, but it wasn't a complete ruin. Each crystal structure was preserved by frost that covered everything in thick layers. The air was sharp with chill, stabbing every inch of skin. My eyelashes, along with exposed hair, stiffened like they would during a ride through Stromhold's plains. The streets, wide and purposeful many years ago, glinted mockingly from under the frozen surface and I knew one careless step could lead to a broken ankle. The majority of the houses were blanketed under a thick crust of ice and their vaulted roofs, fortified by stone columns, leaned drunkenly to one side.

'We should head for Sirili,' Mirable said. 'I should think the most important structure in Antaya would be well preserved.' Unlike the rest of us, he didn't struggle to balance on the slippery path and skipped lightly across the ice. When our quest was over, I promised myself to question him about this sudden agility and bursts of energy, considering the injuries Hyllus inflicted upon him.

The silence in the city was disturbed by the muffled sounds of the Great Atlantic mixed with echoes of our footsteps and I felt like a ghost trapped in the past. This place was unreal and I was afraid that we fell under a spell of some kind, a spell that would ensnare us here for all eternity.

We passed more statues of crystal mages in various forms and it seemed like every street was guarded by one of them to remind people of who ruled Antaya. Some kneeled, with their heads bowed, and others stood tall, hands raised towards the sky in a pleading gesture.

I stopped in front of a tall building that looked like a frozen temple with a triangle-shaped roof supported by wide columns, and some unseen force urged me inside. When I obeyed and crossed the threshold, the sight stopped me mid-stride. A set of extensive steps spread before me with crystal statues of Skaldir on either side, shimmering with bluish light. The goddess's palms rested on the hilt of her sword and her face was veiled by a thin layer of ice. I stood in the place of her worship, the very temple where mages summoned her with their ancient magic. Despite the cold, a hot wave rushed through me and my hand sought my sword—it was hers and so was I. The thought woke the old anger.

Who was she to make a claim on me?

I climbed the steps to the dais where another statue of the goddess loomed, but this time her arms were widespread, the point of her sword reaching towards the icicles that hung from the high ceiling. A blue flame flickered in her left palm.

'It's best to leave it.' Fjola's voice startled me. I didn't see her following me inside the temple. 'We don't know what seals were placed upon Antaya to keep the ocean at bay.'

I regarded the goddess. 'Why me?' My voice rang off the crystal statues. 'What's so special about me?' I asked louder, but only her hard stare answered back.

'Pure coincidence, fate, or maybe other reasons,' Fjola said. 'What does it matter?'

I turned on her. 'It matters. Everyone wants a piece of me. Skaldir…Witches…I didn't ask for this.'

'We don't get to choose. Do you think Skari asked to die? He met you and suddenly his life was no longer his own, but still, he accepted his fate. What matters is what you decide.'

I recoiled from her tone. 'I'm being told by everyone there's no escape from my destiny, no way to resist her call. Do you agree? Perhaps you too think me weak.'

She looked thoughtful for a moment as if considering what lie would hurt me the least. 'No one is judging you but yourself. My father once said that anything is possible if you have a strong desire burning inside the walls of your heart.' She brushed her fingertips across my cheek, filling me with a sudden longing to return her touch. 'If anyone could resist Skaldir it's you.'

I pressed my palm to hers. 'You've always believed in me. Njall was sent by Torgal to accompany me, Skari joined us to watch over you, but you…you didn't act at anyone's behest. How a man without a soul, and with the heavy burden of Skaldir's mark, could ever deserve your trust?'

Her eyes were deep forest pools and in them I glimpsed a possibility of what could be if I were a free man. Her hand in mine suddenly turned into a hot coal fresh from the fire and ready to set my skin alight. The sensation travelled through me, prodding every place touched by Lumi and thawing the chills she left behind. Fjola parted her lips to answer when Mirable popped his head through the opening.

'You have lingered enough,' he said.

Fjola jumped away, taking the warmth with her and leaving me cold again. 'Better hurry before Njall starts waving his spear at unseen apparitions.'

'My brother isn't a coward, and he's faced dangers far greater than this city,' Fjola said. She cast me one more glance then followed Mirable out.

We carried on through the streets, among the frozen buildings that dreamed their eternal dreams, and I forced myself not to think about the mass of water rushing around and above us, kept at bay only by a thin veil of magic. Looking at the empty houses it was hard to imagine that once upon a time people walked the same streets, trading and extending courtesies to one another. How did Antaya look before she was submerged beneath the ocean? If it glimmered so much in the darkness, what would it look like on a full summer's day, with the Vestern sun shining upon its towers and sunlight reflected in the crystal walls? Stromhold, Hvitur, and even Vester didn't come close to it and I wondered why nobody thought to recreate the city following its demise. The only crystal structure I'd ever seen was the floor atop Hyllus's tower.

I couldn't say how long we walked because time in Antaya didn't seem the same as back in the world. There was no sun here to guide us and no moon to warn us of the upcoming night.

At last, Mirable stopped at the base of the great building we saw from the tunnel's opening. Four towers spiked towards the ocean and the entrance was set deep under the archway resembling a carefully made arrowhead. In all my travels, I never saw a structure which came close to this one. It was like looking at the entrance to Himinn. Above the gate, runes and symbols were set into the crystal, shimmering with a blue light similar to that in Skaldir's palm back in the temple. Unlike the rest of the buildings in Antaya, Sirili was untouched by ice and the frost moved no further than the base of the steps, as if fearing to cross the boundary set by an invisible force. Two statues guarded the entrance, their crystal bodies glinting silver like the rest of the statues of the city, with scrolls and staffs clutched in their hands.

'Can you read the runes?' Fjola asked Mirable. Her cheeks burned bright red and I couldn't tell if it was from the chill or our moment in the temple, but I hoped for the latter.

'Yldir would twist my tongue if I tried to speak the words written in the forbidden script,' he said.

When I took the first step, Mirable caught my arm. 'Are you certain of this? We don't know what evil lurks in these walls and the gods may punish us for setting foot in this place.'

I shrugged him off. 'Stay here then.' Lumi's heart was within my grasp, I could feel it, and I wasn't about to turn around for fear of the gods. I turned to look at Njall and Fjola who, like Mirable, shifted uneasily at the base of the steps. 'I would never challenge your faith or force you to disobey the gods, so if you wish to stay behind, do so.'

Without a word, Njall walked up to my side and Fjola unsheathed her daggers, but she couldn't hide the doubt that wrinkled her face. Despite their strong faith, they followed me without hesitation, and more than ever I wanted to prove I was worthy of their devotion. I drew my sword, surprised to see it shining with a faint green light.

'You have the blade,' Mirable exclaimed and his eyes widened in either fear or astonishment—I couldn't tell.

'It's a long story and this isn't the place for it.'

'Whatever it is, you should destroy it.' He made a gesture as if to grab it.

In a flash, I was onto him, pinning him against the wall, the sword at his throat. 'No one touches the blade,' I hissed in his face. Rage rose in me, flooding my veins and clouding my vision. My jaws clenched so hard I thought my teeth would shatter. Whatever overtook me was more powerful than my will to resist it. 'It's mine by right and I'd sooner destroy you than let you touch it.'

'Jarin!' Fjola's voice reached me through the fog of my anger.

Mirable's eyes bulged, but this time it wasn't because he feared Hyllus's tortures, but because of the person he chose to follow into the depths of Antaya. The rage that burned in me so strongly a few moments ago dissipated. I didn't know how I let myself act with such hatred. It was unnatural.

I pushed Mirable away and Fjola's eyes met mine. Her face was full of bewilderment and she clutched her daggers to her chest in a protective gesture. I gripped the sides of my temples. 'It's this place…it must be,' I said, rushing through the doorway. I wasn't sure what happened, but the presence that filled me moments ago was gone, leaving me trembling and gasping for the chill air. Deep down the voice whispered that I wasn't as strong as I thought, and here, in this place full of Skaldir's magic, the sword woke, shining with its own life. It took control over me.

If this was the manifestation of the goddess's power, I stood little chance to resist her call when she summoned me. The sword, which I regarded as a symbol of my father's strength and his gift to me, turned sinister in my grip, but even though every part of me urged me to cast it aside, I couldn't bring myself to do it.

'Are you well?' Njall asked, and in his face I glimpsed a mixture of concern and suspicion.

I straightened up and forced myself to meet his gaze. 'I want to leave here as soon as the heart is destroyed.'

Fjola entered with Mirable cowering behind her, but none of them said anything. Sirili was a vast, tall building made of crystal, like much of Antaya. It was a perfect depiction of those who lived here before the fall of the city. I had to stretch my neck to see the high ceiling with crystal shards suspended like frozen icicles. A number of doors, set in a semicircle, beckoned us to open them. A staircase wound up in a tight spiral, with a handrail made of pure gold and balusters shaped like hourglasses. Silver light cascaded onto the crystal floor from a window set in the back wall, glimmering like moonlight on a river. At the end of the hall, a circular platform rose under the archway with a small crystal chest upon it, guarded by two giant columns from which shards jutted out in all directions, sharp as ice picks.

Clutching Hyllus's key and with my heart hammering against my ribs like a giant demanding to be set free, I walked towards it. Echoes of my boots reverberated off the walls. I stopped at the edge of the platform and steadied my breath.

The surface of the chest was covered in a fine layer of dust-like powder. It wasn't grey, but white like frost. I brushed it off with my quivering fingers to reveal a blue heart inside the chest, beating in a steady rhythm.

I froze, transfixed, unable to pull my eyes away. Until this moment, I'd distrusted Kylfa's words. How could a heart survive outside the body? But now, looking at the steady beating beneath the lid, my doubt vanished and I knew my oath to my mother would be fulfilled. I felt for the lock, set Hyllus's key to it, and it turned without hesitation. I never knew my hands to shake so much as I placed them on the lid and opened it.

I remember the cooks in Stromhold's kitchens dressing rabbits, dividing hearts and other organs into separate bowls, but Lumi's heart was unlike any I had ever seen. Dark blue veins spread through the muscle like branches of a dead tree, pumping blood of the same colour to keep the owner alive.

I hesitated. This was the heart I had desired for so many winters and now, when it was in my grasp, a strange sadness settled in me for I was about to shatter the life out of it. Gently, I lifted it from the chest and it felt cold and solid, like holding a crystal pear in my palm. As if spurred by the warmth radiating off my skin, its beat quickened. My own heart rushed to answer the rhythm of Lumi's, the world around me slowed down and in an instant I was plunged into another time and place.

Sirili disappeared and I stood in a long, narrow corridor, facing multiple archways erected from red stone and shaped like a horseshoe. I looked around for my companions, but there was no sign of them. It was as if some force plucked me out of Antaya and plunged me into this empty place. I took a careful step forward and when my feet crossed the threshold under the first arch, invisible energy pulled me forth.

Clutching Lumi's heart in my palms, I found myself back in the Citadel of Vester, in the chamber where we found Mirable, witness to an exchange between Hyllus and another man who's features were concealed in darkness. I don't know how, but I knew he was the man Lumi spoke off in the midst of the storm—her master, Goro-Khan. She called him the Laughing God and warned me not to cross him.

'Make me a demon worthy of the task,' Goro-Khan said, and I shuddered at its baleful tone. 'A demon who won't fail us.'

Hyllus's mad laugh carried across the room. 'Yes, Master.'

A demon…They spoke of Lumi, of her creation, and my heart sank deep in my chest. Somehow, I still hoped she was just like me, a misguided human being who committed a terrible act, but the vision before me wiped away the last traces of hope.

Just as swiftly as it pulled me here, the energy wrapped me again and I was back in the corridor and in front of another archway. I didn't know what magic lived in these walls, but being pushed and pulled at will woke a terrible fear in me.

But there was nowhere to go but forward, so with a deep breath, I crossed the second threshold.

I was pulled into another place and time—a forest in the middle of winter. A group of riders came from the north and among them, my father. He was wrapped in furs and rode his black horse. I would recognise his confident stance and the assured way he gripped the reins anywhere. I took a step towards him, but some great force held me firmly in place. Uncontrollable sobs escaped my lips. All I wanted was to run up to him and throw my arms around him just like when I was a boy, to ask his forgiveness for everything I had done.

'Father!' I cried out in the foolish hope that he would turn my way and the vision would become a reality, but he wasn't aware of my presence—and how could he when his soul was wandering the passages of Himinn?

'Halt.' Father raised his hand and pointed at the snowdrifts.

'Who's that?' Argil asked, and my eyes welled up with tears at the sight of my old friend.

'A girl?' Orri said, standing up in his stirrups. 'In this cold?'

I followed his gaze to a girl wearing a white dress, her black hair tousled by the wind, and joy jolted through me at seeing her familiar face. Lumi…

Before I could call out to her, the invisible energy gripped me and thrust me back into the corridor.

'Take me back!' I screamed, and without hesitation I hurried through another archway with one thought only—to warn them, to avert the doom that would follow if they took Lumi back with them.

Instead, I was sent to Lumi's room on the day I was getting ready to leave for Elizan with Father and his warriors. She stood by the fireplace, blue dress hugging her lean body, the same dress I found thrown across her bed when I returned to a Stromhold full of dead bodies. Lumi crossed the chamber and looked up at me with that smile of hers I used to love so much.

'You found me.' Her voice was a whisper and I reached out to touch her face, but my fingers grasped at the air. She was an image, conjured up by the magic of Antaya. She placed one hand on her heart and pressed another to my own and her emotions stormed my senses, pouring into me like a flood through a broken dam. More images charged through my mind—Lumi using her powers to freeze her bedchamber before a confrontation with my mother...Lumi watching me fight Argil in the training yard in Stromhold...how she acted with such delight and wonder during our first horse ride...Lumi standing at the window and watching me leave for Elizan.

'Is this how it feels to be a human?' someone whispered, but Lumi's lips remained still. The voice came from somewhere deeper than the illusion. She looked into my eyes and the blue storm in hers woke again, pulling me deeper into her soul. 'I need it. Without my heart, my feelings are but a shadow of your own. I don't want to be a shadow...' She turned her head to the side. 'I can't do it. To hurt him so much would be unbearable even to someone like me.'

I didn't know who she was talking to as we were alone in her chamber, but before I could ask, another voice rang in my ears. 'You can and you will if you ever want to be whole again. We all have our orders. Remember what you are. You have but one purpose: to destroy.'

She looked at me and the pain in her eyes cut through me like a scythe. I reached out to comfort her but she pushed me away and dissipated like a mist. I groped after her, but the vision was fading and my senses were flooding back to me.

Fjola shook my shoulder, calling my name. It was like waking from a dream I didn't want to leave. Lumi's heart still rested in my palm, so small and fragile, beating and full of memories and feelings. Kylfa said that to destroy Lumi, I had to shatter her heart, but now I knew if I did, my own would shatter along with hers.

'Jarin!' Njall, shook me with force. 'The columns—they're coming alive!'

I snapped back to reality, struggling for air with black circles clouding my vision. Splashes of red dotted the edge of the box—I was bleeding from my nose. Fjola and Njall had their weapons drawn and Mirable cowered behind them, eyes wild and mouth wide open. In the silver light of the hall, the columns to either side of the platform cracked and stretched, pieces of crystal tumbling to the floor in large chunks. I placed the heart back in the box and slammed the lid shut.

'Keep it safe,' I called, and pushed the box towards Mirable.

It slid on the even floor and stopped at his feet. He grabbed it and made for the exit, but the door was blocked by a wall of thick ice.

'We're trapped!' Mirable cried out as a claw ripped free from the column.

With the air creaking and splitting, the crystal giants came alive, tearing away from the seals which bound them. The columns collapsed when their bodies took shape.

'They must be the guardians of Sirili,' I said, trying to stop the bleeding and cursing my naivety for believing I could enter such a place as Antaya and leave unscathed.

But my blade continued to shimmer with green light, filling me with courage and hope. I carried magic of my own.

The giants were covered in scars jutting out from their crystalline flesh, and their heaving breaths were a mist, freezing the space around them and turning the air itself into ice. A frost-coated claw plunged at me, sending a shower of splinters into the air. I leaped out of the way, slipping on the crystal floor. The giant advanced on me and the ground shattered under his weight. Without much choice, I pushed myself up and swung at him, but the blade made a ringing sound as it bounced off the solid crystal—our human weapons stood little chance against these giants.

A shrill cry split the air, like ice smashing into a million pieces, but despite knowing that my efforts were in vain, I tried again, slashing at the shards on his feet. Small pieces chipped away, but the giant didn't sway. Instead, he dealt a blow to my ribs with his fist and sent me flying across the hall where my back hit a pillar.

Pain seared through my chest and I tasted blood. The chamber spun about me in a dizzying dance, but the giant didn't hesitate, closing the space between us in two long strides. He raised his powerful leg to crush me and even though my blade was no match against the solid crystal, I stabbed at the splinters jutting out from his foot. The pressure caused him to stagger, gaining me a precious moment to roll away. I was on my feet again, and with a scream, plunged my sword into the crystalline body. It caught, breaking the shell and releasing blue liquid from the crack.

As nimble as a cat on a hunt, Fjola ran up to the giant. Using the shards on his body, she skipped across and stabbed her daggers into the oozing wound. He flung at her and she fell to the ground. One of her daggers spun across the floor towards where Mirable shrank away by the sealed door, the chest clutched in his arms.

I rushed to Fjola's side when another blow sent me crashing down. The giant ripped a shard free of his body and aimed. I could almost feel the piercing pain stabbing through my heart when a scream tore the air and Mirable sprang on the creature's back, Fjola's dagger in his hand. He scaled the crystal body with agility even she would struggle to match and went about stabbing the blue eye.

The shard clattered to the floor, smashing into pieces, and the giant slapped Mirable off him. I stabbed at the giant's wound again and the chamber trembled with his shriek. From the power of it, the ice blocking the entrance shattered in a shower of flakes, filling the air with a sharp rattle that seemed to vibrate through every inch of the crystal walls.

My ears rang and I could hardly hear myself yelling to the others to run for the door. Our only chance was in escaping the giants before their enormous bodies crushed us into dust. I raced to Mirable, grabbed his shirt, and pulled him to his feet. He dashed down the steps after Fjola.

Njall was locked in his own struggle with the second giant, who overpowered him with ease while the building continued to shake. Pieces from the walls crashed to the ground. I rushed to his aid just as he delivered a blow to the giant's trunk of a leg, and with a final *snap*. His spear splintered in two.

The first giant advanced on Njall and I got there in time to push him out of the way of the great fist. Panic turned his eyes feral.

'They're too powerful, we'll never fight them off,' I yelled.

We sprang for the door. Weaving between the two giants felt like weaving between two towers, but due to their size, they were slow and we managed to outrun them. We raced through the streets with the guardians in pursuit, causing earthquakes in their wake. The frozen buildings tumbled down around us and the ground cracked, shooting out fractures in all directions. The air pierced with another shriek, powerful enough to cause the ground under my feet to splinter.

Struggling for balance, I slipped and fell across the ice, scraping my hands and face, and my eyes filled with white dust.

The giants thundered close behind, one step to five of ours. Ahead, Mirable, with one hand clasped over his turban, dashed for his life, Njall and Fjola close behind. I scrambled to my feet and ran after them. The ancient streets flew past me and when I dared to glance over my shoulder, the earth was crumbling and sliding into the abyss—Antaya, the lost city of mages, shattered, taking her mysteries and magic with her.

I forced myself to a greater speed, my eyes on the archway where Fjola and Njall waved their arms, shouting. Mirable joined them moments before a chasm opened up. The crack in the earth twisted and turned like a sea serpent, widening the gap between me and my companions. Sharp air cut through my lungs and the cracks began opening all around me until I had to jump to avoid falling through.

When another powerful cry echoed through the city, I knew the giants were no more, swallowed by the earthquake of their own making.

Njall waved for me to jump and with no time to consider my options, I raced to the edge, pushing my feet off the ground and sending my body leaping into the air, vaguely aware of my arms and legs flailing above the abyss beneath me.

But the gap was too wide and my chest hit the icy wall, cutting my breath short. I grasped at the slippery surface, heart flogging in my chest, and now I knew the terror Skari felt with his body suspended over blackness.

Njall and Fjola grabbed my arms. 'We won't let go,' she said, straining against the weight of my body. I thrashed at the wall with my boots, struggling for a grip and slipping further down, but Njall pulled me harder until together, they managed to haul me over the edge. When we got to our feet, the ground still trembled, sinking Antaya deep into the bowels of the Great Atlantic. The mighty crystal wall that had guarded the lost city crashed and fell, taking the archway with it.

'Hurry! The cave is falling!' Mirable yelled.

We ran as the world around us shivered like a leaf in the eye of a hurricane. Inside the tunnel the crystal walls were already cracked and splintered, letting the ocean in. Water poured through the gaps, no longer contained by the magical barrier, forcing further fissures to widen under pressure and filling the cave with sounds of thunder.

I didn't remember the tunnel being so long, but it seemed never-ending as we raced for our lives while the vicious ocean hindered our escape. The flood tore down the walls and bit away at our knees like a wild beast in a rush of frenzy.

Mirable's cries mingled with the surging waves as he begged Yldir to spare him—and moments later he lost his balance and fell underwater.

I dived after him and grabbed his turban, all the while fighting against the powerful force that tried to pull us under and back into the city to meet our deaths. Mirable wiped his eyes and coughed out the salty water, but there was no time to linger and I pushed him forward. Fjola was slipping and falling, and Njall fought against the currents to keep them both afloat. It was becoming more difficult as the water reached as high as my chest and I was sure we would never escape as Antaya dragged us into the abyss with her.

When at last the gate appeared, a sharp *bang* filled the cave and the barrier holding the ocean at bay ruptured completely, setting the Great Atlantic free. It snatched and slammed us against the gate until the wall gave way under pressure. The force of the water threw us through the doorway where Blixt reared up and the other horses strained against their ties, nickering in terror. I caught Blixt's saddle and dragged myself up whilst Mirable scrambled behind me. Njall and Fjola spurred their horses after us and we raced away with the Great Atlantic raging at our backs, swallowing the statues of mages and the trail leading to the lost city.

XXVI

When we were sure the ocean could no longer reach us, we halted the horses at the edge of the forest. The waters guarded the path to Antaya like a jealous mother guarding a new-born child, spitting foam in all directions and daring us to try our luck against the angry waves. The Great Atlantic waited for centuries to conquer the lost city and now it had claimed its prize.

'So much hardship, and all for nothing,' I said. 'We braved the Great Atlantic and the magic of Antaya to be chased away by waves. This journey was in vain.' Lumi was lost to me, destroyed, perhaps, in the depths of the seething ocean.

Mirable regarded me with a shadow of a smile on his lips. His turban was undone and the loose folds flapped about his face, animated by the morning wind, exposing his curly hair. 'When we left for Antaya, I told you I was hoping to find precious trinkets in the streets of the lost city, and true to my word, I did.' He fumbled in the folds of his soaked tunic. 'I retrieved the most valuable item Antaya had to offer.' He presented me with the heart, still concealed in its chest. 'You saved my life in the Citadel of Vester and ever since, I have been looking for a way to repay my debt.'

I snatched it from him, unable to believe it survived our ordeals unscathed, but one look inside assured me the heart was still beating in a steady rhythm, keeping Lumi alive. I embraced Mirable, ignoring his struggles against the force of my gratitude.

'There's no debt between us, my friend,' I said.

'Enough. Before you strangle me,' he said, squirming.

'Are you going to destroy it?' Fjola asked and her voice carried a note of disapproval.

'When I touched it in Antaya, I had visions, images of the past. It was as if Lumi was there, right next to me, whispering in my ear, and I could feel everything she felt.'

'You mean, the demon,' Fjola corrected me.

'I thought you wanted revenge,' Njall said. 'You travelled this far to find the heart. We almost died trying to retrieve it. Shatter it just like the witch advised and your mother shall know peace in Himinn.'

I traced the blue veins across the transparent lid. I no longer knew what I wanted. Before my palms savoured the coolness and life of Lumi's heart, vengeance was the only thing that occupied my mind. It spurred me forward like a rider spurring his horse when it falters during the chase. But its force abandoned me now, leaving emptiness in its wake. No matter how hard I tried to deny it, Lumi was still there, scratching at the walls of my heart, her sweet face nestled behind my thoughts only to emerge at night, pulled forth with the power of my dreams. I knew I had to see her one last time to understand the visions and the reasons behind her actions in Stromhold. I could never forgive Lumi for slaying my family, but my heart called out to her across the Great Atlantic, leaving me no choice but to follow.

Part of me felt a strange relief that she still meant so much to me, but another part accused me of being a fool and I chastised myself for my inability to hate her. How could I even consider having feelings for someone who destroyed my life? I hated to think what my mother and father would've said to that, and I was sure they would've been deeply disappointed by my weakness. Throughout my journey I was always focused and confident in my tasks, but with Lumi's heart beating in my palms, I was no longer sure of anything.

'I need to know the truth about what happened,' I said, struggling to find a better explanation for the whirlpool of emotions flooding my heart.

'Your mother was killed along with your warriors,' Fjola said. Her cheeks turned crimson and her eyes glistened like dew on morning grass. 'What truth are you hoping to find?'

'There was a man in my visions, concealed in darkness, and he spoke of destruction. His name is Goro-Khan, and from what I know of him, he is more powerful than Hyllus, who, it seems, was merely a pawn, obeying orders. Lumi was right when she said there are more powerful forces at work, and if we're to stand a chance against them, we must act. I'll sail east, to Shinpi. We must learn all we can about Goro-Khan and what he intends. I fear it has something to do with me and the Day of Judgement.'

'How can you trust the vision of a demon?' Fjola asked. 'She tricked you before and she can do it again. How many lies will it take for you to realise that all she's ever done is deceive you?'

There was hurt in her voice and part of me wanted to reach out and console her, but how could I explain the closeness I experienced when Lumi shared her emotions with me? To my companions she was just a demon. Unlike me, they had no memories of her.

'I have no choice. Lumi is the only link we have, and I must pursue it.' My words sounded weak even to me, but Lumi was the only person who could lead me to Goro-Khan and betray his intent. Perhaps she was the only one who could help me alter the prophecy and save the world.

Without a word, Fjola turned away and headed for the shore.

'She's hurt,' Njall said when she was out of earshot.

'I know, and it pains me to see her this way, but I can't destroy the heart. Not yet. There's too much at stake.'

'Your reasons aren't for me to judge.'

I mustered all my courage to ask the question, 'Will you sail with me?' I had little hope that he would, and even though he said nothing to me, I sensed that deep inside he questioned my reasons for going after Lumi.

'Must you always doubt my loyalty, Jarin? I promised to stand by you until the end, regardless of what the future holds for us, and I intend to keep my word. We're brothers now.'

'And Fjola? You know I can't make promises I could never keep.'

'Your feelings are between you and her,' he said.

We stood in silence, watching the eastern sky turn pink before the sun poked its head above the waters. Mirable rattled the pans, mumbling about the supplies we lost during our mad ride from Antaya, and after a while Njall offered to get wood for the fire.

'My thanks. It's a long ride back home and I don't intend to make it on an empty stomach,' Mirable said, starting after him.

I caught his arm. 'How did you do it?'

'You asked me to keep it safe, remember? Just before the guardians woke.'

'Not the box. I'm talking about your leap at the giant. You were so fast, climbing up those shards. What is it that you're hiding from us?'

He narrowed his eyes. 'You were pinned to the ground. What would you have me do? Let the beast crush you?'

'I saw the swelling on your arm when we left the citadel. What did Hyllus do to you? Are you becoming one of the Varls? Please let me help you. Together we might find a way to reverse the transformation.'

'Hyllus did nothing to me,' Mirable snapped back and pulled his arm free of my grip. 'You keep your secrets and let me keep mine.' And with that he followed Njall into the forest.

I could force the truth out of him, but I came to regard Mirable as my friend and didn't want to press him. He'd suffered much in Hyllus's hands, and I hoped he'd share his secret with me when the time was right. I only hoped it wasn't too late.

Then I walked down the beach to where Fjola stood, a crisp breeze tugging at her rusty hair.

'Your blade saved my life,' I said.

'You should thank Mirable.'

'I worry about him. Ever since we left the citadel, he's been acting strange.'

'He could say the same about you.'

'The blade is simply a token from my father,' I said in a firm voice.

She shrugged. The waves splashed at our feet just to pull away and come back with more spirit. I tasted salt on my lips.

'I'm sorry,' I said.

'Don't be. I'm the one to blame. We all fell victim to our hearts. Perhaps it's a punishment for Skari, for the way I treated him. I cast away his devotion to follow my selfish desires.'

I brushed her cheek, soft against my fingertips, and in that moment, I wanted nothing more than to let go of Lumi. How could one hunger for cold and for warmth at the same time?

Fjola pushed my hand away and her eyes turned to stone. 'I followed you, hoping you would choose me, that you would destroy the heart and accept mine in place of hers, but I was a fool. I cannot understand why you love her so much after everything she's done. Even though it hurts me beyond measure, I can no longer be a part of your journey.'

'Fjola…'

She shook her head. 'This is where we part, Jarin Olversson. I hope you will find what it is that you are looking for.' She turned away from me and walked back to the camp.

I watched her mount her horse and a great sadness welled up in me. Before she rode off, Njall rushed to her side and caught the reins. They exchanged a few sharp words then she spurred the horse towards the forest.

I wanted to go after her, beg for her forgiveness, and ask her to stay with me, but how could I? Lumi took away more than my family and home, she made me a prisoner to her heart. No matter how much I longed for Fjola, I couldn't give her what she wanted. Despair ate at me like a sickness and there was no cure for it.

The Night of Norrsken loomed closer and I had to find a way to free myself from Skaldir's grip. With my soul under contract I had limited tomorrows left, so it was time to focus on saving the lives of the people I loved.

The Great Atlantic shimmered as the morning light caught its waves, and the horizon looked back at me with a promise to unravel the mysteries of Shinpi—the land no one had set a foot on, and where Lumi hid amidst the wintery slopes. It awaited me and all I needed to reach its shores was a boat—and courage.

Bonus Content:

Get your free fantasy adventure!

*"An emotionless warrior.
A journey across four lands.
A quest to uncover the power of the human heart."*

Visit ulanadabbs.com to subscribe and receive your free copy of:

Storms of Tomorrow

Note from Jarin:

Thank you for reading *Lumi's Spell*.
I would very much appreciate your feedback!
Please leave me an honest review on Amazon or Goodreads, so I can use it to improve my skills as a warrior and prepare for my next adventure.
Your feedback means a great deal and will help other readers discover my story.

—Jarin, the Guardian of Stromhold

Acknowledgements

I would like to thank Philip Athans for his excellent editing advice, support, and for helping this story shine.

My coach, Fiona Longsdon, for always pushing me to go deeper and find the true heart of the story.

Lauren Nicholls, for her diligent proofreading.

Mario Wibisono for bringing Lumi to life with his magnificent cover art.

Printed in Poland
by Amazon Fulfillment
Poland Sp. z o.o., Wrocław
31 October 2022

a1737cc1-7ff6-4727-a184-6296daf3c11fR01